Resounding Accla
BARBARA

BLAMELESS

"AN ABSORBING, NO-WAY-OUT STORY THAT KEPT ME TURNING PAGES BREATHLESSLY"

Phyllis A. Whitney

"NERVE-WRACKING . . . BONE-NUMBING SUSPENSE . . . THE COMPELLING STORY WILL GRAB YOU BY THE NECK AND PROPEL YOU TO READ WITH INCREASING SPEED"

Boston Herald

"BARBARA SHAPIRO HAS CRAFTED A WINNER!"

Katherine Hall Page, author of *The Body in the Basement*

SHATTERED ECHOES

"A GRIPPING TALE THAT WILL KEEP YOU ON THE EDGE OF YOUR SEAT."

Judith Kelman, author of *One Last Kiss*

"*SHATTERED ECHOES* REPEATEDLY TOUCHES A RAW SPOT THAT CAN BE SOOTHED ONLY BY TURNING EVERY PAGE UNTIL IT'S OVER."

Boston Globe

"I READ THIS IN ONE SITTING . . . IT WAS THAT GOOD."

Mystery News

Other Avon Books by
Barbara Shapiro

BLAMELESS
SHATTERED ECHOES

BARBARA SHAPIRO

SEE NO EVIL

AVON BOOKS NEW YORK

SEE NO EVIL is an original publication of Avon Books. This work has never before appeared in book form. This work is a novel. Any similarity to actual persons or events is purely coincidental.

AVON BOOKS
A division of
The Hearst Corporation
1350 Avenue of the Americas
New York, New York 10019

Inside cover author photo by Marc Holland
Published by arrangement with the author
Library of Congress Catalog Card Number: 95-95177
ISBN: 0-380-77421-6

First Avon Books Printing: May 1996

Printed in the U.S.A.

RA 10 9 8 7 6 5 4 3 2 1

To Robin and Scott,
who always remind me what is really important

ACKNOWLEDGMENTS

A theme appears to be emerging on the acknowledgment pages of my books: the same people keep showing up. My writers' group: Diane Bonavist, Jan Brogan, Floyd Kemske, Rachel Plummer, and Donna Baier Stein. My family: Dan, Robin, and Scott Fleishman. My parents: Norman and Sandra Shapiro. My agent and editor: Nancy Yost and Ellen Edwards. To all of you, as before, my deepest thanks.

For their professional expertise, manuscript critiques, or just plain great ideas, I want to thank Amy Agigian, Margie Bogdanow, Steve Corr, Deborah Crombie, Tamar Hosansky, Phyllis Kapken-Silverman, Larry Starr, Kelly Tate, and Steve Womack.

And to Ellen and Nancy, although you have already been mentioned, double thanks are indeed appropriate.

It is no more surprising to be born twice than once.

—VOLTAIRE

One

SHIVERING IN THE NIGHT AIR, REBEKA HIBBENS PUSHED aside the reeds and the brush at the river's edge, at the place where firm ground flowed into mud and marsh and then on into the ocean's sandy shore. Her dress was torn and her cloak streaked with dirt. Oblivious to the mud that sucked at the ankles of her boots, she knelt and, using her hands as a trowel, searched for the shallow grave she knew lay in the soft ground.

The others stood on the sand, gathered around a large bonfire and a bush whose exposed roots resembled a knot of sleeping snakes. Including Rebeka, there were seven: six women and one man. All had been convicted of witchcraft and had just escaped from Cambridge Prison. All were being pursued by the righteous goodmen of Massachusetts Bay Colony. And all were to be hanged at dawn the following day.

"The Immortalis must be done," Millicent Glover called to Rebeka, but her words were shredded by the wind and Rebeka heard only a few snippets of sound.

Groping in the dirt, Rebeka's fingers finally hit upon the soft object she sought. Gently pulling against the sucking mud, she brought forth a soiled bundle the size and heft of an infant born a few months before its time. Peeling off the binding cotton shroud and letting the muddy cloth drop away, Rebeka exposed a naked doll to the cold moonlight.

She looked down at the misshapen thing: a sorcerer's poppet she had hurriedly crafted from old rags and stuffed with boar bristles. The doll's pewter eyes, which in her haste she had affixed slightly askew, gleamed dully back at her: flat and empty and ominous.

She held the poppet heavenward, revealing it to the stars and the waxing crescent moon that stood out against the ebony sky. Although she felt an abiding sadness at having to speak the words, nonetheless Rebeka said,"Those who risk the sanctity of the coven shall be punished by eternal death."

"Mahala," Millicent called to Rebeka again. "We must make haste. They shall soon be upon us."

Rebeka nodded and dropped the poppet into a deep pocket in her skirt. As she approached the group around the bonfire, Rebeka saw how weak and low they all were. Dirt outlined the deep wrinkles etched into Millicent's skin, and one of Abigail Cullender's eyes was swollen shut, swallowed by a purple and black bruise. Bridgit Corey's arm hung at an odd and useless angle as she leaned into Foster Lacy—he in ripped breeches and a single boot. Mercy Broadstreet stood on Foster's other side. Rebeka was overcome with an aching tenderness for them all. Even for her cousin, Faith Osborne, who was the cause of it all.

Faith's hair was full of leaves, and the dirt on her face was streaked with the tears she had shed, and was still shedding, over the death of her only child, Dorcas, who had been hung a fortnight ago on Gallows Hill. Looking at Faith, Rebeka was stirred to empathy: how terrible to have watched the life being smothered from the one for whom you cared the most.

And yet, Rebeka knew, Dorcas would not have been hanged but for Faith's own folly. Nor would the rest of them be in such danger, forced to make quick business of what Rebeka and Millicent had intended to be a prolonged and glorious event.

Rebeka touched the magic lancet that hung from her neck on a braided chain of human hair and reminded herself that Faith was not one of them, that Faith should not be here, partaking of this sacred ritual; it was Dorcas who was of the coven, Dorcas whose power, if it were present, would allow the coven to unchain itself from humanness and ascend to immortality. But now that Dorcas was lost to them, three more Immortalises would have to be performed and three more human lifetimes would have to be endured before the coven could regain the power necessary to reach eternal life among the sages.

Rebeka entered the circle, promising herself that, care as she might for Faith, she would complete the poppet's curse before this Immortalis was done. Although vengeance was not in her nature, the sages had made it known to her that Faith must pay for her deeds.

With the crescent moon to her back, Rebeka lowered a wooden dipper into the pockmarked pot. She lifted the full dipper and turned to Millicent, offering her the first sip of the liquid. "Heliotrope, sage, malaxis, christianwort, heart of lubin, aconite," she chanted as Millicent drank, her voice vibrating with power. "To live, one must die." Although Rebeka knew the goodmen would soon be upon them with their rifles and their dogs and their chains, she spoke the words she had written with clarity and deliberation. "To die for future life is the privilege of the few."

As Rebeka passed the dipper around the circle, the hem of her cloak dragging along the ground, Millicent began the story of the Immortalis. "We come to this ocean that carves the edge of the earth, to perform the first great Immortalis," she said. "It is a deep magic Rebeka and I have crafted to insure that our seven souls shall be reborn together again, and again, and again.

"One plus zero plus one," Millicent continued. "One hundred and one. Every one hundred and one years until the great millennium, in 1793, and in 1894, and in 1995,

we shall meet upon the ocean's sand under a waxing crescent moon to perform the Immortalis: to give up our present forms, to meld our souls and our energies, until we are able to reach the sages and our immortality."

The wind picked up and brought with it the whooshing sound of movement: the sound of something, or someone, approaching. Millicent froze.

Rebeka held her arms wide in a gesture of comfort. "'Tis only a bird," she said as a long-necked heron dove between the killdeer and the pickerelweed at the water's edge. "Only a bird."

Millicent sighed and concluded her story. "And in each new incarnation our coven shall grow in knowledge and in power and in the magical crafts," she said. "Until we have learned all there is to learn, until we are able to leave behind the shackles of our human carapace."

As Millicent's words were carried away by the wind, Rebeka turned to the dark water, its waves pulled by the force of the new moon. Slowly, she walked across the sand and into the ocean, stopping when the water flowed just above her waist; her cloak swirled as it rode the restless waves. She turned and beckoned for the others to follow.

They stepped into the sea: Millicent and Mercy held hands to keep from stumbling on the slippery rocks; Foster helped Abigail; Bridgit and Faith clutched each other tightly. Slowly, the six made their way to where Rebeka stood.

When they were a circle once more, enfolded and rocked by the bone numbing water, Rebeka stepped into the middle and tugged the ribbon that gathered the neck band of her cloak. As the cloak fell open, she pulled out the lancet. It was a physician's lancet, and concealed within its wooden case, carved with serpents, pinecones, frogs, and a winged caduceus, were four keen-edged blades. Reverently, Rebeka opened the lancet and fanned the knives above her head. "I wield the lancet of heaven," she whispered into the fog that hung in ghostlike wisps over the ocean. "The touch of this divine blade shall carry us high."

"To die for future life is the privilege of the few," the coven chanted.

"The touch of this divine blade shall ensure breath be with us for all eternity," Rebeka said, touching each of the four blades to her nose, to her lips, and to the soft spot at the base of her neck. "To live, one must die."

"No!" Faith cried, pulling her hands from the circle. "'Tis against God's will."

Rebeka reached out and took Faith's hand in hers. "This must be done," she said softly.

Muffled sounds from upriver interrupted Rebeka. This time the sounds were not the natural noises of the marsh; this time they were the cries of men, the thud of horses' hooves. Rebeka turned to Faith. "Look at me," she ordered. When Faith raised her eyes, she was caught within Rebeka's unblinking stare. "You shall do as we do," Rebeka said.

"I-I . . ." Faith stuttered.

"You shall do as we do," Rebeka repeated, her gaze burrowing deeper and deeper into Faith's eyes, deep into the core of Faith's being. "You shall say what we say: 'To live, one must die.' "

Faith's eyes were fixed on Rebeka, trancelike and dazed. "To live, one must die," she repeated in a stilted and disembodied voice. "To live, one must die."

Torchlights flickered through the naked tree branches and the sound of barking dogs was carried by the wind. Rebeka turned from Faith to Millicent. "Faith will follow my will," Rebeka told her friend. Then she bowed her head in a gesture of both respect and farewell. "Go to new life, Millicent Glover. We shall meet again soon."

At Rebeka's words, Millicent plunged a single blade into the soft spot at the hollow of her own neck. Deep red blood spurted into the dark waters as she twisted the knife to cut the shape of the crescent moon into her skin. "To live, one must die," she whispered as she handed the lancet to Faith. Then Millicent waded toward the deep channel, lay back upon the moving waters, and let herself be carried out to sea.

Faith stood motionless in the frigid water, the lancet in her open palm.

"Go to new life, Faith Osborne," Rebeka said, her eyes searing into Faith's, ordering her to do her bidding. Faith remained frozen, the lancet at her side. Rebeka lifted her cousin's hand and, with Faith's fingers wrapped around the hilt, Rebeka placed the knife to the younger woman's neck. Rebeka glanced over her shoulder; the torchlights were growing brighter and the horses' hooves louder.

"The sages have rendered judgment upon you," Rebeka told Faith. "You must sacrifice your life. And you shall be cursed to be with us, to make this same sacrifice, in every succeeding lifetime and at every succeeding Immortalis—until we have achieved our immortality and your soul is lost forever."

With her free arm, Rebeka pulled the sodden poppet from her skirt pocket and held it up to the heavens. The moon caught the dull shine of the doll's pewter eyes and, for a moment, the thing seemed to come alive. One silver eye flashed her a roguish wink, while the other pierced straight into her soul with its depraved stare.

"Those who risk the sanctity of the coven shall be punished," Rebeka said to Faith. Then she threw the doll into the ocean.

Faith gave a feeble kick as Rebeka guided the knife to the hollow of her neck, but it was apparent to all who watched that the young woman's spirit had been broken. Rebeka pressed the blade home, slicing a deep crescent into Faith's taut skin. With a slight tremor, Faith slipped from her grasp. Within moments, she was gone.

The other four followed in quick succession. Rebeka was the last to go. Standing alone as the frigid waves lapped at her waist, she watched the first of the goodmen break through the birch and pine trees, knowing she would be gone before they were able to detect her form upon the water. As the throng of horses and dogs and men thundered toward the long spit of sand, she cut a deep crescent into her own neck and cast the sacred lancet back toward shore.

As she knew it would, the lancet flew as if it had wings over the water and the sandy beach, until it dropped into a crevice between a large outcropping of rocks. Rebeka noted exactly where the lancet had set down and then lay herself upon the waters, thinking of Faith Osborne, cursed to unwillingly sacrifice her life in 1793 and again in 1894 and again in 1995.

It had to be done, Rebeka thought as she let the swiftly moving waves carry her far into the night. Justice had to be done.

Deborah Sewall carefully closed the cover over the yellowed parchment pages from which she had been reading. Placing her hand on the book's leather spine, she raised her eyes and gazed into the five rapt faces before her. Although she and Rebeka shared the same soul—were, in essence, the same person—the intervening centuries had hardened that soul. For Deborah had been forced to endure, as Rebeka Hibbens never had, the consequences of Faith Osborne's deed.

Deborah's eyes peered into the shadowy darkness of the small room. "And as we did in 1692 and 1793 and 1894," she told those assembled at her feet, "so too shall we do in 1995."

Two

LAUREN FREEMAN DROPPED TO AN EMPTY BENCH AND inspected the small health food store on the other side of JFK Street. *RavenWing* was etched into the shop's window in elongated letters that filled the plate glass, serifs dripping into the casing. The store was one of many squeezed into two matched gray and orange buildings, each twin outlined by octagonal bays crowned with pointed roofs and orange dental molding. Half a dozen restaurants, two boutiques, a psychologist, and a résumé service were layered above and below as well as next to RavenWing. In front of the buildings, two groups of students were distributing fliers; one set of "flier people" accosted passersby with green sheets of paper, while the other group taped pink ones to lampposts and street signs. Lauren couldn't help smiling: Harvard Square at its best.

"Meet me at RavenWing at three," Jackie Pappas had told her that morning. "I think Deborah's going to come across with *the chronicle*." Jackie's voice had italicized the words. "This could be our big break," she had added before hanging up. Lauren shook her head, wondering how she had managed to get herself into a position where her "big break" was meeting a woman who claimed to be the reincarnation of a seventeenth-century witch.

It wasn't as if she didn't have enough to do in the twentieth century: She needed to get a batch of books from Jackie's house for the graduate seminar in historiography she was auditing; she had fifty quizzes to grade for Dr. Conklin's "Making of the Modern World" course; her son Drew needed to be picked up from his extended day program before she got a late fine—again; not to mention her empty refrigerator, the pile of dirty laundry next to her bed, and the ever expanding dust balls that were threatening to take over her apartment. She stood and dashed across the street, cutting in front of a slow moving pickup truck and scowling at the driver when he honked at her.

Reaching the half flight of stairs that led up to RavenWing, Lauren scanned the sidewalks for Jackie, although she had little hope her friend would be on time: Jackie was always breathlessly and apologetically late. Waving away the flier people, Lauren leaned against the wrought iron railing. These witches were Jackie's contacts, and Lauren was disinclined to enter the store without her.

When Jackie had first proposed they coauthor a book together, Lauren had been flabbergasted that a woman of Jackie's caliber would even consider her. Only twelve years Lauren's senior, Jackie was aeons further professionally. Jackie was a well-respected, tenured full professor, while Lauren—although thirty-eight with a son and a soon-to-be ex-husband—was just another graduate student struggling to complete her dissertation, get her PhD, and enter a world with little use for green historians. So when the history department had consented to accept the book in lieu of her doctoral dissertation, Lauren had jumped at the project.

A cold wind was blowing off the Charles River, more reminiscent of January than of late October. As a frigid blast hit her from behind, Lauren climbed the stairs with the unrealistic hope that Jackie had been early and was waiting for her inside. Wind chimes rang gently as Lauren pushed the door open. She looked around expectantly, but aside from a businesswoman engrossed in a book, a teenage girl with bad teeth stocking shelves from a stepladder, and a canary in a graceful bamboo cage, the store was empty. As the door closed softly behind her, the chimes pealed again.

Although disappointed that Jackie was nowhere in sight, Lauren was pleasantly surprised by the store itself. It was lovely: the rose-colored walls and soft recessed lighting; the slightly burnt, pungent smell of sandalwood; shelves of books clustered around a few beanbag chairs in the far corner; Mozart playing softly in the background. Somehow, this wasn't what she had expected.

Lauren took a deep breath of the spicy-sweet air. Had she really expected the place to be dark and cave-like, filled with glowing talismans and mandrake roots and pin-studded voodoo dolls? This was nothing like that. It was comforting and earthy, almost erotic, like having all of her senses pleasantly, but subtly, stroked.

Wandering down a crowded aisle, she saw it was stocked with normal enough looking lotions and shampoos—although everything seemed to be made from bee pollen and to have names like Brainstorm and Waterfall. Then she noticed an entire section devoted to aromatherapy: tiny bottles of clary sage, neroli, and bergamot for tension relief; other concoctions to enhance meditation and well-being. Was she going to have to talk seriously with a woman who believed in aromatherapy?

Lauren glanced at her watch and headed toward a niche formed by two ceiling-high bookshelves along the back wall. The shelves were filled with books as ordinary as *Diet for a Small Planet* and as extraordinary as *Witches Heal: Lesbian Herbal Self-Sufficiency*. Some were classic, leatherbound editions; others were obviously self-published. She pulled out an herbal encyclopedia and began to flip through it.

"If all goes well, our book'll be on these shelves soon," a soft voice said in Lauren's ear as she was enveloped in a huge bear hug. Pressing Lauren to her with one arm, Jackie waved the other at the book niche.

Despite her apprehension about the project, Lauren felt a leap of exhilaration at the thought of a book with her name on the jacket. She disengaged herself from Jackie's voluminous wool cloak and smiled at her friend. Jackie was a handsome woman whose comfort with herself exuded from her every pore; she wore no makeup and no dye streaked her silver-white hair. Jackie's attractiveness lay in her intelligence and enthusiasm for life—and she was astute enough to know it.

"Can't you just see it?" Jackie asked, her eyes shining. "*The Lost Coven of Rebeka Hibbens: Hoax, Sorcery, or Social Psychology?* by Jackie Pappas, PhD, and Lauren Freeman, *PhD*."

"As long as we don't end up with a book that doesn't need 'hoax' or 'social psychology' in the title," Lauren said. "Not to mention the question mark."

Jackie's laugh pealed across the store. "Your open-mindedness is staggering."

"Well, you've got to admit this is getting pretty far from our original idea," Lauren said in what she knew to be a vain attempt to buttress her position. Their initial concept for the book was a multidisciplinary investigation of an actual historical event: six women and one man convicted of witchcraft in Cambridge in 1692, who vanished from their prison cells on the eve of their executions and were never seen again. The original proposal had set out an outline for the first half to contain a description of the events, followed by chapters posing historical, social psychological, anthropological, feminist, and supernatural explanations of the disappearances. But ever since Deborah Sewall—the co-owner of RavenWing and the self-proclaimed reincarnation of Rebeka Hibbens—had told Jackie about *The Chronicle of the Coven,* Jackie's plans for the format and content of the book had changed.

Jackie studied Lauren carefully with her open, childlike gaze, a gaze that was strangely congruous with the fine web of lines around her eyes. "You can't possibly believe we shouldn't take a look at their chronicle," she finally said, shaking her head at Lauren in mock despair. "Even a 'rational' scholar couldn't resist a little peek."

"Of course I want to look at it," Lauren said. "I just think there's a danger if we begin to take the chronicle, or this Deborah and Cassandra, too seriously." Cassandra Abbott was the other owner of RavenWing; she claimed to be the reincarnation of Millicent Glover, also a member of the lost coven.

"I'm just keeping an open mind." Jackie's tone clearly stated that Lauren was not.

Lauren looked down at the herbal encyclopedia she still held in her hands. Immortality and reincarnation—as well as the power of the herb violaceae to "reduce growths, benign and malignant"—were a bit much for her to buy. "How come no one ever claims to be the reincarnation of a garbageman or a peasant?" she asked. "How come they're always the reborn soul of some extraordinary person?"

Jackie sighed. "I just got off the phone with Nat.

That's why I was late. He's talked to a few people in the publishing house and apparently they're all very excited about our new slant on *Rebeka Hibbens.*"

"Aren't you all jumping the gun a bit?" Lauren asked. Nat Abraham was their editor at Boylston Press. He had already told Jackie that if the chronicle contained even a fraction of what Deborah had hinted at, he wanted the supernatural explanation to be integrated throughout the book rather than relegated to a single hypothetical chapter. And now it sounded as if he had the publishing house behind him. "We haven't even seen the chronicle—let alone read it. The whole thing could be complete bunk." Lauren closed the encyclopedia and placed it back on the shelf.

"That's why we're here."

"I don't know, Jack," Lauren said. "I'm just afraid that if we put too much supernatural in *Rebeka Hibbens,* we're going to lose our credibility."

"Is this book about *our* credibility?"

Lauren ran her finger along the binding of a book written by someone named Starhawk titled *The Spiral Dance: A Rebirth of the Ancient Religion of the Great Goddess.* "Without knowing you're reading the work of a credible source," she finally answered, "what's the point of studying history at all?"

"Maybe historical research is about pushing limits—or maybe it should be," Jackie said. "Getting people—and ourselves—to think in ways we've never thought before."

"I suppose."

It was a hopeless argument: Lauren's commitment to the painstaking, rational amassing of historical data based on primary sources was as strong as Jackie's was to radical experimentation. She would never convince Jackie—and Jackie would never convince her. "So where's Rebeka?" Lauren asked in the hope of changing the subject, though she couldn't help adding, "I've never met a three-hundred-year-old soul before."

"Don't be so sure," said a deep voice behind her.

Lauren whirled around and saw a tall woman with a wild mane of curly dark hair that was liberally sprinkled with gray. The woman's eyes were an eerie white-brown, nearly transparent, and they were looking at Lauren with disquieting intensity. "I'm Deborah Sewall," she said, holding out her hand.

Automatically, Lauren held out her own hand, but her eyes never left Deborah's. The woman emanated a commanding energy. Her presence was so powerful it seemed to vibrate around her. Like her almost colorless eyes, she was simultaneously seductive and repellent.

"Hi," Lauren finally said. "Lauren Freeman."

Deborah nodded and took Jackie's hand in both of hers. "Please come with me."

"Where's Cassandra?" Jackie asked.

"Cassandra's on a knowledge quest—a stained-glass course in Vermont. We all do it toward the end," Deborah said. "Knowledge gained at the tail of a lifetime is the most enduring."

Lauren tried to catch Jackie's attention to share her astonishment at the confident manner in which Deborah had delivered this decidedly odd piece of information. But Jackie was watching Deborah with an inscrutable expression and did not meet Lauren's eye.

After pausing to give a few instructions to the teenage girl, Deborah ushered them into a back room that obviously served as both storage chamber and office. The room was long and low and lit only by a small, dirty window on the rear wall. Deborah snapped on a floor lamp; the occult symbols cut into the lamp shade threw odd shapes of light over some portions of the room, while casting deep shadows into others.

Following Deborah and Jackie, Lauren stepped around burlap bags covered with strange letters and stamps denoting their place of origin: the Maldive Islands, Benghazi, Dondra Head. Shelves, loaded down with books, candles, and hundreds of wax figures, circled the room. The shelves held so many dark pockets that the pieces hit by the irregular light were edged with a sharpness that seemed to expand them beyond three dimensions. So this was RavenWing's dark underside, Lauren thought, wrapping her arms around herself. She wondered if Deborah had an underside also.

Deborah cleared cartons of incense and vitamins from chairs at a long table, then motioned for Lauren and Jackie to sit. She remained standing. "We've never shown our chronicle to an outsider before," she began. "But I had a vision the sages wished us to share our knowledge with you." Deborah turned her intense gaze from Jackie to Lauren. "Although this gift is not without danger."

Lauren shifted her eyes to the shelf behind Deborah. It overflowed with wax forms: normal-looking tapered candles; waxen pentacles and pinecones; a very tall, winged caduceus. A life-size mask of a man who appeared to be breathing leaves was highlighted by the lamp's beam. Meeting the mask's deep-set, shadowy gaze, Lauren shivered and quickly pulled her eyes back to Deborah's.

"I see you're going to have difficulty with what I'm about to tell you," Deborah said, looking at Lauren. "But you're an historian—you've studied religion, seen its power, its mystery. Tell me," she demanded, "what is a religion?"

"You want me to answer that question?" Lauren asked. Deborah nodded, and Jackie gave her a whimsical smile. "Well," Lauren began slowly, "I guess you could say it's a system of beliefs about how to live life. A set of constructs explaining the unexplainable. . . ."

Deborah nodded again. "And to explain the unexplainable, one must have faith. All religions—Christianity, Judaism, Islam, whatever—depend on it. One must believe in miracles, whether they be the virgin birth or the parting of the Red Sea. And our religion is no different."

"Although your miracles are," Jackie said.

"I know it's hard for people to believe, but you're exactly right." Deborah ran her fingers through her hair, pulling it into an even wilder mass around her head. "*The Chronicle of the Coven* is similar to your Bible. It's full of knowledge, history, philosophy, religion, magic. It contains the story of our founders. Morality tales. Fables."

Jackie leaned her elbows on the table and looked up at Deborah. "Fables like Moses receiving the Ten Commandments? Like Lot's wife turning to salt?" she asked. "Can you tell us one?"

Deborah's irises paled to a dusty white as she looked past Jackie into a place and time far beyond the walls of RavenWing. "Our most sacred artifact is Rebeka's lancet. We have many tales of its power to bring forth our immortality—or to destroy us."

"Rebeka Hibbens?" Lauren asked.

Deborah grinned and Lauren was jolted by the seductiveness of her smile. "Rebeka Hibbens was a very powerful witch," Deborah said. "Her magic created the lancet that will allow us to break free from the chains of humanness."

This time Jackie met Lauren's eye; she shook her head slightly.

"But according to our lore," Deborah continued, "if the lancet is ever lost or destroyed, the coven will be too. Every member will cease to exist and every soul lose its chance at immortality."

"Did the lost coven lose the lancet?" Jackie asked. "Is that what happened to them?"

"The coven was never lost," Deborah said patiently. "And neither was the lancet. One part of the chronicle, 'The Book of Mahala,' tells the story of what did happen—"

"Mahala?" Jackie interrupted.

"Mahala is what Rebeka was—is—called by the coven. It's a term of reverence meaning 'wise one,' but it also connotes deep respect and affection."

"And 'The Book of Mahala'?" Jackie prompted.

"The book describes what life was like in 1692. Why the coven was arrested. How the escape was accomplished."

Lauren's heart began to pound as she listened to Deborah. She glanced at Jackie. How stupid she had been, focusing on the supernatural angle and Deborah's slightly deranged behavior. She had missed the whole point. This was a primary source from the time in history that fascinated her the most: an account of day-to-day life in the late 1600s written by someone who had lived then, using paper and ink made then, in her own words, with her own misspellings.

Lauren had spent the better part of the past five years reading and studying Colonial history—so much so that she sometimes felt as if she were actually living in the seventeenth century, especially in her dreams, when she imagined she was wandering through smokehouses hung with huge hams or sitting at a foot wheel, spinning flax thread into linen. Even if ninety percent of this so-called chronicle was bunk, it could still provide incredible insights. To discover a new primary source was the stuff of a scholar's dreams. "Who wrote this book?" she asked.

"Rebeka Hibbens."

Lauren clasped her hands together; her palms were damp. "What kind of condition is it in? Can we turn the pages? The last three-hundred-year-old document I used was kept under glass and had to be read at the library."

"The chronicle isn't actually that old," Deborah said

slowly. "It was written in the late nineteenth century by Harriet Reardon Smith—one of Rebeka's reincarnations."

"Oh," Lauren said, letting her breath out in a rush.

"As the daughter and wife of wealthy men, Harriet got to study art, literature, and history—but wasn't allowed to use her knowledge," Deborah continued. "So she poured all her learning and all of what she knew of the past into the chronicle. It's a masterpiece of social and historical interpretation." She looked at Lauren as if her colorless eyes could see into Lauren's soul. "If I do say so myself."

Lauren's shoulders slumped and she closed her eyes for a moment. Was Deborah saying she was both the reincarnation of Rebeka and of Harriet? That a book written in the nineteenth century was a primary source from the seventeenth? "You mean this Harriet Reardon Smith wrote down what she remembered from her life two hundred years before—when she actually *was* Rebeka Hibbens?"

"That, along with the collective memory of the coven," Deborah said as calmly as if she were commenting on the weather.

Lauren stared at the poised woman before her. How could someone intelligent enough to offer a cogent argument on the functions of religion, someone together enough to run a successful business, be so clearly delusional? Unable to come up with even a semblance of an answer, Lauren turned to Jackie. "It isn't a primary source."

"It all depends on your definition." Jackie's voice was thoughtful and deliberate. "Although I guess it really is something new altogether: a primary source written two hundred years after the fact."

"But isn't that a contradiction in terms?" Lauren argued. "If it's *after the fact,* it's not a primary source."

Deborah cleared her throat. "*The Chronicle of the Coven* is much more than just narrative history. The chronicle also tells of magic spells and potions and reveals the mysteries of reincarnation, as well as the rites for consummating the Immortalis—the ritual we reenact at the ocean's edge, under a waxing crescent moon, every one hundred and one years. The ritual that will ultimately secure our immortality." Deborah paused for a long moment. "And it is here that the danger lies."

Lauren and Jackie stared at Deborah.

"Something so powerful must have a means of protecting itself." Deborah looked closely at them both, a slight smile tugging at the edges of her lips. "It is said that anyone who reads the chronicle and isn't a member of the coven will either die or go mad."

Lauren forced herself to maintain eye contact with Deborah. "Do you believe that?"

Deborah turned and walked over to a cupboard. She knelt and opened a lower door. "I believe in the message of the sages."

Lauren watched Deborah warily. Cursed chronicles and visions and messages from the sages. Deborah's argument about religion and faith and magic notwithstanding, this woman was on the edge.

"Normally, this is kept well hidden." Deborah pulled an oversize book from the cupboard and placed it on the table. It was a beautiful object, bound on the spine and corners in a rich butter-colored leather, its front and back boards protected by a darker skin. Rough-edged parchment pages poked from between the covers. No title marred the face of the book, for no words were necessary; this was clearly an important and much-cherished artifact.

"One week," Deborah said, her fingers lingering on the spine. "You may have it until next Thursday—and no photocopying."

Lauren and Jackie looked down at the handsome book, but neither moved toward it. Finally, Lauren reached out for the thick volume. But as soon as its smooth leather touched her skin, she was overwhelmed by confusion; she felt light-headed and a little bit dizzy.

The book was warm and worn and smelled of aged paper and secluded library stacks. It drew her as old books always drew her, but this book unsettled her in a way she had never experienced before. As she pressed it between her palms, she felt as if she were surrounded by shadowy figures, disembodied torsos bobbing above dark, rippling waters. She recoiled at the odor of dampness and fear.

Lauren thrust the chronicle at Jackie and stood up. "Thanks," she said to Deborah. "We really appreciate this, but we've got to get going." As soon as her hands were empty, her apprehension disappeared, but she noticed Jackie and Deborah were looking at her closely.

Lauren was relieved when Jackie stood too. As they stepped aside to let Deborah lead them into the store, Lauren accidentally pressed up against the chronicle Jackie held to her chest. When the book grazed her back, her relief vanished. For from somewhere inside her head, Lauren heard a faraway chorus of voices chanting words she couldn't discern. And for a moment, she thought she saw the sliver of a crescent moon, shining against an ebony sky.

Three

As far back into time as she could remember, Deborah had been blessed with visions. As the years passed, the visions became more frequent and she became more adept at interpreting them. Watching Jackie Pappas and Lauren Freeman descend the stairs to the sidewalk, Deborah smiled. Her vision would now be fulfilled. She had given Jackie the chronicle, and as a result Faith Osborne's arrival was assured. Although a plummeting raven had accompanied Faith in the vision, Deborah felt no responsibility for the death the raven foretold. The loss of a human life was of no more significance to her than the loss of a grain of sand from a beach.

She opened the latch on the bamboo bird cage and Summerland jumped out onto her finger. She had named him for summerland, the home of the sages, the place where the soul rests between lives, where it is refreshed and made young once again. While canaries were usually high-strung and difficult to tame, Deborah had a way with animals and Summerland would sit on her shoulder for hours. She had even trained him to select Tarot cards for her customers by pecking at them with his beak. The bird's Tarot choices were startlingly accurate.

"When will Faith arrive, little fella?" Deborah cooed to the canary, running her finger over the soft feathers on his breast. "Will it be soon?" Her questions were not rhetorical: The sages spoke to her through the bird. The coven had to have Faith Osborne—or, more accurately, the body in which Faith's soul now resided—to perform the Immortalis. For until the lethal crescent was carved into Faith's neck with Rebeka's lancet, the coven's ascendence to immortality could not occur.

Summerland's intelligent black eyes met Deborah's. He tilted his head and opened his beak. The store was filled with his sweet, gurgling song. The canary stopped singing for a moment and looked at her. Eight short chirps trilled through the air, then he was silent once again.

Deborah nodded. Eight days. The sages were letting her know that Faith would arrive within eight days, assuring her that the Immortalis would take place. She ran her tongue along the top of Summerland's head and deposited him back in his cage. Then she picked a few leaves from the packet of fresh greens she kept nearby and sprinkled them in his dish. "Thank you, little one," she said, closing the latch.

As Summerland ate, Deborah thought of the past three Immortalises, when, after sacrificing Faith Osborne, the coven found themselves born once again as human. This Immortalis would be different. With the fourth sacrifice of Faith, the cycle would be broken. In this, their fourth incarnation, the six had finally amassed enough power to escape from the bonds of humanness. The sages had promised Deborah that eternal life in summerland awaited them on the other side of this year's ritual.

Deborah's hands clenched into fists as she thought

of the squandered time. Had Faith not caused Dorcas to be separated from them, the coven would have had enough power to reach summerland after the first Immortalis. It had taken 300 years—and many human lifetimes for each of them—to amass what would have been theirs if Dorcas's power had not been lost. A combined total of eighteen hundred wasted years lay upon Faith Osborne's head.

Deborah looked at the antique ink block print of Dorcas by the artist Deodat Willard. Jackie Pappas had given her the small picture, and she had hung it across from the cash register so she could see it often. It brought back bittersweet memories of the immense power lost to the coven because of the blindness and stupidity of the girl's mother, Faith, and the narrow-minded depravity of her stepfather, Oliver Osborne, a powerful magistrate who was the primary architect of the witchcraft hysteria in Massachusetts Bay Colony.

Deborah had been mesmerized by the ink block when she had seen it in Jackie's kitchen, for Deodat Willard had caught the essence of Dorcas. Seated on a craggy boulder, the young girl beckoned to a field of towering corn that bent in obedience to her command.

Actually, Dorcas had been able to seduce far more than cornstalks. Livestock and birds and wild animals from the forest had all responded to her power. But Dorcas's soul had been ripped from the coven when, at seven years of age, she had become the youngest "witch" to be hung on Gallows Hill. And although Deborah had searched for her in, and between, every lifetime, Dorcas's soul was lost in the eddying tides of time.

When Deborah had seen the print at Jackie's, Dorcas's unexpected presence had evoked such powerful emotions in Deborah that she had been stunned into silence. Watching Deborah carefully, Jackie had lifted the picture from the wall. "I can see this touches something in you," Jackie had said. "I want you to have it."

Late that same evening Deborah had had the vision. She was sitting on her mat in the small closet behind her living room, doing her shibboleth, magic that thinned the veil between the worlds and opened contact with the sages. She drifted into a deep trance. *Kamalo,* she repeated to herself. *Kamalo.*

She saw herself wearing a long black dress. She was carrying the chronicle and climbing a snaking path up the side of a mountain. At the crest of the mountain, Jackie waited. When she reached Jackie, Deborah held out the book. Jackie took it, pressed it to her breast, and then slipped down the other side of the precipice. Suddenly, a black raven filled Deborah's vision. The bird was large and shiny. Its unblinking eyes met hers, luminous with life. Then the eyes clouded and rolled upward and the raven fell into the dark river, disappearing without a splash.

Where the bird had entered the water, RavenWing arose, an Atlantis in reverse. She, Deborah, was standing at the cash register. A tall woman, her face obscured by shadow, approached. When the woman lifted her face, Deborah saw the countenance of Faith Osborne, and Deborah knew the sages were instructing her to draw Faith to the coven by giving Jackie the chronicle.

Coming back to herself, Deborah blinked at the Deodat Willard. Touching a finger to the smooth cheek of the young Dorcas, Deborah headed toward the book corner nestled in an alcove in the back of the store. She retrieved an oversize paperback on herbal home health care that had been left on a beanbag chair and replaced it on the shelf. Then she told the clerk she could go home, that she, Deborah, would handle the store by herself.

Within moments of the clerk's departure, Bram

Melgram pushed open the door and threw himself across the threshold. "Did it happen as you had seen?" he asked, the gold hoop piercing the skin below his right eyebrow quivering in his excitement. "Did she come? Did you give her the chronicle? Will everything work out as we need it to?"

"Of course." Deborah's voice was icy. "Did you ever doubt it?"

"I'm sorry, Mahala," Bram mumbled. "Of course I never doubted you. I was just worried. There's barely a month left and no sign of Faith."

Deborah looked at the young man, his shoulders tense and his face flushed with embarrassment at having questioned her. Bram's had always been an insecure soul, in need of constant reassurance. But the soul had improved much over time, she reminded herself, remembering how uncertainty had rendered Foster Lacy almost powerless, but how now, in this fourth incarnation, Bram had grown into an impressive sorcerer. "Perhaps there is no sign," Deborah said. "And perhaps there is."

"Another human came with the Pappas woman?" Bram asked, his shoulders dropping in relief.

Deborah grabbed a handful of fliers lying on the table and began to hang them on the bulletin board near the door. "Someone else came." She stabbed pushpins into the cork.

"Was it Faith?" Bram demanded, then his face flushed again at the impertinence of his tone.

"It is not clear to me yet," Deborah told him impassively.

Bram nodded and lowered his eyes.

Deborah placed her hands on Bram's head. He trembled under her fingertips. "Faith Osborne will come to us within eight days," Deborah told him. "Of that I am certain. She will stay among us until the twelfth waxing crescent moon of 1995. Then, together, we shall all consummate the Immortalis." Deborah stretched her arms toward the heavens. "When her soul is destroyed, we will finally be free."

Bram raised his eyes and they smiled at one another.

"It will happen as it was foretold," Deborah said. "Now go and tell the others."

Bram touched the crescent-shaped scar at the base of his neck and left the store.

Four

"WELL, THAT SURE RANKS RIGHT UP THERE WITH THE weird experiences of *my* life," Lauren said, leaning across the wide table toward Jackie. They were sitting in Jackie's dining room–office, having gone there directly from RavenWing so Lauren could borrow a few books. "What do you make of her?"

"She's not your ordinary shopkeeper, that's for sure," Jackie said.

Lauren absently tapped the pile of papers in front of her. "It's the contradiction that amazes me. How can someone who's so obviously intelligent, someone capable of presenting a reasoned argument and running a successful business, also believe in cursed chronicles and magic lancets? Or that she's the reincarnation of a seventeenth-century witch?" She shook her head. "Is there a kind of mental illness where you can be so deluded and still function?"

"Maybe it's not a mental illness—and maybe there's no contradiction," Jackie argued. "Maybe Deborah just sees what the rest of us are too blind to see."

"Do you really believe that?"

"Probably not," Jackie admitted. "But it might explain what happened to our coven."

Lauren walked to the vast fireplace at the far end of the room. Its deep, gaping opening was at least eight feet wide and its lintel came to just below her eye level—and Lauren was over five foot eight. She used her fingernail to trace the words *Friends and Publick* etched into the leather of an old fire bucket hanging from a hook imbedded in the rough-hewn lintel. *Their* coven. The people they were researching weren't even a coven—for a coven was comprised of actual witches. Their seven were just ordinary souls, convicted of a ridiculous crime in an absurd time.

People so ordinary, in fact, that Rebeka Hibbens might have lived in this very house, Lauren thought as she played with a set of old toasting forks hanging next to the bucket, twirling them around on their chain, snapping the two pieces closed then opening them again. Rebeka might have used the fire bucket and the toasting forks and the bread box inside the fireplace. Or the spinning wheel in the corner. But Rebeka, and the six other ordinary people, had disappeared from their prison cells without a trace.

Rubbing her arms, Lauren looked around the room. It was the perfect repository for Jackie's antiques—and for Jackie. The house was well over 300 years old and the wide fireplace marked this room as the original kitchen. In keeping with the earliest use of the room, Jackie had suspended iron pots, copper kettles, and all kinds of wooden and pewter kitchen utensils—some period and some not—from chains inside the chimney. The computer and fax machine on the table gave the place a jumbled, anachronistic spirit, although a quite pleasant one.

Lauren picked up a cracked wooden ladle from the mantel and lightly tapped a pockmarked copper pail that hung from the longest chain; the hollow copper made a reassuring clank as it hit the black iron pot hanging next to it. Could Rebeka have served her family's porridge with this ladle or boiled sap into sugar in this pail?

"Are you saying you believe in reincarnation?" Lauren asked.

Jackie rested her hand on the chronicle's leather cover. "Right now, more people in the world believe in reincarnation than in Jesus Christ." She regarded Lauren over her reading glasses.

"Hey, I'm Jewish," Lauren said, holding up her hands. "I don't have to believe in either."

Jackie walked to the front window, which was small and made of a thick, wavy glass. The autumn sun fell on her face, highlighting the signs of age her wide eyes and thick hair denied. "Sometimes I just don't understand you," she said softly, playing with a mottled green glass bottle, one of dozens that filled a triangular shelf wedged into the corner. She kept her back to Lauren. "Don't you *want* to push beyond what we think we know? Push into that great unknown? We have a chance to use history as a key to the present—as a way of enlightening our world—not just as a place to hide." She turned and looked at Lauren.

"What do you mean 'hide'?"

"Sometimes I think you use the past—your books, your work, your fascination with what was—as a way to escape the present," Jackie said. "And even though, as your professor, I'll admit your amazing ability to grasp the essence of seventeenth-century life is what made me want to work with you on *Rebeka Hibbens*, as your friend I've got to warn you that it's a mistake to use this skill to hide behind. You can't keep running away from the things that scare you."

"I'm not scared and I'm not escaping into the past," Lauren declared vehemently, staring down at the chronicle. "And I never said I didn't want to read their book. I'm a historian. I study Colonial America, for God's sake. Of course I'm curious to see what's in there." She looked up at Jackie and smiled. "Even if it isn't a primary source."

"History is more than primary sources." Jackie tossed her eyeglasses onto the table. "Come on. Let's have some tea. Then there's something funny I want to show you."

Relieved by this reprieve, Lauren followed Jackie into the kitchen, which fit snugly under the roof that started at two-and-a-half stories at the front of the house and sloped steeply to almost ground level in the back. She sat down and watched Jackie fill the kettle with water, thinking how deeply she loved and respected this woman, and how much it hurt to disappoint her.

Despite her assertions to the contrary, Lauren knew she *did* turn to her work whenever life—especially her current problems with her husband, Todd—began to overwhelm her. And she *did* like things predictable and stable, preferring to reexamine old ideas from a new perspective rather than strike out in a new direction. Todd was always telling her to "let go," but Lauren just wasn't the "let go" type. It had taken him years to convince her to give up her job and go to graduate school—a decision that had brought her many positive results, Jackie's friendship being one of the best.

Jackie poured their tea and, grinning slyly, pulled a paper bag from a cabinet. She offered Lauren some carrot chips, well aware that Lauren was fonder of the high-salt, high-cholesterol type. Lauren reluctantly popped one in her mouth; she was forced to acknowledge that it was actually quite good.

Jackie sat down across from Lauren. "You've got to give these women a chance, Lauren. They could hold the key to our whole book."

"Level with me, Jack," Lauren said. "Do you really

believe Deborah's the reincarnation of Rebeka Hibbens or that Cassandra woman is Millicent Glover? Don't you have a problem with evil curses and magic lancets—not to mention how they remember all the details of their previous lives?"

"I'm agnostic," Jackie said. "I've no proof that it's true—and I've no proof that it's not."

Lauren groaned. When Jackie became "agnostic" about something, her mind was made up: She was going to be open-minded to the end.

Jackie reached over and tapped the table in front of Lauren. "I've done my bit in the straight historical world. I've more than paid my dues. This book is my great adventure. It's as if we're exploring a new world—or at least a new way of looking at the old one."

"Maybe I just don't have the pioneer spirit."

"Beats working your way through graduate school waiting table like I did." Jackie's voice was gentle but firm.

Lauren nodded and sipped her tea. She *was* grateful to Jackie—extremely grateful indeed—for involving her in this project and making her the envy of her fellow graduate students. Jackie had handed her a great dissertation topic and enough money to last until she finished her degree—although she had spent most of her share of the modest advance.

"When I spoke with Nat this morning," Jackie was saying, "he hinted that if Deborah's chronicle pans out we might be talking a much larger print run."

"I'm not doing the talk shows," Lauren joked, waving a carrot chip at Jackie. "I can just see it now. They'll have us on with women who have had sex with the reincarnation of their husbands' brothers."

Jackie looked at Lauren sadly. "This is serious scholarship—it's just scholarship in an area that, because of our society's narrow views, isn't usually studied. This book contract is a gift—and you of all people should know I would never let it be turned into a circus."

Sufficiently chastised, Lauren studied her teacup. "You had something funny to show me?"

"Oh, right," Jackie said, jumping up from her chair. "You've got to see what Paul Conklin sent me." Paul Conklin was a professor in their department who specialized in modern American diplomatic history—and practical jokes.

"Another one of his less than amusing pranks?" Lauren called as Jackie went into the living room.

"This one's pretty amusing," Jackie said as she returned to the kitchen carrying a narrow shoe box. "And quite clever."

"I thought he swore off his jokes after the last one backfired and Gabe Phipps's car ended up getting towed."

Jackie placed the box on the table. "Apparently not," she said, shoving it toward Lauren.

A dank, not unpleasant odor reminiscent of hayrides and childhood visits to her grandmother's farm rose from the box. Lauren hesitated. Although she had no tolerance for practical jokes—finding them at best stupid and at worst hurtful—more than her lack of appreciation of Paul Conklin's humor gave her pause; she somehow knew that she didn't want to see what was in the box.

"Go on," Jackie coaxed, laughing. "It's Paul at his best."

Lauren didn't move for a long moment, then she slowly raised the lid. Inside was a naked doll: a misshapen, sloppily made doll, constructed of old rags and straw. Its eyes were crooked and it stared up at her with a lopsided, slightly demented grin.

"Oh," Lauren cried, pushing the box away. "That's awful."

"Here's the note that came with it," Jackie said, handing Lauren a white note card.

Lauren opened the card. *Those who risk the sanctity of the coven shall be punished with eternal death: Do not touch the chronicle.* She dropped the card to the table. "I don't think that's funny at all."

"Oh, come on, Lauren," Jackie said, laughing again. "Lighten up. Everyone in the department knew we were picking up the chronicle today—he was just joking around." Jackie was not one to keep secrets, whether in her personal or professional life. She shared everything from her latest historical breakthrough to where she kept the spare key to her house.

Reaching into the box, Jackie lifted the doll. "Where do you think he ever found a poppet? And such an authentic-looking one at that." She turned the doll over a few times, admiring it, then placed it carefully back in the box. "The guy's amazing—it's perfect."

Lauren frowned. "You're the amazing one. Paul sends you a voodoo doll with a threatening note and you think it's 'perfect'?"

"It's a joke, Lauren. A joke." Jackie threw her hands up in exasperation. "Let go a little, will you?"

Lauren forced a chuckle. "You sound like Todd."

"I always did like that guy." Jackie moved the box to the counter and sat back down. "Heard from him lately?" she asked, taking a sip of her tea.

"He called last night. . . ." Lauren stretched her long legs under the table and inspected her fingernails.

"And?"

"And he says people change," Lauren answered with a sigh. "That he has."

"But you're afraid." Jackie's question was a statement.

Lauren looked up at her friend. "I don't think I could stand being hurt again."

"I understand." Jackie covered Lauren's hand with her own. "But he's a wonderful man."

"Wonderful men don't always make wonderful husbands."

"At least you got one out of two." Jackie smiled as only those who have been long divorced can when discussing their ex-spouses. "Simon actually threatened to go to court to get custody of Matthew if I don't stop writing this book. He's afraid that the notoriety about my 'weirdness' will negatively affect Matthew's academic progress—but you and I know all Simon's really worried about is how it might reflect on him." She chuckled. "Thank goodness Helene's out of school and married."

"It's amazing that after all these years the man just can't let it go."

"A man of Simon's towering ego doesn't like being left for a woman," Jackie said with a mischievous twinkle in her eye. True to form, Jackie had never hidden the fact that she had divorced Simon because she had fallen in love with a woman, Andrea Molineaux. She and Andrea had lived together in Jackie's house until Andrea had died of breast cancer three years before.

"But I've got to admit, I'm kind of guilty of not letting go too." Jackie waved her hand toward an empty spot on the wall above the stove. At Lauren's confused look, she explained, "I got immense pleasure out of giving Deborah the Willard print that belonged to Simon's mother."

"You gave Deborah the Deodat Willard?" Lauren was incredulous. Although far from a household name in the twentieth century, Deodat Willard had been a well-known and respected scholar in the seventeenth, dabbling in painting and ink block as well as in historical study. Lauren stared at the bare wall where the print had hung. Jackie had told her that when she had stumbled on the Willard in her in-laws' garage, Simon's mother had been more than happy to give her the strange little print. Unaware that the seductive young girl beckoning to a field of towering corn was supposed to be a witch, Simon's mother had nonetheless confessed to Jackie that the piece had always given her the creeps.

Jackie shrugged off Lauren's surprise. "Deborah was entranced by it when she was here the other day. She said it was an inspired portrayal of the Colonial love-hate relationship with women and witchcraft." She shrugged again. "So I gave it to her."

"Isn't it valuable?"

"It was mine to give," Jackie said, draining her cup and dropping her mug in the sink. "Let's go get your books. I'm anxious to get rid of you and take a look at that cursed chronicle."

Lauren glanced at her watch as she started to follow Jackie. "You're in luck—I've only got a few minutes. I can't be late picking up Drew again. His teachers are no more pleased with me than they are with him."

Jackie raised her eyebrows.

"Drew's been acting up lately. His teacher says he's having trouble concentrating. And he's been misbehaving. Apparently, he's been drawing violent pictures for his classmates—women and children hanging by nooses from trees and such." Lauren sighed. "Last week he input a bunch of swear words into the class's spelling test file—which Mrs. Baker then printed up and distributed to twenty-two highly amused seven-year-olds."

Jackie burst out laughing. "Doesn't sound too serious to me."

"She also mentioned something about him ripping another child's art project." Lauren shook her head. "Anyway, she figures he's acting out because of the divorce, and she wants to talk to me about it tomorrow morning."

"Sounds all too familiar." Jackie touched Lauren's sleeve as they entered the dining room. "Kids are tougher than you think."

"Yeah, I'm sure he is," Lauren said, although she was far from certain. Drew had been having a difficult time accepting his parents' separation, and she had been trying to compensate by spending more time with him. But it seemed the more time and attention she gave him, the more demanding and out of control he became. "Stability," Mrs. Baker had said. "Kids just need to feel safe."

Jackie picked up her glasses from the table and perched them on the end of her nose. She craned her neck and looked up at the top of the bookshelves. "So what books did you tell me you needed to borrow?" she asked. "You wanted Robert Brown, right?"

"And Thomas Swain's *Mission and Reason in Colonial New England.*"

Jackie pointed to the top shelf. "You'll have to get the step stool. They're all up there."

Lauren laughed. Jackie was barely five feet tall, and whenever she started a new project, she pulled down all the books she might need to her level. The lower shelves were currently filled with books on the historical roots of feminism, the occult, and analyses of European and American witch trials. The fact that the historiography books were on the top shelf was a clear indication of the esteem in which Jackie held them. The study of historical method and philosophy was far too traditional for Jackie's revisionist tastes.

"I like historiography," Lauren said, as she climbed on the stool.

"You would." Jackie walked over to the table and looked down at the chronicle. "It's probably just as well that you've got to go. I'll read through this quickly to get an idea of what it says. Then we'll know if it's worth our time—and our weekend."

"Do you need me during the day tomorrow?" Lauren asked as she grabbed the Robert Brown from the shelf. "How about after I talk to Mrs. Baker in the morning, I hit the library? I'll read up on some of that paranormal stuff you've been after me to take a look at." She climbed down off the step stool and checked her watch. "You get started on the chronicle and I'll come back here—say around five? Aunt Beatrice has Drew for dinner, so I'm free until eight. And we'll have plenty of time over the weekend—I've got no plans."

"It's going to be great fun," Jackie said, giving Lauren a quick hug. "I promise."

As Lauren headed for the door with Jackie's books under her arm, she found herself drawn to the chronicle. She stopped and stood staring down at the book. Gingerly, she moved her hand toward it, then pulled it back.

"It's not going to bite you," Jackie said.

Lauren thrust out her hand and touched the cover. No bobbing shadows. No chanting voices. Relieved, she put down Jackie's books and lifted the chronicle. But as soon as she opened it, she was overtaken by a powerful sense of déjà vu. For a moment, it was as if the plaster walls of Jackie's dining room had been stripped away and the rough-hewn wood exposed. The computer and fax machine disappeared, replaced by pewter tankards sitting on a narrow oaken table board in the center of the room.

Lauren blinked and all was as it had been. Yet she had the strangest feeling that she had been in this room before. That she had stood right on this spot and held a book in her hand—and that it had been a long, long time ago. A furry shiver ran down her spine. She snapped the book shut and dropped it on the table. Then she grabbed her coat off the cobbler's bench in the small foyer and headed out the door.

Five

Books towered over her head. Books everywhere. Lauren reached out her arms and touched the shelves that rose until their tops appeared to tip inward, to bend toward each other, like railroad tracks extending to the horizon. She whirled around, but there was only one way to run. Ahead. She had to keep going. To find her way out of the maze.

But she couldn't move. She tried and she tried, but her feet wouldn't budge. She looked down. Books. Books covered her shoes and her ankles and her calves—she was knee-deep in books! Frantically, she snatched at them: hardcovers, paperbacks, and piles and piles of handsome oversize leather volumes. She flung them to the left. To the right. Quickly. Quickly.

But she was not quick enough. For when she looked up, she saw the man. The man was walking slowly between the soaring stacks, moving silently and inexorably toward Lauren, his muddy cloak brushing dirt on the books as he passed. Lauren cried out, but she was no more able to speak than she was able to move. The man was getting closer. And closer. And closer.

At first Lauren had no idea who the man might be, but then, with the terrifying certainty of nightmares, she knew it was Oliver Osborne. Oliver Osborne, the one who had masterminded the Cambridge witch trials, the one who had arrested and prosecuted the coven.

Oliver's bushy hair was filled with dirt and leaves. His eyes were filled with hatred. As he drew nearer, Lauren saw a flash of metal. Many flashes of metal. Oliver held a fan of knives in his hand, undulating and unfolding, shiny and sly. Then Oliver was upon her.

Lauren's eyes flew open and she sat straight up in bed, her heart pounding, sweat running between her breasts. Whoa, she thought as she grabbed her dream journal and the little flashlight she kept by her bed. This coven was not only disrupting her life, it was beginning to seep into her unconscious. Lauren flipped open the notebook, and just as Jackie had instructed, she scribbled down a few key words to remind her of the dream in the morning.

Lauren had started the journal two years before, on Jackie's recommendation, as a way to release her creativity and perhaps, as Jackie put it, "to crack open her rigid mind-set." Although most of Lauren's dreams were a mishmash of her day's activities and worries, she was surprised that some actually did give her interesting insights. Unfortunately for Jackie, there hadn't been any noticeable changes in her mind-set.

Lauren closed the notebook and checked the clock. Then she flopped back onto the pillow, contemplating her dream and the absurd notion of graduate education. One of the problems with doctoral programs was that the faculty's major goal—aside from inflicting as much misery as possible—was to immerse a graduate student in the subject matter to such an extent that the academic discipline and the pupil became one. In Lauren's case, the idea was to imbed Colonial history so deeply into her psyche that it became a part of who she was, of how she would think and view the world for the rest of her life. Lauren smiled without humor. Given the nightmare from which she had just woken, she was in the running to be her department's greatest success.

She tried to will herself back to sleep, but it was no use. In the year since Todd had moved out, she had suffered bouts of insomnia and she now recognized all the signs of impending wakefulness. In an all too familiar ritual, she climbed out of bed, walked over to the window, and pulled up the shade. She stared at the street below. It was full of handsome houses and majestic trees, its stillness belying its closeness to both Porter and Harvard squares. But the calm moonlight bathing the silent pavement did little to subdue her anxiety.

She and Todd had been so excited when they had heard that a couple of Todd's friends were moving from their rent-controlled apartment on the second floor of an old Cambridge mansion. It was a price they could afford for a place they had never dared hope to live in. They immediately broke their own lease. The apartment was half the original bedroom wing, with four large rooms—two with turrets—flowing around what had once been an open, curved staircase. The top of the staircase was now at her front door. One bedroom had been converted into an airy kitchen and another into a spacious living room with two bays and a fireplace. Lauren used the huge built-in linen cabinet in the hallway for her books.

Moving away from the window, she took her bathrobe from the hook and went to check on Drew. As always, he was sprawled all over the bed, with Bunny, his favorite stuffed animal, clutched to his chest. Drew had slept with Bunny every night since he was a baby. Lauren vividly remembered the frantic searches she and Todd had made for the stuffed rabbit while Drew cried for his toy from his crib.

She stared at the spot under the window where the crib had once stood. Suddenly, it was four years ago, a hot summer day, and she and Todd were taking the crib apart. Drew was jumping on his new bed while he watched their every move, obviously worried about what this desecration might mean.

"Don't hurt crib, Daddy," Drew cried. "Don't hurt."

"Don't worry, slugger," Todd assured him. "I'm not hurting it, we're just taking it apart. We're going to put it in the basement until we need it again." He raised his eyebrows at Lauren and she playfully jabbed the screwdriver she was using into his side. Todd was anxious to start "trying" as soon as possible, but Lauren was starting graduate school in September and wanted to get a year behind her before she got pregnant again. Not to mention that with Todd's fledgling business and Lauren not working, they couldn't exactly afford another child.

Drew looked puzzled. "I have new bed," he said. "No more crib. I'm a big boy."

Lauren and Todd exchanged glances. "You *are* a big boy," Lauren told Drew. "But maybe some other baby will use it some day."

The little boy was silent for a moment and then his face lit up. "For Baby Jonathan or Baby Adam." Jonathan and Adam were Drew's second cousins, the twin sons of Aunt Beatrice's daughter Roz.

Todd slid behind Lauren and pulled her to him so that she could feel him hardening against her buttocks. "Or maybe a baby girl," he said, more to Lauren than to Drew.

Lauren arched her body, pressing even closer to

Todd. She twisted her head and met his kiss. "Maybe," she had said. "Maybe."

As quickly as the vision had come, it disappeared and Lauren was once again in Drew's dark bedroom. No Todd. No toddler Drew. And no hope for her little baby girl.

Lauren straightened the blanket and sheets and tucked them around Drew. She snuggled her face into his neck, breathing in his slightly stale sleeping smell. She kissed him. "I love you," she whispered. But he didn't stir. Drew was a very deep sleeper. Just like Todd.

Lauren wandered back to her bedroom, running her hand along the rich wood of the linen cabinet-bookcase. Sometimes she ached so from missing Todd, like the pain an amputee feels in a lost limb. Todd was just as severed from her life as her cousin Roger's leg was from his. Roger claimed he still felt his leg twenty-five years after it had been blown off in Vietnam. Lauren wondered if she was still going to ache twenty-four years from now.

In the beginning, she and Todd had been so good together: backpacking across Europe, throwing parties in the studio apartment they had painted bright red to disguise the fact that it had only one small window; reading Fitzgerald and Dickens and Tolstoy out loud to each other deep into the night. She had loved that he was a photographer, an artist, able to see what others missed, able to make the ordinary extraordinary. Todd had taught her to appreciate the moment, the living of life, the exquisite pleasure that was now.

Then Todd had changed, or she had changed, or life had changed. Todd's spontaneity and fierce independence, which had so appealed to Lauren, grew into annoying impulsiveness and irresponsibility. He ran off to Peking before *Time* actually hired him—which they never did. He screwed up their tax return and brought on an audit. His business failed, bequeathing a loan they would be struggling to repay into the next millennium. He forgot to pick up Drew at kindergarten, leaving her to stand, passive and repentant, pressing her sobbing child close, as she received a lecture from the teacher on the importance of stability and predictability to a five-year-old. The day Todd tried to explain away his fling with Melissa as a "meaningless mistake" was the day Lauren asked him to leave.

Lauren returned to her post at the window. She stood there for a long time, thinking about love and life and lost chances. Exhaustion finally overcame her and she dropped back into bed without even taking off her bathrobe. She fell into an immediate and surprisingly deep sleep.

She didn't wake until her bedroom door creaked open and Drew peeked in. He was wearing a pair of Celtics pajamas two sizes too big for him. The early morning sun shone like a fuzzy halo behind his tousled blond hair.

"Hi, honey," she mumbled, waving him over. "Want to cuddle?"

Drew shuffled to her side of the bed, managing not to trip over the pant legs that engulfed his feet. Looking down at her, his little mouth set in a straight line, he said, "I'm not going to school."

Lauren sighed. So it was going to be that kind of day. "Well, how about some breakfast anyway?" she asked, sitting up and swinging her legs over the side of the bed. "I'm hungry as a bear." She reached out and pulled him to her. "Grrrrr," she roared. "Better watch out."

Drew struggled out of her arms. "Don't, Mom," he said, but Lauren saw the twinge of a smile at the corners of his lips.

She turned away to give him some time to save face. Keeping her back to him, she stretched her hands to the ceiling and said, "You go pick out your cereal.

I'll be there in a minute." As he scurried toward the kitchen, Lauren headed to the bathroom, preparing herself for what she knew was going to be a difficult morning.

When Lauren entered the kitchen, she was surprised to see Drew sitting at the table, finishing up his cold cereal. She kissed the top of his head and he gave her a hug. "Want seconds?" she asked.

"Okily-dokily," he said, smiling and holding out his empty bowl.

Taking it, she leaned over and kissed him again. Maybe she was going to be spared a temper tantrum after all. Lauren refilled his bowl, put on the coffee, and toasted herself a bagel while Drew prattled on about his camp counselor last summer. Why this would come into his head on a late October morning was a mystery to Lauren. Placing her breakfast on the table, she sat down and smiled at him. When his bowl was empty, she said, "Go quick and do your stuff: clothes, teeth, hair, and bed."

He stood up and crossed his arms in a disarmingly adult gesture. "I'm not going to school," he said, looking her straight in the eye. "It's stupid and I hate it."

Lauren closed her eyes for a moment, wanting more than anything to just say, "Okay, we'll both play hooky and stay home and watch videos." But even if her conscience would have allowed it, she couldn't say it today. Today she was meeting with Mrs. Baker at nine. Today she was studying up on the paranormal. Today she was going to read Deborah's chronicle.

"I'll help you pick out your clothes," she said calmly, standing up and dropping her coffee cup in the sink. "Do you want to wear your Cambridge Camp sweatshirt or the Red Sox one Daddy got you?"

"I'm not going to school."

Lauren turned him toward his bedroom. "No matter what you do, you still have to get dressed. Let's go into your room and—" Lauren was cut off by the ringing of the telephone. "Now," she said to Drew as she picked up the receiver.

It was Jackie. Her voice was breathless and charged with excitement. "I'm so glad you're still there. I've been up all night reading this chronicle—I just couldn't bear to stop. It's unbelievable. Completely enthralling. Magnificent! I can't wait for you to read it. Although I sure hope Deborah meant what she said about just *reenacting* the Immortalis."

"Why? What's the deal with the Immortalis?"

"Nothing, if you don't mind—"

"Hold on a sec, Jack." Lauren turned to Drew, who hadn't moved. "Scott will be here in fifteen minutes. You go do your stuff right now or no TV tonight." Drew and his friend Scott had been walking to school together since the beginning of the year, both very proud of the new independence their mothers had reluctantly bestowed upon them.

Drew looked down at his foot, turned his ankle a few times, then looked back up at her. "I don't care about TV."

"If Scott gets here and you're not ready, I'm going to send him off and I'll walk you to school myself," Lauren said in her don't mess with me voice. When Drew sauntered slowly out of the room, Lauren sighed and returned to the phone. "Sorry," she said. "I'm dealing with the 'terrible sevens' here—and let me tell you, sevens have got it all over on twos."

"Listen, Lauren, you've got to come over here earlier than we planned. I've found something—something really *big*—and I don't know what to do with it."

Lauren rolled her eyes heavenward. She could just imagine what Jackie's "really big" something was. But before she could reply, she heard the sound of Rocky and Bullwinkle blast from the other room.

"Hold on," she said again and went tearing out of the kitchen.

When she got to the living room she found Drew, still in his pajamas, standing defiantly in front of the booming TV set. "Just what do you think you're doing, young man?" she demanded, grabbing the remote control and clicking the television off. "I've had enough of your nonsense. No TV tonight—and if you don't get into your bedroom right now, that television is off for the whole weekend."

"Not the whole weekend," Drew wailed. "That's not fair."

"What's not fair is the way you're acting," Lauren said. She grabbed him by the shoulders and pointed him toward his bedroom. "Now get!"

Back in the kitchen, Lauren picked up the phone again. "I'm sorry, Jack, but I've got to run. How about I cut my time at the library short and come over earlier in the afternoon?" Before Jackie could answer, Lauren dropped the phone and leaned out into the hallway. "Are you dressed yet?"

"—not what you think," Jackie was saying when Lauren returned. "It's bad. Really bad. I'm going to call Deborah as soon as I get off the phone with you." Jackie hesitated. "I was reading this section on religion in Colonial life, and it struck me that something wasn't quite right. It's pre-Phipps, yet it posits a much more reduced role for theology than I've ever seen before—"

"Mom!" Drew cried. "Someone stole my Red Sox sweatshirt!"

"I've got to run," Lauren interrupted. "I'll be there by mid-afternoon." She hung up the phone and headed down the hall, wondering how she was going to make it through the day.

Lauren had an image of herself as barely out of childhood, a mere youngster playing grownup, and often wondered why people didn't act more surprised that she was the mother of a seven-year-old. After all, she wore jeans and sweatshirts and listened to the "in" rock-and-roll station. But when Lauren walked into Mrs. Baker's second-grade classroom, she was forced to acknowledge that she had been out of elementary school for a long time.

The room was a whirlwind of activity as clusters of children worked at different "learning stations": Three girls were sprawled on the floor reading a single book, a group of boys was throwing various sized metal weights into the pan of a beam-balance scale, Drew and Scott were pouring sand all over each other's hands.

Although Mrs. Baker had explained the school's educational philosophy at Parent's Night—as had Ms. Anderson in the first grade—Lauren had difficulty believing children could learn amidst what appeared to be unsupervised chaos. Not that she had such fond memories of being one of the silent, prim children doing rote arithmetic drills in her own second-grade classroom, but somehow she thought there had to be a middle ground.

"Mrs. Freeman," Mrs. Baker called cheerfully, turning from two children at a computer. "As soon as I get Seth and Rachel outfitted for their trip to Oregon, I'll be right with you."

Lauren nodded and waited by the door. Drew shot her a look that clearly told her she was not to approach him, and a few of the other children glanced at her curiously. But most of the class appeared oblivious to her presence, obviously comfortable with parents walking in and out of the classroom—another change since Lauren's school days.

"Come," Mrs. Baker said, touching her arm. "Let's go to the cafeteria—there'll be no one there at this hour. The aide will watch the class."

As they walked down the hallway lined with colorful self-portraits and maps of New England, Mrs. Baker—Ellen, she had told Lauren to call her—chatted about what an interesting mix of children there was in the class this year and how much she was enjoying getting to know them all. But when they were seated at a table at the far end of the cafeteria, Ellen grew serious. She folded her hands and said, "I'm concerned about Drew. He's a very bright boy, and happy much of the time, but there are occasions, more and more lately, when nothing seems to interest him. He withdraws from me, from the other children. He seems so sad. . . ." She let her words trail off and watched Lauren intently.

"How, how often has this been happening?" Lauren asked, trying to get the words out from around the huge lump in her throat.

"It was only periodic during September. But there's been a gradual increase this month, and now I'd say, oh, at least three or four afternoons a week."

Lauren looked at the mural of happy primary-colored children riding trains and planes on the wall across from her. What were she and Todd doing to the poor little guy? How could they have thought he'd be capable of calmly accepting the dissolution of his family, of the only world he had ever known? "You know his father and I are getting divorced?" she asked softly.

The teacher's gaze was compassionate. "That's why I was so concerned about the incident with the family portrait. That's why I wanted to talk to you."

Lauren took a deep breath. "What exactly happened?"

"The assignment was to draw a picture of your family. As you know, we allow many opportunities to complete an assignment, but after three days, when almost all the other children had finished theirs, Drew still hadn't begun." Ellen ran her fingers through her fashionably short hair. "It was partly my fault. I wasn't thinking—if I had been, I'd have let the whole thing slide—but instead I told him he had to have it done or he'd lose afternoon recess. The next thing I knew, Kisha Liebhaber, the girl who sits next to him, was crying hysterically. Apparently unprovoked, Drew grabbed Kisha's painting from her desk and ripped it in half."

Lauren closed her eyes against the pain. "I suppose Kisha's family is happily intact."

Ellen reached over and touched Lauren's hand. "Things happen to kids. Friends move away. Grandparents die. Marriages break up. I simply want to help Drew adapt to the situation."

Lauren opened her eyes and smiled at the teacher through the tears in her eyes. "Thanks."

"Which is why I'm suggesting you give him lots of TLC at home and that you and your husband—and Drew too—talk with Dr. Berg, the school psychologist."

"Psychologist?" Lauren demanded. "Isn't that a bit extreme?"

"Not at all," Ellen said calmly. "Drew's behavior is a cry for help—and I think we should give it to him."

Zipping her parka up to her neck and throwing her backpack over her shoulder, Lauren walked slowly down the wide library steps and turned onto Cambridge Street. She couldn't remember an October so wintery. It must be well below freezing, and the gathering clouds foretold an early dusk and possibly snow. Raising her eyes to the darkening sky, she saw the day was working itself toward evening. Where had the hours gone? she wondered and then thought back on her meeting with Ellen Baker. Were Jackie and Todd right? Was she using her work to avoid confronting the problems with Drew?

Right now Drew was at Aunt Beatrice's, getting all the TLC he could stand from his "on-site grandparent." Both her parents and Todd's lived in Florida. Friday nights were "Aunt Beatrice night" and had been since Drew was an infant, when she and Todd had lived for those few precious hours of privacy each week. Lately, Lauren had taken to spending the early hours of Friday evening wandering around her empty apartment, watching the news—and then the clock—until it was time to pick up Drew.

At least she had somewhere to go tonight, Lauren thought as she sidestepped a gaggle of undergraduates giggling their way to the square. She jammed her hands in her pockets and thought of her own undergraduate Friday night sprees in the days before Drew and divorce and dissertation. At least she had Jackie. For without Jackie, Lauren knew this difficult time in her life would be almost unbearable.

She thought of how pleased Jackie would be with the research she had done. She had skimmed Carl Jung's discussion of the collective unconscious and Ian Stevenson's anthropological study of children who remembered previous lives. And she had found herself strangely intrigued by an odd little book by Brian Weiss, a well-known psychiatrist, that described his encounters with "spirit entities" who controlled reincarnation and revealed to him the secrets of immortality. She wondered if Dr. Weiss's entities were anything like Deborah Sewall's sages.

Walking briskly through the university's netherlands—where the outer reaches of campus pushed their tentacles into an old residential area of Cambridge—Lauren thought of Jackie's excitement on the phone that morning. Maybe Jackie had found something that would make it all click, that elusive concept or piece of information that would hold their book together, giving it coherence and shape.

But as she turned the corner onto Trowbridge Street, Lauren remembered the tension underlying Jackie's voice. *"Not what you think,"* Jackie had said.

"It's bad. Really bad." The sky darkened and the street lights switched on in a vain attempt to fend off the gathering gloom. Suddenly, Lauren was filled with a premonition: Jackie had found something that invalidated their book. Lauren just knew it.

Hurrying up the steps, she banged the wrought iron door knocker against the grimacing countenance of a bearded Colonial farmer—the face of the stingy man who had built the house, Jackie liked to say, the one who made the ceilings too low and the stairs so steep and narrow. But Lauren heard no motion inside. Standing on her toes, she tried to see through the mottled bull's-eye glass of the two small windows in the door. But it was useless.

Damn, she thought, Jackie must have given up on her and gone out. It was her own fault for procrastinating. She thought about using the spare key in the mailbox, but she decided against it and knocked again. Then, in a last futile gesture, she pressed the door latch. To her surprise the door swung inward, creaking slightly on the old hinges.

"Jackie?" Lauren said, sticking her head into the entryway. A lone lamp on the dining room table cast a circle of light over Jackie's cluttered desk, and a small fire licked at the last remnants of a log in the living room fireplace, but the house had an abandoned feel.

"Jack?" she called again, her voice echoing through the quiet rooms. Thinking she heard the back door closing, Lauren stepped tentatively forward, drawn into the shadowy house by a sense of unease—followed by a sudden and gripping fear.

Groping for a light switch, Lauren walked cautiously toward the dining room. "It's me. Are you—" Her words were cut off as she found the switch. As soon as light flooded the room, Lauren saw Jackie. She was sprawled on the floor, her broken eyeglasses just beyond her outstretched arm and the step stool toppled at her feet. Lauren stood frozen in the open doorway, unable to scream, unable to move, as she tried to understand what she was seeing.

There was blood on the table leg and blood on Jackie's forehead. But worst of all, Jackie's chin was pulled sideways, twisting her neck into an impossible position.

Six

Lauren dropped down next to Jackie's still body and grabbed her hand. The bones of Jackie's wrist felt so small and fragile that Lauren feared they would break under her clumsy probing. Lauren's heart pounded and the blood was rushing so loudly in her ears that it drowned the street noise outside. *Please,* Lauren said to herself, or to the God she didn't really believe was listening. *Please.* But she felt nothing under her trembling fingers. Jackie's hand lay in hers, pale and limp and tiny.

Then she felt it: a faint flicker that reminded her of Peter Pan's dying Tinker Bell. *Clap your hands,* she thought idiotically. *Clap your hands.* Lauren pushed her finger more forcefully to the spot below Jackie's thumb. Yes. There was a pulse. But she didn't appear to be breathing. It was clear Jackie needed medical help. And fast.

Lauren leapt up and then froze, her mind numb. What to do first? Frantically trying to remember the first aid course she had taken as a Girl Scout thirty years earlier, she looked down at her friend's frighteningly white face. There didn't seem to be much blood, so a tourniquet wasn't necessary. Don't touch her, they always said. Call the police and cover her with a blanket. Police, she thought, still frozen in place. Phone.

Launching herself toward the kitchen, Lauren skidded through the pantry and grabbed the phone from the wall next to the sink. She punched 911. Waiting through the two longest rings of her lifetime, Lauren stared out the window. For a moment, she thought she saw a shadow slip through the hedges that divided Jackie's backyard from her neighbor's. "Come quickly!" she screamed into the phone when a crisp, tinny voice answered. "I think my friend's dying. We need help right away!"

"Please try and take it easy," the voice said calmly. "Now tell me where you're located."

"I-I . . ." Lauren stuttered, her mind suddenly blank. "Cambridge," she finally said.

"What street in Cambridge?"

The cool competence of the operator cleared Lauren's head. "Trowbridge," she cried triumphantly. "Trowbridge Street!"

"And the house number?"

"Just come," she pleaded. "I don't know the number. I'll meet you in the street."

"Do you see any mail?"

"Mail?" Lauren was completely baffled.

"For the address. Look around for some bills or letters—they'll have the street address and apartment number."

Lauren frantically scanned the kitchen. A teacup sat in the sink. Herbs grew from dozens of jumbled pots on the windowsill. An assortment of neatly labeled keys hung from the wall. But she saw no mail. Then she looked down. Directly beneath the phone was a wicker basket filled with unopened envelopes. Lauren grabbed a fistful. "Forty-six," she read off the phone bill. "Forty-six."

"Is there an apartment number?"

"No," she said, tears running down her cheeks. "There's nothing but us. Please send someone right away."

There was a moment of silence and then the tinny voice returned. "The ambulance has been dispatched," he said with composed professionalism. "Now, I need you to tell me the exact nature of the problem so the paramedics can be prepared."

Lauren took a deep breath and forced herself to calmness. She needed to stay in control. Jackie's life depended on it. "She appears to have fallen. There isn't much blood, but her neck is twisted funny."

"Is there a pulse?"

"Yes," she said, her voice shaky. "But I don't think she's breathing—and she's awfully pale."

"Now what I want you to do is go to the front door and open it," the operator instructed. "Turn on the outside light and wait for the ambulance. They should be there in a couple of minutes—the fire department's right down the street. You may be able to hear the sirens already. Please wait outside and don't try to move her."

"Okay," Lauren said, letting her breath out in a rush. "Thank you."

"You did good," the voice said, suddenly turning human. "I hope your friend's all right."

Lauren hung up the phone and ran to the front door. She found the switch for the outside lights and, although she hated to leave Jackie alone in the house, she raced down the porch stairs. The house was only a few feet from the sidewalk, and by the time she reached the street, she could hear the approaching sirens. When the ambulance made the tight turn from Cambridge onto Trowbridge, Lauren stood in the middle of the road and waved it down.

The vehicle screeched to a stop and a paramedic jumped out. "Where is she?" the woman asked.

Lauren pointed to the house as the driver climbed down. She motioned them to follow her. As soon as they saw Jackie and the narrowness of the small rooms, they told Lauren to go sit in the kitchen.

The next few minutes were a blur of terrifying sensory tumult. Flashing lights and crackling cellular phones swirled around her. A stretcher and all kinds of equipment were brought in. More medics appeared. Someone starting administering CPR.

Finally, they had Jackie on the stretcher. Her head was held rigid by a plaster contraption under her chin and her arms were clamped down. An oxygen mask covered her face. Lauren watched from the kitchen. Jackie looked so pale and so still.

"Is she going to be okay?" Lauren asked the woman who had been the first off the ambulance.

"We're taking her over to Cambridge City," the medic said, touching Lauren lightly on the arm. "You can follow us there and talk with the doctors."

Lauren's blood turned to ice at the way the medic had avoided her question. "Can I go with her?" she asked.

"The hospital's just around the block. Why don't you walk over and we'll meet you there."

"But—" Lauren began.

The woman looked over at her partner, who was hooking up an IV. "She's not going to know you're with her, honey," she said. "It'll be easier all around if you're not in the ambulance." Turning back to Lauren, she touched her arm again. "Believe me."

Lauren's protests were silenced by the tired compassion in the woman's eyes. She nodded and headed out the door.

Lauren beat the ambulance to the hospital. When it finally arrived, they wouldn't let her see Jackie and no one would tell her anything. Yelling something about "code," two hospital employees in blue scrubs rushed Jackie through double doors marked *No Admittance.* The nice medic from Jackie's house seemed to have disappeared, and although the receptionist at the emergency room desk was sympathetic, after she had gotten what little information Lauren knew about Jackie's health insurance, she had no answers to Lauren's questions.

"One of the doctors will be out to speak with you as soon as there's any information," she said.

Lauren went into the waiting room, which was tastefully furnished with cushioned sofas and love seats, two television sets, and a bank of telephones complete with a full complement of telephone books. It was also empty. Helene and Matthew, Lauren thought. She had to call Jackie's children.

But as she approached the phones, Lauren realized that she had left her backpack at Jackie's. She had no money. When she explained her predicament to the receptionist, the woman smiled reassuringly, reached into a drawer, and handed her two quarters. Lauren's eyes welled with tears as she thanked her and turned back to the waiting room.

Which one to call first? Lauren wondered. Neither call was going to be easy. Jackie's daughter, Helene, was in her early twenties and lived with her husband just around the corner. Helene was extremely close to her mother and quite high-strung. Matthew was the more mellow of the two, but he was still in high school and was staying with his father for the month of October in a complicated joint custody arrangement; given the hour, he was apt to be home alone. Helene, Lauren decided, grabbing the Cambridge phone book. Maybe her husband, Dan Ling, would answer. He was a grounded, steady guy—and a newly deputized Cambridge policeman to boot.

Please, she prayed as she dropped the coin into the slot, *let Dan answer.*

For the first time that day, luck broke on Lauren's side and Dan picked up the phone. When he heard Lauren's story and her description of Jackie's symptoms, he was quiet for a second. "We'll be right there," he said, his voice breaking slightly. "I'll call Matt and Simon."

After hanging up the phone, Lauren paced the small waiting room. A part of her was nauseated and terrified, while another part was removed from herself, watching the nauseated, terrified Lauren from the protection of the corner above one of the television sets. Then the scene began to replay in her head: Jackie's gruesome door knocker; the silent, shadowy house; her growing sense of unease; Jackie sprawled on the edge of the dining room rug.

Lauren closed her eyes against the pictures. Then her eyes flew open. The chronicle. Deborah had warned them of the curse. "*Anyone who reads the chronicle and isn't a member of the coven,*" she had said, "*will either die or go mad.*"

Lauren shook her head. It was too ridiculous. And anyway, Jackie wasn't going to die. She had just hit her head on the leg of the table. It happened every day. If everyone who hit their head died, there'd be no people left on earth.

Yes, she comforted herself, in a few days they'd be sitting around Jackie's dining room table arguing over historical method and the possibility of reincarnation. Just a concussion, Lauren thought, tears pricking the backs of her eyes. It had to be. She dropped onto one of the couches and rested her head in her hands.

It could have been hours, or only minutes, when Helene and Dan came rushing into the room and swallowed her up in hugs and tears and questions. She told them what little she knew, and Dan went off in search of an update. He explained to the receptionist that he was a Cambridge policeman, but he didn't get any more information than Lauren had.

"They'll let us know as soon as there's something to know," he told them, flopping onto the couch next to Helene and putting his arms around her.

Lauren had expected Helene to be hysterical, but except for the fact that she kept asking the same question over and over again, she was surprisingly composed. "She didn't move at all?" Helene asked Lauren for about the fourth time since she arrived. "Not even a little?"

Dan saved Lauren from having to answer again by pulling his wife to her feet. "Let's go see if we can find a vending machine," he said. "I need a cup of coffee." When Helene began to protest, he gently turned her toward the door. "We'll only be a minute, Hel. Lauren's here."

So Lauren was in the waiting room alone when the doctor approached. She stood and faced him. He looked awfully young and awfully tired, and she knew from the expression on his face that his news wasn't good.

"It happens sometimes." He shook his head in bewilderment. "Sometimes people walk away from car crashes that by all rights should've killed 'em, and other times a simple fall is all it takes." His eyes were filled with genuine sorrow. "I'm sorry," he said. "We did what we could, but it was over before she got here."

Lauren dropped onto the couch as Helene and Dan walked into the room. One look at Lauren's face and Helene let out a wail. It was an awful, keening sound, full of a child's hurt and an adult's loss.

Lauren didn't understand how it could be so cold and still rain. It was well below freezing, yet rain poured from the heavens, drenching her hair and her face and her parka. But she cared little that she was soaking wet. Jackie was dead. Nothing else mattered.

Trudging down Trowbridge Street, Lauren couldn't believe that just a few hours ago she had walked this same sidewalk, worrying about the lateness of the hour. Worrying about whether Jackie had found something in the chronicle that might negatively impact their book. As if their book mattered.

Lauren stopped in front of the house, her hand resting on the gate. All the lights were blazing, and the medics had left the front door wide open. The farmer on Jackie's door knocker grimaced in the hallway light.

Lauren didn't want to go inside, but she had to get her backpack—it contained her wallet and keys. And she had to close the door before someone stole all of Jackie's precious belongings. Through the open doorway, she could see Jackie's rag rug and her butter churn at the edge of the staircase. The tears Lauren hadn't allowed herself to shed in front of Helene rolled down her cheeks. Jackie wasn't going to need her belongings anymore.

As she forced herself up the porch stairs, Lauren decided she should probably take the chronicle home with her for safekeeping. Deborah had said it was valuable. Lauren figured she owed it to Jackie to protect—and to read—the damn book.

Stepping into the foyer, she closed her eyes against the images of the last time she had crossed this threshold: the shadowy room; the fading fire embers; Jackie dying on the floor. "*Anyone who reads the chronicle will either die or go mad,*" she heard Deborah say.

Lauren's eyes flew open and she looked at Jackie's workplace at the dining room table. Although there were piles of books strewn all over the table, the spot in front of Jackie's chair was empty. The chronicle was gone.

Seven

LAUREN HAD MANAGED TO PUT ON STOCKINGS AND A navy wool dress, but she was stymied by her shoes. She sat on the edge of her unmade bed and stared at her toes, all squashed and misshapen inside their tight nylon cocoon. They didn't look like her toes at all, she thought. They looked like her mother's.

She glanced at the clock and, somewhere deep inside her, realized that if she didn't put on her shoes, she was going to be late for the funeral. Jackie's funeral. Resting her heels on the floor, Lauren lifted her feet toward her. Actually, now that she thought about it, her toes looked like Aunt Beatrice's. Aunt Beatrice always wore stockings.

Lauren stared at the sunlight pushing through the cracks in her yellowed shades. On the bottom of the far shade, the light splinters formed a design resembling chips of ocean waves. Todd would be here soon. He had promised to come by ten. He would find her shoes and put them on her feet. Then he would guide her into the car and drive her to the funeral. Todd would be her anchor, as he had been during Drew's meningitis scare and her father's heart bypass surgery. His very presence would allow her to sink into thoughts of squished toes and fractured waves, permit her to bob and drift through this terrible day.

Lauren stood in the corner of Simon Pappas's condominium, her back toward the crowd, sipping a drink she didn't want and staring through a wall of glass at the high-rise office buildings of Kendall Square on the Cambridge side of the Charles River. The river was so bright and festive, sparkling under a cloudless autumn sky; it was painful to look at such a scene after having just buried her dear friend. From within the depths of her grief, Lauren knew that she had only begun to miss Jackie, that she hadn't even started to understand the hole that had been rent in her life.

Lauren turned away, forced back into the huge, soaring room she knew Jackie must have hated. It was a peach and teal monstrosity, two stories of chrome and glass and marble in which even the subdued voices of the mourners bounced harshly off the hard surfaces. The furnishings were so perfectly coordinated that she could imagine the word DECORATOR stamped in huge letters over everything. Nothing appeared to have been in existence prior to 1990. Lauren supposed that was the point.

At least the funeral had resonated of Jackie: the dark, rich wood of the eighteenth-century chapel set on the edge of the university's wide quad; the sunlight pouring through the stained-glass saints and casting jewel-colored shadows on the old pews; the regal procession of long-robed priests and serious-faced altar boys swinging smoking metal baskets.

Lauren scanned the room for Jackie's family so that she could say her good-byes. She was completely wrung out from the emotion of the day, for aside from her overwhelming sorrow, she was furious at Todd.

A little before ten o'clock, as she had waited for him, bereft and shoeless in her bedroom, he had called to tell her he wasn't going to make it. Although he'd had three days' warning, he claimed his shoot had been "impossible to reschedule." He was going to miss the funeral, but he had promised to come to Simon's as soon as he was finished. Lauren wanted to leave before he arrived.

Simon was standing on the other side of the bar, surrounded by a large group of men in dark suits. Lauren guessed from their clothes that they were business associates, then realized that all the men in the room were wearing dark suits. Helene was huddled in a corner with Dan, but Matthew was nowhere to be seen.

Lauren squared her shoulders and headed toward Simon. But as several people stopped her to talk, she realized that walking across the room was a mistake. All day she had been treated like a macabre celebrity. Not only was she Jackie's close friend, but she had been the last person to see Jackie alive—and the one who had found her body.

At the funeral it had seemed that everyone wanted a word with her: her fellow graduate students, Jackie's neighbor, the department secretary. And now Gabe Phipps, the chair of her department, the man whose craggy, handsome features were gracing this week's cover of *Time* magazine, the man who usually just nodded in a distracted manner when they passed in the hall, was walking directly toward her.

Gabe had always been well respected in the academic community for his many insightful articles in *American Historical Review* and the *Journal of American History*, and in 1990 he had achieved big man on campus status with the publication of his groundbreaking book, *A New Social History of Colonial America*. Now the surprising success of his PBS special on the Revolutionary War—currently running in eight parts on public television stations across the country—was catapulting him to national celebrity.

Gabe seemed to be comfortable with his newfound fame, smiling and nodding as the crowd parted to let him through. A woman Lauren didn't recognize reached out and touched the back of his jacket as he passed. Lauren felt heat rise to her face as he approached. She took a quick sip of her wine, spilling a few drops on her blouse.

"Lauren." Gabe came up beside her and took her empty hand in both of his, his usual charisma dampened by the strain clearly etched on his pale face.

Lauren was touched by how shaken he was. Tears pricked behind her eyes and the lump that had been lodged in her throat for three days seemed to expand. She swallowed. "Dr. Phipps," was all she could manage to say.

"Please," he said, "call me Gabe." He glanced over her head at the panoramic scene outside the window and then turned quickly away from its brightness, just as she had. "Did you know Jackie and I started teaching the same year?"

Lauren nodded awkwardly, wondering how she was supposed to respond and if he would ever let go of her hand.

"How're you doing?" he finally asked.

"I'll be better when this," she extracted her damp hand and waved it, "is all over."

"So will we all."

Lauren took a sip of her drink and eyed the door. "Life must go on," she finally blurted.

For a moment Gabe's worried face was transformed by his famous eye-crinkling grin. "Clichés can be surprisingly comforting at times like these," he said.

Thrown off guard by his smile, Lauren smiled back. She realized with a start that this must be the first time she had smiled since she had found Jackie four days ago. Dr. Phipps's—Gabe's—grin had that effect on people: It demanded an equivalent return. And although she knew it was both inappropriate and ridiculous, she felt a jolt of attraction when he looked into her eyes—despite the thirteen-year difference in their ages, and despite the fact that he was an inch or two shorter than she. Quickly downing her drink, she raised her glass and slipped toward the bar. He seemed reluctant to let her go.

While the bartender poured her another glass of wine she didn't want, Lauren edged closer to where Simon was standing. But before she could reach him, a second-year graduate student whose name Lauren couldn't remember came up to her.

"How're you holding up?" the blond woman asked, morbid curiosity in her voice. "It must have been just awful." Her eyes begged Lauren to share all the gruesome details.

Reaching for her drink, Lauren shrugged and shook her head. "I'm on my way home," she said before she realized how her actions contradicted her words.

"Was that weird woman at the funeral one of the ones?" the young woman demanded.

Lauren turned her glass between her palms and donned a perplexed expression, although she knew exactly to whom the woman was referring—Deborah. Lauren didn't want to think about Deborah's bizarre actions, or the fact that they might be linked to the missing chronicle. It was highly unlikely that the chronicle was actually missing, Lauren reminded herself. The more she thought about it, the more sure she was that the medics had moved the book in the tumult, that it was still somewhere in Jackie's dining room. She was so sure, in fact, that she had arranged with Dan to get into the house this coming Thursday so she could get the book and read it before returning it to Deborah, as promised, by that evening.

"Well, was she?" the woman pressed. "You know, one of *the* ones in your book?"

Lauren was filled with a growing unease as, despite her attempts to push away the image of Deborah at the cemetery, the episode came back to her with frightening clarity. The mourners had been huddled around the raised coffin, wrung out after the long mass, chilled by a cold wind off the ocean. The priest said a few words, then he took two roses from the lid of the casket and handed one to Helene and one to Matthew. Matthew clenched his jaw and stared straight ahead as befit a sixteen-year-old boy at his mother's funeral; Helene flung the flower to the ground and buried her face in Dan's chest.

Just as the priest seemed to be ending the service, Deborah, her hair blown wild by the wind, sprang forward and placed a repulsive black-and-white "thing" on top of the casket. It was a plant of sorts, for there were white leaflike growths on its outer edges, but it was mostly a mass of exposed black roots, intertwined coils, serpentine and creepy, almost mobile in their sliminess. There was a collective gasp as the disgusting thing tottered on the coffin's lid. The priest swung around in surprise.

"Christmas rose," Deborah said. "To ward off the evil spirits."

Lauren had stepped back, warily watching this woman who thought herself the reincarnation of a wronged spirit, who believed in black magic and cursed chronicles. Then Lauren found herself stepping forward again, her unease mingling with a compelling desire to draw closer. There was danger here. And power. It was almost palpable—and disturbingly seductive.

The priest grabbed Deborah's arm and tried to thrust her back into the crowd. But Deborah shook him off as if he were a pesky insect and, raising her arms wide, began to chant unintelligible syllables in a low, husky voice.

"Silence!" roared the priest. "That's enough!"

"I only pray you are right," Deborah said. Then she melted back into the crowd and disappeared.

The priest flung the plant to the ground and quickly ended the service. But as the mourners dispersed, there had been a tense silence, born of more than the usual funereal sorrow.

Lauren blinked and looked at the nameless graduate student who was watching her expectantly. She took a large gulp of wine. "No," she said. "I don't know who she is."

The woman smiled knowingly. "If that's the game you want to play."

Lauren was saved from any further discussion by Simon, who threw his arm over her shoulders. "Could you excuse us, please?" he asked. When they were alone, he glanced down at Lauren and smiled sadly. "Sorry you weren't able to give a eulogy," he said. "I'm sure Jackie would've liked it."

Lauren turned so that he had to drop his arm and stepped away from this distinguished-looking man who had given her friend so much trouble with his childish and miserly wrangling. Simon Pappas was all too accustomed to getting his own way, and Lauren knew she couldn't trust his pseudopoliteness.

"I wasn't up to it," she said. Although she felt a bit guilty for having turned down Helene's request, Lauren recognized she was far too upset to talk about Jackie in public, not to mention that her discomfort at speaking in public bordered on being phobic.

Simon leaned toward her, putting his face uncomfortably close to hers. "I won't have Jackie's memory or Matthew's future besmirched by a bunch of lesbians spouting witchcraft."

She took another step backward, stunned into silence. Even knowing that Simon had never recovered from the blow of being left for a woman, Lauren was still surprised by the hostility underlying his words.

"I want Jackie's name off the book—no authorship

credit," he said. An elderly woman walked by and touched his arm. He bent over and, murmuring softly, kissed her papery cheek. But when the woman moved on, he straightened up. "I'd buy her off the contract if I had the cash, but I've got my own troubles," he said as smoothly, although his eyes were like ice. "And when her estate's settled, it'll probably turn out that she gave everything away to some antique society. So you're the only one who can do it."

Suddenly, Simon's eyes softened and he draped his arm lightly over Lauren's shoulders. "Gabe Phipps!" he called out in a voice guaranteed to carry across the room. "I can't tell you how pleased we all are by the success of one of our own. Your TV show is just wonderful—and the cover of *Time* magazine! Well, all I can say is that I'm extremely impressed." He grabbed Gabe's hand in both of his. "It's good to see you again, old man."

Gabe nodded politely and withdrew his hand. "I only wish we were meeting under happier circumstances."

Simon quickly bowed his head in pseudosorrow, as if just remembering the purpose of the repast. "It's a difficult time for us all."

Disgusted, Lauren tried to slip toward the door, but Simon tightened his grip on her shoulder. "Lauren and I were just discussing the witchcraft book," he said. "Boylston's your publisher too, right? Same editor?" When Gabe nodded, he continued. "Do you think they'd have a problem with turning the whole project over to this attractive young lady here?"

Jerking herself away from Simon, Lauren shot Gabe a glance that clearly indicated her aversion to the man.

Gabe smiled uncertainly at Lauren and shrugged, as if unclear about Simon's contact with reality. Then he turned back to Simon. "Lauren's a very capable scholar," he said slowly. "One of our best. And frankly, I don't see that there's an alternative."

"They could try to keep Jackie on as primary author because of her name value." Simon smiled affectionately at Lauren. "But that wouldn't be fair to Lauren here. She would be the one doing all the work, so she should be the one getting the credit."

"Or they might cancel the whole project." Gabe paused and turned to Lauren. "What do you think?"

Lauren looked into the depths of her wineglass. She had been so upset about losing Jackie that she hadn't given much thought to how Jackie's death was going to affect her professionally. She blinked back the tears that welled in her eyes.

"Lauren?" Gabe touched her arm lightly. "You okay?"

She nodded and blinked again. It was unthinkable to cancel the book. She would have no dissertation, and there was the small issue of returning money she had either already spent or had earmarked for rent and food for the next six months. *"This book contract is a gift,"* Jackie had said. *"My great adventure."* How could she turn her back on what meant the most to her dead friend? On the other hand, how could she, a conservative, agnostic scholar, write a book using the supernatural as an explanation for an historical event?

Simon squeezed her shoulder. "This is a difficult time for us all," he said again. "But we must get on with the banalities of day-to-day business."

Lauren twisted away from Simon. "Yes," she said slowly, stalling for time. The answer was to get Nat to go back to the original plan—retaining the supernatural as one of many possible explanations, but not focusing on it—and to keep Jackie on as primary author just to spite Simon.

"The truth is," she said to Gabe, avoiding Simon's eyes, "I've never been comfortable with making the supernatural a large part of the book. And now that I've got to handle it by myself . . ." She glanced down again and ran her fingers along the damp stem of her wineglass, feeling like a heel for taking advantage of Jackie's death to alter the book for her own purposes. She looked up at Gabe and was reassured by his smile. "Do you think I could convince Nat to drop the supernatural as the focus of the book? To maybe relegate it back to a single chapter?" She purposely left out any direct mention of authorship.

Both men beamed at her. Gabe said, "I don't see why not. Want me to call Nat?" he offered. "He owes me a favor or two. I could tell him I'd be very grateful if he'd consider dropping—or significantly condensing—the supernatural piece of the book."

Lauren hesitated for a second. Jackie had been the one who had handled all the business dealings with Boylston, and Lauren had been more than happy to leave it that way. But things had changed and, although she would have preferred to sink back into her research, the book was her responsibility now. Jackie would want her to take charge.

"Thanks," she said, "but I'll call myself. You can be my backup." As she spoke the words, Lauren was uncomfortably aware that her first act of mastery, an act motivated by her desire for Jackie's approval, was also an act against Jackie's vision of their book.

"I'm here if you need me," Gabe said, smiling into her eyes. "Call any time." He squeezed her hand, then slipped around the bar.

Lauren stared after him, still feeling the imprint of his hand on hers. But before she could wonder about her response or Gabe's, Simon pressed his face so close to hers she could smell the alcohol on his breath. "Just make sure her name isn't on that book," he said. Then he let go of Lauren's arm and walked briskly across the room to Helene.

Lauren watched Simon kiss his daughter's forehead

and sit down next to Dan. The three of them pressed closely together, forming a perfect tableau of a grieving family. Lauren decided she'd call Matthew and Helene later in the week and slipped toward the door.

She searched through the jumble of coats piled on a narrow marble bench running along one side of the entryway. Over the bench hung a huge white canvas, empty except for three tiny overlapping green rectangles. She had to get out of here, away from all this pretension and deceit. She needed to be alone, needed space to think.

Just as she was pulling her jacket from the pile, she felt two hands on her shoulders. She jerked away sharply and whirled around.

"Todd," she cried in relief, forgetting she was furious with him. She threw her arms around her tall, lanky husband and buried her face in his coat. It smelled like fresh air and autumn. And Todd.

"Hey," he said, running his hand down her long hair in a familiar, soothing gesture. "Hey," he said again.

She wanted to stay there forever, buried in his safety, in his protection. But she knew that Todd offered neither safety nor protection. That his arms were an illusion she couldn't trust, couldn't depend upon. She pulled away and grabbed her coat, pressing the wool to her eyes. "I was just leaving," she said stiffly.

He reached out and touched her cheek. "Sorry I couldn't be here earlier."

She slipped her coat on. Todd was always sorry. And he was never there. She shook her head and walked quickly out the door.

Lauren took Memorial Drive, hoping that the prettier route, with its view of Back Bay town houses rising above the fiery autumn trees, would cheer her. But neither nature's magnificent palate nor man's magnificent architecture could touch her grief. The bright sun, highlighting the scullers as they pulled on the river like choreographed centipedes, depressed her even more.

She had a terrible longing to be with Drew. She needed to touch his skinny shoulder blades, feel the satiny plumpness of his cheek against her own, to smell his innocent, little-boy smell. She needed to know there was life to be lived, sweetness to be savored. But it was only one o'clock and Drew was still in school. Then she remembered it was Tuesday, Todd's night with Drew, and that she wouldn't get to see him until tomorrow. A single tear slid down her cheek.

She considered visiting Aunt Beatrice. But she knew at this hour Aunt Beatrice was either playing bridge or having lunch with her cronies. Maybe she should just wallow in her sorrow, Lauren thought as she took the series of quick turns that would put her at her house while avoiding the traffic of Harvard Square. She had every right to be miserable. She had lost her best friend—her two best friends, if you counted Todd.

The lump in her throat expanded until it felt as if it would burst through her skin. Lauren swallowed hard and blinked back her tears. No, she told herself, she would not wallow. She turned the car toward the university. She would take advantage of the afternoon and get some work done.

But when she got to the library, Lauren found herself wandering through the stacks as if she had never been there before. Her Oliver Osborne nightmare came flooding back to her, and she looked up at the tall bookshelves, almost expecting them to tip inward as they had in her dream. She glanced furtively down the long rows of books, alert for flashing knives. When she saw nothing but a couple of students whispering in the medieval section, she felt foolish and slipped over to where the American history books were shelved.

Lauren breathed in the familiar scent of glue and dust and old leather bindings, but she couldn't find her usual comfort in them. So instead of reaching for the dry tomes she knew she should be reading, she went over to her favorite books: *Everyday Life in the Massachusetts Bay Colony, Letters and Notes on Colonial Days, Manners and Customs of the Early American Settlers, Life in the Shop and Home of Captain Joseph Weld.*

Running her finger along the thick books, she finally withdrew *Manners and Customs* and brought it to a nearby study table. She flipped open to a chapter on the duties of children and was soon lost amidst the details of a Colonial girl's occupations: hatchelling and carding, spinning and reeling, weaving and bleaching. There was a fascinating segment from the diary of a young girl from Colchester, Connecticut, in which she had recorded her daily work.

> *Fix'd gown for Prude,—Set a Red Dye,—Milked the cows,—Hatchel'd flax with Hannah,—Made a Broom of Guinea wheat straw,—Made Soap with Mother . . .*

Lauren leaned back in her chair. It had been so different then. What must it have been like to spend a childhood milking cows and hatchelling flax and making soap? Never really able to be a child, to laugh or to run or to play silly games? Never to be free from the punitive cramp of life in the seventeenth century? Lauren closed her eyes and imagined a mother and daughter doing their chores on a spring morning in 1690.

"Come roundabout and help me set the leach," the mother said. "We must make the lye."

A young girl, perhaps five years of age, in a long skirt and bonnet, smiled up at her mother. "Must we,

Mama? It would be much nicer to walk in the woods. 'Tis such a pretty day."

"Thou art a mischievous and troublesome girl," her mother grumbled, but there was warmth in her voice and the crinkle of a smile played around her tired eyes. "The winter's fires have given us sufficient wood ash and grease. 'Tis time to make the soap."

"But we must have some sport," the child cried gleefully as she danced around the barrel of ash. She stopped and stared up at her mother. "Making soap is the most loathsome of chores."

The mother shook her head fondly at her high-spirited daughter. "With your dear father gone, there is not much time for sport, I'm afraid. Come, help me fill this barrel. Then together we shall pour the water through."

"But, Mama," the child whined, "it takes so many pours 'til it is lye—and the odor is vile."

"We shall sing as we work," the mother cajoled. "Come do as I say."

And sing they did. Through the morning as they turned ash into lye. And through the afternoon as lye and grease were boiled into soap. As they lifted and stirred and lifted and stirred once again. "Dry sun, dry wind, safe bind, safe find," the woman and girl sang together. "Go wash well, saith summer, with sun I shall dry . . ."

As the singsongy voices faded away, Lauren opened her eyes. She blinked in confusion for a moment, then smiled. Once again, she had been able to slip into the seventeenth century, to immerse herself so completely that it had felt as if she were living there. Despite Jackie's warning about the dangers of escaping into the past, Lauren knew it was this skill that set her apart from her fellow graduate students. It was her ability to lose herself in time that allowed her to write so vividly about Colonial life, that had landed her the coauthorship of *Rebeka Hibbens*.

Jackie, Lauren thought as she rubbed her sore shoulders. It was going to be so lonely without Jackie. Glancing down at her watch, she saw that two hours had passed since she had entered the library. She quickly gathered her things and left.

As she walked across campus, every building, every bench, every turn reminded her of her lost friend. She and Jackie had stood in that doorway, arguing about the chances that ergot poisoning in the wheat had caused the hallucinations that started the witchcraft hysteria. . . . She and Jackie had sat on that bench, eating red-pepper subs in the noon sunshine. . . . She and Jackie had walked along that path the day Todd left, Jackie rubbing her arm and telling her that she was there whenever Lauren needed her. . . . Lauren swiped at her tears with the sleeve of her jacket as she climbed into her car.

She headed toward home, barely aware she was driving. A yellow light suddenly loomed before her and she slammed on her brakes, evoking blasting horns and raised fingers from the cars behind her. Lauren dropped her head to the steering wheel as a wrenching sadness overwhelmed her. She needed to be home. She needed to enfold herself in misery, to cry for everything that had been, for all she had lost that could never be again.

A furious honking roused her from her reverie and she stepped on the gas. When she finally pulled up to the curb in front of her house, she had decided she'd walk down to the White Hen Pantry on the corner of Mass Ave. and buy a big bag of cookies—Vienna Fingers, her favorites. Then she'd curl up on the couch and cry as hard and as loud and for as long as she wanted. And she'd eat every cookie in the bag. Lauren felt consoled for the first time in days. Her step was a little lighter as she headed for the store and lighter still as she returned home.

The last rays of sunlight shot into the large foyer,

warming the dark oak wainscoting that circled the room and climbed the curving stairway. The house seemed to wrap itself around her, welcoming her home, comforting her. Lauren quickly sifted through the mail piled on the table at the foot of the stairs, separating her bills and catalogs from her neighbors'. There was a package the size of a narrow shoe box. It was wrapped in brown paper and addressed to her.

Lifting the carton, she noticed the handwriting was unfamiliar and that there was no return address—although it was postmarked "Cambridge" and dated October 27. Three days before Jackie had died. Lauren was startled by the realization that she had begun dividing events into "before" and "after."

Shaking the box, Lauren felt something soft and light shift within it and caught a fleeting odor that reminded her of farm animals. She placed the box under her arm and carried her mail and cookies up to the apartment.

In the kitchen, Lauren grabbed a knife and cut the string from the box. As she ripped the paper, she saw that it was indeed a shoe box, and as the odor became stronger she was suddenly filled with foreboding. She didn't reach to lift the lid for a long moment, then with a jerky motion she flipped it off the box.

Inside was a poppet. Only this doll was even more hideous and deformed than Jackie's had been. Its pewter eyes were more mismatched and askew. Its left arm grew from its stomach.

Lauren opened the white note card resting on the chest of the horrible thing. *Those who risk the sanctity of the coven shall be punished with eternal death,* the card said. *Do not touch the chronicle.*

Eight

WITH A GNARLED BROWN CANDLE, DEBORAH LIT THE christianwort packed inside the incense holder. As soon as she replaced the copper cap, black smoke poured from triangular holes cut into the metal; she breathed in the bitter vapors, concentrating on aiding Bram with his mission.

Deborah had dreamed of the raven every night since Jackie's death. In one dream, the black bird sat motionless on top of a towering flagpole, watching her every move. In another, he shattered into a flock of insect-sized ravens that rained down on her head in shiny black pellets. And in the dream she had had that morning just before sunrise, he swooped from the rafters of a shadowy barn and swallowed the chronicle whole.

She had dispatched Bram to Jackie's house with the order to get the chronicle. She and the others now awaited his return in the back room of RavenWing—Deborah at the small altar she had erected behind the sacks of bulgur, and the other members of the coven seated at her feet.

The storage room was narrow and cluttered and teeming with shadows. Burlap bags and crates were squeezed into corners and piled on top of each other, overrunning what little floor space there was. Deborah breathed in the vapors again, relishing the smoky bite as well as the cavelike sensation created by the low ceiling and murky light. Cupping her hand, she directed the smoke toward herself, then blew it away. "Talisman, talisman," she chanted. "Return to us what is ours."

"Mahala, Mahala," the others answered. "Return to us what is ours."

Deborah smiled benevolently upon the flock of souls she had gathered around her, all of whom had willingly separated themselves from their lives and their families to follow her into immortality. Cassandra, her eyes hooded and her face etched with the wrinkles of her eight decades, steepled her arthritic fingers beneath her chin. Tamar, her skin as smooth as Cassandra's was creased, lowered her eyes in reverence. Robin beamed up at Deborah, her euphoria almost a visible aura surrounding her; looking at the dear girl, Deborah knew Robin had spoken the truth when she said that, as a member of the coven, she was the happiest she had been in the six years since her parents had been killed. And Alva, their mute, innocent Alva, with her tiny frame and chocolate skin, played a few sweet notes on her flute.

"Bram is coming," Deborah said.

Within moments Bram entered the room. His face was pasty white and the eye ring that pierced just below his brow bounced against his upper lid. His eyes flitted to Deborah's for a moment, then he looked down at his empty hands. "I have failed you."

Deborah said nothing. She picked up the twisted brown candle she had used to light the christianwort and held it between her palms. The flame flickered with her breathing as she waited for Bram's explanation.

"I did everything you asked, Mahala," Bram said, still looking down at his hands. "I took the key from Jackie Pappas's mailbox and then searched her house. And when I was sure the chronicle wasn't there, I took Lauren Freeman's key from where it was hanging in the Pappas person's kitchen and searched the Freeman person's apartment." He raised his eyes; they were large and dark with fear. "The chronicle wasn't there either—I looked everywhere."

"Where else have you been?" Deborah demanded.

"I, ah, I . . ." Bram stuttered. "I've been waiting for the people to leave the Pappas person's house so I could return the Freeman person's key to its place on the wall—which I did." With trembling hands, Bram reached out and took the candle from Deborah. Holding it in his right hand, he placed his left palm in the flame. The room was silent as Bram endured his punishment for failure to carry out the will of Mahala.

"Enough," Deborah said when the skin of Bram's hand began to bubble and blacken. Although she knew the punishment was both important and necessary, she believed it should never be too harsh. She took the candle from him.

"Thank you, Mahala," he answered, sweat running down his face. "For allowing me to serve you."

Deborah reached over to a shelf and pulled down a glass pot labeled *plantain and burdock root*. As she scooped the ointment from the jar and spread it on Bram's palm, she said, "You have done the coven a great service. In my vision, it was the powerful raven who swallowed the chronicle. I thought it unlikely the raven would signify either Jackie Pappas or Lauren Freeman, but we had to be sure. And you did that for us. Now we know magic is the only means through which the raven can be bested."

Bram hung his head. "Because of my failure, we cannot have the recitation."

"The recitation shall commence as planned," Deborah said.

"But we don't have the chroni—"

"I told you the recitation shall commence as planned!" Deborah slammed the pot of burdock root on the table, and Bram shrank back. "In the forty days prior to the Immortalis, 'The Book of Mahala' has always been read—and this year shall be no different."

Cassandra stood and pulled a length of gauze made from cinquefoil from a drawer. She wrapped the woven grass bandage around Bram's wounded hand and motioned him to join the circle. As he sat, no one said a word.

"Last week we read the fourth chapter of 'The Book of Mahala,' the story of the first Immortalis. Today we read the third, which tells of our escape from Cambridge Prison, from the shackles of evil." Deborah smiled and reached under the velvet drape of the altar. "We always begin at the end and end in the beginning, to signify that there *is* no end and no beginning, that the cycle continues to cycle." She pulled out a packet of photocopied papers and raised them for all to see. "Forty-eight hours before the Immortalis we shall read the first chapter."

The coven released a collective sigh and looked up at Deborah in adoration. They joined hands and settled themselves to listen.

Placing the pages before her on the altar, Deborah looked at her flock. "From *The Chronicle of the Coven,*" she said. " 'The Book of Mahala.' Chapter III." Then she began to read.

Even the walls were weeping, so musty and wretched was it there; the bricks' tears ran down the mortar and added themselves to the river that rose above Rebeka's boots. She kicked out at something slimy and cold as it swam past her calf, knowing not whether it be rat or snake—or worse. By misfortune, Rebeka hit Abigail Cullender, who stood shackled to the brick no more than a foot beyond her own chains; Abigail groaned quietly and then was still.

"Abigail," Rebeka cried to the lass who had been bright of eye and salty of tongue just a single month past, to the young girl she now feared was dead. "Abigail, thou must remain strong. We have lost Dorcas and her power, and without you there is no hope of reaching the sages." But Abigail neither answered nor moved, and fear twisted in Rebeka's belly.

Then Abigail shuddered and Rebeka felt the warmth of the young girl's sour breath tickling her neck. She dropped her head in thanksgiving. A sign from the sages that all was not lost.

Although Rebeka was weak and low, she knew she would not die in this place with its wetness and its cold and its miserable wretches packed close against her. She, the great Mahala, who had harnessed the power of heliotrope and malaxis to carry them to eternal life among the sages, would not succumb amidst the putrid smells of disease and despair. Help was coming; she knew it to be so.

Abigail groaned again and raised her head. "Mahala," she called, her voice barely a whisper. "Is it thou?"

"Yes, child," Rebeka replied. "It is I."

Abigail sighed. "Thanks be to the Lord that thou are alive. That Oliver Osborne's pillory did not kill thee."

"My powers are far greater than Oliver Osborne's evil." Rebeka thought of the hours she had stood in the icy rain, her arms outstretched, as Oliver read from his Malleus Maleficarum, *prancing and preening for the crowd gathered to watch her pain. But Rebeka had showed no pain; she had stood tall, neither flinching nor crying. Oliver had renounced her for causing Goody Warren gripping pains and for making the old woman vomit crooked pins and twopenny nails. Rebeka had shaken her head sadly at his accusations, for she had done no such things.*

"The Immortalis," Abigail gasped. "Can it be done?"

"It shall be done," Rebeka assured her. And she knew it to be so, for as she stood at the pillory that morn, her brother Ezekiel had passed behind her. "All is as thee planned," he had whispered in her ear. "Be of brave heart and quick wit, for aid shall come tonight." But before Rebeka could further comfort the frightened Abigail, the goodmen of Cambridge were upon them.

By lantern light, the men sludged through the mire to search for witches' teats upon their bodies, for any unnatural protrusions of the flesh that signified the women had been marked by the devil—a freckle or burn or boil would do.

Ripping the ragged clothes from their bodices, the goodmen burned Rebeka and Abigail with their flames and heckled their shriveled breasts. "These not be godly goodwives," they cried. "They not be hale and well-looking. They be dirty and foul and full of the devil!" They pointed to the insect bites that covered Rebeka's skin as proof of their accusations.

Rebeka pulled her small body to its fullest height. "Foolish men," she admonished them softly. "Can thou not see that these be the bites of the bugs that infest the water in which we stand? These markings are not the work of the devil—lest you think thine own hands are under the command of Satan."

But the men would have none of her, and they continued past, their laughter bouncing harshly off the brick walls.

Rebeka cared not that the goodmen found marks upon her, nor that they had laughed. For these foolish men believed Rebeka and Abigail, along with Millicent Glover, Foster Lacy, Bridgit Corey, and Mercy Broadstreet, would be hanged by the morning's light, and Rebeka knew it would not be so. She knew they would be saved, that the coven would be consummating the Immortalis well before the next sun's rise.

And it came to pass just as Rebeka knew that it would. As she was falling into a dazed stupor somewhere between sleep and hell, a hand gripped her shoulder. "Awake, Goody

Hibbens," an unfamiliar voice whispered in her ear. "Awake and follow me."

The sweet scratch of metal upon metal filled her ears as his key unlocked the shackles that bound both Rebeka and Abigail. Weak with hunger and fatigue, both women fell to their knees in the putrid water, their legs having forgotten how to support their bodies.

"Rise," the voice hissed in the darkness. "Time is short."

With one arm around Abigail and one hand grasping the man's coattails, Rebeka sludged through the dungeon, the pitiful moans of the other prisoners echoing in the darkness. It seemed to take forever before they crawled out of the abyss and into the night. When the sweetness of the air hit her face, Rebeka sucked it deeply into her lungs, as a greedy baby will suck at his mother's breast.

"Make haste," the man said. "The others await us at Brattle Wood."

His words filled Rebeka with great gladness; the Immortalis would be held. Her flock awaited her, awaited her magic and her cunning, awaited her to lead them to eternal life. Although Abigail shivered as the cold air chilled her wet clothes and body, Rebeka was flushed with warmth and vigor; she flew over the fallen branches and brambles and rocks covered with slippery moss. She was going to her future.

When the man led them to the place deep within the forest where the others waited, Rebeka found six bodies sprawled upon the ground instead of the five she had expected. Off from the others, Faith Osborne lay huddled against a towering oak tree.

"'Twas a grievous mistake in the darkness, Mahala," Millicent said quickly, pulling herself up from the ground and coming to take Rebeka's hands in hers. "She, she . . ." Millicent looked at Faith and spat on the ground three times. "She was rescued from Cambridge Prison along with Foster and Mercy. But it is of no consequence. She is of no consequence. I thought we should leave her here to die the death she deserves."

Rebeka looked sadly upon her cousin. She had had such love for the young woman, had had such love for her child. Faith cowered under Rebeka's gaze and pulled her body even more tightly into itself.

As Rebeka bent toward Faith, a raven circling overhead caught her attention. She lifted her eyes to follow the bird's restless flight. Finally settling himself on a branch above Faith's head, the raven locked his beady eyes into Rebeka's. He cawed three times—two long and one short—then flew off into the dark sky.

Rebeka nodded, then turned from the empty branch to Millicent. "The sages think not," she said. "Faith shall come with us to meet her destiny."

As Deborah's voice faded away, the room was filled with a dense silence. Deborah replaced the pages under the altar and said softly, "Our chronicle is more than our heritage, more than our shared history. It is our shared memory." She met the eyes of each of the coven members in turn. "What I have read to you is no mere story—it is our life. For as I remember being there in 1692 as Rebeka, Bram remembers being there as Foster, Cassandra as Millicent, Robin as Bridgit, Tamar as Abigail, and Alva as Mercy."

"I remember Faith cowering under your gaze," Cassandra said.

"I remember being shackled to the brick," Bram added quickly. "And all those horrid insects."

"I remember being so weak I fell into the water."

"And I remember how the walls of Cambridge Prison wept for us."

Alva played a lilting trill on her flute.

"Now that we all remember who we are, and what has been done to us," Deborah said, "it is time to retrieve our chronicle." She went to a far corner of the room and pushed a bag of bulgur with her foot. "Never forget, our power continues no matter who the raven personifies. We shall best the raven—the lancet proves it!" Deborah's voice thundered through the low room.

"The lancet?" Robin repeated, her face filled with awe.

Rebeka's lancet was the most hallowed of the coven's relics and it was rarely removed from its hiding place. With the exception of Deborah, each of the coven members had seen it only once before—at the initiation when it was used to cut a shallow crescent into the soft skin at the base of each member's neck.

Deborah slipped her finger into a small notch between the floorboards and raised a narrow piece of wood. Lifting more pieces of flooring, she exposed an opening about three feet square. She reached in. After a few twists of her wrist, there was a soft click. Deborah pulled a metal door toward her and retrieved a long jewelry box. She flipped open the case, revealing Rebeka's lancet lying upon the velvet. Reverently, she lifted the lancet and held it out to them.

"Behold the power," Deborah said. "Behold the power of our most sacred sacred, the lancet that finds us in every lifetime. Behold the power and know it is far greater than any other."

One by one, each coven member raised a finger to his or her neck, to the crescent-shaped scar that lay at the site of the 1692 death wound.

Deborah closed her fingers tightly around the familiar hills and valleys, exploring as if blind the carved serpents and pinecones, feeling the lancet's heft—and its power. The power that allowed the coven to reincarnate together every 101 years, the power that would finally, with the great Immortalis of 1995, lead them into immortality. She touched the crescent-shaped birthmark on her own neck. "The chronicle shall be ours once again!"

Deborah stared off into the distance, across time and space, well beyond the bounds of the back room of RavenWing and her life in the twentieth century.

She heard Dorcas Osborne giggling as she hid amid the tall rows of Rebeka's herb garden. She saw Millicent carving pinecones into the hilt of the lancet, which she, Rebeka, had received as a gift from the village doctor, Foster Lacy. She felt the icy water of Cambridge Prison rise above her boots as she stood shackled to the cell wall.

"And Faith Osborne shall be ours too!" Deborah closed her eyes. She needed to invoke a very powerful magic to draw both the chronicle and Faith, but she knew the energy to perform magic was a finite fuel. It could be dissipated, even for the very powerful, by casting a particularly complex spell or by performing too many incantations within too short a time. One of the signs of a great witch was the ability to cast efficient yet powerful spells. Deborah opened her eyes. She knew she was a great witch.

Deborah held Rebeka's lancet over the symbolic objects before her: the rock of black obsidian, the vial of bird ashes, the ritual knife, the cup of blood. Before she spoke, she considered which chant would be the most potent but used the fewest words—how to ask for the least while receiving the most. After a long silence, she nodded.

"Black-luggie, hammer-head, rowan-tree, red-thread," Deborah chanted. "Bring to us what has always been ours. Return to us our chronicle and return to us our Faith." Then she raised the cup of human blood to her lips and devoured every drop.

Nine

LAUREN BANGED THE WROUGHT IRON KNOCKER FOR the third time; the stillness inside Jackie's house remained solid and undisturbed. She stood on her toes and tried to peer through a bull's-eye pane, but, just as the last time she had waited for the door to be answered, she could see nothing through the wavy glass. She was waiting for Dan, not Jackie, she reminded herself. It was morning, not evening. The breeze and sky were crisp and invigorating, not heavy and dank. But still, the situation was all too familiar.

Lauren pulled her jacket closer around her, although she wasn't cold. She supposed she could use the key in the mailbox to let herself in, but somehow it didn't seem right. She sat on the short slate stoop. The stoop was so close to the sidewalk, she had to pull her legs in whenever anyone walked by. She stretched while she was able, then glared at the toes of the Nikes or wing tips or boots that forced her back into a crouch.

Lauren yawned. In the days since Jackie's death, she had fallen into a semidazed lethargy. She was somehow making it through the motions of life: getting herself up and dressed, making Drew go to school, even managing the two-block walk to the Star Market in Porter Square a couple of times. But she wasn't really there. She was in a dream world where she could reach for the phone and call Jackie whenever she wanted, where she could sit in Jackie's snug kitchen and drink tea and argue about whether some of the seventeenth century witches might actually have been guilty, or how aggressive she should be in the meeting with Dr. Berg, the school psychologist, next Tuesday. She lived in a world where Jackie was still alive and where she, Lauren, didn't need to wait for Jackie's son-in-law to help her gather the materials she would need to finish Jackie's book by herself.

Lauren pulled her legs in again, thinking that this was probably a much more pleasant spot to sit in Colonial days. Originally, Jackie's house must have been set back by itself on a lazy dirt road or cow path. But now progress had shoved two taller and much uglier buildings almost on top of it, and it stood barely a foot from the well-traveled sidewalk. It would be a much more pleasant spot today if Lauren weren't so conflicted about Deborah's chronicle.

She wanted to find the book—she needed it for Nat and for *Rebeka Hibbens* and to see if she could find the "really big" something Jackie had alluded to on the phone just before her death. Not to mention that they had promised Deborah they would return the book tonight. On the other hand, Lauren couldn't forget Deborah's words: *"It is said that anyone who reads the chronicle and isn't a member of the coven will either die or go mad."*

Jackie wasn't of the coven. Jackie had read the chronicle. Jackie had died. She, Lauren, wasn't of the coven. She was here to read the chronicle. She would then . . .

Lauren shifted on the hard stoop and scanned the

sidewalk. Dan was nowhere to be seen. She twisted the new turquoise ring she had picked up at a dress shop for a few dollars to replace the wedding band she now kept in her jewelry box. As she pulled her legs into her chest, Lauren was once again reminded of that terrible night, of the click of the back door, of the shadow in the hedges. No, Lauren told herself, there are no such things as evil curses. She had imagined the click and the shadow. Paul Conklin had sent the poppets.

But Paul had denied it when she had asked him. "It's a tough addiction to kick," he had said after a long pause, "but I swore off practical jokes after Gabe's BMW got towed." When Lauren pressed him, he had added, "I've got to admit it's a good prank—one I'd be proud to claim—but I can't." But the shame that had colored his voice, and his indirect denial, had left her uncertain.

Lauren felt a tap on her shoulder and swung around.

"Helene's having a tough time," Dan said as if they were in the middle of a conversation rather than starting one. He was tall and slight and his face was very pale. He pushed his black hair from his forehead with a weary gesture. Dan had explained at the funeral he had next to no bereavement time, and Lauren figured between his regular shifts, taking care of Helene, and dealing with the aftermath of Jackie's death, the guy was working the equivalent of at least two full-time jobs.

"Sorry I'm late," he said, his hair falling back to where it had been before.

Lauren jumped up. "No problem."

Dan nodded and flipped open Jackie's mailbox. He retrieved the key and twisted it in the lock. "Helene's barely slept since last Friday," he said over his shoulder as he opened the door. "And I don't think she's eaten a thing."

Lauren followed him into the tiny foyer, instinctively turning toward the dining room, Jackie's room. Dust motes danced in the narrow rays of light that shot through the half-closed curtains, highlighting Jackie's clutter: her spinning wheel and the toasting forks hanging from the fireplace lintel; her books, computer, and Colonial bottle collection. But despite the comfortable jumble, the room felt unused, deserted.

Lauren took a step backward and tripped on the edge of the rag rug. She lurched toward the steep stairway and grabbed a narrow baluster for support. Jackie was really gone—and she wasn't ever coming back.

"Want to sit for a minute?" Dan asked, futilely pushing his hair back again. "Wouldn't mind myself. I'm bushed." He pointed toward the living room.

Lauren nodded gratefully, but when she reached the threshold she stopped as a pain knifed through her stomach. Moving cartons were scattered everywhere. Some were sealed and stacked neatly in the corner, but most were open-mouthed and half packed, their future contents strewn around the room: Jackie's Betty lamp collection, the first lamps brought to America, small, shallow repositories with projecting spouts for the burning of whale oil; Jackie's candle molds; her framed samplers; her iron pots, copper kettles, and wooden and pewter kitchen utensils. Jackie's life, all the things she had loved, lay at Lauren's feet.

"The Cambridge Antiquarian Society was here 'til past midnight yesterday," Dan said. "Jackie left the house to Helene and Matthew—along with any of the contents they wanted. Everything else is going to the society." He paced the tiny entryway, crossing and uncrossing his arms. "Matthew wants the computer and Helene some jewelry, but neither of them seems interested in much else. The society's thrilled."

Lauren shook her head. "It feels so, so—oh, I don't know. So carnivorous, or cannibalistic, or something."

"The house is going up for sale next week. My father-in-law's very anxious, and we've all agreed that the sooner this stuff is all sorted out, the sooner everyone'll be able to get back to normal." Dan leaned against the nail-studded front door. "Simon's particularly keen on getting Matthew back into his regular schedule of hyper overachievement."

Pushing thoughts of Simon and the unpleasant conversation they had had after Jackie's funeral from her mind, Lauren looked around the room. But seeing the half-packed cartons filled her with such sadness, with such a piercing sense of loss, that she raised her eyes to the ceiling. She focused on the huge wooden beams that formed rectangles across the plaster, trying to think of anything but Jackie. She reminded herself that the large middle beam was called the summer-piece and that the joists were the cross-beams. But she could still see Jackie's body lying so motionless.

She turned abruptly, almost knocking into Dan. "Why don't we just get this over with?" she asked, pointing back at the dining room. "Let's take a look at what she's got in there—and hopefully find that book I need."

He nodded and stepped aside to let her pass through the narrow foyer. "Helene said to take anything you need—and she means it. The less stuff there is for her to go through, the easier it'll be."

Lauren looked at the mounds of materials and shook her head. Slowly, she walked around the table, searching for the large leather volume. She checked the chairs. She looked under the table. Starting from the left, she ran her eyes methodically along the rows of bookshelves. No chronicle.

Dan leaned against the chair rail and watched her in silence. "She'd been working really hard on this book," he finally said. "She was really into it."

"Your mother-in-law was a very organized and thorough woman." Lauren picked up a pile of folders from the far end of the table. It didn't seem possible all of Jackie's energy could be gone. Vanished as if it had never been.

Dan stared out the dining room window at the busy Cambridge street, his hand resting on a stack of books. "It's really kind of strange." He turned and looked at Lauren. "About the step stool, I mean."

"She must've needed a book," Lauren said, flipping open a file Jackie had labeled "Concord Wicca." Inside were notes on a coven of witches Jackie had found in a western suburb of Boston. Modern day Wiccans referred to themselves as witches and practiced an earthy, feminist religion based on pre-Christian pagan beliefs. Lauren shut the file and opened another. It contained notes on sorcerers and black witches, descriptions of their use of wax pentagrams, and voodoo, and snakes stuffed with hair and fingernail parings. A shiver ran up her spine.

"You know how organized she was about her books," Dan said. "She even showed me how everything she needed for *Rebeka Hibbens* had been moved to the lower shelves."

Lauren nodded, not really listening. For although Jackie's files filled her with unease, she was also strangely mesmerized by their exotic contents. Observations of the Sabbat Rite. The Invocation of the Horned God. The Casting of the Circle. Between two pages, she found a note Jackie had made to follow up on a rumor of a group of sorcerers in Cavendish, Vermont, who, just like the seventeenth-century black witches, used poppets and mandrake roots to cast their voodoo spells. At the bottom of the paper was a fax number.

"I'm sorry, Dan," she said. "What were you saying?"

"Nothing, I guess." He shook his head. "I'm just tired."

Lauren stared at the manila folder in her hand as if it held some magic answer. The chronicle wasn't here. The chronicle—the irreplaceable, priceless chronicle for which she was responsible—was gone. She thought she had seen it on the table the night Jackie died, but she couldn't be sure.

Could someone have taken it? It didn't seem likely. Lauren dropped the folder onto the table and looked at the exposed scars in the old wood, at the deep crack that ran almost the entire length of the table. The colonists had called them turn tables, she thought idiotically. One side of the table was used for cutting and cooking, then when company arrived, the table was turned smooth side up. Lauren scanned the room one last time. Things were very rarely what they seemed. "I don't see my book."

"There's a box of weird stuff in the living room," Dan said. "Maybe it's in there."

"What kind of weird stuff?" Lauren asked, rubbing her arms.

He shrugged. "Witchcraft stuff, I guess. Candles, stones, incense, a creepy doll . . ."

"Made from rags with crooked eyes?" Lauren asked.

"How did you know?"

"Because Jackie showed it to me—and because I got one just like it."

His eyes widened. "With the same note?"

Lauren nodded. "But it was all a joke. A dumb joke that backfired—and my guess is the guy who came up with it is feeling pretty bad about now." She told him about Paul Conklin.

"How can you be so sure it wasn't the witches?" Dan asked.

"The witches are the ones who gave us the chronicle in the first place," Lauren said.

"Did you get an ugly brown urn too?"

Lauren shook her head. "What kind of urn?"

"Some sort of pottery, I guess. Kind of big with a fat stomach. There's a man's face on it that looks half wolf and half human." He shuddered. "Strange symbols. And something rattling around inside." He gave her a sheepish smile. "I didn't open it."

Lauren nodded. "A Bellarmine urn. They were used by sixteenth-century sorcerers. Black magic at its finest."

"Black magic," Dan murmured as he began absently fiddling with the nails hammered into the front door. "This whole thing is starting to weird me out." He pressed the tip of his finger to a doornail in the top left corner, then methodically worked his way down the uneven row.

Dead as a doornail, Lauren thought as she watched him. The saying was actually derived from the Colonial practice of hammering nails into their front doors as a display of their affluence. The wealthier a house, the more nails in the door. And because nails were a limited, and therefore valuable, commodity in the seventeenth century, the resourceful colonists cut off the ends of the nails so that they couldn't be removed—or ever used again. Hence, if someone or something was "as dead as a doornail," their usefulness had passed. Just like Jackie, Lauren thought, tears welling in her eyes.

"Black magic only has power over those who believe in it," Lauren said more harshly than she intended.

Dan stared past her into the living room. He shrugged. "It's all in there," he said, waving toward the cobbler's bench in front of the couch. "Go look for yourself."

But despite her words, Lauren wasn't ready to face the "weird stuff" in Dan's box. She turned her back on the bench and walked to the fireplace on the opposite side of the living room. Although this fireplace wasn't as deep or as wide as the one in the dining room, it had the comforting aura of long-ago meals and families and laughter—of continuity, of the cyclical rhythms of living.

Lauren was reminded of the Wiccan concept of the wheel of life. Just as the year was a cycle of spring, summer, autumn, and winter, so too did life go through birth, growth, fading and death. And, just as nothing really died in nature, so too, the Wiccans believed, the life of a human soul was never over.

Lauren glanced toward Dan, but he was lost in his own sadness, staring despondently at an open carton. She turned back to the fireplace, thinking of a book she had read by Ian Stevenson describing how people remember snippets of their previous lives, how phobias and talents can cross from one life into the next, how birthmarks are often the site of an earlier death wound. Lauren also thought of Deborah's sages and Brian Weiss's entities, living on a higher spiritual plane, refreshing souls and then sending them back to earth to work through their destiny. She pressed her palm against the fireplace's rough-hewn lintel.

The moment her hand touched the lintel, she found herself standing off to the side of a room with weathered wood for walls. She was watching a pretty girl who was sitting on a three-legged stool, the gray skirt of her dress pulled above her ankles. The child dropped a log onto the roaring fire, then threw a worried glance over her shoulder, as if to check that no one watched her. Obviously convinced she was alone, the girl smiled mischievously and leaned into the fire, twisting her head among the pots and kettles hanging from the lug pole. The child raised her eyes into the huge throat of the chimney. The heat of the blaze reddened her cheeks and her face was filled with awe as she watched the sparks of the fire float up into the night sky.

Lauren blinked and she was back in Jackie's living room. She yanked her hands from the fireplace and pressed them together. "Let's see what we've got here," she said with a heartiness that startled both Dan and herself. She marched across the room and looked into the carton.

The objects were pretty much as Dan had described them: long tapered candles; black stones; small bunches of coral. She reached into the open carton and pulled a wooden amulet from the box. It was shaped like a hand and covered with intricate carvings: snakes and frogs and pinecones. "Weird, all right," she said, putting the amulet on the bench.

Dan walked over and stood next to her. "There's your voodoo doll," he said, pointing to the shoe box.

"And another handsome fella." She lifted a wax mask out of the carton. It looked familiar, a man's face breathing leaves, but she couldn't quite place it. She shivered as a wisp of a dream returned to her of something, or someone, flying through a dank, low-ceilinged cave. Lauren dropped the mask on the bench. The thing was definitely creepy.

"Where's the urn?" she asked, lifting the carton and putting it on the floor so she could see into it better.

Dan reached into the box and wordlessly raised the urn. He held it out toward her.

Lauren scrutinized its large body and rather narrow neck. "That's a Bellarmine, all right," she said, tentatively touching its nose. The fierce, bearded face stared angrily back at her. "Though I've never actually seen one outside of a book," she added, dropping her hand. "These are called Bellarmines because some people say the face is a likeness of a sixteenth-century sorcerer, a cardinal named Bellarmine. Others say it's Satan."

Dan shook the urn. A raspy, hollow rattle filled the quiet room. "Should we open it?"

Lauren sat down on the couch and looked up at

Dan. The urn appeared larger and more ominous from this angle. *"You can't keep running away from the things that scare you,"* Jackie had told her.

She reached up and took the urn from him. He didn't move as she placed it on her lap. "Oh, what the hell," she said, pulling the wide cork from the urn's neck. The odor of dirt and dampness and long-dead animals assaulted her nostrils. She hesitated and looked up at Dan again. He nodded.

Lauren upended the urn and spilled its contents onto the bench. A braid of white hair—the exact color of Jackie's—studded with sharp nails slid across the shiny wooden surface. A scattering of fingernail parings followed. Lauren shuddered and shook the urn again. A red felt heart, pierced through with pins, fell on top of the fingernails. Embroidered across the center of the heart were the words "Jackie Pappas: Silence or Death."

Ten

LAUREN STARED IN HORROR AT THE CONTENTS OF THE urn strewn on the cobbler's bench.

"Jesus H. Christ!" Dan cried, taking a step backward.

"You don't think that could actually be Jackie's hair?" Lauren's voice was a hoarse whisper as she inched her way to the far side of the couch. "Or her fingernails?"

Dan shook his head. "It looks like the same color, but how the hell . . ." He stood motionless for a few minutes, then he began to pace the room. "Remember what I was saying about the step stool?" he asked. "Why would she need a step stool if all the books she wanted were on the lower shelves?"

"Well," Lauren said slowly, pulling her eyes from the gruesome objects on the table, "you never know *exactly* which books you're going to need when you're working on a complicated project—"

"I had a strange feeling about this right from the start," Dan interrupted, his dark eyes blazing. "And now with this voodoo doll and this urn—something's not right here, Lauren. I can just feel it."

Lauren dropped her gaze back to the table and met the hollow eyes of the wax man breathing leaves. She looked up at Dan. "Are you saying what I think you're saying?" she asked, unable to bring herself to speak the word.

Dan stopped in front of the bench, his legs wide apart. "Yeah," he said, crossing his arms over his chest. "I guess I am." Although he was not in uniform, there was something about his stance and the cut of his bomber jacket that gave him the look of a policeman.

"But no one would want to hurt Jackie," Lauren argued. "Everyone liked her. It doesn't make any sense."

"It does if you figure someone wanted her out of the way because she was messing where she wasn't supposed to." Dan stared pointedly at the cobbler's bench and then looked back up at Lauren. "Messing with witchcraft."

Lauren met his eyes but said nothing. Dan was a cop—an overeager rookie, to boot—and, as a surgeon would propose surgery as the means of curing a back problem while a chiropractor would propose chiropractic, Dan was apt to see a crime where there was none.

"But how could the research Jackie was doing be a threat to anyone?" Lauren asked. "Granted, the witches and sorcerers she was meeting with might have been a bit odd, but their religion isn't about black magic and evil. It's mostly just pagan: worshiping nature and goddesses and such."

"I don't think Jackie fell from any step stool," Dan said.

"So does that mean she died from voodoo?"

Dan sat down on the couch. "Did you see anything strange when you got here that night?" he asked in what Lauren assumed was his professional voice. "Hear anything out of the ordinary?"

Lauren inspected her fingernails. She didn't want to think about that night. She didn't want to relive it, even in words. The pain was still too raw. She raised her eyes and shook her head.

"Tell me," Dan said softly. "What we don't know can be much more dangerous than what we do."

Lauren looked at Jackie's white hair studded with nails and felt a tremor of apprehension. There was no denying that Dan's words jibed with thoughts she had been trying to suppress since Jackie's death. Slowly, haltingly, she told Dan what she knew. She told him about the click of the back door and about the shadow that had cut through the hedges. She told him about Jackie's phone call, about her "really bad" something. She told him about the curse of the chronicle and about the book's strange disappearance. And she agreed it was highly unlikely that Jackie would have had any interest in a book on a high shelf that afternoon. Jackie had been completely consumed with the chronicle.

When Lauren was finished, she rested her elbows on her knees and leaned toward Dan. "But if we assume there's no such thing as black magic and evil curses, where does that leave us? Do you really think there could be some crazed murderer running around?"

"Crazy people can be far more dangerous than any curse," Dan said.

Lauren thought about Deborah's visions and sages and magic lancets. But she also remembered Deborah's thoughtful discussion of her religion. "*To explain the unexplainable one must have faith. All religions depend on it . . . Our religion is no different. . . .*"

"It won't hurt to check it out," Dan was saying, his face set and serious. "I'll go over to the station right now and talk to the lieutenant detective. See if we can get an investigation opened. Then—"

"An investigation?" Lauren interrupted. "Shadows in the dark. Step stools. Cursed chronicle. Is anyone going to believe you?"

"All I can do is try." Dan slapped his thighs and stood. "There's a cult expert on the force. Zaleski. I'll ask him if he's got any information on these RavenWing women or their lost coven. And I know an autopsy was done—I'll get the report." He paused and regarded Lauren thoughtfully. "You know, in a strange way, this actually makes me feel better. Like maybe there's something I *can* do for Jackie. Maybe there's someone I can punish."

"*If* she was murdered."

"Right," Dan said, although Lauren could tell from the look in his eye that he no longer considered accidental death a possibility.

"I've got to go to RavenWing and tell Deborah I've lost the chronicle," Lauren said slowly, more to herself than to Dan. She dreaded the task, but she didn't see any way to avoid it.

"Stay away from them," Dan warned her. "Let me handle this."

"I don't have a choice."

Dan shook his head emphatically. "Even if it turns out that there was no murder, whoever sent Jackie this stuff"—he waved his hand at the cobbler's bench—"had some kind of evil intent. At the very least, this was sent to frighten Jackie because she was prying where she wasn't wanted." He frowned and crossed his arms. "It sounds to me like you're planning on prying in exactly the same places."

After filling the trunk of her car with Jackie's books and files, Lauren went directly to RavenWing. Although she had tried to talk herself out of it, her sense of responsibility won out over her fears. Deborah was neither crazy enough to be dangerous nor did she have supernatural powers, Lauren consoled herself as she climbed the stairs to the store's entrance. But her palms were damp and her heart was pounding.

The wind chimes rattled and the canary warbled as she pushed the door open, but she didn't see anyone in the store. Maybe Deborah and Cassandra were out. Maybe she could leave her message with a clerk and get the hell out of there. Lauren forced herself forward. "Hello?" she called out.

When no one answered, she took a deep breath and walked toward the far end of the store. All the things that had seemed so ordinary just last week suddenly took on an ominous cast: steel cut oats and chandrita ayuredic soap and a vitamin called candicidin corynefum. Could these women be insane? Could they have given Jackie the chronicle and then killed her to get it back?

Lauren stopped abruptly as she came face-to-face with Jackie's Deodat Willard print. After recovering from the initial shock, she took a step closer. A feeling of power emanated from the young girl in the picture. Lauren reached out and touched the hand that directed the corn. She dropped her hand and looked more closely. She had seen this girl somewhere before. She knew that she had. With a start, Lauren realized the girl in the print looked a lot like the girl she had imagined making soap—and the girl at the fireplace.

Lauren turned from the picture and moved toward the back of the store. As she walked through the aromatherapy section, she couldn't help overhearing a conversation on the other side of the shelf.

"It's the chemo that's getting to me," said a soft, tired voice. "The doctors say there isn't much they can do."

"Too bound to western medicine," a husky voice answered. "There's a lot that can be done."

Deborah, Lauren thought, her heart beginning to hammer. She was here after all. Lauren pretended to inspect the label on a box of unbleached pancake mix as she eavesdropped on a conversation about the use of bitterworm to combat nausea and sea salt to draw toxins from the body. Lauren was encouraged by the compassion in Deborah's voice. If Deborah was so understanding of the woman's problems, maybe she'd be understanding of Lauren's too. Of course, the woman wasn't telling Deborah that she had lost one of her most priceless possessions.

Comparing the unbleached pancake mix to the unbleached flour next to it, Lauren waited for the woman to complete her purchase. When she heard the wind chimes on the door, Lauren took a deep breath and strode resolutely to the front of the store. Still holding the pancake mix, she turned from the aisle and faced the register.

Deborah looked up. She nodded but didn't say anything.

Lauren was unprepared for Deborah's coldness. Did she already know about the lost chronicle? Lauren wondered. Was she planning some ghoulish punishment? "I-I want to buy this pancake mix," Lauren stuttered.

Deborah silently rang up the purchase on an old silver cash register. She didn't offer Lauren a bag along with her change. When Lauren took the pancake mix but didn't move toward the door, Deborah stared over Lauren's head at the Deodat Willard print, as if by pretending that Lauren wasn't there, she would disappear.

"I have some bad—" Lauren said, but she stopped when an elderly woman with a long braid came up behind Deborah.

"I'm Cassandra Abbott." The old woman stared at Lauren through the narrow fissure below her wrinkled eyelids. "I'm sorry about your friend."

"Thank you," Lauren said uncertainly, stepping back. There was a slightly unpleasant burned odor emanating from the woman, and Lauren didn't like the chill in her beady eyes. But she was the most shaken by the fact that Cassandra had known who she was.

Before Cassandra could say more, the door of the store flew open. A stocky man with a greasy ponytail and a pierced eyebrow entered. He bowed slightly to Deborah and turned to Cassandra. "Did my Welsh valerian root come in yet?"

"No," Cassandra said.

The man brushed past Lauren and placed himself in front of Cassandra. "You promised it would be here today."

Deborah turned to him. "She promised no such thing, Bram. Cassandra said either Monday or Tuesday of *next* week." Pointing down the first aisle, she added, "There's some local valerian on the shelf—use that. Northern Hemisphere isn't so different from European."

Bram bowed to Deborah once again, then he clutched at Cassandra's arm and pulled her off to the side. "You know I need my European valerian," he said urgently, lowering his voice, "if I want to stay off the Prozac."

Deborah nodded to Lauren in what was clearly a dismissal.

"I need to talk to—" Lauren began.

"Do you think you could call Wales?" Bram asked Cassandra, his voice rising.

"You'll either have to wait or get your valerian root elsewhere," Deborah answered before Cassandra could speak.

Bram's eyes widened in fear and his face paled. He backed slowly toward the door. If he'd had a tail, he would have left with it between his legs.

"I can't find your chronicle," Lauren blurted out as

soon as the door had closed. "I think it was stolen from Jackie's house."

"It was returned," Deborah said, sharing a knowing smile with Cassandra. "Just this morning."

"But, but . . ." Lauren stuttered. "I don't understand."

"Deborah's powers are extraordinary," Cassandra said, looking up at Deborah with undisguised reverence on her face. "She has brought the chronicle back where it belongs."

Puzzled, Lauren looked from Deborah to Cassandra. "But who took it?" she asked. "And who brought it back?"

"I called for it and it came—that's all you need to know." Deborah rested her hands on the trestle table and leaned toward Lauren. "The chronicle is neither your responsibility nor your concern any longer," she said, her soft voice as tough as iron.

"Of, of course not," Lauren said, relief spreading through her. She wasn't responsible for the loss of the chronicle—and it wasn't lost to her as a research source. "I'm so glad you've got it," she began to babble. "I was just so worried—afraid it was my fault. And disappointed. I haven't gotten a chance to read it yet."

Deborah stepped around the table. "It's clear that it's not possible for you to read the chronicle," she said to Lauren. "We warned you about the curse."

"But I don't believe—" Lauren began.

"We can't help you with your book—or with anything, for that matter," Deborah said, her tone brooking no argument. "It's best if you go now."

Lauren nervously fingered her necklace. "If you could just—" she started, then stopped, for Deborah was staring at her necklace, a look of extreme satisfaction on her face.

Dropping her hand self-consciously, it took Lauren

a moment to realize that Deborah wasn't interested in the necklace, that Deborah's pale eyes were searing into the skin behind the gold chain, locked onto the crescent-shaped scar at the base of Lauren's throat.

Eleven

IT WAS FRIDAY AFTERNOON, EXACTLY ONE WEEK AFTER Jackie's death, and Lauren was at her desk, trying—rather unsuccessfully—to keep from thinking about what she had been doing last week at this time. She had spent the morning in an uncharacteristic frenzy of activity, but neither bill paying nor dish washing nor bathroom scrubbing had been able to keep the memories at bay. Last week I was arguing with Drew about getting dressed, she thought as she mulled over how much of the balance she should pay on her MasterCard. Last week I was meeting with Ellen Baker.

After managing to swallow a quarter of a tuna fish sandwich, Lauren settled down to make a list of some of the things Drew had done lately that demonstrated he was a healthy, well-adjusted boy. She wanted to prove to Dr. Berg that there were many sides to Drew—and that most of them were of no interest to a child psychologist.

1. *Built a forbidden island with his pirate Legos.*
2. *Made up a secret language with his friend Scott.*

3. *Said he liked dirty fingernails.*
4. *Complained that making his bed was useless because he was just going to mess it up again the next night.*

But even as she was smiling at her list, Lauren couldn't help glancing at the clock. Last week I was at the library.

She hastily scribbled that Drew liked playing on the computer and occasionally ate too much ice cream, then she stood and stretched, almost glad it was time to get ready for her appointment with Nat Abraham. Although she had been dreading this meeting, which she had set up after Jackie's funeral to try to convince Nat to let her write *Rebeka Hibbens* her way, Lauren was now relieved just to have someplace to go.

She went into her bedroom and stared forlornly into her closet, hoping the appropriate outfit would somehow materialize, yet knowing it wouldn't. Aside from buying underwear and socks, she hadn't spent money on clothes since she had begun graduate school. As she reached for her man-tailored white shirt with the frayed left cuff, the phone rang. It was Dan Ling.

"Bad news," he said. "Lieutenant Conway nixed the investigation."

Lauren didn't say anything for a moment, surprised by the disappointment Dan's words produced. "I guess we shouldn't have expected anything different."

"Conway gave me one of those you-overeager-rookies-are-all-alike smiles. Then he patted my shoulder and told me to stay focused on my duties. 'Your time will come,' he tells me. 'Your time will come.' " Dan's voice was bitter. "So I guess we're on our own."

"I don't know, Dan," she said. "Maybe we do have it wrong. . . ." Lauren wasn't at all sure how she felt about being on their own in a murder investigation.

Granted, there were a lot of suspicious aspects to Jackie's death, but if a police lieutenant didn't think them sufficient cause for concern, maybe they shouldn't either. "What can we even do?"

"Well, we can't do anything immediately," Dan said. "I wrangled a little time off, so Sunday I'm taking Helene out to the Berkshires for a few days. We'll be back late Tuesday, so let's plan on meeting first thing Wednesday morning."

"Sounds good to me."

"It's just for three days," Dan said, apparently thinking she needed reassurance. "So don't let it worry you. Until I get back all you have to do is lie low. Don't work on that book. Don't get near those witches. And keep your doors locked."

* * *

"I had a friend," Nat Abraham said, putting his legs up on his desk. "Forty-two. Gets on the commuter train one morning. Drinks his coffee. Reads his newspaper. Wham—aneurysm. He's gone." He shook his head. "Makes you think about chucking it all and heading for Tahiti."

Lauren pressed her palms to her skirt. She had been thinking similar thoughts herself, not so much about running away as about the fragility of life.

Nat swung his arm out wide, pulling her from her reverie and directing her to look at his cubbyhole of an office. Piles of manuscripts crowded his desk, more cluttered the floor, others tottered on the listing bookshelves next to his narrow window. There wasn't much space for him, nor for her, nor for all the pink telephone slips and yellow stickies that were strewn on top of the manuscripts and stuck to the walls.

"Ever see the movie *Romancing the Stone*?" he asked.

Confused, Lauren tried to remember the movie—from the early eighties, she thought—but kept coming up blank. Nat's habit of jumping from one topic to another seemingly unconnected topic always threw her off balance. That was one of the many reasons Jackie had always dealt with him.

"Michael Douglas?" she finally guessed.

"And Kathleen Turner." He grinned. "Anyway—remember in the movie she's a writer?"

Lauren nodded, although she remembered nothing of the sort.

"And she goes to her editor's office?"

Lauren nodded again. What was he getting at?

"And remember what it looked like?"

Suddenly, Lauren did remember: Kathleen Turner's editor had an elegant, spacious office with color-coordinated couches, lots of large windows, and not a manuscript in sight. She smiled. "Nothing like this office."

"Tahiti."

"I wish I could go with you," she said, settling back into her chair, starting to feel a bit more comfortable, beginning to understand why Jackie and Gabe liked Nat so much.

"I wish I could go with me too." He looked out his small window for a moment and then dropped his legs from the desk and swung toward Lauren. "You want an extension—right?"

"That, uh, that would be great."

"Can't give you much, but I'll see what I can do." He leaned closer. "You want something else too." His question was a statement.

"Well, as a matter of fact . . ." She tried to smile, but she knew her attempt was anemic. Once again, she heard Dan's admonition: *"Don't work on that book. Don't get near those witches."*

"Spit it out," Nat prompted.

"Gabe Phipps and I were discussing *Rebeka Hibbens* the other day." Lauren folded her hands in her lap and tried to look scholarly and thoughtful. If Nat thought for a minute she was actually afraid of the project, he'd never take her request seriously. "We were thinking that a bit of restructuring might be in order."

"Oh, you were, were you?" Nat leaned back and put his legs up on the desk again. "And just what does the great Dr. Phipps think about *Rebeka Hibbens*?"

"We both feel quite strongly that the supernatural portion of the book should be cut back," she said firmly. "That reverting to the original outline and concept will make it much stronger and more credible."

"That's what you and Gabe Phipps think?" Nat's voice had a poking-fun tone to it that Lauren chose to ignore.

"Yes." She paused and smiled brightly, too brightly, she thought, pulling her lips closed. "Gabe said there should be more than enough interest in my feminist and social-psychological interpretations of witchcraft to make for a strong book without a primary focus on the supernatural." She figured that was what Gabe would say if he were given the chance.

"But a unique book? A commercial book?" Nat demanded. "Is there enough in your 'feminist and social-psychological interpretations' to support the print run we have in mind?"

Lauren sat up straighter in her chair. "Witchcraft is very popular."

"The spooky side, yes."

"I could give it an interesting new twist," Lauren said. "Come up with a unique interdisciplinary perspective—"

He held up his hands. "We bought a book about witchcraft and the supernatural, and that's the book we want—especially now that you've got the witches' bible—that chronicle. You know how many feminist books there are by legit academics? How many books on social psychology?"

"That's not the—"

"It's exactly the point," he interrupted, then paused for effect. "How many books do you think there are by established historians that posit the occult as the cause of a real historical event?"

Lauren played with her necklace and avoided Nat's eyes. She was a good historian. She had a great memory and her mind easily grasped large historical concepts. She was a thorough researcher and a strong writer. But she wasn't a particularly good businesswoman. She hadn't thought a historian had to be.

"The supernatural would still be a part," she argued. "Still a possible explanation."

"Not enough!" Nat cried, swinging his legs off the desk and facing her. "Boylston's excited about *Rebeka Hibbens* because the supernatural's more than just a possibility. But," he paused again, "now that we've lost our 'established' historian, we've got a problem."

"A problem?" she repeated.

"We've now paid quite a bit of money for a book by an unknown."

"Jackie can still be primary author," Lauren said quickly. "That would be fine with me—more than fine. I'd really like to do that for her," she added, thinking how annoyed Simon would be if he could hear this conversation.

"Nice sentiment, but not enough." Nat shook his head sadly. "We plan to keep Jackie as primary author—but we need something else too. Something to make up for her lack of input." His eyes sparkled and Lauren's heart sank.

Lauren had known it was coming, but somehow it was still a blow to hear the words. "You want material from the chronicle to form the core of the book," she said dully.

"Exactly." He leaned back in his chair, crossed his arms, and regarded her carefully. "Have you seen it?"

Lauren pressed her hands together and tried one more time. "You liked the original proposal," she reminded him. "Isn't there any chance we could go back to it?"

"No can do," Nat said, shaking his head. "Everyone here's too psyched about that bible—and remember, we've lost the input of our primary author."

Silently apologizing to Jackie, Lauren said, "What if we made a new deal for a new book and I returned the difference between the advances?"

"Okay, let's see how that might look." Nat began scribbling on a pad and muttering encouraging phrases such as "unknown without a PhD" and "never go mass market." He paused and tapped his pencil on the desk. "With luck, maybe I could convince them to give you a couple thousand dollar advance."

Lauren was horrified. She thought of the balance she was carrying on her credit card, of the new pair of sneakers Drew needed, of the note she'd received from Mrs. Piccini, the landlady, complaining that Todd's half of the November rent had not been paid. "That's all?" Her voice came out as a hoarse whisper.

"That's if I could sell them on the idea of yet another feminist reinterpretation of witchcraft—and for that I give you no guarantees." Nat jumped up and went to a tall file cabinet shoved behind his door. He rummaged through a drawer and pulled out a file. "Look, I know Jackie was the one who was into this occult shit," he said, flipping through some papers, "but you don't have to believe the stuff to write a good book about it. Just start with what she already did—all those meetings with mediums and fortunetellers and those new earth-mother witches—what do they call themselves?"

"The Wicca," Lauren said dully.

"See? You know all about this already. And with her latest breakthrough . . ." Nat looked up at Lauren and his eyes clouded. "I talked to her about that chronicle a little over a week ago. Damned shame. Damned shame."

To her amazement, Lauren was overcome by a powerful blast of anger. Anger at Jackie for dying and leaving her alone with this mess. Anger at Deborah for suddenly believing in the stupid curse. Anger at Dan for putting crazy ideas into her head. Lauren wished she could grab a manuscript from Nat's desk and rip it to shreds the way Drew had ripped Kisha Liebhaber's picture, stomping her foot and screaming out her fury at the unfairness of it all. But that would be ridiculous and futile. She slumped in the chair. As ridiculous and futile as her anger.

"Anyway," Nat was saying, "when I talked to Jackie she was tremendously excited. Told me all about the reincarnated women and their bible. Can you beat it?" He shook his head. "You've seen the book, haven't you?" he asked again.

Lauren nodded, thinking of the last time she had seen the chronicle. How she had held the thick leather volume in her hands while Jackie happily jabbered. *"It's going to be great fun. I promise."*

"If you can do something with it," Nat was saying, "if you can find any sliver of truth in their story—well, do that, and all your problems will be solved!" He chuckled. "That Jackie. You've got to hand it to her—finding nutsos who actually think they're the reincarnation of your lost coven. What was she—some kind of a kook magnet?"

Lauren stared at him. "Kook magnet," she repeated. And now she was being drawn in as well.

Nat touched her shoulder. "Look, Lauren, don't take it so hard. Just go read it—" He paused, a worried frown crossing his face. "You do have the book, don't you?"

Lauren wondered once again what the real story was. Who had taken the chronicle from Jackie's house—and who had given the book back to the witches? There was something about the smile that had passed between Deborah and Cassandra that led Lauren to believe the two women knew more than they were saying.

"Lauren?" Nat interrupted her thoughts.

Lauren knew there was no way to keep from telling him the truth. She took a deep breath. "The witches have it—and they've changed their minds and won't let me read it," she said quickly. "Deborah told me they don't want any part of *Rebeka Hibbens*."

"So your job's to get them to change their minds, kid," Nat said, unperturbed by her news. "All you've got to do is convince them of your sincerity and the historical importance of their book. A little cajoling, a little flattery . . . You'll be amazed at what you can do. And who knows—maybe you'll get into it."

Lauren stood up, trying to convince herself that this was what Jackie would have wanted, that this was the right thing to do. She reminded herself that Lieutenant Conway didn't think there was anything suspicious about Jackie's death. "Would you get into spending your time with a bunch of women who thought they were the reincarnations of three-hundred-year-old witches?" she asked.

Nat looked at her thoughtfully for a moment. "Not that I'm suggesting this or anything," he finally said, "but you can always cancel the contract and give the advance back—that would get you off the hook."

She shook her head. "Not when the money's already been spent."

He smiled and turned his palms to the ceiling. "Hey, look at the bright side. This'll force you to write the book and maybe it'll make us all rich. One more best-seller like Gabe's and I could be sitting in Kathleen Turner's editor's office!" He draped his arm over her shoulder as he led her to the door. "Spending that money could be the best thing you ever did."

Somehow, Lauren doubted it.

* * *

"Nat? Gabe Phipps," Gabe said into the telephone. "How's it going?"

Lauren sat silently in the chair opposite Gabe's desk, listening to him attempt to charm Nat.

"You'll have to deal with Nancy on this second serial rights bit," Gabe was saying. "Have your contracts people talk with the agency's people—I stay out of these financial finaglings." He chuckled. "After what happened with the audio rights for *A New Social History,* Nancy ordered me never to speak to you again." Gabe nodded and winked at Lauren as he listened to Nat.

Lauren wasn't happy about being here. After her futile discussion with Nat on Friday, she had brooded all weekend about whether to take Gabe up on his offer to help her change Nat's mind. Despite Dan's advice to the contrary and a gnawing fear in her belly, Lauren had decided to try talking to Deborah before approaching Gabe. But when Gabe had grabbed her in the hallway first thing this morning and reiterated his offer, Lauren had agreed to let him give it a try. So here she sat, in "the inner sanctum of our great leader," as Terri, the department secretary, always referred to Gabe's office.

"Sure, sure," Gabe was saying. "Of course I have no problem. Braille is fine. You think I want to gouge blind people for a few bucks?" He laughed. "What kind of a guy do you take me for?" He paused and then laughed even louder at Nat's response. "Just don't tell Nancy that."

She looked around the large corner office, midmorning sunlight flooding the comfortable clutter and the Oriental rug that had faded to muted perfection. Gabe *had* offered to call Nat, she reminded herself. Twice. She had never actually asked him to do it. It had been *his* idea. Nevertheless, she felt like a commoner groveling before the nobility—and hated it.

"There's one more thing," Gabe said after setting up a golf date with Nat. "Lauren Freeman stopped by to see me the other day." He winked at her again. "Yeah, yeah, I know. We're all taking it pretty hard." He listened for a few minutes. "Yeah, Lauren told me." He listened again and laughed. "Got to agree with you there." He scribbled a note and handed it to Lauren.

She looked down at it. "He thinks you're cute," it said. Glancing up from the note, she saw that Gabe was grinning at her. When he smiled like that, he really was an incredibly attractive man.

"I understand," Gabe was saying. "It's all very intriguing. But you've got to remember we're talking history here. Not fairy tales. We're talking respected historians—" He listened for a minute before continuing. "I'll give you a whole list of reasons. One: It's all hogwash. Two: It's all hogwash. Three: It's all hogwash. And four: If your name is associated with hogwash you'll never get that promotion—or that corner office—you're always pining after."

Lauren leaned forward in her chair, as if that would enable her to hear Nat's side of the conversation. Gabe had charmed all of America; he could certainly charm Nat Abraham. That grin could charm anyone.

"Nat," Gabe said in his perfectly modulated, expert lecturer voice, "you're missing a valuable point here." He listened. "No, no, I completely appreciate your position, it's just that—"

Lauren's heart sank. Apparently, Nat Abraham was tougher than all of America. And, of course, he couldn't see Gabe's grin.

"Okay, okay, pal," Gabe said. "Listen, I'll probably run into Lauren sometime soon. Let me talk to her. Until then, let's leave it that you'll think about it." He burst out laughing. "You know me, I always get what I want in the end." He listened, then sobered. "I'm telling you, I know what I'm talking about, and you're making a big mistake."

Lauren stared at the intricate design of the Oriental rug. There were patterns within patterns within patterns. Each one caught inside the other, defined and confined by the one larger than itself. Lauren heard Gabe's sharp intake of breath and looked up.

"I'm going to do you a favor and forget you ever told me that," Gabe said softly. He listened for a moment then hung up the phone.

"What?" Lauren asked.

"Nat was just 'making a business observation,'" Gabe said bitterly. "He was noting that authors who 'die under unusual circumstances' often sell extremely well."

Dumbfounded, Lauren stared at him. "Nat said that?"

"Anyone who thinks publishing is a gentleman's business shouldn't be writing books." Gabe swiveled his chair and stared out the window at the graceful quad crisscrossed with sidewalks and students rushing to class. Lauren could see the determination carving his features. "We've lost a battle," he said, swinging back toward her, "but that doesn't mean we'll lose the war."

Lauren was touched by his concern. She had never seen this side of Gabe; she had always assumed he was too caught up in his own ambition to care much about the problems of others. She had misjudged him. Apparently being rich, famous, and brilliant didn't mean you couldn't be a good friend.

"Thanks for the try," she said, standing up and forcing herself to smile. She rapped on the desk with her knuckles. "I mean it, thanks a lot."

He leaned forward. "What will you do now?"

"This really is what Jackie would've wanted," Lauren said, striving to be upbeat. "Part of me is actually relieved to do it her way."

"You mean you'll do Jackie's part? Hunt down witches and sorcerers? Badger those reincarnated crazies until they show you their chronicle?" He waved her back into the chair. "It doesn't sound like you."

Lauren sat down, once again surprised by Gabe's interest. She raised her chin and reminded herself that she had done many things in her life that she hadn't wanted to do: she had spent every Christmas vacation at Todd's parents' tiny apartment in Fort Lauderdale; had labored for thirty-seven hours to give birth to Drew; she had filed for divorce; and now she was living through the loneliness of having lost her best friend.

"May not sound like me," she said, keeping her voice light, "but when you've spent the advance, you've got to write the book."

"Ah," he said, frowning.

"Unless you have any other ideas?" Her question was rhetorical—another attempt at lightness.

Unexpectedly, Gabe's face filled with his famous grin. "You could have dinner with me tonight."

Lauren was caught by surprise. "That's, ah, not exactly the kind of idea I meant," she finally stuttered.

"But is it a good idea?" His dark eyes gleamed mischievously, almost shrewdly.

Was he asking her out on a date? Lauren wondered. It had been well over a decade since anyone had asked her for a date; she didn't know the rules anymore. No, this clearly wasn't a date. He was just being nice, trying to cheer her up. "It's not a bad idea—I mean it's a good idea," she said. "Just a bad time."

"I understand." He nodded, his grin gone, his face full of the serious empathy Lauren often saw when she told people she and Todd were getting divorced.

"No, no. It's not that. It's Drew—my son," she said. "I don't like to leave him more than I have to. The poor little guy's having a tough time adjusting."

Gabe turned his palms up. "I was spared that." Department gossip had it that Gabe had been through a particularly messy divorce about ten years ago, and that he never spoke of his marriage—or of his ex-wife. "Although I often regret never having had a child," he said softly.

"Maybe we could have dinner some other time?" Lauren surprised herself by asking.

"Does Drew like Chinese food?"

"As long as it's Peking ravioli," Lauren answered.

"How about I pick up some Chinese and bring it to your house?"

"Tonight?" Lauren asked, thinking of how excited Drew would be. Peking ravioli was his favorite, but money had been so tight lately that eating out or taking in had assumed "special treat" status.

"Isn't that what we're talking about?" Gabe's irresistible grin flashed again. "We'll strategize. Maybe come up with a new game plan that will avoid excessive contact with crazy witches and still keep Nat happy."

Both relieved and surprisingly disappointed, Lauren smiled. This wasn't a date. "Sevenish?"

"White wine or red?"

"Either is fine," she said, walking to the door and giving him a foolish little wave before escaping into the hallway. Why had she said that? she wondered. Red wine gave her a headache.

Twelve

GABE ARRIVED PROMPTLY AT SEVEN, CARRYING TWO bottles of red wine and a large bag on which *Chinese Food* was written in tapering brush strokes intended to resemble Oriental characters. He looked handsome—and years younger—in his bright-colored rugby jersey and blue jeans. She was used to seeing him in tweed jackets and oxford shirts. Dressed like this, his daily workouts showed.

"Am I too early?" he asked almost shyly.

"No, no," she said, taking the wine bottles from him. "It's a fine time," she added as she led him up the stairs. A fine time? she asked herself. What the hell did that mean?

"Great place," Gabe said, running his hand over the thick mahogany banister. "Beautiful wood."

As she pushed the door open with her elbow and waved him into the hall, Lauren decided she liked that he wore his hair unstylishly long. The way it curled around his collar was appealing, if perhaps too reminiscent of the sixties—a decade of which he must have much stronger memories than she.

"It actually reminds me a lot of your house," Lauren said. Then, afraid that she might be insulting him by comparing his mansion to her small apartment, she added quickly, "Except, of course, that yours is the whole thing—the real thing. Mine's only a small piece of what this place once was."

He shrugged and inspected the cornice molding.

Lauren tried to keep herself from rocking back and forth on her feet. She knew she should lead him into the living room, but then they would have to pass the kitchen. And suddenly she didn't want him to see the little table she had set for three. In some moronic way, it embarrassed her, made her feel exposed and silly, as if she were a little girl playing grown up.

Just as Gabe turned and looked at her expectantly, Drew came up behind her. Relieved to have an object of conversation, Lauren pulled him to her. Drew stood with half his body pressed into his mother's leg and stared at Gabe. The genes had mixed strangely, for he was small for his age, while both she and Todd were quite tall. People either assumed he was exceptionally bright and articulate or guessed him to be one or two years younger than his current age. The latter did not sit well with Drew.

"Did you bring the Peking ravioli?" Drew demanded.

"Drew! Don't be rude," Lauren said. "Say hello to Dr. Phipps. Do you remember him from the department picnic at his house last summer?"

"You made me watch him on TV last week instead of 'The Simpsons.' " Drew leaned on the toe of one sneaker.

"Well, say hello anyway," she ordered.

Drew didn't say a word. He just continued to stare at Gabe and rotate his foot.

"You're going to be watching him tonight too—it's the last segment of his series," Lauren said. "And if you don't say hello, you won't be watching 'The Simpsons' for a week after that either."

"I'm with Drew on this one," Gabe said, winking at the boy. "I'd really like to get away from it all for an evening—Homer and Bart sound much more appealing than listening to myself pontificate on the American Revolution."

"But I want to see it," Lauren protested.

Gabe smiled at Drew and rolled his eyes. "Hasn't your mom ever heard of a VCR?" he asked.

Drew giggled. "She doesn't like TV all that much, but I can tape it for her."

"Next time I'll try not to be on TV during 'The Simpsons,' " Gabe said to Drew as Lauren led them into the kitchen.

"That'd be good." Drew nodded emphatically. "You're boring."

"Drew!" Lauren cried.

Gabe laughed as he put the food on the counter. "Really, Lauren, you can't believe I'd be insulted because an eight-year-old prefers 'The Simpsons' to events that happened over two hundred years ago?"

"I'm seven."

Gabe looked at Drew carefully. "You look eight to me. Nine maybe. Are you sure you're not mistaken?"

Lauren watched Drew puff up with pride. Perhaps Gabe had failed to charm Nat, but he sure was doing a great job on Drew—no small accomplishment. And now that she was standing next to Gabe in her stocking feet, she realized he was much taller than she had thought; they were about the same height. She busied herself taking cartons from the bag, wondering what Jackie would think of this new twist in departmental relations.

"Want to meet Herman?" Drew asked Gabe.

"Herman?" Gabe squatted down so he was at eye level with the boy. "I didn't know you had a brother."

"Not a brother," Drew said, tilting his head shyly.

"Herman's my turtle." He turned and dashed down the hallway. "I'll go get him."

Within seconds Drew was back with Herman in his hand. He held the turtle out proudly for Gabe's inspection. About twice the size of a silver dollar, Herman was the kind of small green turtle that had been popular in the fifties and sixties—until the species was banned from the country for spreading salmonella poisoning. Todd smuggled Herman in from Spain as a consolation present after he missed Drew's seventh birthday. Drew loved Herman so much he had immediately forgiven Todd. Lauren had not.

"He's a beaut." Gabe ran a finger along the ridges of Herman's shell; Herman pulled in his head and limbs.

"Don't you think it looks like a birdhouse?" Drew asked, tracing a rough square of slightly darker green along the turtle's carapace.

Gabe considered the turtle's shell carefully. "I sure do," he declared, cementing Drew's approval. Most of Drew's friends, as well as his parents and Aunt Beatrice, had a lot of difficulty seeing the birdhouse.

"Why don't you bring Herman back to your room?" Lauren suggested, throwing a smile of thanks at Gabe. "And wash your hands. Dinner's ready."

Lauren thoroughly enjoyed dinner. Gabe and Drew discussed turtles and exactly what kinds of guns and other weapons the minutemen had used at Lexington and Concord. Lauren and Gabe discussed a juicy bit of gossip about Terri, the department secretary, and a popular movie they had both seen and hated. They finished off both orders of Peking ravioli.

By the time she put Drew to bed, Lauren had decided to show Gabe the poppet she had received in the mail. As she pulled the shoe box from the linen cabinet bookshelf, the phone rang. With the box under her arm, she went into the living room, where Gabe was sitting, to answer it. She was surprised to find the call was for him.

He walked over to her desk. "I hope you don't mind that I had my calls forwarded here." He shrugged sheepishly as he picked up the receiver. "Hollywood's three hours behind us, so there are always deals cooking in the evening."

Lauren wondered whether she should go into the kitchen to give him some privacy. But then, figuring it was her house, she sat down on the couch. Feigning disinterest in his conversation, she lifted a glass of wine and took a sip. Then she opened an old copy of *Newsweek* and began flipping through it.

"You're kidding!" Gabe exclaimed, a wide grin animating his face. "That's great, Nance. Good job."

Lauren remembered that Nancy was his agent. Her heart beat faster and she gave up any pretense of inattention. Something important was happening.

Gabe burst out laughing at something Nancy said. "Maybe you're right."

When he finally put down the phone, he smiled at Lauren the way Drew did when he was particularly proud of himself but didn't want her to know. "'The Tonight Show,' " Gabe said. "They want to fly me to L.A. to be on the show."

"The *real* 'Tonight Show'?" Lauren asked, incredulous. As much as she admired and respected Gabe, it was difficult to imagine that Jay Leno wanted to talk to him on national television.

"The very real one," Gabe said, flashing his irresistible grin. "Nancy said it was no joke—they actually want boring l'il old historian me!"

"That's fabulous," Lauren said, handing him a glass of wine. She had never known anyone who had been on "The Tonight Show." "To your success as a popular icon."

He touched her glass with his and his face glowed with happiness. "What an absurd—but admittedly appealing—concept." He took a large gulp of wine and came to sit next to her on the couch. He looked at the shoe box. "What's this?"

"Oh, nothing," she said, putting it under the coffee table. "It seems so silly and unimportant after your news."

"No, no," he said. "Remember I said I wanted to get away from it all for an evening?" He ran his hands through his thick hair. "This 'onstage' stuff gets to be a bit much after awhile."

"Well, if you're sure . . ." she said, reluctantly putting the box on the table. "It's a Paul Conklin joke—I think. He sent one to me and one to Jackie."

Gabe lifted his eyebrows. "I thought he swore off the practical jokes after he got my car towed."

"See for yourself."

Gabe flipped off the lid and stared impassively at the doll. He read the note and looked up at her; his eyes were dark and brooding. "Jackie got one of these too?" he asked, his face paling as the full impact of the poppet and Jackie's death hit him. "Poor bastard'll never pull another prank again."

"So you think Paul sent them?"

"He knew you and Jackie were going to get the chronicle—and it sure seems like his kind of gag." Gabe picked the poppet up and inspected it more closely. "Ugly sucker," he muttered. "Did you ask him about it?"

Lauren told him exactly what Paul had said. Then she told him about Deborah's curse.

Gabe sipped his wine and stared at the poppet as she spoke. "So what did you think of Deborah?" he finally asked.

"Intense," she said slowly. "But very smart—and maybe very off her rocker. A real enigma."

Gabe nodded. "She's an enigma, all right."

"You know her?" Lauren asked, surprised.

"I used to." He swallowed the remaining wine in

his glass and poured himself another. "Why do you think it was Paul instead of your reincarnated witches who sent the poppets? The witches are more likely to mix their historical metaphors."

Lauren was intrigued and impressed by Gabe's point. Historically, poppets weren't found in the home of the victim; they were kept by the sorcerer, who, through spells and incantations, used the dolls as conduits to work evil on his or her prey.

"These new witches do things differently," Lauren said thoughtfully. "My knowledge of contemporary witchcraft is pretty limited, but I do know that covens are encouraged to make up their own spells and incantations. To do things their own way." She shrugged. "Maybe someone wanted to scare Jackie and didn't care—or know—if it was 'historically correct.' "

"Seems logical."

"But it couldn't have been Deborah. She's the one who gave us the chronicle in the first place—and who else would care? I figure it must've been Paul," Lauren said, realizing she was trying to convince herself as well as Gabe. "Even if he's aware of the intricate details of Colonial black magic—which, given his specialty, is unlikely—my guess is he would take poetic license for a good practical joke." She looked down at the deformed doll and shuddered. Replacing the lid on the shoe box, she pushed it under the couch with her foot.

Gabe nodded. "My guess too."

"But the worst of it is," Lauren continued, "because of Jackie's death, Deborah and Cassandra are now convinced their curse has come true. And, as long as they believe that, no chronicle for me—or Nat."

"And Nat's not a man who's easily swayed," Gabe said, refilling her glass.

Once again touched by his interest, Lauren took another sip of the red wine; it tasted quite bitter on her tongue. "Nat's obsessed with that chronicle—he wants supernatural, reincarnation, spooky, weird. I want history, feminism, social psychology." She shrugged, feigning a nonchalance she didn't feel. "He's got all the power, all the money, and all the control."

Gabe ran his finger around the rim of his glass; she liked the tight, hard look of the muscles along his arm. "So what's your plan?" he asked.

"Figure out a way to keep Nat happy." Lauren sipped her wine and wondered why she kept drinking it. "Sometimes I feel like I'm just a caboose—being pulled along by everyone else. Reacting to situations that other people create." She took another sip, but as soon as the taste registered she put the glass down on the table. "And I don't want any more wine," she added emphatically.

"Okay," he said, shifting his weight so that he was slightly farther away from her on the couch. "You don't have to have any."

"Sorry. I guess it's been a long day." She looked down at her hands, thinking that if this had been a date, it surely wasn't any longer. She noticed that the turquoise stone in her ring had fallen out. The ring hadn't been expensive, nor did it have any sentimental value; nonetheless, Lauren felt a pang as she slipped the ring in her pocket. It seemed she was losing so much lately.

Gabe leaned toward her. "But how can you do what you're told when Nat tells you one thing and your witches tell you another?"

"I'm just going to have to give Deborah and Cassandra time to cool down and then ask again for permission to read the chronicle." She shrugged. "Nat's the boss—he has to win."

Gabe looked over at Lauren's desk, heaped with books and file folders. "What about Jackie's other leads?"

Lauren followed his gaze. "There's plenty of weird stuff, but none of it's as relevant or commercial as the reincarnated witches."

"So make it relevant," Gabe said. "Make it commercial." He tapped her leg with his finger and she felt a jolt flow from the spot he had touched. "There's got to be great stuff in there. Stones and circles and curses. Amulets and chants and magic symbolism. Things your coven did in 1692 that are still being done today. I'll bet you can come up with an interpretation that'll explain why the coven disappeared."

"One that's good enough to satisfy Nat?" Her voice was full of doubt. "As good as the chronicle?"

"Why not?" Gabe stood up and grabbed a few files. He flipped through them. "This is great stuff: the black mass sequel, the necromantic invocation, the conjuration of a girl . . . Hey, look at this—she's got a list called 'local witches.' Can you believe the woman? There are even phone numbers," he said triumphantly. "Call them all. I'll bet you can find what you need for Nat without ever having to go back to that crazy store."

Despite his persuasiveness and her desire to believe, Lauren was still skeptical. "But what if it's not linked enough—or spooky enough—for Nat?"

Gabe grabbed Lauren's hands and sat down next to her, closer than before. "Oh, it's spooky enough," he said. "All you have to do is find a connection. And if there's one thing I've learned about historical connections, it's that if you look long enough, you'll find them. I just never give up until I get what I want." He grinned at her. "You can do this, Lauren. I know you can. As a matter of fact, I'm so convinced you can pull it off that I'd be willing to work with you on it."

Mesmerized by both his words and the touch of his hands, Lauren didn't move. The great Gabe Phipps, willing to work with a lowly graduate student? The man who was going to be flown to L.A. to be on "The

Tonight Show"? As her mind whirled, a part of her remained acutely aware of the strength of his grip, of the thick dark hairs on his forearms.

"Thanks—that would be great," she said, trying to match his enthusiasm, although she held out little hope for success. Gabe hadn't seen Nat's face when he had described the excitement at Boylston Press over the "witches' bible." "I guess there's nothing to lose by giving it a shot."

"Good." Gabe leaned back on the couch and crossed his arms over his chest, a satisfied smile on his face. They sat in silence for a few minutes as he glanced around the airy room, casually inspecting its double bay windows, its gaping fireplace, its wild and obviously uncared-for plants, its mishmash of furniture and functions: living room, study, playroom. "I like it here," Gabe finally said.

"So do I."

"You know, you're a very comfortable person to be around." He smiled—not his usual public grin, but a warm, intimate smile that touched something deep inside her.

Lauren picked up her wineglass and took a sip. When the bitter taste touched her tongue, she burst out laughing.

Gabe leaned over and took the glass from her hand. "You don't want any more wine."

"Right, I don't want any more wine," she repeated, her eyes close to his.

He set the glass on the table. "Guess it's time for me to get going." His statement was obviously a question.

Lauren studied a lock of hair curling over the collar of his shirt. She wanted to reach out and touch it. "I guess it is," she said.

Gabe stood up. "I've got a few more hours of work to put in anyway." At Lauren's surprised look he added, "I'm a real night owl."

Disappointed, Lauren followed him through the hallway. Now that she really looked, she realized he might even be an inch taller than she was. She pulled open the door. "Thanks for the Chinese—" she started to say as he put his arms around her and kissed her.

After the awkwardness of the past few minutes and the tension she had felt all evening, it was so comfortable, so right, to relax in his arms, to be kissing him instead of just thinking about it, to feel his muscular body instead of just wondering about it. As she pressed closer, she realized she had been thinking about kissing him all day.

They stepped apart and smiled shyly at each other. "I had a great time tonight," Gabe said. "Better than I've had in a long time."

This man is a charmer, Lauren reminded herself. And what they were doing right now might even be against university policy. She surprised herself by reaching out and running her finger along the strong line of his chin. She pulled her hand back. "Me too," she said softly.

"It's probably not a good idea . . ."

"Probably not," she agreed, longing to lean over and kiss the spot under his chin where she could see his pulse throbbing.

"So, how about a real dinner?" he asked. "Saturday night?"

"I'd love to," she said before her wiser self could intercede.

Gabe touched her cheek. "I'll call you later in the week." Then he turned and walked down the stairs.

Thirteen

LAUREN SIPPED HER COFFEE, HOPING IT WOULD EASE the headache that neither the previous cup nor the aspirin she had taken earlier had been able to soothe. It was the damn red wine, she thought as the pain hammered behind her eyes.

Somehow she had managed to get Drew off to school and had even called Aunt Beatrice to ask if she could baby-sit Saturday night, but she didn't feel up to convincing Dr. Berg that Drew was just a normal little boy struggling to deal with adult problems. Rubbing her temples, Lauren glanced at the clock and noted that her appointment was in half an hour. Next time she would tell Gabe to bring white wine.

Gabe. Just saying his name to herself caused her stomach to squeeze with nervousness—and her spirits to rise. There was no denying the attraction. On her side it was indisputable and, although she was no expert on men, Lauren was pretty sure that what she had felt from his side of that kiss had been real. She rubbed the goose bumps that rose on her arms at the memory. There was no way he would ever have agreed to help her with the book if he wasn't attracted. Gabe Phipps had far better things to do with his time than guide lowly graduate students through their dissertations. He never even sat on anyone's dissertation committee; she had heard he had a special exemption in his contract.

As she dropped her coffee cup in the sink, the telephone rang. It was Todd.

"I'm running a bit late, hon," he said. "But I promise I'll be there on time."

Lauren pressed her eyes closed for a moment. "You've got less than half an hour," she couldn't keep from reminding him.

"I'm in Cambridgeport finishing up a shoot. Not even ten minutes away. It's one of those architectural projects where the early morning light is crucial—and the light's gone."

"Please just be there, Todd," Lauren said. "It's important we present a united front to this psychologist. That we show him there's nothing wrong with Drew that a little time and love won't cure. Once a kid gets labeled in a school system—"

"I'm not so sure we should minimize this problem," Todd interrupted. "Drew's never acted up in school before. And I'm real concerned about his destroying another child's property—not to mention the part about him drawing pictures of dead people hanging from trees. If the teacher considers it bad enough to refer him to a doctor, don't you think we should take it seriously?"

Lauren heard Ellen Baker's voice: *"Drew's behavior is a cry for help—and I think we should give it to him."* "I guess," she said listlessly.

"There's another way to solve this problem, you know." Todd's tone was playful.

"Please," Lauren said. "Not now."

"Baby girls are awfully cute. . . ."

"I said, not now!" Lauren's voice was sharp. There

was silence on the other end of the phone. "Look," she began. "I didn't—"

"I'll see you at the school," Todd said. Then the phone clicked in her ear.

Lauren slowly replaced the receiver as tears filled her eyes. Why couldn't they ever get anything right? Why did every encounter end in an argument? Pushing thoughts of Todd away, she searched through the mess on her desk for Drew's "normal" list, as she had begun referring to it. When she found the list, she ran her eyes down the items. If this list didn't prove to Dr. Berg and Ellen Baker—as well as to Todd—that Drew was a normal seven-year-old boy, nothing would.

Lauren stuffed the list in her purse and headed out the door. Thatcher Elementary School was only five blocks away and, given the mildness of the morning as well as her still-throbbing head, Lauren decided to walk. According to the radio, a northern swing of the jet stream was bringing in a late Indian summer: It was supposed to hit seventy by afternoon and perhaps get even warmer tomorrow. As she filled her lungs, pushing the sweet-tasting air deep within her, Lauren had the fleeting thought that this was the first real breath she had taken since Jackie's death.

When she was escorted into Dr. Berg's office, Lauren was surprised and then slightly ashamed by her sexist assumptions: Dr. Berg was a woman. A woman who couldn't possibly be as young as she looked—for she appeared to be only about twenty. A woman who, although she smiled as she shook Lauren's hand, had a very serious expression in her large dark eyes.

"Is my husband here yet?" Lauren asked. A quick look around the small, windowless office answered her question. As she dropped into the chair the doctor indicated, she felt her blood pressure rise. She noticed the primary-colored drawings taped to the walls and the worn toys tumbling from a red and purple carton in the corner, but all she could think about was Todd's lateness.

Dr. Berg closed the door, on which hung a large envelope with the words *Please leave me a note to let me know you came by* written across it in blue magic marker, and sat behind her desk. A small nameplate informed Lauren that her first name was Margie. A diploma on the wall indicated she had received her PhD from Brandeis University.

"As we've only got half an hour," the doctor said, "I think we should get started. We can fill Mr. Freeman in when he arrives."

Lauren barked a laugh that contained no humor. "*I promise I'll be there on time,*" Todd had said. "He'll be here any minute, I'm sure," she said, not wanting Dr. Berg to think there were bad feelings between herself and Todd. "He called me just a few minutes ago."

"Then he won't miss much." Margie Berg folded her small hands on the desk. "Sounds like there are some issues with Drew," she said. Despite her youthful face, Dr. Berg was poised and self-confident. She regarded Lauren with both intelligence and compassion. "I've heard a bit from Ellen Baker, but why don't you let me hear it from you. What's going on?"

"I think what's going on is pretty simple. Drew's a seven-year-old boy trying to come to grips with his parents' divorce," Lauren said. "The little guy's feeling pretty bad, but we've tried very hard to explain that, although we've fallen out of love with each other, we still love him very much."

"It can be a very difficult thing for kids to understand."

"I've tried to teach Drew to express his feelings—to recognize his emotions and to talk about them. And I think that's what he's doing now. He's confused and upset and sad—and he's acting out a little." Lauren paused. "Just the other day I was sitting in my editor's office, and I was so frustrated by what he was telling me that I wanted to rip the manuscripts on his desk the same way Drew ripped that little girl's picture. Frankly," Lauren smiled at the psychologist, encouraging her to agree, "Drew's actions don't seem all that inappropriate to me."

The psychologist didn't smile back. "There's a difference between feeling and doing," she said gently. "You may have *wanted* to rip up the manuscripts, but you didn't. You controlled yourself. What we need to do is help Drew control himself by teaching him appropriate ways to act out his feelings."

"You mean like rip up his own picture?" Lauren asked.

"Or perhaps a blank piece of paper. Something that doesn't harm anything." Dr. Berg leaned forward. "Kids aren't born knowing how to control themselves—we need to teach them to set limits before their behavior escalates into something more problematic."

Lauren reached into her purse and placed her list on the desk in front of the psychologist. "Look at this," she said, smoothing it out. "These are some of the things Drew's done in the past few days that Ellen Baker doesn't know about."

Dr. Berg studied the list for a long while and then a wide smile creased her face. "This is great," she said. "It's great that you're keeping in touch with what Drew's doing right—with what a normal kid he is most of the time. Now what we have to do is look at these isolated instances of negative behavior and be detectives. Kids communicate in nonverbal ways, so we have to study Drew's actions and ask ourselves: 'What is he trying to tell us?' "

"But is this concern really necessary?" Lauren tapped the list with her finger. "If he's perfectly normal most of the time, do we really need to focus so much on these isolated instances? Wouldn't he be fine if we just gave him lots of love and let him work it out himself?"

"Very possibly he would—and I most certainly hope that's the case. Lots of kids exhibit aggressive behavior when they're struggling with difficult issues, and Drew's behavior in class may be just that. But I'm concerned about where it could go."

"And just where do you think this 'could go'?" Lauren tried to keep the edge from her voice by reminding herself that Margie Berg's education had immersed her in problematic behavior the same way her own was immersing her in the seventeenth century. The power of graduate programs could be a truly frightening thing to behold.

Dr. Berg gave a little laugh. "If you read the newspapers, you know as well as I do how kids can get out of—"

"Now wait just a minute," Lauren interrupted.

The psychologist raised her hands to fend off Lauren's comment. "And that's why it's so good that we're dealing with this now. So we can teach Drew how to handle his conflicted feelings in a positive manner. So he can learn how to act out in a way that doesn't hurt people."

"You make it sound as if he beat up someone instead of just ripping a piece—"

At that moment, Todd knocked and entered the room. Lauren could barely contain her anger. She glared at Todd and crossed her arms over her chest. He raised his eyebrows at her and shook hands with the doctor. "Sorry I'm late," he said, sitting down. "I got hung up at work."

Lauren swallowed the biting comment on the edge of her tongue.

"We've only got a few minutes left," Dr. Berg was saying, "so I'll let your wife fill you in on the details later. The bottom line is that I think we need to give Drew a little help controlling his anger. Show him more appropriate ways to express his feelings."

"So he doesn't become a serial murderer," Lauren mumbled.

Todd turned to her. "I don't think you should be so flip about this, Lauren. If Mrs. Baker and Dr. Berg think we've got a problem on our hands, maybe we should listen to them."

"It's not clear whether we've got a problem," Lauren said, "or just a mixed-up little boy who needs a lot of love and attention."

"You're right, Mrs. Freeman," Dr. Berg interjected smoothly. "He does need a lot of love and attention—but maybe a little instruction too."

"I'm very concerned about what's been going on," Todd said. "My wife tends to put on her rose-colored glasses in such situations."

"If you're so concerned," Lauren snapped, "how come you showed up five minutes before this meeting's supposed to be over?"

"You know I can't control my shoots."

"For something you're so *concerned* about, I'd think you might try—" Lauren stopped when she noticed the psychologist was watching them closely. "Anyway," she said, "the point is that we're here to help Drew."

Dr. Berg nodded. "I propose that I see Drew a few times over the next couple of weeks. To work with him on acknowledging his feelings but limiting his behavior. To show him how his behavior can affect himself and others. And I'd like you both to do the same at home." She glanced at her watch and stood. "I hope this was helpful," she said, shaking their hands. "I'll call you in a few weeks to schedule another meeting to reassess the situation, okay?"

Lauren and Todd nodded.

"I'll be in touch," Dr. Berg said as she walked out the door, leaving Lauren and Todd standing alone in the small room.

Todd turned to Lauren. "I think this is the wrong time to go into your denial mode," he said. "Despite your take on it, this whole business sounds pretty bad to me."

Lauren was so furious she could barely think straight. After taking a few deep breaths, she collected herself enough to speak. "You missed the part where Dr. Berg said this happens to lots of kids and that it's probably not a big deal. If you can't get here on time, you can't pass judgment," she said in a controlled whisper. "And you might also think about sending Mrs. Piccini your rent check."

Then she swung her purse to her shoulder and walked out the door.

Motioning Cassandra to join her at the altar, Deborah reached under the velvet covering and brought out a small turquoise stone. She held it in her open palm. "It's Lauren Freeman's. She dropped it when she was here last Thursday."

"You really think this is necessary?" Cassandra asked.

"Yes," Deborah said as she aligned the turquoise into a pentagram with a chunk of obsidian, a half-burned candle, a knife, and a cup of human blood. It was just before opening time, and they were alone in the back room of RavenWing. It had been four days since they had seen the mark on Lauren's neck, four days in which Lauren had not contacted them. "We must bring her to us."

"Bram's incantation is set for tonight," Cassandra reminded Deborah. "We promised him no magic within forty-eight hours."

Deborah dismissed Bram with a wave of her hand. "I want her at this ritual, and I need you to work with me."

Deborah had decided to invite Lauren to the waxing crescent moon ritual to be held that evening. They were participating in a Wiccan ceremony with a number of other covens, and the event promised to be tame and spiritual and earthy—in a word: Wiccan. A perfect mechanism, Deborah had gleefully concluded, for developing Lauren's trust, for encouraging her to believe they were as harmless as the Wiccans.

Cassandra bowed her head. "As you wish, Mahala."

"Let us begin," Deborah said, spreading her hands over the implements on the altar and closing her eyes. Within seconds she felt the power rising from the ceremonial objects; this was a good sign. As Cassandra placed her hands over Deborah's, Deborah watched the old woman's aura change from a silvery sheen, which denoted resting power, to a fiery orange.

After casting the circle and invoking the goddess, Deborah handed Cassandra the cup of blood. They each took a sip and Deborah returned the vessel to its place on the altar. She dipped the end of the knife into the cup of blood, then, raising the turquoise, she pointed the bloody blade into the heart of the stone.

"Consecrated knife, magic weapon, fly true and fly straight and inform Lauren Freeman that I hold the key to all she wishes to know."

Cassandra placed her hands on the hilt of the knife, adjoining her power to the spell. "Oh Mitra, oh Varuna, tell Lauren Freeman we await her call."

"And wipe from her mind what is best left forgotten," Deborah added.

Deborah knew it was a risk bringing Lauren to the ritual, for it was being held at White Horse Beach, the site of all the Immortalises. Her presence there might summon memories of the past. As everyone had lived many times prior to their current life, it was common to experience flashbacks of places one had been to, or of people one had known. These flashbacks were often triggered by returning to the site of an important event in a previous lifetime; they were often mistakenly referred to as "déjà vu" by unaware human beings. The last thing Deborah wanted was for Lauren to remember what had happened to her at the past Immortalises.

"Oh Mitra, oh Varuna," Deborah called, "protect our coven's immortality above all else." She then quickly dismissed the invoked powers, opened the circle, and she and Cassandra returned to ordinary consciousness. It was time to open the store.

As Lauren flipped through a thick, dry tome on the Puritan mind, she sipped yet another cup of coffee. Her headache was back with a vengeance. Closing the book with a thud, Lauren stood and walked over to the bay window. She flipped the sash lock on one of the windows and, after a little tugging, lifted it. Leaning her elbows on the sill, she looked through the web of branches at the elegant Victorian house across the way. Even with most of their leaves missing, the thick trunks and limbs of the ancient oaks that lined the street gave this very urban place a sense of the rural.

Drew was going to be fine, she told herself, she just knew that he was. And it wasn't just her "denial mode," as Todd had called it. She was the one who spent the most time with Drew; she was the one who knew him best.

Lauren drummed her fingers on the windowsill as her thoughts turned to Gabe. Gabe had promised he would help her find the historical connections between her present research and the lost coven. Lauren smiled as the sunlight warmed her face and the pounding in her head receded; she couldn't help wondering what else Gabe might help her with. Without thinking, she reached for the phone to call Jackie and talk with her about Gabe. Freezing her hand in midair, Lauren stared at it as if it belonged to someone else, horrified that she had forgotten for even a second that Jackie was dead.

Making an effort to calm herself, she sat back down at her desk and resumed reading, but this time she chose a book more to her liking—*Ordinary People in Pre-Revolutionary America.* Although well aware that life had been very difficult in Colonial times, a part of Lauren longed for the simplicity of hard physical work, of abiding religious conviction, of a clear sense of right and wrong. She closed her eyes, wishing herself there, far away from her modern-day problems.

It was a vividly bright fall day. The sun kindled the leaves to fiery bursts of red and orange, and the sky was a dome of the most perfect blue. She heard a high tinkling laugh.

"Mama!" a child's sweet voice called. "Come roundabout and see what I can do."

She was standing on the edge of a cornfield, surrounded by the rich odor of dirt and growth and harvest. She was wearing a long gray dress with a bodice of crossed linen stays and lace cuffs at the sleeve. Her daughter was at her side.

"Watch!" the child ordered. She drew her hands to her chest and, as if on command, the tall stalks of corn bent toward her. Then she threw her arms forward and the stalks bent away. The little girl turned and grinned proudly up at her mother.

"You would do well never to do such a thing again!" she cried, filled with horror at the scene before her. "'Tis evil and most dangerous."

The child's laughter tinkled again. "'Twas just for sport, Mama. I must have some sport."

She knelt and pulled her daughter to her. "Your stepfather shall be most distressed," she said. "He has been so very kind to us, and it would be grievous folly to incite his wrath."

The child stared over her mother's shoulder. "I don't like him nor his fancy house," she said. "I wish to be in our little house." Her face crumpled and she began to cry. "With Papa."

"The Lord hath chosen to take Papa to him," she said softly, folding the sobbing child in her arms. "But I would belie myself if I did not avow I long for him too." She pushed her daughter gently from her so she could look the child in the eye. "But thou must heed my words: These be dangerous times, full of wicked people who mind nothing that is good and fear things they know not. Thou must never meddle with the corn again—nor or do other tricks for sport. I know thee to be as clear as a child unborn, but another might think differently."

The child shook her head and pressed her face into her mother's breast. She sobbed as if her heart were being rent in two.

Lauren blinked and found herself back in her living room. The clock on the desk told her three hours had passed. Three hours in which she had been standing in a cornfield comforting a daughter she didn't have. Three hours in which the seventeenth century had been more real to her than the twentieth. Although she had purposely put herself in the past and had been doing it for years, the experience in the cornfield had been somehow different. Something about how real it had felt, that she had been a participant, not just an observer. And she had been gone for so long. . . .

It occurred to her that this had been happening to her a lot lately, odd, fuguelike states that gobbled time. It was as if the hours had never existed—or as if she had never existed within them. She thought of the book she had found in her refrigerator the other day; she still had no idea how it had gotten there. With a flush of embarrassment, she remembered the full grocery cart she had left in the Star Market parking lot; it hadn't been until hours later, when she went to make dinner, that she realized she had forgotten to load the groceries into her car.

No, she thought, there was nothing wrong with her

that a little less stress wouldn't take care of. And the truth was, she rather enjoyed getting lost in the past. Her real problem at the moment was more academic. She was finding little historical information on Rebeka Hibbens and her cohorts.

Historians were as fickle as the present-day media, arbitrarily choosing one person to make a star and relegating another—who was just as talented or interesting or important—to the oblivion of a footnote. The members of the lost coven were footnotes at best. Aside from Rebeka Hibbens, hardly any of the others had achieved even that distinction.

Lauren pushed her chair away from the desk and stretched. If only Dorcas Osborne had been a coven member rather than her mother, Faith. The books were full of information on Dorcas. At age seven, she'd been the youngest "witch" to be put to death by the Massachusetts Bay Puritans. That damn chronicle was probably the only source of solid information on the coven, Lauren thought in disgust. The chronicle that Deborah and Cassandra would no longer share.

Lauren looked over at Jackie's files on the occult and realized the headache that the seventeenth century had held at bay was once again pounding in her brain. She went to the kitchen to take a couple more aspirin. But standing only seemed to make her feel worse, so she slipped into her bedroom and lay down on the bed. Within minutes, she was asleep and dreaming—and back in the seventeenth century.

She was running through a garden, but it was a garden full of giant plants, plants so tall they cut off the sunlight above. And she was frantic to find Dorcas. For if Lauren couldn't find her, Dorcas would die. Pushing the tall branches aside, Lauren called out for her child, but only the buzzing of insects answered her cries. The garden was a maze and Dorcas was in the center. She needed the key. But the key belonged to Rebeka Hibbens. And Lauren was afraid of Rebeka.

Suddenly Gabe Phipps appeared beside her; he was wearing a red frock coat lined with large wooden buttons and matching breeches. "Don't be a foolish wench," he said. "Rebeka is crazy—as dotty as they come. She'll never give you the key. She'll only betray your trust."

As Lauren turned from Gabe and ran off, a yellow canary flew above her head. "Gabe Phipps is only concerned with himself and his words are false," the canary called down to her. "Rebeka is there to help you. She is waiting for you." Then with a melodic warble, the canary flew away.

Lauren's eyes opened. Momentarily disoriented by the alien look of her bedroom in the afternoon light, she blinked and then reached for her dream journal. "Dorcas," she wrote. "In maze. Gabe says no. Canary says Rebeka has the key." Then she lay down and closed her eyes, trying to find the thread of the dream to follow it back before the images were lost to her.

As she lay there, quietly letting the dream return, Lauren had to smile at the success of her professors and the directness of her subconscious: Dorcas obviously represented the book, the maze was her conundrum, Rebeka was Deborah, Gabe was the voice of rationality, the canary was Jackie. Nor was there any doubt as to the interpretation of this dream. Her subconscious was telling her to call Deborah. To give it one more try.

Without allowing herself time to think about what she was doing, Lauren got up and went into the kitchen. She grabbed the phone book from the top of the refrigerator, quickly found the number for RavenWing, and dialed it.

Deborah answered on the first ring and, after Lauren identified herself, greeted her warmly. "Why, Lauren Freeman," Deborah said, as if she were repeating Lauren's name for someone else's benefit.

"I'm so pleased you've called. Let me put you on hold for a quick second. I'll be right back." Before Lauren could answer, the line was filled with Beethoven.

Flabbergasted by Deborah's unexpected friendliness, Lauren listened to the complicated melody, unable to imagine what might have caused the woman's change of heart. Did this mean that Deborah and Cassandra were now willing to help her with the book?

"We've had second thoughts about helping you with your book," Deborah said, coming back on the line. "We never read history—male-biased, patriarchal conjecture about events by old white men who weren't there is always wrong and of no interest to us whatsoever—but, on reflection, we thought that perhaps your book might be of a different sort."

"You did?" Lauren was incredulous.

"So we have an invitation," Deborah continued, apparently oblivious to Lauren's surprise. "How would you like to be our guest tonight at a Wiccan waxing crescent moon ritual to be held at White Horse Beach?"

"A Wiccan new moon ritual?" Lauren repeated, trying to get a handle on what Deborah was saying. She knew that being invited to a ritual was no small thing, that outsiders were usually not welcome. While part of her wondered why they were willing to include her, another part knew she should jump at this chance to get her hands on some solid information for her book. "I don't know what to say."

Deborah's laugh tinkled across the phone line. "Then say 'yes.' There are a lot of people who want to meet you."

Fourteen

THERE ARE MANY STRETCHES OF SAND ALONG THE oceans of the world called White Horse Beach. The name is thought to derive from an ancient tale of a white stallion galloping through the darkness, invoking nightmares. There must be at least a half dozen White Horse Beaches in New England alone; the one to which Deborah directed Lauren was just north of Boston.

Lauren didn't know whether it was because of her abysmal sense of direction or her not-so-subconscious desire to avoid the ritual, but there was no doubt about it: She was lost. She passed the Moorscott Presbyterian Church and pulled into the small parking lot of the Cloyce House Inn; a *Closed for the Season* sign banged against the porch railing. She flicked on the interior car light and reviewed Deborah's map and directions. White Horse Beach straddled the Lynn-Moorscott line, a tiny wisp of land jutting out between Lynn Beach and King's Beach. She had somehow missed the turnoff for Shore Drive and was now well into the next town.

Lauren rolled down her window, letting the warm air play with her hair. Staring at the shadowy lines of the dark inn, she decided that getting lost was a clear sign that coming here was a mistake. Then again, if every time she got lost it meant that she wasn't supposed to reach her destination, she might as well stay home. Lauren never made it anywhere on the first try.

Heading back toward the southwest, she finally caught sight of a sign for Shore Drive. Within minutes her headlights lit up a dirt road with a pair of white birches standing sentinel on either side. The road was narrow and rutted, more a path or a trail. She took it slowly, as Deborah had advised. It ended abruptly in a grassy circle just large enough to hold the dozen cars parked there.

Lauren squeezed in between a small pickup truck and a new Lexus and saw about twenty people enjoying the unseasonably warm night. Although mostly women, there were a few men in the group. If it hadn't been for the secluded spot and the white clothes worn by almost all of them, Lauren would have thought she had stumbled onto a football tailgate party. Everyone was chatting and smiling and pulling baskets and other paraphernalia from their trunks. Lauren couldn't help being surprised by how unwitchy the group looked—whatever a witchy group was supposed to look like.

Feeling better because of the apparent normality of her companions, Lauren climbed from her car. Reaching down to lock the door, she noticed Deborah separate herself from the crowd and stride briskly toward her. Cassandra, wearing a white tunic over billowing white pants, and Bram, the man with the pierced eyebrow, followed more slowly. Deborah was also in white, a long dress that grazed the ground as she walked, but Lauren was relieved to see that Bram had on a brown and blue serape over a pair of faded blue jeans. At least she wouldn't be the only one wearing dark clothing.

"No need to lock up." Deborah waved her arm in a graceful arc that encompassed the thick birches and pines. "This time of year we'll have the place all to ourselves."

Lauren thrust her hand forward. "Thank you for inviting me," she said. "I really appreciate the privilege."

Deborah grasped Lauren's hand in both of hers. "It's our pleasure."

Bram came up behind Deborah. "So this is Lauren Freeman," he said, his eyes drifting down to Lauren's neck.

Lauren raised her hand to the high mock turtle collar of her shirt, a style she had favored ever since "the accident," as it was referred to in her family. When she was eleven, she and her parents had been in a car wreck that had left her father with two broken legs, her mother in a coma for several days, and Lauren with a semicircular scar at the base of her throat. She tugged at her collar self-consciously. What was it with these people and her neck? she wondered, suddenly not quite so certain of their normality.

"Lauren's the mother of a seven-year-old son," Deborah was saying to Bram, linking her arm through Lauren's. "Her energy will be a powerful force to add to your incantation." She nodded to Cassandra and Bram, waving her hand at the others, who were beginning to make their way toward the beach. "Go on ahead. I'd like to talk to Lauren—and it looks like Robin could use some help."

Bram nodded and left, but Cassandra didn't move, holding Deborah's gaze for a long time. Lauren had the impression the two women were communicating with one another—but that their conversation was going on at a frequency to which she was unable to tune. Then Cassandra turned and went to catch up with two tall women as they entered a narrow path between the trees. She relieved the more slender of the two of a burlap backpack.

"Shall we?" Deborah asked, taking a step toward the path.

Lauren had no choice but to walk beside Deborah, whose grasp on her arm was surprisingly strong. She felt as if she were being driven by more than politeness or the strength of Deborah's grip. She was being compelled by Deborah's will. Compelled toward the beach, and the rites, and whatever else she might find there.

It was an esbat, Deborah explained to Lauren as they followed the snaking path through dense pines occasionally studded with startling white birches. Sometimes referred to as the rites of the crescent moon, this lunar ritual celebrated life and birth and regeneration. It also celebrated woman, whose tie to the moon was ancient and deep. Its colors were white and silver, its letter S, and its numbers three and nine. "The night of the waxing crescent belongs to the goddesses Artemis and Nimue," Deborah said.

Lauren was intrigued as she listened to Deborah's deep voice recounting the ancient pagan rituals of this almost ageless religion, its ceremonies and beliefs born before recorded time. As a historian, Lauren had a respectful appreciation for the power of religion—for good and for evil. Throughout recorded history more battles had been fought and more lives lost in the name of someone's "god" than for any other reason. But many hearts had also been soothed and many troubles made endurable by the answers and the connections of faith. These people seemed to personify the worthier side.

Lauren stepped carefully around a crop of birch saplings and followed the bobbing flashlights of those walking ahead. She could hear the soft lapping of the waves, smell the nip of salt in the air. When they stepped from the woods and the white sand opened wide before them, Lauren stopped. The ocean. She couldn't swim and was nervous near all bodies of water, but the ocean filled her with a deep and primal fear.

"Come," Deborah said, gently pushing her forward, a strange and knowing smile on her face. "There's nothing to be afraid of."

Including Lauren, there were twenty-one celebrants on the shore of White Horse Beach. They were members of two covens and a few "solitaries," witches who worked alone, Deborah explained. They had come together to pay homage to powers greater than they and to share in the wonder of the earth and her cycles. Logs and kindling had been piled halfway between the woods and the ocean. The witches were gathering around the unlit bonfire.

Deborah turned Lauren over to Cassandra, who, holding one of Lauren's hands in her own, placed the other into the plump grasp of a young woman in white lace. "Tamar," Cassandra whispered.

Tamar gave Lauren's hand an enthusiastic squeeze with her soft dimpled one. "Madeline's completely wild—and, as far as I'm concerned, the fact that Elysia's here tonight proves Madeline's point," Tamar said, as if Lauren had known her for years—and as if Lauren had a clue as to what she was talking about. "It's good that you're here."

Lauren forced a feeble smile in Tamar's direction and pulled her hand away from the strange woman.

"Between you, me, and the goddess, Elysia's got nerve," Tamar said, grabbing Lauren's hand again.

Lauren didn't know what to do or say, so she left her hand in Tamar's small one and kept her mouth shut.

When everyone had gathered to form a circle, Deborah stepped into the middle. Silently, she walked to the eastern edge of the circle and raised a small knife.

"It's a consecrated knife," Cassandra whispered. "An athama."

Lauren watched the gleaming blade. As it caught the reflected starlight, a wisp of memory skated across her mind. A dream perhaps, an elusive glimmer. But as Deborah traced a pentagram in the air with her knife, Lauren's memory trace disappeared.

Robin, the slender woman who had walked to the beach with Cassandra, pulled bamboo pins from her hair and it fell in a thick black cape to below her knees. As she twirled in a wild dance around the unlit bonfire, her hair lifted with her movements. Lauren was relieved when Robin stopped dancing and handed Deborah a small pot.

Deborah took the pot and flung what appeared to be droplets of water into the air. Her long skirt skimming the ground behind her, she walked to the south, west and north edges of the circle, sprinkling water to invoke the power of the four directions. When she returned to the east, she pressed the athama to her lips and then walked to the center. She grazed the top piece of wood on the unlit bonfire with the knife, then put it down in the sand.

"Tonight the veil that divides the worlds is thin," Deborah said, touching a lit candle to five spots within the pile of branches.

"The veil is thin," chorused the witches.

The bonfire roared to life, and Deborah dropped the candle into its center. "The circle is cast," she cried, raising her arms heavenward. "We are between the worlds."

"She's created a sacred space for us to work in," Cassandra whispered in Lauren's ear as Deborah rejoined the circle.

Tamar dropped Lauren's hand and walked to the center of the sacred space. Holding her arms above the fire, she called to the goddess Artemis.

Bram took her place and called to the goddess Nimue.

Robin raised a cup of saltwater and passed it around the circle. Everyone flung a few drops into the air. When the cup came to Lauren, she self-consciously threw water too.

Cassandra drew a series of pentagrams in the sand with a long stick, then she melted back into the circle.

There was chanting and some singing and a tiny woman, her skin a beautiful chocolate brown, began to play the flute. "Alva," Cassandra whispered, identifying the flute player. "She's a mute."

Lauren stood silent and stiff, one hand in Cassandra's, one held by Tamar.

At some unseen command, everyone sat down on the damp sand. Tamar told the story of the white stallion. This was followed by the tale of the seasons, of Demeter's bargain with Pluto to save her daughter, Persephone, from a lifetime in the dark underworld. Then someone began free-associating with the terms "woman" and "mother." All around Lauren, in waves of words, womanhood and motherhood were exalted. Earth. Birth. Fertility. Growth. Love. Crone. Care. Feed. Soft. Safety. Seasons. Cycles. Comfort. Sex. Breasts. Family. Affinity. Warmth. Kinship. Blood.

Lauren thought of how Drew had pummeled her stomach from within. Once he had kicked so hard she actually saw the impression of his little heel on her skin. Although she didn't say anything, she smiled and sat taller, her conviction growing that these people could have no connection with evil or black magic.

When the sounds ebbed and the circle was silent, Bram rose. Carrying a backpack, he walked to the bonfire and stood staring down into the flames. His eye ring glinted in the fire's light. "I need your help," he said simply. "I need the help that only you can give. You, who understand as no outsider can that the world doesn't have to be like this." He raised his head. "We have a different world vision. A vision of a world in which men and women are held responsible for their deeds. A world in which the guilty are punished."

Offers of help rippled through the circle. "His nephew was sexually molested, and the court let the man who did it go free," Cassandra whispered to Lauren. "The boy's seven years old."

"Oh," Lauren said, a shiver running through her body. She would kill anyone who hurt Drew.

"I want to bind him," Bram continued. "This man named Nigel Hawkes. I want to invoke the spirits to punish him as humans are powerless to do." He stared fiercely around the circle, his unblinking eyes boring into each person's in turn. Lauren shivered when his eyes met hers, glad she was not the object of this man's vengeance. "And I want Nigel to live forever with the knowledge of what he has done—the knowledge of who he truly is." Bram reached into his backpack and pulled out a long coil of rope. "Let us bind our hands as we hope to bind Nigel Hawkes."

Bram returned to the circle and started the chain. He looped the rope around his wrists, then raised his bound hands to Deborah. Lauren noticed he had a tattoo of a face that looked a bit like Cardinal Bellarmine cut into his forearm. "May he be punished in a manner fitting his crime," Bram said. Deborah took the hemp from him and bound her own wrists; passing it, she repeated Bram's wish.

As the rope went around the circle, Cassandra explained what was happening. "What you send returns three times over," she told Lauren. "She who casts the spell becomes one with she who receives it. So you can't wish for anything you wouldn't wish for yourself."

When the rope reached Lauren, she bound it tightly around her wrists. "May he be punished in a manner fitting his crime," she said, her voice loud and strong.

When the rope returned to Bram, he dropped the remaining coil to his lap. "May he be punished in a manner fitting his crime," he said, closing the circle. No one spoke or moved for a long moment, their silence made deeper by the soft, lapping waves.

Then Bram began to disentangle the rope from his hands. As the unraveling traveled around the circle, he pulled a series of objects from his backpack: a mirror, a mason jar, a lock of hair.

Fascinated, Lauren watched him. "What's he doing?" she whispered to Cassandra.

"I don't know," the older woman said. "The Craft—the Wiccan—encourages the creation of personal spells—he's doing something that's meaningful to him. But he must have stored up a large amount of energy to cast two powerful spells so close together."

Carefully, Bram placed the hair and the mirror inside the mason jar. He pressed the metal latch and locked the jar shut. Then he stood and walked to the bonfire, holding the jar above the flames. "This is the hair of Nigel Hawkes," he said. "So this is Nigel, caught in this jar with this mirror—with his own reflection. He's locked in forever, forever faced with himself. Forever seeing what he has done—and who he is."

Watching Bram and listening to his words, Lauren could not help but be moved. This man was trying to right a wrong in a way that made sense to him. He believed in the magic of his religion, in the power of his rituals and of his people—more than in the power of the state. And perhaps, given the circumstances, he was right.

Bram raised the jar over his head. "There is no escape for Nigel Hawkes."

A smattering of applause for Bram's clever spell came from the circle. "Nigel Hawkes is locked in forever," they began to chant. "There is no escape." The chant was repeated with greater and greater volume, and everyone swayed in rhythm to the words. To her amazement, Lauren found herself swaying too.

Deborah broke from the circle and walked slowly toward the bonfire. She raised her arms. Mesmerized, Lauren followed Deborah's movements and, as she looked heavenward, she suddenly saw another heaven; she was in another place. This moon stood out more starkly against a much darker sky, and the Milky Way was so clear and distinct that it formed a vaporous backdrop for the closer stars. Fascinated yet strangely unafraid, Lauren looked down. Rather than the running shoes she had put on that morning, her feet were covered by roughly crafted leather boots, and the hem of her long coat was ragged and muddy.

Lauren raised her eyes. The woman who stood at the bonfire, her arms lifted to receive the power of the stars and the moon, wasn't Deborah. And yet, in some way, she still was Deborah, even though she was suddenly old and tiny and frail. After a long moment, the old woman lowered her arms and turned toward the water. The ocean was dark and compelling, its waves pulled by the force of the new moon. It beckoned with its beauty and its promises, and Lauren felt its force within her. Her usual fear of water gone, she was pulled by an irresistible desire to walk into the waves, to become one with their power.

Lauren broke from the circle and started toward the ocean. But as soon as she took a step, the old woman transformed into a much younger one, her dark curls wild and free. "Bury it," the dark-haired woman said. "Bury the jar far from the child."

Bury what jar? Lauren wondered, blinking at this new reality. Far from what child? Disoriented, she stood motionless as waves of words rose around her, words she knew were English but made no sense. Then bodies slid by her, parting like a school of fish as they swept past, rushing toward the woman and a man in a brown and blue serape. Arms whirled before her. Soon, so many arms were entwined with each other that it was hard to tell where one person stopped and another started.

Then the group began to disentangle and separate people emerged: The man in the serape reverently placed a glass jar in his backpack; the woman with the dark curls picked up a knife from the sand; a tiny woman started to play a flute. Stumbling backward, Lauren reached a rock near the edge of the woods and sat down. Soon the whole group was dancing around the bonfire, singing and laughing and throwing their arms in the air. She sat alone, suddenly chilled, struggling to comprehend what had just happened.

Taking a series of deep breaths, Lauren watched the dancers and the flames being whipped high by the ocean wind. As she came back to herself, she saw the scene before her from a fresh perspective. Despite eye rings and binding spells and consecrated athamas, were these witches any more irrational than the people at Jackie's funeral taking communion, symbolically tasting the blood and body of Christ? Was their dance any more absurd than that of her own great-grandfather and his minyan: ten Jewish men wearing embroidered shawls, bobbing rhythmically before a hand-lettered scroll? Was their esbat bonfire all that different from midnight mass or the Passover seder or the feasts of Ramadan?

And yet, if these witches were no different from Jews and Christians and Muslims, then what had just happened to her? They believed in their magic and, Lauren had to admit, in the throes of Bram's spell, she too had believed. It had seemed so sane, so logical. Staring into the flames, chin resting in her hands, Lauren watched the dancers' earthy grace and clearly saw their connection to each other—and to their spiritual beliefs. For a moment, feeling the mesmerizing power of the bonfire and the lilting notes of Alva's flute, she could almost believe that their ritual *had* caused her to go into some kind of trance. That the witches had put her in touch with some other reality.

Suddenly, the wind picked up and brought with it the whooshing sound of movement. Lauren whirled around but saw nothing. Returning her gaze to the spiraling dancers, she couldn't help thinking that maybe Carl Jung wasn't so far off after all. Maybe there *was* a collective unconscious—and maybe she had just tapped into it.

Muffled sounds rolled in from behind her. Something or someone was coming. Lauren turned again. This time she heard the pounding of footsteps, the barking of dogs. Startled, she jumped up. Lights were bobbing down the path through the trees. "Hey!" she yelled as half a dozen policemen raced onto the beach.

"You folks got a permit for this fire?" demanded the first cop to reach the group, a smirk of derision on his face. He waved Lauren over to the bonfire. She obeyed immediately.

The dancers stopped abruptly. Dazed, they all turned to confront the policeman; no one answered his question.

"Well then," he said, crossing his arms over his chest in obvious satisfaction, "you're all under arrest."

Fifteen

LAUREN STARED THROUGH THE FOUR-INCH-SQUARE window. If she twisted her neck just the right way, she could see a small slice of the sergeant's desk through the matching window of a door that stood at a ninety-degree angle to the door of her cell. The cell in which she was locked. In jail. She took a long breath, forcing air deep into her lungs, but when she released it, she felt as if she hadn't breathed at all.

Looking around her, Lauren noted that the Moorscott jail didn't look anything like jails on television. Her cell had no bars, no seatless toilets, no bug-infested mattresses hung from the wall by rusted chains. It was a narrow cinderblock room, ugly and cold but clean. On the way over, the talkative young cop had explained that the jail had only two cells: one large and one small. Lauren assumed that, because only five of them were in here, she was in the small one and all the others were in the larger. Taking another ragged breath, Lauren ran her hand along the edge of the door, along the metal plate that was screwed in where the handle would normally be. It was smooth. There was nowhere to grip. There was no way to get out. She pressed her nose to the glass.

Through her strip of window, Lauren watched a blue sleeve moving back and forth across a scarred wooden desk. She was overwhelmed by the intensity of her claustrophobia and surprised by her hunger to follow the motions of someone who was free. Rebeka Hibbens would understand. An image of the squalor and misery of a seventeenth-century dungeon flashed through Lauren's mind: snake-infested water leeching up through the mud floor, bugs, shackles, frigid cold. What must it have felt like being confined in a place like that for a crime she hadn't committed? A humorless laugh caught in Lauren's throat, the irony of the situation not lost on her.

She knew it was all a mistake. She knew that Gabe would arrive and arrange for her release soon. She knew that when she told this tale in years to come, she would pause to build up the suspense of the approaching flashlights, lean forward when she told of their capture at gunpoint, chuckle as she described the "criminals" entering the police station. Nevertheless, her stomach churned.

She looked at her watch. Gabe should have been here by now. He had promised to leave right away. Gabe. Even as she yearned for him to come and free her, Lauren was uncertain. She didn't really know him well, and there was a good chance he'd be annoyed at her presumptuousness. Who wouldn't be annoyed to be asked to drive twenty miles in the middle of the night to make bail for someone he hardly knew?

But she hadn't been able to think of anyone else to call. All of her friends had young children or had been in bed for hours. Todd was taking care of Drew, and Aunt Beatrice would faint dead away if she ever saw Lauren behind bars. If Jackie had been alive, Lauren would have called her, but as it was there had been no one else but Gabe.

Gabe Phipps, the well-known night owl and liberal. Gabe Phipps, who had kissed her just last night and with whom she was having dinner on Saturday. Lauren took another deep breath and pressed her palms together. He hadn't sounded annoyed on the phone.

The snide policeman's sleeve reached into Lauren's vision to pick up the phone; it disappeared and then reappeared to put the receiver back down. His hand jotted a quick line in a loose-leaf notebook, then picked up the telephone again. She knew it was the snide cop because she recognized his ruby ring. She remembered how it had hurt when he grabbed her and pushed her into the Jeep. She rubbed her forearm; the band of skin he had gripped would be black-and-blue tomorrow.

What was taking Gabe so long?

"Can I look for a while?" Robin stood at Lauren's shoulder, her hair once again pinned up with the bamboo clips. While they were in the Jeep, Robin had told Lauren she was a transportation planner. She worked for a consulting firm and traveled around the country designing transportation systems for the disabled.

Lauren moved reluctantly away from the window. "Not much to see."

Robin shrugged and stationed herself exactly where Lauren had been standing. She pressed her nose to the glass, saying nothing as she watched the blue sleeve.

Lauren almost tripped over Alva, who was sitting on the floor, cradling her flute like a baby and staring off into space with the glazed look of one who is listening to her own inner music. Lauren edged toward the cot at the opposite end of the cell; the cot was exactly the width of the cell and was the only piece of furniture in it. Tamar was huddled on one end, crying; Deborah was sitting next to her, an arm around her shoulders. Now that Lauren got a closer look at Tamar, she could see that the girl was even younger than she had guessed. Deborah nodded for Lauren to sit down with them, but she shook her head and leaned against the wall. She rubbed her damp palms against her jeans, not wanting to eavesdrop but unable to do anything else.

"My mother'll kill me," Tamar was wailing.

"We'll see if we can keep her from finding out," Deborah said.

"No way." Tamar shook her head vigorously. "This will be all over the papers."

Robin turned from the door. "Tamar's right, you know. I can see the headlines now: 'Witches Arrested During Weird Moon Ritual.' " She snorted and turned back to the window. "I'm surprised the reporters aren't here already."

"Maybe your mother won't see it," Deborah suggested, glancing up at Lauren to see if she was listening. When Deborah saw that Lauren was, she smiled, including her in their conversation.

"She reads the *Globe* every day." Tamar began to cry harder. "I told her this was a sorority."

Deborah shook her head. "Such unnecessary prejudice and ignorance."

"Some things haven't improved much in three hundred years," Lauren surprised herself by saying.

Deborah raised her eyebrows and smiled slyly at her. "Far less than one might think changes over time. People stay remarkably the same."

Lauren played with the collar of her shirt, wondering if everyone at the ritual knew Deborah and Cassandra believed themselves to be the reincarnation of seventeenth-century witches. "It's all too true," Lauren said, purposely choosing to misunderstand Deborah. "Human beings seem to have a tremendous capacity to hate anyone who's a little bit different from themselves."

"Karma returns three times over," Deborah told Lauren. "The ones who persecute suffer much more than the ones who are persecuted."

Lauren sighed. "I wish I believed that."

Deborah gave Tamar's shoulders a squeeze and then looked up at Lauren. "If you're interested in learning more about what we believe—and more about us—I'd be happy to spend some time talking with you."

"You would?" Lauren couldn't keep the surprise from her voice. Deborah had never been so warm and forthcoming. "I mean," she corrected herself quickly, "I mean, that would be great. Terrific. Name the time."

"We don't open the store on Sunday 'til noon," Deborah said. "If you want to come by, say about nine, that would give us plenty of time."

"Don't get near those witches." Dan's warning reverberated through Lauren's head, but she chose to ignore it. If Deborah had had second thoughts about helping with the book, perhaps she would also change her mind about the chronicle. "I have to drop Drew off at Sunday school in Porter Square a little before nine," she said. "I can be there by nine-fifteen."

"It's all set then." Deborah nodded at Lauren, then turned and offered Tamar a tissue.

Robin, her face still pressed to the window, said, "I'm afraid this is going to cost me my job." She twisted around and threw a glance at Lauren as if she, like Deborah, wanted to make sure Lauren felt included in their discussion.

Mothers and jobs, Lauren thought. It was all so incredibly ordinary. These women were just normal people with the same mundane concerns as everyone else. And what had happened to her out on the beach hadn't been magic; she had merely been moved by

Bram's ritual. The power of the ritual must have created her dreamlike illusion. The more she thought about it, the less vivid and clear the experience became. Actually, nothing that strange had happened at all.

"Would they really fire you for something like this?" Lauren asked Robin.

"They might." Robin shrugged and turned back to the window. "Most of the work we do comes directly or indirectly from the feds. And they can be—Hey," she interrupted herself, "there's some guy here who seems to be stirring things up."

Lauren jumped from the cot. "What does he look like?"

"Hard to tell," Robin said. "Good-looking. Older. Seems important."

"Let me see." Lauren was at the window in a few long strides. As Robin turned away, Lauren glimpsed a suede elbow patch on a tweed jacket, followed by the emphatic wave of a hand. "Thank God," she said, relief overcoming her apprehension about confronting Gabe. She didn't care if he was annoyed with her; she was going to be free.

Twenty minutes later, Lauren climbed into Gabe's car. Leaning back against the soft leather seat, she stared up through the sunroof at the clear sky above. The sliver of crescent moon returned her stare; a Cheshire cat grin shining down on the earth. Could only one day have passed since she and Gabe had sat drinking wine in her living room? Could it be only hours since she had turned onto the narrow dirt road leading to White Horse Beach? It didn't seem possible.

"They had no right to treat you like that." Gabe slid under the steering wheel and crossed his arms. Glaring out at the small parking lot, he said, "I'm going to call my lawyer first thing in the morning. We'll file charges. Wrongful arrest. Assault and battery. Police brutality."

"It's really nice of you to come all the way down here at this hour," Lauren said. "And I'm really sorry that I had—"

Gabe waved her words away. "My lawyer's top-notch—Allysa St. Gelais at Hubbard and Hobbs. You've heard of her?" Gabe seemed disappointed when Lauren shook her head. "She'll make sure these small-town hackers get what they deserve."

"I don't know, Gabe," she said. "Maybe we shouldn't make a fuss. No one was hurt."

He turned to her and their eyes met. "Pushing you into the back of a paddy wagon?" he demanded. "Throwing you in a cell like a common criminal? That's plenty hurt in my book."

"It wasn't a paddy wagon," she said with a smile. "It was a Jeep." The closeness of Gabe's body and the seclusion of the sensuous sports car brought back the previous night: his incredible smile, the hair curling over his collar, their kiss. The inside of her bones felt hollow, and it was suddenly very warm.

Gabe's eyes didn't leave hers. "Whatever," he said, reaching over and touching her cheek lightly.

"Thanks for putting up everyone's bail." Lauren turned away and hooked her seat belt, purposely breaking the mood. She had had enough emotion for one day; there would be time for Gabe on Saturday night. "I'll pay you back Saturday."

"No need," Gabe said, slipping the key in the ignition and starting the car. "It's an issue of civil liberties." When she persisted, he held up his hands. "The sergeant told me everyone'll be processed by one o'clock at the latest. Then they'll all be free to go."

Lauren watched Gabe slip the car into reverse and then into first. He had such nice hands, the fingers long and tapered but strong looking. Powerful. "Do you think you'll be able to keep Robin and Tamar's names out of the paper?" she asked, picking lint off her black jeans.

"I've got a good friend who's one of the most powerful reporters at the *Globe*." Gabe pulled to the end of the driveway. They were facing the center of Moorscott, a rustic New England town with squat brick buildings, soaring church spires, a diamond-shaped town green, and, of course, a McDonald's. "I can keep your name out of the paper too, if you want," he continued, resting his arms on top of the steering wheel. "But if Nat finds out I helped you avoid this publicity opportunity, he'll probably kill me." He raised his eyebrows. "Which way?"

Lauren pointed to the right. "Is Lynn that way?"

Gabe shook his head and laughed; he turned to the left. Once they passed out of town, he glanced at her from the corner of his eye. "So, you apparently took my advice and followed up on some of Jackie's leads," he said. "Want to tell me how you managed all this so quickly?"

A tremendous surge of relief poured over Lauren, relief at being out of jail, relief that Gabe wasn't angry, relief that she had someone with whom she could share her strange tale. She laughed for what felt like the first time in a long while. Then she sobered and began to tell him what had transpired since he'd left her apartment the previous evening.

"So," Lauren said in conclusion, leaning back against the seat and allowing a sweet exhaustion to seep in where all her tension had been, "then Deborah invited me to their Wiccan moon ritual."

Gabe's jaw tightened and he looked over at her. "I thought we'd decided you were going to stay away from those women."

Lauren sat up, surprised by both his intensity and the possessiveness of his words. She wasn't at all sure she liked either. "I was wrong," she said. "This was just a bunch of people doing their own thing."

"What does that mean?" he demanded.

She stared out the window at the empty road and the almost leafless trees, lit up for a moment by the car's headlights then sucked back into darkness once they had passed by. She didn't know how to begin to answer Gabe's question.

"Didn't they tell you to stay away from them?" The incredulity on Gabe's face was heightened by the eerie red glow of the dashboard lights. "What about their cursed chronicle?"

"Something must have happened to make them change their minds," Lauren said, pointing to the sign for Shore Drive, amazed that he had found it the first time around. "I'm meeting Deborah at the store first thing Sunday morning."

Gabe twisted the wheel hard. "Deborah's going to help you with the book?"

"Slow down," Lauren said, watching for the dirt road and wondering if maybe Gabe *was* angry at having to come get her in the middle of the night. "One of them was a transportation planner," she added in an attempt to steer the discussion away from Deborah.

He frowned. "One of your witches?"

She shook her head. "They're not real witches—not in Nat's sense of the word. There's no black magic, no supernatural powers. They're just ordinary people. They worship goddesses, that's all." She shrugged. "They're just—" she resumed, trying to make him understand, then interrupted herself. "There," she said, pointing to the space between the twin birches. "There's the road."

"I think you're making a big mistake," Gabe grumbled as he took the turn. They jostled down the rutted road in silence. When they reached the circle of cars, he parked and turned off the ignition. "There's something I've got to tell you," he said slowly.

Here it comes, Lauren thought, folding her hands

in her lap. She had pushed Gabe too far, and he was withdrawing his support. She was surprised at how deeply disappointed she was, both at losing his help with *Rebeka Hibbens* and losing the fantasy of falling in love with him.

"I, ah, I don't know quite how to say this. . . ." He hesitated and looked down at his hands.

Lauren was amazed; she had never seen Gabe at a loss for words before. "It's okay," she began. "I knew how you felt—"

"If there's one thing my marriage taught me, it's that secrets will destroy a relationship faster than anything else," he interrupted, raising his eyes and spitting out the words as if he had finally found his courage. "There's more behind my warning you away from Deborah than I let on."

"What do you mean?" Lauren asked, completely mystified.

"I know for a fact that the woman's certifiable." He sighed the sigh of the damned. "I know this because I once had to have her committed—to a locked ward at McLean."

"*You* had Deborah Sewall committed to a mental institution?" Lauren was even more confused than before. "The woman from RavenWing?"

"I should have told you about this earlier, but the time just never seemed right." Gabe reached over and took Lauren's hands in his. "Prepare yourself for a shock: Deborah Sewall is my ex-wife."

"That's impossible!" Lauren gasped. "You two are just, just . . ." She stared at him. "I can't believe it."

"I often have trouble with the concept myself." Gabe shrugged and gave her a self-deprecating smile. "It was a long, long time ago. We were very young. She was very different—although I'm sure she'd say I was plenty different too."

"And she was so crazy that you had to have her committed?" Lauren asked, still having trouble making sense of Gabe's disclosure. "But she seems so normal—in a bizarre way," she corrected herself.

"All part of the disease—or at least that's how it was explained to me." Gabe leaned over and kissed the end of Lauren's nose. "Look, it's late and it's been a tough day all around. How about we save this discussion for Saturday night? I promise you more details on the strange Ms. Sewall than you ever wanted to hear."

"But—"

Gabe shook his head to cut off her question. "Is seven o'clock okay?" he asked. When Lauren nodded, he climbed out of the car and came over to her side. With a gesture of exaggerated gallantry, he opened her door.

"You sure are full of surprises, Dr. Phipps," she said as he wrapped her in his arms.

"And I hope to remain that way," Gabe said, still smiling. Just when Lauren thought he was going to kiss her, he released her and motioned for her to get into her car. He waited until she had started her engine, then climbed into his own car, threw it into reverse, and headed back down the dark road.

Lauren followed, the events of the evening weighing heavily on her mind. But rather than attempt to comprehend the incomprehensible, she concentrated on keeping Gabe's taillights in sight. She was very much relieved when he led her safely back to Cambridge.

Sixteen

"YOU DID WHAT?" DAN LING DEMANDED, HIS DARK eyes wide with disbelief.

"My editor made it clear he'd accept nothing less than the chronicle," Lauren answered. "So when Deborah called and invited me to the ritual . . ."

It was four o'clock the next afternoon. Lauren and Dan were sitting on a wooden bench at the Braybrook playground watching Drew and his friend Scott swoop down a spiral slide and then chase each other across a swinging walkway that connected a turreted room with a long tunnel.

Braybrook was one of the famous Leathers's fantasy playgrounds. It had been designed by Robert Leathers with input from the neighborhood children and then built by their parents in a weekend marathon reminiscent of Colonial barn raisings. Todd had been a member of the organizing committee. The *Boston Globe* had run a photograph of Todd standing atop one of the turrets, an electric screwdriver in his hand. Drew had tacked the picture to the bulletin board in his bedroom.

Dan was wearing jeans and a sweatshirt and looked incredibly young, despite the stern expression on his face. "Don't you see what's going on here? I'm pretty sure Jackie was killed because she was mixed up with these witches—and now you've gone and marched right over to them."

Lauren watched Drew and Scott scamper across the sand. "You've got to understand that I'm caught in a no-win situation," she said. "I've got to write this book—I need the money. Badly."

"At the risk of your life?"

"Hey, Mom," Drew called, hanging from the monkey bars by one hand. "Look at me!"

"Great," Lauren shouted, smiling at Drew. "Good job." Her smile disappeared as she turned to Dan. "Gabe Phipps might be able to help me." She told Dan about Gabe's offer to help her write the book without Deborah and Cassandra.

"The few times I met Phipps, he struck me as street smart as well as book smart," Dan said. "And it was damn nice of him to go all the way up to Moorscott to bail you out last night. My advice is to do the book his way."

Lauren noticed Drew leaning precariously far out of an opening at the top of the play structure. "Drew!" she called to him. "I've told you before not to do that—get back inside or you'll have to take a time-out." Drew immediately disappeared from view. "If Gabe's way works," she said to Dan.

"Based on how successful Phipps is getting, I'd say doing it his way is a pretty safe bet."

"I'm having dinner with him Saturday night," Lauren said, as much to change the subject as to assess Dan's reaction to herself and Gabe as a couple.

Dan raised his eyebrows. "I didn't know you were dating."

"Drew!" Lauren yelled, jumping up from the bench and walking over to where he was pulling the same leaning-out-of-the-opening stunt. "Get down here right now."

Drew disappeared inside the structure and reappeared a few seconds later in front of Lauren. "Sorry," he said, looking at the ground and digging his toe in the sand. "I forgot."

Lauren pointed to a tree a few yards from the play structure. "Five minutes," she said. "One more trick like that and we're going home."

Drew kicked the sand a couple of times, then turned and did as his mother had ordered. Scott jumped from the monkey bars and ran over to where Drew was sitting. "Can I just stand here with Drew, Mrs. Freeman?" Scott asked. "I promise I won't talk."

"Okay," Lauren said to Scott, then held up her hand and spread her fingers at Drew, indicating five minutes. He nodded glumly, and she walked back to Dan.

Lauren sat back down on the bench. "So, if your lieutenant won't help us, how can we figure out if Jackie really was murdered?"

"Zaleski—he's the cult expert on the force I was telling you about—is checking out the RavenWing women for me, and the autopsy report is on the way." Dan pulled his legs up on the bench and rested his chin between his knees. "There's more we can do too."

"Like what?" Lauren asked, casting a watchful eye on Drew and Scott. They weren't talking to each other, as promised, but they were both digging in the dirt in a way that made her suspicious.

"Like talking to Jackie's neighbors to find out if anyone else saw your shadow in the backyard. Like figuring out who else might have had a motive: Jackie's other occult contacts, colleagues, friends, family members . . ."

Lauren watched Drew and Scott carefully; now they seemed to be putting something into their pockets. "I can tell you right now that the colleagues, friends, and family route is going to turn up empty. You know as well as I do how much everyone liked Jackie." As she was speaking, Lauren suddenly remembered Simon Pappas on the day of Jackie's funeral, pressing his fingers into her arm and whispering with icy fury: *"I won't have Jackie's memory or Matthew's future besmirched by a bunch of lesbians spouting witchcraft. . . ."*

Drew and Scott approached cautiously, and Lauren nodded her permission for Drew to resume playing. Giggling, the boys ran to the play structure.

"You're probably right," Dan said, "but I still think it's worth a try. I'll start talking to neighbors, and if you could go through the notes you got from Jackie's house and compile a list of all the people she talked to about the book, I'll tackle them next."

"Couldn't you get into trouble with your lieutenant for this?" Lauren asked.

Dan grinned. "That's the least of our worries. The other thing I'd like you to do is check out that poppet and urn. Is there anyone beside the RavenWing women who might know anything about them?"

Lauren thought for a moment. "Not that I can think—"

She was interrupted by a high-pitched scream, followed by the sickening thud of a body hitting the ground. Terrified, she whirled toward the sounds.

A young couple who had been sitting on a bench holding hands jumped to their feet. "Amanda!" they screamed in unison as they ran toward the still form of a little girl crumpled on the sand. White faced, Drew and Scott scurried down a ladder and stood off to one side.

Dan was right behind the parents. "I'm a police officer," he said as he knelt by the girl, reaching for her wrist.

Lauren followed more slowly and went to stand

next to Drew. She put an arm around his shoulder; he leaned slightly into her hip. Lauren was relieved to hear Amanda crying, but she could see that the girl's arm was bent at an unnatural angle. Dan asked if anyone had a phone. A woman standing behind Lauren pulled a flip phone from her purse and dialed 911.

"It's just a precaution," Dan told Amanda's distraught parents. "She's conscious, and that's a good sign, but she might have suffered a concussion. It's always best to have a doctor take a look after a fall."

Amanda began to cry louder. "He threw worms at me," she said, pointing at Drew. "And then he pushed me!"

Horrified, Lauren dropped her arm and stared at her son. "Did you push her?" she demanded.

"He's at my school," Amanda sobbed to her mother. "He's always mean to me."

"Did you?' Lauren asked again. Everyone was staring at them in stony silence. Amanda's parents were glaring at Drew, and even Dan's expression was cold.

Drew crossed his arms and looked Lauren in the eye. "I might've thrown a couple of worms at her," he said, "but I never pushed her—I wouldn't push a *girl*." He said "girl" with such disdain that Lauren was inclined to believe him.

"Well, we'll see about that, young man," she said, grabbing his shoulder and turning him toward the crowd. "Right now you march right over there and apologize to Amanda." Lauren could see that Drew was mortified by this request, but she also knew he would comply. She followed him to where Amanda was now sitting up, resting against her father.

"I'm sorry," Drew mumbled to the ground.

"We're both very sorry," Lauren said, looking first at Amanda and then at her parents. "I'll find out exactly what went on here, and I promise you Drew will be punished accordingly. Do you want us to give you a ride to the hospital?" she offered, forgetting she had just watched a woman call for an ambulance. "Is there anything I can do to help?"

As the sound of approaching sirens filled the air, Amanda's mother looked up at Lauren. Her face was pale and streaked with tears. "You can make sure your son stays away from my daughter," she snapped. "And you can get out of my sight."

Lauren decided to wait twenty-four hours before talking with Drew, figuring if she was going to get the truth out of him, he needed time to calm down. She called Amanda's house first thing the next morning to apologize again and find out how the little girl was doing. Amanda's mother was just as caustic as she had been at the playground, but she did tell Lauren that, although Amanda didn't have a concussion, her arm was fractured in two places.

Lauren felt terrible. The only bright spot was when Scott's mother called to tell her that Scott claimed Drew's story was true. He and Drew *had* been throwing worms, but Drew had never touched Amanda. Lauren recognized that this was not much of a bright spot.

When Drew came home from school, he was quieter than usual. He went straight to the kitchen to fix himself a Pop-Tart. Lauren poured him the glass of milk he had conveniently forgotten and sat down across from him.

"How was school today?" she asked.

"Okay, I guess." His usual answer.

"You know Daddy and I went to see Dr. Berg at your school the other day," she began.

"I didn't push Amanda."

"I didn't say that you did," Lauren said soothingly. "But both Mrs. Baker and Dr. Berg think maybe you're feeling angry a lot in school. Is that true?"

"She wasn't in school today." Drew twirled the remains of his Pop-Tart on the table. "Someone said she was hurt really bad," he added, his voice wavering. When he finally looked up at Lauren, his eyes were filled with tears. "I didn't push her, Mommy, I swear I didn't." Then he started crying and ran over to Lauren.

She opened her arms and pulled him into her lap. "I know you didn't, Mister Boy," she said, rubbing his back and kissing the top of his head. "I know you didn't."

"But, but I did throw the worms," he stuttered. "And, and that's prob'ly why she fell—so it really *is* my fault. The same as if I did push her." He began to cry even harder. "Is she going to d-die?"

"Oh no, honey," Lauren said, taking his face in her hands and looking into his eyes. "She broke her arm, that's all. It's bad and I'm sure it hurts her a lot, but she's not going to die." She pressed Drew to her. "She's not going to die."

"Will I have to go to jail?" he asked in a small voice.

Lauren held Drew even tighter, her heart aching with empathy for his guilt and fear; being a parent was so much harder and more complex than she had ever imagined. "You did a bad thing, honey, but it was a little-boy bad thing, not a grownup bad thing. Little boys don't go to jail for throwing worms."

After he calmed down and finished his snack, Lauren sat Drew next to her on the living room couch. She took a deep breath, hoping she was handling the situation correctly. "You know how you feel bad when I yell at you?" she asked, pressing one of his hands between her own. "Or if some kid says something mean to you at school?"

Drew nodded uncertainly and withdrew his hand.

"Well, everyone has feelings the same way that you do, and part of being a big kid—part of being a good grownup too—is thinking about how what you do and say is going to make other people feel."

"Like not throwing worms 'cause it'll make somebody scared?"

"Just like that." Lauren smiled at Drew and rubbed his cheek with her knuckle. "Can you think of any others?"

Drew bit his lip and looked up at her questioningly. "Like when I tell you I hate you just 'cause you won't let me go over to Scott's?"

"It does make me feel very sad when you tell me you hate me, so that's a good example."

"I don't hate you, Mommy," Drew said, his eyes beginning to well with tears again. "I'm sorry. I'll try not to say it anymore."

"I know you don't hate me, honey—and it would make me feel very happy if you didn't say that anymore." Lauren's heart filled with such love for her sad little boy that she didn't know how she could contain it within her body. She blinked back her own tears and tried to speak around the lump in her throat. "But just as important as being careful of what you say is being careful of what you do. Both to other people and to things that belong to them."

Drew was silent for a minute and then he reached down and took one of his action figures from the coffee table. Turning the figure's silver and black head until it was facing backward, he said, "I told Kisha I was sorry I ripped her picture."

"It's good you apologized." Lauren gently took the figure from his hand. "But it's more important that you don't do it again. It's wrong to hurt other people—and it's wrong to hurt their things. When you destroy something that belongs to someone else, it's the same as stealing from them."

"I didn't steal anything," Drew protested, his face filling with anger. "I wouldn't—

"I know you didn't steal anything," Lauren said quickly, seeing she had taken a wrong turn. "I'm just trying to show you how bad it felt to Kisha."

"It was just some crummy picture."

Lauren knew she had lost him. Her only hope was that he had been sufficiently scared by the thought of inadvertently killing Amanda that he would take more care with other people's feelings. "You know I'm going to have to punish you for ripping the picture and throwing the worms, don't you?"

Drew stared straight ahead.

"What do you think would be an appropriate punishment?"

He shrugged, still avoiding her eyes.

"One week without television," she said, standing up to emphasize the firmness of her decision. Expecting violent protest, she turned and looked at him. One week without television was the most severe punishment he had ever received.

But Drew didn't say anything, he just looked at her and nodded.

"Good," Lauren said. "Then we understand each other." She grabbed The *Boston Globe* from the coffee table and went into her bedroom to give him some time alone.

Lauren threw herself down on the bed and stared at the ceiling, hoping she had said the right things, that Drew had understood, that she wasn't going to be the mother of a serial murderer. Before she could slip too deeply into neurotic fretting, she pushed herself up against the wall and began to flip through the newspaper.

An article about the Cambridge school system caught her eye and she pulled out the Metro/Region section. As she heard Drew stomping into his bedroom, Lauren noticed another article: "Somerville Man Jumps To Death." She skimmed the first paragraph and let out a gasp. The newspaper fell from her trembling fingers.

> The body of a forty-three-year-old man was recovered from beneath the Tobin Bridge early

last evening by the Boston police diving squad. He was identified as Nigel Hawkes, an unemployed carpenter, residing at 732 Broadway. . . .

Seventeen

LAUREN HAD BEEN LOOKING FORWARD TO THIS EVENING with both curiosity and trepidation, as well as more than a bit of hormonal agitation. But now that she was sitting next to Gabe, watching him taste his wine and nod his acceptance to the waiter, curiosity was rapidly overwhelming her other emotions. She could barely keep from demanding that Gabe tell her the story of Deborah's stay in one of the premier mental institutions in the country.

Despite Nigel Hawkes's suicide and Dan's suspicions, Lauren had decided she was going to meet with Deborah tomorrow, and she wanted to be armed with as much information as possible. Over the last couple of days, she had been forced to the unpleasant conclusion that she didn't have the luxury for either superstition or fear. She had to write *Rebeka Hibbens*. She needed the advance money to finish the book, and she needed to finish the book to get her degree and find a job. Being a single parent reduced life to simple equations.

Gabe smiled as the waiter finished filling their

wineglasses. After leaving the bottle to chill in the ice bucket next to their table, the man backed off with the promise to return soon with their appetizers. They were seated in a back corner of the elegant French restaurant Villemomble, a quiet place tucked into a side street on Beacon Hill. Lauren had never been here before, but she had heard of it. Aunt Beatrice, a gourmand who had a floor-to-ceiling bookcase in her kitchen just to hold her cookbooks, had instructed Lauren to order the house specialty, veal Languedoc, a veal and grape dish she claimed was "beyond superb."

Gabe lifted his glass. "To *Rebeka Hibbens,*" he said.

Lauren touched her glass to his and wondered whether he was aware of the multiple meaning of his toast: to her book and to the real Rebeka Hibbens—and, if one were to take Deborah seriously, to his ex-wife as well.

"May it be completed on time," she said, trying to think of a way to tactfully introduce Deborah into the conversation. Lauren took a sip of her wine—white this time—and looked at Gabe. When their eyes met, she felt a warmth spreading outward from between her legs that made her forget all about Deborah. She coughed and took another sip of wine. It had been a long time since she had been on a date.

Noting the appealing crookedness of Gabe's smile and the elegant fit of his jacket, Lauren couldn't help comparing him to Todd. This evening was a perfect example of how different the two men were. Gabe had shown up on time and made reservations at this extraordinary restaurant. And Lauren was somehow convinced that when they returned to his car after dinner, there would be no boot immobilizing it because of unpaid parking tickets—as had happened the last time Todd took her out for what was supposed to be a reconciliation dinner.

Lauren put her glass down and turned it slowly on

the linen tablecloth. "So," she said, deciding she might as well just ask, "you promised me all the gory details about Deborah. . . ."

"Yes," Gabe said. "Let's get it over with so we can enjoy the rest of our evening." He cleared his throat and folded his hands. "I met Deborah when I was in graduate school—I had a teaching fellowship and she was one of my students." He gazed somewhere beyond Lauren's right shoulder; somewhere far beyond the wall of Villemomble, Lauren thought. "Deborah had an amazing talent for history," Gabe continued. "Although the last time I talked to her, she said something about history being 'patriarchal bullshit' conceived of, and perpetuated by 'old white guys.' "

Lauren smiled. "She told me something very similar."

"It's such a waste of talent," Gabe said, shaking his head. "Such a waste." He then went on to tell Lauren the story.

He and Deborah had been married in the early seventies and struggled through graduate school together—Deborah getting a master's degree in history and education, he continuing on for his doctorate. Deborah supported them by teaching history at a junior high school while he finished his degree and launched his career.

It was a classic tale of the struggling young couple, drinking chianti in a tiny apartment full of plywood and cinder block bookshelves. Then, about eight years into the marriage, just when Gabe was finally getting established and Deborah was talking about returning to school for her PhD, Deborah was in a plane crash.

"Do you remember reading about an airplane that ran off the runway at Logan?" Gabe asked. "The thing broke in half and the people in the front were pulled into the ocean?" When Lauren nodded, Gabe continued, "Well, Deborah was in the back of that plane and she never got over it. After the accident she was very depressed—couldn't do much of anything except sit around the house. So when she got involved with a woman's group advocating feminist causes—going to meetings, organizing rallies—I was hopeful she'd soon be her old self again.

"But it wasn't to be." Gabe sighed. "Deborah lost interest in the political aspects of feminism and she started spending time with a fringe group of religious fanatics—and let me tell you, those people were really weird. Somewhere along the line they convinced her that she was the reincarnation of Joan of Arc." He smiled wryly. "But that was a bit much even for Deborah to buy. It was she who decided she had been Rebeka Hibbens—Rebeka being, ironically, the topic of her master's thesis."

"And she used the reincarnation theory as an explanation for her interest in the subject in the first place," Lauren couldn't resist interjecting.

Gabe smiled, obviously pleased with Lauren's take on the situation. "I figured it was a stage she was going through and tried to ignore the whole thing. Then I happened to read what I thought was a paper she was writing about life in pre-revolutionary Massachusetts—and it scared the shit out of me."

"You don't mean the chronicle?"

"Deborah tried to tell me it was written by some woman in the nineteenth century, but I saw her working on it."

"A large leather book with parchment pages? Old-style handwriting?"

"That one came later," Gabe said. "I think she had it copied over to impress the weirdos she gathered around her after the divorce. When I read the chronicle, it was typed on our IBM Selectric typewriter."

"But why didn't you tell Jackie this when you knew Deborah was giving her the chronicle?"

Gabe looked into the depths of his wineglass and sighed. "Jackie was there when Deborah and I fell apart. She knew how distraught Deborah could make me. How crazed." He looked up at Lauren. "I figured Jackie would never believe me—that it would be a waste of my time to get into it with her."

Lauren nodded slowly. If what Gabe said was true, then the chronicle was completely bogus. On the other hand, Deborah might have had a reason for retyping a portion of the real chronicle. Lauren carefully looked at Gabe. There was no way to know if his version of events was accurate. It was possible he wasn't the most reliable narrator. In her experience, both as a participant and an outside observer, neither party involved in a divorce ever saw things as they really were.

"But it was what was on the pages that spooked me," Gabe was saying. "There were descriptions of weird rituals involving suicide and murder—and what appeared to be plans for more. All I could think was that there was going to be another mass suicide like the one at Jonestown—with Deborah as the next Jim Jones.

"So I took her to a psychiatrist a friend recommended, and Deborah readily admitted her beliefs. She told him she was the reincarnation of Rebeka Hibbens, that she was a powerful sorceress, and that her life's mission was to find the other members of her coven and perform the great Immortalis, thereby freeing them to achieve eternal life among the sages.

"As you might expect," Gabe continued, "Dr. Bluestone told me she was a very sick woman. That she was psychotic and paranoid. Preoccupied with suicide and delusions of grandeur. He said she needed to be hospitalized because she was a threat to herself and to others. Although I was concerned, I was amazed at the seriousness with which he took the situation; it wasn't as if Deborah were hallucinating or losing touch with reality. But Bluestone explained that her problem wasn't like schizophrenia, that it wasn't uncommon for people with Deborah's disorder to be 'highly functional.' Still, he was anxious to get her started on a regimen of antipsychotic drugs as soon as possible."

Lauren remembered back to the conversation she and Jackie had had about the seeming contradiction between Deborah's delusions and her ability to run a successful business. Dr. Bluestone's diagnosis explained the incongruities.

"Of course, she wouldn't agree to the hospitalization." Gabe lowered his eyes and twirled his wineglass. "We had to 'pink paper' her and—"

" 'Pink paper'?" Lauren interrupted.

"Commit her against her will." Gabe finished off his wine, and immediately a waiter appeared to refill his glass. When the waiter left, Gabe resumed his story. "They gave her a diagnosis of 'psychotic disorder NOS'—whatever that means—put her in a locked unit at McLean, and started dosing her with medication.

"At first she was completely wacked-out from the drugs, but even doped up, Deborah was too smart for them." He smiled sadly at the memory of his brilliant ex-wife, and Lauren had a fleeting flash of jealousy. "She told me later that she realized the only way out was to play along. So she 'cheeked her meds'—pretended to take her medication—and changed her story. Thrilled with their success, the doctors released her." He shook his head as if to shake off a bad dream. "As soon as she got home, she began hanging out with a band of misfits who bought into her madness."

"The coven," Lauren said.

"Cult is more like it," Gabe corrected. "They're a sorry lot—she even met one of them, the guy with the ring in his eyebrow, at McLean."

"Bram," Lauren said, relief flooding through her. Mental illness would explain why Bram believed himself to be a powerful sorcerer. But, she thought, her relief vanishing, it did nothing to explain Nigel Hawkes' suicide.

"Whoever." Gabe waved his hand dismissively. "They're just a bunch of life's losers who need someone to tell them they're special—and I guess Deborah does that. As long as she doesn't talk them into killing themselves, I try to convince myself that no harm's being done." He raised his glass in a mock toast.

"So that's why you were so adamant about steering me away from the chronicle."

"At first, I didn't feel right telling you Deborah's story—it's pretty personal stuff." He rested his arm on the back of Lauren's chair. "But now that things appear to be changing between us, I just couldn't let you believe that a manuscript I knew had been written in the twentieth century was a seventeenth-century primary source—especially when it was written by someone who's been diagnosed by some of the best doctors as delusional and psychotic."

Lauren felt the warmth of his hand against her shoulder. Although she agreed with and was touched by his remarks, there was a complacency to his argument that annoyed her. "But is it really that simple? Do the 'best doctors' always agree? Or always know the truth?" she asked, leaning forward. "A friend told me the other day that her doctor at Beth Israel—one of the best hospitals—recommended an herbal remedy from a health food store because it worked better than anything he could prescribe."

"A friend you met at the Moorscott jail?" Gabe asked, removing his arm from her chair.

Lauren glanced quickly at him, but she saw from the twinkle in his eye that he was teasing. "As a matter of fact," she said, crossing her arms over her chest, "a friend I ran into at Wiggins Library."

Gabe threw his head back and laughed. Lauren

joined him. Gabe possessed a laugh that demanded company, a laugh that pulled all those around him into his circle of charisma. A few of the other diners turned and smiled at them.

An elegantly dressed woman, her blue-tinted hair perfectly coiffed, rose and came over to their table. "Please excuse my interrupting your dinner, Dr. Phipps, but my grandson is a history major at Cornell. He's such a great fan, and his birthday is just next week. . . ." She held up a small notebook and pen, her face flushing slightly. "I was hoping you wouldn't mind—"

"Of course not," Gabe said, quickly taking the book to cut short the woman's embarrassment. "I'd be honored." When she left, he turned back to Lauren with a wide smile. "I'm not knocking herbal remedies," he said. "I've even been known to take a bit of seaweed and miso when I have a cold. I'm just saying that I don't see a place for the supernatural in serious scholarship."

"I agree with a lot of what you've said." Lauren paused and took a sip of wine. "But I'm still committed to talking with Deborah tomorrow."

Although she knew it wasn't what Gabe had intended, his story had actually made her feel better about Deborah and Bram. They weren't powerful sorcerers controlling the mysteries of black magic; they were just a litter of sick puppies. And it all jibed with the conclusion she had reached about Nigel Hawkes.

After the first shock of reading about his death in the *Globe,* Lauren had carefully reread the article, hoping Nigel Hawkes was a more common name than she had thought. She quickly realized that it was unlikely there were two Nigel Hawkeses in the Boston area who had been recently acquitted of sexually molesting a young boy. But when her eye caught a quote from Nigel's mother, her spirits lifted. "He was so happy after the trial was over," Mrs. Hawkes had told the reporter. "But then his boss got all bent out of shape and fired him for something he never done, and he got real depressed again."

Lauren was sure that depressed people without jobs had been known to commit suicide without the benefit of a witch's incantation.

Gabe was watching her closely, frowning and tapping the back of his fork on the table. "After everything I've just told you, how can you have any use for anything Deborah has to say?"

Before Lauren could answer, the waiter arrived with their appetizers. When she ordered the veal Languedoc, the waiter bowed and told her it was an excellent choice. After he left, Lauren turned to Gabe. "Do they ever tell you it was a lousy choice?"

Gabe smiled in response and put a couple of stuffed mushrooms on each of their plates. "So explain to me why you still want to see Deborah tomorrow."

Lauren speared a mushroom, but instead of eating it, she twirled the fork and watched the mushroom spin, wondering how much she should tell Gabe. "It's more than just academic curiosity—Dan Ling thinks somebody might have murdered Jackie." She popped the mushroom into her mouth.

Gabe looked alarmed, and Lauren thought he might be ill.

"Are you all right?" she asked, glad she had decided against telling him about Nigel Hawkes.

Gabe coughed and waved away her concern. He reached for his water glass, then drank. "Something went down the wrong way." He sipped again. "I thought Jackie fell off a step stool."

"Dan thinks there may be more to it than that."

"Meaning?" Gabe asked, his mouth set in a thin line.

Lauren put her fork down and met his gaze. "Meaning that maybe she was messing where she shouldn't have been messing."

"You think Deborah and her hapless band killed Jackie?"

"That doesn't make any sense. If Deborah wanted Jackie to stay away, why would she have given us the chronicle? Maybe it was one of the other witches Jackie was talking to. . . ." Lauren felt slightly foolish for having brought up the subject, but now that she had, she decided to push on. "Remember the poppets and the Bellarmine urn I was telling you about the other night?" When Gabe nodded, she told him about the shadow in Jackie's hedges and the click of the back door. "Dan's convinced Jackie was killed because she was getting close to something someone didn't want her to know. Something involved with witchcraft."

"Is this just Dan's theory, or do the police think something's up too?"

"He couldn't convince his lieutenant to open an investigation, so Dan's going to dig around on his own."

Gabe leaned back and cleared his throat. "That's one hell of a theory," he said. "And even more reason for you to stay away from RavenWing."

"But Deborah or Cassandra might know who's using poppets and Bellarmines," Lauren persisted. "And it does seem highly unlikely either of them had anything to do with Jackie's death. Actually, now that I think about it, Cassandra couldn't have—she was in Vermont taking a stained-glass course at the time."

"With the sorcerers you mentioned?" Gabe asked.

Lauren looked at him in surprise. "I don't know," she said, making a mental note to check them out for Dan. "I hadn't thought of that."

Gabe reached over and took her hand in both of his. "You don't really believe any of this, do you? A cursed chronicle and voodoo and shadows in the dark?"

"I don't know what to think," she said. With his

hands warming hers, she was having trouble thinking about anything except how soft his lips had been the other night, how comfortable she had felt in his arms. "Dan's convinced something's not right."

"You've got to remember Ling's a cop and trained to be suspicious of—"

"Well, well, well. Look who's here," a booming voice interrupted Gabe. "It's our own famous man." With a few long strides, Simon Pappas was at their table, grinning down at them. A petite woman who had to be half his age, wearing perfectly applied makeup and far too much jewelry, came to stand shyly behind him. Simon neither introduced her nor indicated he was aware of her presence. "Is this kosher?" he asked. "Professors fraternizing with students?"

"You mean like Jackie and me?" Lauren asked, although she pulled her hand from Gabe's. It was obvious Simon had had a few drinks.

Gabe squeezed her knee under the table. He stood and held out his hand. "How're you doing, old man?" he asked. "Good to see you."

Simon waved Gabe back into his seat. "Seriously," he said, "isn't this against university policy?" He leered at Lauren, his eyes dropping to her breasts.

"University policy against fraternization between students and faculty is intended to discourage abuses of power," Gabe said smoothly. "And since Lauren's completed her course work, and I'm not on her dissertation committee, I've got very little power over her."

Lauren smiled at Gabe and he gave her a wink she felt in the pit of her stomach. Thinking again how different he was from Todd, she wondered how much power he might actually have over her. In this situation, Todd would most likely be on his feet yelling, perhaps even swinging, at Simon. Gabe was composed and reasonable, besting Simon with logic and a cool head.

"How's the book coming?" Simon asked Lauren. "Did you get Jackie's name off it?"

"I met with Nat Abraham just the other day," she said, her voice sugarcoated. "The details of authorship are being worked out."

"It's funny I should run into you, Lauren," Simon said, apparently accepting her evasive answer. "I was planning to call you. My son-in-law Dan tells me you've been going through some of Jackie's things."

Confused, Lauren nodded.

"I'm looking for something—a valuable painting—that seems to be missing. It belonged to my mother."

"The Deodat Willard," Lauren said.

"The one she had in the kitchen?" Gabe asked. "With the witch and the corn?"

"It isn't a witch," Simon snapped, glaring at Gabe. He turned back to Lauren. "Do you know where it is?"

Unwilling to tell Simon the truth, Lauren slowly turned her wineglass on the tablecloth. She hated to lie—and wasn't particularly good at it—but she didn't know what else to do under the circumstances. "Last time I saw it," she said, raising her eyes for a moment, then lowering them, "it was hanging on Jackie's kitchen wall."

Simon narrowed his eyes at Lauren. "I hope you're telling the truth, young lady, because I was told that painting is now worth a lot of money."

Lauren looked up at him. "Didn't your mother give it to Jackie?"

"Yes," Simon said, crossing his arms over his chest, "but Jackie and I were still married then, and Mother had no idea what it was worth. That painting's been in my family for generations, and that's where it belongs now."

"I'm sure it'll show up," Gabe said, his tone indicating that the conversation was over.

"I just hope those twits at the antiquarian society haven't got it."

Lauren and Gabe exchanged a glance that Simon caught.

"And I hope the rumors of your troubles with NEH don't materialize," Simon told Gabe, a smirk on his face. "Because if you're counting on Jackie's records to help you, you're in deep trouble. She couldn't keep track of her household expenses, let alone a grant budget."

As Gabe's face paled, Simon's smile widened. He punched Gabe on the shoulder. "Have a nice night, famous man," Simon said and then headed toward the door. The young woman followed closely behind him, her gold bangle bracelets clanking loudly.

As she watched Simon leave, Lauren was reminded of Dan's search for motives among Jackie's family and friends. Although Simon was undoubtedly a jerk, she couldn't picture him as a murderer. She turned to Gabe. "What did he mean about the National Endowment for the Humanities?" she asked. "I didn't even know you had an NEH grant."

"It was years ago," Gabe said, the color beginning to return to his face. "Ancient history. Simon's just being a prick."

Lauren shook her head. "I've always found it hard to understand how Jackie could have been married to him."

"Believe it or not," Gabe said, as the waiter arrived with their entrées, "he was once a pretty good guy."

The veal Languedoc was as superb as Aunt Beatrice had promised, as was the rest of the evening. They didn't talk about Deborah or Jackie or the supernatural—although they did agree that they both detested Simon Pappas. Instead, they drank another bottle of wine and gossiped about the department. Then they had a heated discussion about the president's foreign policy and discovered a mutual passion for travel, film noir, and mystery novels. Lauren hadn't felt as alive or as happy in a long time. She was completely caught up in Gabe: in his conversation; in his charm; in his long, lingering glances. They skipped dessert and went to Lauren's house.

"Would you like to come up for a nightcap?" Lauren asked Gabe as they stood in the foyer, her heart beating wildly at her boldness.

Gabe wrapped his arms around her and pulled her to him. "I'd love to," he said. They walked up the stairs with their arms around each other, but they broke apart when they entered the apartment.

Aunt Beatrice came out of the living room to greet them. She was a tall, wiry woman with the no-nonsense air of one who doesn't have time for foolishness. She was very fond of Todd and, after Lauren introduced them, gave Gabe an appraising look as she shook his hand. She acted as if she had no idea who he was.

"Drew was talking about *his father* all evening," Aunt Beatrice told Lauren, although it was clear she was speaking for Gabe's benefit. "About Todd's new camera and how if Todd gets some project in Washington, he might take Drew with him for a few days."

Lauren kissed her aunt and thanked her for babysitting, shooing her down the stairs. When she turned from the door, Gabe pulled her into his arms.

"Wait," she said softly. "Let me check on Drew."

Acutely aware that Gabe was watching her from the doorway, she picked Bunny up from the floor and placed him in the crook of Drew's arm. The boy murmured a few unintelligible syllables, then he drew Bunny to his chest and curled his body protectively around the stuffed animal. Lauren kissed him and tiptoed to the door, leaving it open a crack.

"Deborah never wanted any kids," Gabe said, his eyes sad.

Lauren touched his arm. "Ready for that drink?"

Gabe was suddenly uninterested in a drink. Instead he gently removed her coat and draped it over a small table in the hallway. Then he began to unbutton her blouse. "It's strange," he murmured, tracing the crescent-shaped scar on her neck with his tongue.

Lauren pulled his shirt from his pants and ran her hands along his back, pulling him closer. "What's strange?"

"I know someone with a birthmark that's the same size and shape—and in exactly the same place—as your scar."

But Lauren didn't care about birthmarks. All she cared about was making love to Gabe, of feeling his flesh along the length of hers, of his hands, his tongue, his body inside hers. "Come with me," she said.

His laugh emerged from deep in his chest. He took her hand and followed her to the bedroom. She closed the door firmly and turned to him. Within minutes they were naked.

Gabe was a wonderful lover, gentle and slow and caring—almost too slow for Lauren. He kissed her long and deep, and when he finally touched her breast, she moaned so loud he laughed again. "Don't laugh at me, you stinker," Lauren said, poking him in the side. "It's been a long time."

He ran his hand down the length of her body and kissed the inside of her wrist. "That's a deprivation we'll have to keep from ever happening again," he said. Lauren was more than willing to comply.

Afterward, lying in Gabe's arms, Lauren asked, "So who's got a scar just like mine?"

"Birthmark," he corrected. "And you probably don't want to know."

He was right. Lauren didn't want to know. "Sorry

I asked," she said. "I really don't care where Deborah's birthmarks are."

"I just want to start this relationship being honest." Gabe sat up and pulled her closer. "Everything out in the open. I have a feeling we could be really good together." He ran his finger along Lauren's cheekbone and touched her lips. "Really good."

Lauren looked at Gabe closely. He seemed to mean it. Gabe Phipps, *the* Gabe Phipps, sounded like he wanted a serious relationship with her. She leaned over and kissed him. His lips were so warm and enveloping that she wanted to stay in this moment forever. But thinking of Drew in the next room, as well as her early morning appointment, she said, "You really should go now."

He cupped her chin in his hand and smiled at her. "Okay."

"I had a great time," she whispered, her voice husky.

"Me too," he said as he climbed out of bed. Gabe dressed quickly and Lauren slipped into a robe. "Is there a night when Drew stays with his father?" Gabe asked as they walked together into the hall. "I'll make dinner for you at my house—I'm actually not a half-bad cook."

Lauren smiled. "Would Tuesday be too soon?"

"Perfect," Gabe said. "And if you must go to RavenWing tomorrow, please don't stay too long—and don't read that chronicle."

"I thought you didn't believe in curses," she teased.

"I don't," Gabe said. "But suddenly I don't want to take any chances."

After Gabe left, Lauren stood pressing her ear to the closed door, keenly aware of the blood pulsing through her body, breathing in the musky male scent that clung to her. She thought about sex and love and lust, and wondered exactly what she was feeling right now. For a moment, she thought she heard a rustling sound coming from Drew's room, but when she peeked through his doorway, he was fast asleep.

Humming softly, she floated back to bed.

That night Lauren dreamed she was in jail again. She was in a dungeon, a true dungeon filled with a bone numbing dampness and the odor of fear. Her feet were sunk into an oozing, clinging mud and shackles chained her to the wall. Fingers tore at her dress, oily and callused, their nails and knuckles caked with dirt. Repulsed and terrified, she twisted and turned but was unable to move. She was at the mercy of the groping, marauding hands.

Voices screamed and heckled her. The laughter and taunts grew until they echoed off the walls and the water, and Lauren thought she would be encased forever in the monstrous clamor. "Full of the devil," the voices shrieked. "This witch must die!"

A bloated face rose before her, its teeth black and its breath putrid. It was Oliver Osborne. He began screaming in agony, holding first his gut, then his head, then his gut again, pleading with the Lord to let him die. As the Lord granted his wish, Osborne collapsed to the ground, knocking over an urn with the triple face of a bearded devil carved onto it. The urn tipped and opened, spilling human hair and fingernail parings onto the floor.

"They say it be witchcraft," Gabe Phipps told Lauren as he walked nonchalantly down a long hallway into what was her living room and yet not her living room. As he approached her, his voice began to change and his face molted until he grew twisted and deformed, and his laughter became the laughter of the men in the dungeon. Gabe shrieked and, when he opened his mouth, his teeth were all black and his breath smelled just like Oliver Osborne's.

Lauren bolted upright, icy sweat gluing her nightshirt to her back as Gabe's voice from her dream slipped into her waking. "All witches must die," he cried. "Hung at dawn until dead."

Her hand was trembling as she groped for her dream diary, but when her eyes grazed the clock, she dropped the book and leapt out of bed. In her lust-induced fog, she had forgotten to set the alarm last night. Drew was due at Sunday school in less than thirty minutes and she was supposed to be at RavenWing in forty-five.

"Drew!" she called as she raced down the hallway. "We've overslept. It's time to get up."

But when she got to the boy's bedroom, she skidded to a stop in surprise. Drew was already up and dressed, sitting on his bed and staring at the floor.

"Oh," she said, pushing her hair out of her eyes. "I guess I'm the only one who overslept. Want to be my alarm clock from now on?" she asked as she leaned over to kiss him.

He didn't say anything. He just shrugged, his eyes focused on the floor.

"Come on, Mister Boy." Lauren ruffled his hair. "Come with me and I'll whip you up a mean bowl of Rice Krispies." When Drew still didn't move, Lauren looked at him more carefully. "Are you feeling okay?" she asked, pressing her wrist to his cool forehead.

He shrugged again and his eyes skittered toward his desk.

Lauren followed his gaze, then walked slowly to the corner of the room. The desk was its usual mess, piled so high with Legos and drawing paper and stacks of old copies of *Boy's Life* and *Adventure* that not a sliver of its red top could be seen. Finding nothing unusual, she turned back toward Drew, but as she did, she glimpsed something in his wastebasket.

"What the . . . ?" Lauren dropped to her knees, hoping that what she was seeing was not actually there. But it was. Sticking out of the wastebasket was a jumble of dark brown stuffed arms and legs and other body parts. Wisps of cotton batting littered the floor.

It was Bunny. Bunny had been slashed and dismembered and thrown away in the trash.

Eighteen

As Lauren climbed from the bowels of the Harvard Square subway station into the gray morning light, she found the dismal weather a perfect reflection of her mood. Drew had destroyed Bunny in a horrible and violent way, and she was terrified Mrs. Baker and Dr. Berg's concerns were well placed—that there might be something seriously wrong with her son.

When she had questioned Drew about Bunny, he had glared defiantly at her. "Stuffed animals are for babies," he said, crossing his arms over his chest in a heartbreakingly adult gesture. "You told me not to hurt other people's things. Bunny's mine and I can hurt him if I want."

"But you love Bunny," Lauren said, her voice breaking. "You've always loved Bunny."

"Not anymore," Drew had told her.

Lauren blinked back tears and looked up at the sky, which was the same color as the concrete beneath her feet. Glancing at her watch, she took the subway stairs two at a time. She was late to meet Deborah. She frowned at the bulky shopping bag she carried on her arm. Although she had remembered to bring the Bellarmine urn, in her haste and distraction she had forgotten the poppet.

The square was eerily still as she reached the street. A solitary cab was taking a wide turn in front of the Harvard Coop and a fortress of unsold newspapers stood sentinel around the Out of Town kiosk. As the sky began to spit something between rain and snow, Lauren hurried to RavenWing.

When she got there, the sign in the window read CLOSED. But when she pushed the latch, the door opened, setting off tinkling wind chimes and the canary's song.

"Lauren?" Deborah's disembodied voice called from somewhere deep in the store. "Could you bolt the door behind you, please?" she asked before Lauren could identify herself. When Lauren came back through the small vestibule, Deborah was standing next to the trestle table smiling at her.

Deborah held out her hands and pressed Lauren's free hand between them. "You're frozen," she said. "Come, I've put on some tea." She waved Lauren toward the book corner. "Go sit down in the niche—it's so much nicer than in the storage room. I'll be right back."

Lauren looked nervously around the empty store, remembering everything Gabe had told her the previous evening. Things that, despite Deborah's "normal" appearance this morning, Lauren was sure were true. Thinking about Jackie's admonition to keep an open mind, Lauren placed the shopping bag on the floor and took off her jacket. She sank into one of the beanbag chairs and shifted around, trying to get comfortable. But long-legged people and beanbag chairs don't mix. With her knees in the air and her shoulders angled back toward the wall, Lauren felt like an overgrown Alice in a very uncomfortable wonderland.

"Milk or lemon?" Deborah called out through the door to the back room.

"Plain's just fine." Lauren didn't care how her tea was accessorized. No matter what was in it, it was one of her least favorite beverages. Just as, she thought wryly, psychotics were one of her least favorite sources of information.

But when Deborah entered the niche, smiling as she balanced two steaming mugs and the bird cage, Lauren found herself smiling back. Deborah seemed so ordinary in her blue jeans and sweatshirt, so likable with her toothy grin and unruly hair. Doctors had been wrong before.

"I hope you don't mind?" Deborah asked, motioning to the cage. "Summerland gets lonely. He's much happier if he's around people." The little canary began to sing a melody that clearly indicated his happiness at being near them. "Aren't you, darlin'?" Deborah cooed to her pet. "Aren't you?"

"He's beautiful," Lauren told Deborah, just to be polite. But as she looked at the canary more closely, she saw that he was indeed an exceptionally handsome bird. He appeared to be smiling.

"I'm so glad you've come," Deborah said as she settled the bird cage on the floor and herself into the other beanbag chair. "I feel badly about what happened in Moorscott." She took a sip of tea and put the mug down on the table between their chairs. "If there's anything we can do to make it up to you, just say the word."

"Let me read the chronicle?"

Deborah threw back her head and laughed. "How about we start a little more slowly?" She pointed to the bag at Lauren's feet. "What's in there?"

Lauren leaned awkwardly to her right and pushed the bag over to Deborah. "I found it at Jackie's—and I want you to tell me it doesn't mean anything."

"Let's see if I can oblige." Deborah pulled the shopping bag onto her lap and looked inside. She drew the urn out slowly and placed it on the floor, running her hands over the bearded face and the strange symbols below him. She put it to her ear and shook gently. Throwing an inscrutable look at Lauren, she popped the wide cork and carefully poured the contents onto the floor. The dead animal odor seemed an almost visible cloud, pushing itself into the spice-ladened air. Summerland stopped singing and stood completely still on his swing. When Deborah saw the felt heart, she caught her breath.

Lauren grabbed her mug and took a large gulp of tea. The hot liquid burned her tongue. She put the mug back on the table. "I was thinking maybe it was some kind of mass-produced novelty item," Lauren said to break the tense silence. "You know, one of those things you can have made up as a birthday gag or something?"

Deborah, examining the braid of hair, didn't appear to hear her. "Do you keep a dream diary?" she asked.

"As a matter of fact I do," Lauren said, startled by Deborah's question. "How did you know?"

"Did you ever wake to find a dream recorded in an unfamiliar hand?"

"Of course not," Lauren said.

Deborah gingerly turned the braid to avoid sticking herself with the nails. "Do you think this could have been Jackie's hair?" she asked.

"It seems to be the right color," Lauren said slowly. "But how could anyone have gotten enough of Jackie's hair to make a braid?"

"Practitioners of black magic are very patient and resourceful people." There was respect in Deborah's voice as she picked up the pin-studded heart.

"So you think this comes from an actual sorcerer?" Lauren asked. "That it's a real tool of voodoo?"

Just as Lauren began to squirm under the gaze of Deborah's strange but hauntingly beautiful eyes, Deborah waved her hand in the air and said, "It's as real as these books and these walls. As real as you and me."

Lauren took a deep breath and told Deborah about the poppets. "Do you think they came from someone who actually wanted to hurt me and Jackie?"

"I hardly think they came from a friend." Deborah scooped the fingernail parings into her hand and dropped them into the urn. As soon as the urn was corked, Summerland resumed his song. Deborah wiped her hands on her skirt and turned back to Lauren. "There's so much out there that so many of you don't allow yourselves to see. The belief that you can know and understand everything—that you can figure out the rules and then apply them—keeps you from knowing and understanding. There are hidden relationships between all elements of the cosmos."

Annoyed by Deborah's condescending tone, Lauren demanded, "Hidden relationships like yours and Gabe Phipps?"

"Ah," Deborah said. "I wondered when the great Dr. Ego would force himself into our conversation. Never underestimate the power of a man with limitless ambition."

"It was me who forced him into the conversation," Lauren said. "He's not even here."

"I suppose he told you I spent time at McLean? That I suffer from paranoid delusions? That I'm psychotic and unstable and dangerous to both myself and others?" Although Deborah's words were harsh, her voice was amused.

"Is it true?"

"Mark my words," Deborah said, all signs of amusement gone. "Gabe Phipps is far more dangerous than I'll ever be. Don't be fooled by his power and charisma—the man is evil. Evil surrounding a hollow core of ego."

"Aren't you exaggerating just a bit?"

"Truth can never be exaggerated." Deborah's pale eyes scoured Lauren's. "Have you ever gone scuba diving?"

Lauren blinked, taken aback by Deborah's rapid change of subject.

"Bear with this psychotic for a moment, if you will," Deborah said. "We nut cases often make more sense than people like to admit."

Lauren regarded Deborah warily. "I don't swim."

"You're afraid of water." Deborah spoke with a knowledge that Lauren found unnerving.

Lauren pushed herself up in the chair. "What does my swimming ability have to do with Gabe Phipps or Bellarmine urns?"

"When you scuba dive, you're a visitor in another universe," Deborah said. "The aquatic world coexists with our own, but most of us live our lives virtually unaware of its existence. And the physical laws that govern there are completely different from those of the land. Air, which is life to us, is death to most sea creatures. Water, which defines their existence, is just a part of the planet on which we can't live." She placed the braid on one palm and the felt heart on the other. She held them out to Lauren. "What makes sense in one place, makes none in the other."

Lauren silently studied Jackie's name sewn across the felt heart, awed by Deborah's power to logically explaining the illogical. She remembered Jackie's words: *"Maybe Deborah just sees what the rest of us are too blind to see."*

"Oh, I'm far from crazy," Deborah said. "In some ways I'm all too sane—for I can see what their rigid belief system doesn't allow human beings to see: that magic and reincarnation are real."

Taken aback by the similarity between Deborah's words and her own thoughts, Lauren blurted, "The doctors at McLean couldn't see what you did either?"

"Doctors aren't trying to *see* anything," Deborah

said. "They're too consumed with validating themselves and their theories to try to understand anything else."

"Are you saying you think magic was involved in Jackie's death?"

"It's a possibility," Deborah said as she put the urn back into the bag and placed it at Lauren's feet. "These things often don't work out as the practitioner plans. And they're rarely simple." She handed Lauren her mug of tea as if she had asked for it. "Were you a precocious child?"

Stalling for time, Lauren took a long sip of the now lukewarm tea. It was clear that the doctors at McLean had not been as blind as Deborah believed. Deborah's view of reality was definitely warped.

Sighing, Lauren decided that if she was going to get the information Nat wanted, she would have to play along. "I'm an only child," she said. "According to my parents, there was no one more precocious."

Deborah seemed pleased with this answer. "I usually have many siblings. But I've never had any children."

For a moment Lauren was confused by Deborah's choice of words. Then she understood. "You mean in every lifetime it's the same?"

"Although it's not always true for *every* soul in *every* lifetime, it's not uncommon." Deborah rested her hands in her lap and looked at Lauren closely. "For example, in each incarnation, Faith Osborne's been an only child who gives birth to only one of her own."

Lauren nodded. "Her daughter Dorcas was hung in 1692."

"Seven years old and proclaimed a witch," Deborah said, shaking her head. "The poor child thought it was all a game. She didn't know any better than to admit to bewitching Elizabeth Cloyce's cow and spoiling the milk. And her own stepfather, Oliver Osborne, didn't know any better than to believe her."

The nightmare face of Oliver Osborne rose before Lauren, bloated and full of black teeth; the stench of his putrid breath filled her nostrils, his angry voice filled her head. The room grew unbearably warm and seemed to swirl around her. She pulled at the turtleneck of her shirt and gasped for air.

"Lauren?" Deborah called, her voice sounding as if it were coming from the end of a long tunnel. "Are you all right?"

Lauren blinked and the face disappeared along with his foul smell. She took a deep breath of the spicy air and noticed that Deborah was staring at her neck.

"I'm fine," she said, tugging at her collar again. "I guess I was up too late last night." Lauren felt a flush rise on her cheeks, for she had the unsettling sensation that Deborah knew exactly why—and with whom—she had been up too late. She busied herself digging into her backpack for a notebook and pen, hoping these props would put this meeting back on a professional plane. After she found her place in her notes, she leaned forward, her long body awkward in the low chair. "Can I be frank with you?"

"Please."

"In order to make my book work, I need a better understanding of reincarnation," Lauren said. "It's all so amorphous, so hard to grasp. Like trying to hold fog in your hand."

"Most people feel that way about spiritual ideas. The truth is, reincarnation's no harder—or easier—to grasp than heaven or God or Jesus Christ." Deborah watched Lauren closely over the rim of her mug. "How can I help you get your mind around this?"

"Tell me about you," Lauren said. "How did you know you were Rebeka Hibbens—and when?" She tapped her pen on her notebook, wondering if this was really a good line of questioning but curious despite herself. "And what about Cassandra? Was it the same for her? The same for everyone in the coven?"

"Fair enough," Deborah said, putting her mug on the table. "Did you ever hear of a man named Ian Stevenson? He's a physician, a serious scientist—and he's studied thousands of cases of reported reincarnation."

"The children who remember previous lives book," Lauren said excitedly. "I read it a couple of weeks ago as part of my research for *Rebeka Hibbens.*" She had skimmed Ian Stevenson's book on the day Jackie died and hadn't been able to get herself to read it since. Whenever she saw the black and red cover, it brought back that awful afternoon with such vividness that she was forced to turn away.

"Then you know he's found lots of cases of young children who, when they first begin to talk, tell stories about lives they've lived in other places and times. Sometimes they even speak foreign languages."

"But didn't he have trouble confirming most of the stories?"

Deborah nodded. "But he also found many cases he *was* able to confirm. Children who remembered families in faraway places who, when Stevenson took them there, named all these 'unknown' people and even commented on changes that had occurred in the surroundings since their own 'death.' "

"And that's what it was like for you?"

"Except much more vivid—and my memories have never faded, as did most of the subjects' in Stevenson's research. I remember all my lives the way you remember your childhood."

Lauren pondered this information, but she wrote nothing in her notebook. "And it's the same for everyone in the coven?"

"All the real witches."

"Did you tell your parents?"

"I was born into a family of fundamentalist Christians in rural Texas. I had six brothers who were as rowdy and as conservative as they come—sometimes the sages have quite a sense of humor. On the other hand, Cassandra was born to a mother who was a clairvoyant, so she was out of the 'broom closet' at a very early age."

Deborah must have seen from the expression on Lauren's face that she was losing her, so she switched to a more serious note. "When I was about three, I explained to my mother that I had been lots of people who had lived in other places—I told her some stories about Rebeka and then I did a few pagan chants for her." Deborah paused and began to laugh. "I spent a week in the cow shed for my 'blasphemy.' After that, I kept my knowledge to myself. I knew all along that I'd come to Cambridge and meet up with the rest of the coven, that my childhood was just a place to practice my craft and to hone my skills."

Lauren wondered where Gabe and Deborah's marriage fit into this fantasy, but she asked, "What do you mean by 'your craft'?"

"Magic," Deborah said simply. "It's as I told you that first afternoon. The Immortalis allows us to keep our magical skills at the same level they were at the end of our previous life. Those who don't participate in the Immortalis have to relearn most of what they knew in each lifetime. Although," she added, "relearning comes much more easily than learning something for the first time."

"Are you saying there are others?" Lauren asked. "Other people who know they're reincarnated?"

"On some level, everyone knows. Haven't you ever had flashes of another time and place?" Deborah asked, leaning forward and watching Lauren closely. "Images of a person you know you aren't but still feel that you are? Dreams that seem too real and detailed to be just figments of your subconscious imagination?"

Lauren lowered her eyes so Deborah wouldn't see that she had indeed had such experiences. She shrugged nonchalantly. "Sometimes," she admitted. "But I figure it's one of the occupational hazards of being a graduate student in history. You know, like medical students who get every disease they study."

"You dream that you live in the seventeenth century?"

Lauren hesitated. "It's the time I'm most familiar with—the period that's gotten under my skin and into my subconscious."

"Could you tell me one of your dreams?"

"I'd really rather not." Lauren felt a flush of annoyance rising on her cheeks. "Dreams are pretty personal."

"Please?" Deborah pressed. "I don't mean to pry, but dreams fascinate me—and they must fascinate you too if you keep a journal."

Don't mean to pry, Lauren thought. That was a laugh. But she also realized that if she expected Deborah to give her information, she had to be forthcoming in return. "Last week I dreamed I was being chased through the library by Oliver Osborne. And just last night, I had a dream in which I was chained in a Colonial prison—although after Moorscott, I guess it's not too hard to imagine where that one came from."

Deborah's eyes flashed for a moment with what Lauren thought might be fear, but she didn't say anything.

Lauren shifted uncomfortably in the beanbag chair and glanced down at her watch. "Look, I've less than an hour before I have to pick up my son and—"

"Your editor wants the chronicle," Deborah interrupted, "which of course we can't give you. But I can tell you more about our fables. About Rebeka's lancet and magic and the details of how we reenact our Immortalis every one hundred and one years. It might take a few sessions, but we can meet here for the next few Sunday mornings, if you'd like. What do you say?"

"Great." Lauren poised her pen over her notebook and flashed a peppy smile. But as she prepared to listen to Deborah with an open mind, all she could hear were Gabe's words: "*Dr. Bluestone told me she was a very sick woman. . . . Preoccupied with suicide and delusions of grandeur . . . A threat to herself and others . . .*"

Deborah locked the door behind Lauren. She was not pleased that Lauren was dreaming about Oliver Osborne or Cambridge Prison, and she prayed to the sages that Lauren wasn't having waking dreams of the past. Waking dreams would indicate that Faith's memories were breaking into Lauren's consciousness. If Lauren remembered too much of Faith's life, it could jeopardize the Immortalis.

She was also very displeased with the Bellarmine urn and the poppets. Someone was either practicing black magic on Lauren or trying to scare her away from the coven. This too could have a devastating effect on the Immortalis.

Deborah made her way through the store to the back room, where the coven was waiting for her. When she entered, they all bowed their heads. She felt their curiosity pulsing through the silent room. But Deborah had learned long ago that one of the keys to power lay in withholding information. She would tell them nothing about her conversation with Lauren.

Deborah knelt in the far corner and retrieved the chronicle from the floor safe. She walked slowly to the altar and opened the book. "From *The Chronicle of the Coven,*" she said. " 'The Book of Mahala.' Chapter II." She began to read.

Rebeka stood on the edge of a rocky outcropping, her hands pulled painfully behind her back and held fast by a coil of coarse hemp. The sky was steel gray and overcast, the same color as the ocean that lapped at the bottom of the cliff, and the wind cut through her cloak, chilling her in both body and soul. On the rugged hills in the distance, goldenrod and smoky blue asters waved in stark counterpoint to the goings-on of the goodmen of Cambridge.

Rebeka scanned the angry crowd, searching for the members of her coven. For although she had been informed she was not to be hanged this day, she worried that one of the others might be. According to the magic she and Millicent Glover had contrived, the Immortalis would require the energy of seven powerful souls to create the bridge to the sages. There was no certainty that six would ensure the link. Therefore, if any of the others were put to death before the Immortalis could be consummated, all might be lost.

But Rebeka saw no prisoners. She saw only the eyes of her neighbors, burning with self-righteous fury, and eight hangman's nooses dangling from the branches of a great oak tree.

A man Rebeka did not recognize rose before her. "Repent!" he cried. "Renounce the devil and enter into the Kingdom of God."

Rebeka fixed her eyes steadily upon him. "'Tis thou who must renounce the devil," she said softly. "Dost thou not see the grievous error that be done here this day?"

But the man just laughed and continued on.

Human beings were a piteous, confused lot, Rebeka thought sadly. A lot from whom she and her coven would, sages willing, soon depart.

She heard sounds approaching and turned to see a cart rise along the steep side of the hill. The cart was hardly larger than a wheelbarrow, yet it was overloaded with suffering: Seven adults and what appeared to be one small child clung to each other as the wagon jerked up the rutted trail. On foot, Oliver Osborne and Daniel Higgenson led the way, their faces full of themselves and the power they held over the poor souls who followed behind them.

Rebeka squinted as the conveyance drew nearer, hoping

against hope that none of her coven was to be found within. Scanning the faces, she was flooded with both horror and relief. For although poor Goody Warren and Tituba and old Giles Cory were huddled there, neither Foster nor Millicent nor Abigail were with them. Then Rebeka's stomach twisted and she cried out in pain. The child in the wagon was Dorcas Osborne. Dorcas, her precious, sweet Dorcas. Dorcas, whom she had taught all she knew. Dorcas, who could bend the cornstalks with her will and was, aside from Rebeka, the most powerful witch in the coven. Dorcas, whose energy was critical to consummating the Immortalis.

As the cart crested the hill and came to a stop under the thick spreading limbs of the old oak tree, the crowd screamed, "Death to the witches!" Some threw dirt and rocks.

Oliver Osborne walked to the front of the wagon and raised his arms. The crowd grew silent. "The evil hand is upon them," he cried, his face flushed with the importance of the moment, of his place within it. "These eight have been found guilty of consorting with the devil. These eight must die!"

The crowd roared its approval as, one by one, Daniel Higgenson pulled the scraggly souls from the cart. When Susanna Warren was thrown to the ground, she righted herself and stood tall before Osborne. "A grievous mistake has been made, sir," she told him in a strong, steady voice. "I am no witch. I know not what a witch is."

"Goody Warren," Osborne bellowed at Susanna, a wide grin filling his complacent face, "how can you know you are not, what you know not?"

The crowd cheered, and Daniel dragged Susanna to the hanging tree. As Osborne was placing a noose around Susanna's neck, a slender figure broke from the crowd and threw herself on the sole occupant of the cart. Rebeka knew the woman well. It was her cousin, Faith Osborne, trying to snatch her daughter, Dorcas, from Daniel's hands. Re-

beka's heart broke as she watched Daniel push the child behind him and kick Faith to the ground.

"She is but a babe," Faith cried, grabbing Daniel's boots.

"Mama!" Dorcas sobbed. "Mama!"

Faith lunged at Daniel, but Amy Duny and Mary Sibley grabbed her from behind. One held her arms and the other her feet.

"If thee interfere with the work of the Lord," Amy told her, "thou shall be next."

Faith wrenched herself free. "I care not if I am next for I am a witch," she cried, standing before Osborne. "'Tis I who did all Dorcas is accused of. 'Tis I who caused Goody Cloyce's cow to stop giving milk and Goody Sibley's chimney to fall. My specter who came in the night and did bite and pinch. Dorcas has no power. She knows not the devil. 'Tis I who am the devil's consort!"

The crowd fell silent as Oliver Osborne looked down on his wife. Rebeka held her breath. "If thou be a witch," Oliver said softly, his head bent in pious sadness, "then your punishment shall be no different from the others. When this deed is done, I shall declare a warrant against you and you shall be tried for witchcraft under the laws of Massachusetts Bay Colony."

"And Dorcas shall be allowed to go free?" Faith begged, her face streaked with tears.

"Mama," Dorcas bleated in a small voice. "Mama."

Rebeka's heart pounded as they waited for Osborne's verdict.

"I cannot allow the devil his consorts," Osborne cried. "'Tis not only cows and chimneys. Dorcas has been found guilty of using dead snakes to break Rose Easty's leg—of confining a God-fearing woman to her bed, of removing her as an aide to her husband and children. Nay!" he cried even more loudly. "Wife or no wife of mine, stepchild or no stepchild of mine. Justice must be done!" He waved to Daniel. "Take the girl."

"No!" Faith screamed, struggling against the many hands that held her. But the many won out over the one,

and Faith Osborne was forced to stand and watch the noose being tied around Dorcas's neck.

"She's but a child!" Rebeka yelled. "Can you not see this is madness?" But Rebeka's voice was drowned by the cheers of the crowd.

"Take me!" Faith cried. "Take me!"

"Mama!" Dorcas called again, lifting her arms toward Faith, her eyes huge in her white face. "Ma—" Her last word was cut off as the noose broke her windpipe.

She shuddered and then was still.

When Deborah looked up, she saw there were tears streaming down every face in the room. "Don't be sad," she said. "We shall avenge the child. It was Faith who caused Dorcas to be killed. So it is Faith whom we shall punish."

Nineteen

LAUREN WALKED QUICKLY TOWARD THE SUBWAY STAtion as the sky dripped its cold tears on her head. She was anxious to get to Drew—and away from Deborah. Deborah had been a great disappointment. Not only had her belief in the possible link between the Bellarmine urn and Jackie's death proved her to be as delusional as Dr. Bluestone had suspected, but she had also revealed almost nothing to Lauren about the coven. Lauren knew Nat wasn't going to be happy with her morning's work.

She tripped over a raised brick in the sidewalk and swore under her breath. Deborah's discussion of reincarnation and ghostly sages hadn't done much to convey an impression of sound mental health. She had talked about magic dwelling in the mind, about a higher part of the brain—a superconscious—that could see and understand beyond the parameters of the physical world.

When Deborah had launched into a knowledgeable discussion of Carl Jung and his collective unconscious, Lauren had been pleasantly surprised. She had always been fascinated by the Jungian concept of a cosmic folk memory that was genetically transmitted, like the instinct to suckle or the prewired ability to understand the structure of language. But when Deborah had combined Jung with her "superconscious" to account for reincarnation, Lauren had become skeptical.

"Each individual soul obtains wisdom and knowledge through her superconscious," Deborah had explained. "And each bit is added together, person by person, lifetime after lifetime, to form the collective unconscious."

Lauren stopped at the corner of Mount Auburn and JFK Street and waited for the traffic to stop. For Jackie's sake, Lauren had struggled to keep an open mind, but the more Deborah had said, the more unbelievable Lauren had found her arguments.

"Groups of souls tend to reincarnate together," Deborah said in an attempt to illustrate how all the members of the coven could be reborn at the same time in each incarnation. "Together, they work out their destiny—debts owed, lessons learned—over the span of many lifetimes."

Lauren raced across the street, remembering how Deborah had told her souls were guided by sages, who had great knowledge but no physical bodies, who controlled when and where each soul would live its next life. Deborah's sages were unsettlingly similar to Brian Weiss's entities.

Deborah explained that the Immortalis was a sacrament to receive the favor of the sages, who, if the ritual was correctly reenacted with Rebeka's lancet, allowed the souls of the seven to reincarnate together, their collected wisdom and powers intact. The 1995 Immortalis was to be the culmination of all the Immortalises. For if all went as planned, each of the coven members would "cycle out of humanness" at the end of this lifetime and begin eternal life among the sages.

Lauren ducked into the T station and climbed aboard an outbound train that had just arrived. She collapsed on the hard plastic seat and closed her eyes. She believed the coven was going to "cycle out of humanness" about as much as she believed the Bellarmine urn in her shopping bag had caused Jackie's death.

The train lurched forward and the man sitting next to her jammed his arm into her side. She opened her eyes and saw the urn sliding out of the bag. Lauren thrust out her leg, stopping the urn from rolling across the car with her foot. As the triple face of the bearded devil stared up at her, Lauren suddenly wasn't sure what she believed.

Drew was sitting on the wide concrete steps of the Porter Square Synagogue, playing with a puddle of water that had accumulated on a cracked stair, oblivious to the slight drizzle that misted around him. A few adults chatted under the overhang, and a group of children a couple of years younger than Drew played on the sidewalk.

Lauren's heart swelled at the sight of her son. He was such a good-natured child, easily occupying himself with his fantasy games and his Legos and his drawings. Could he really be so troubled? So bad? "Hey there, Mister Boy," she said, dropping a kiss on Drew's head.

Drew looked around to make sure none of his friends were watching. "Hey there, Mister Mommy," he said when he had determined the coast was clear. He jumped up, then beamed at her and did a little jig around the puddles, a puppyish bundle of energy. It was as if he had never destroyed Bunny.

"How was Sunday school?" she asked, giving him a quick hug and propelling him down the stairs.

"Yuckers," he said. "Mrs. Abel's the pits."

Lauren nodded. She was inclined to agree with him. But Todd felt strongly that the boy should learn about his heritage. "It's ethnic, not religious," Todd had argued when she had suggested they skip religious education. "Just think of it as Drew learning about his roots—not about God." She had reluctantly agreed with the proviso that religious instruction was Todd's responsibility.

So, Lauren thought as she took Drew's hand in hers, where was Todd now? Why was *she* picking up Drew and listening to him complain?

"It's sooo boring, Mom," Drew was saying. "We did this stupid project where we cut out paper and glued stuff—just like when we were in kindergarten." He looked up at her and, apparently finding a glimmer of sympathy in her eye, gave her a hug. "Are we meeting Daddy at Friendly's?"

"Yup," Lauren said. "Today's a Friendly's day."

She and Todd had decided that in order to ease the transition for Drew, the three of them should periodically spend time together. Although she often thought these Sunday lunches were a mistake, Lauren was glad they were meeting today. The episode with Bunny had unnerved her and she needed to discuss it with Todd.

Lauren and Drew got to the restaurant early and sat down. "If I eat my whole hot dog can I have one of these?" Drew asked, pointing to a glossy full-color print of a huge hot fudge sundae.

Lauren smiled sadly at Drew and nodded her consent; he appeared to be such a normal seven-year-old.

"Hi, guys." Todd slid into the booth beside Drew and tousled his son's hair. "See," he said to Lauren, "I'm right on time—snowmen in July."

Lauren smiled at his use of one of her mother's expressions—an expression that had driven her crazy as a child because of its illogic.

"I paid Mrs. Piccini my share of both the November and December rent," Todd said quickly.

Lauren nodded. "Thanks."

After wrestling a bit with Drew and finding out that Sunday school was "yuckers," Todd turned to Lauren. "How'd your meeting go?" he asked. "Did you get your witches' bible?"

Lauren shook her head. "I don't think Deborah's going to give it to me. Nat's not going to be happy."

"Do the witches have the story in their bible about God creating the world in six days?" Drew asked.

"No," Lauren said. "Their bible tells their special story just like our Bible tells ours."

"How many bibles are there, Mommy?"

"There are lots, slugger," Todd answered for her. "Like the witches' bible Mommy needs for her book."

"Tell me about your witches," Drew demanded.

After they ordered, Lauren told Drew the story of the lost coven and the chronicle and Jackie and Deborah and Cassandra, omitting, of course, any mention of black magic or poppets or Bellarmine urns, for both Drew and Todd's sakes. Todd, although a risk taker when it came to himself, worried incessantly about both Lauren and Drew. He claimed he had inherited the Freeman worry gene from his paternal grandfather, who had worried himself into a heart attack at thirty-six.

By the time Lauren finished, lunch had arrived. "The whole thing's incredible, Laurie," Todd said. "Absolutely incredible. This is going to make one hell of a great book—even if you can't talk them into giving you their chronicle. People are just going to eat it up." He popped a French fry into his mouth and pulled a face at Drew. "Yum, yum, good book."

Drew giggled. "People don't eat books, Daddy."

"They're going to eat up Mommy's."

Listening to Todd's reaction, Lauren began to feel a stirring of excitement. For the first time since Jackie's death, she was actually beginning to see *Rebeka Hibbens* in a positive way. She heard Jackie's voice: *"Maybe historical research is about getting people—and ourselves—to think in ways we've never thought before."* Maybe it *could* be a good book. An interesting book. A new and unique approach to the overstudied New England witch trials.

"Do you really think people will like the book?" Lauren asked Todd.

"I do." He reached across the table and took her hands in his. "Aren't you glad I nagged you into going to graduate school?"

Lauren pulled her hands into her lap, but not before she realized how comfortable—and how nice—they had felt resting in Todd's. "It does seem to have been a good decision," she said primly.

Todd crossed his arms over his chest and looked at her in mock annoyance. "Admit it," he demanded.

Lauren burst out laughing, thinking of all the times he had demanded she "admit it." The camping trip to the Canadian Rockies. The sex video they had ordered by mail. The water bed. Drew. "All right, all right," she said. "I admit school was a good idea."

"Do you really go to school even though you don't have to?" Drew asked. When Lauren nodded, he shook his head. "I thought you went to school to get smart."

Todd raised his glass of Coke. "To *Rebeka Hibbens,*" he said.

Remembering that Gabe had made the same toast last night, Lauren felt a stab of guilt. But as she touched Todd's glass with her own, she wasn't sure about whom, or what, she felt guilty. She forced the thought aside and popped a nacho in her mouth. "How's your work going?"

"Good," Todd said. "Real good. I think I've finally learned I'm a lot better photographer than a businessman—and that that's where I should concentrate my efforts."

Lauren nodded her agreement. "Jeffrey's been getting you work?" Jeffrey was Todd's new agent.

"Wish I'd found him years ago," Todd said. "I'm still free-lancing for *The Minuteman* and *The Trumpet*—and doing a few portrait jobs on the side—but Jeff's lined me up with some regular accounts that actually pay a decent rate."

"That's great," Lauren said, impressed and pleased that Todd finally seemed to be getting his life together. Watching Drew, who was playing cops and robbers with his French fries, she felt a twinge of sadness. If Todd had managed this feat a bit earlier, it was possible things might be very different today.

"I'm shooting a lot of computers," Todd was saying, his face alive with excitement. "It's not all that artistic—mostly for catalogs—but there are unique challenges and I really like the people I'm working with. And I've been doing some outside work—houses for a developer . . ." His voice trailed off and his face clouded.

"What?" Lauren asked, taking a bite of her salad.

Todd turned to Drew and started up a round of Robin Hood French fries, a game they'd been playing for years in which Drew became Robin, Todd the sheriff of Nottingham, and the French fries swords.

"That's enough, Drew," Lauren said, although she was really talking to Todd. "It's time to eat." She occupied herself cutting Drew's steak and then looked up at Todd. She didn't say anything, not knowing whether she wanted to hear what had happened with the developer or not.

"You're probably not going to agree with me," Todd said and took a bite of his chicken sandwich. He chewed for a while, then looked her straight in the eye. "I walked off the shoot."

Lauren toyed with her salad. Here it came again:

another Todd screwup. She didn't need to hear it. She didn't need to get caught up in Todd's irresponsibility. That's why they were getting a divorce. Not to mention that she was involved in a new relationship—a relationship with a man who was too mature to walk away from his responsibilities.

"You know what, Todd, why don't you skip the story. We're having a nice lunch here, let's not ruin it."

"Is it a good story, Daddy?" Drew asked. "Does it have bad guys and good guys?"

Todd gazed at Drew for a long moment. "Yes, slugger, it does. But I'm afraid Mommy's going to think I'm one of the bad guys."

Drew's eyes grew wide. "Were you?"

"No," Todd said. "I think I was a good guy."

"Tell me the story," Drew demanded.

Todd looked at Lauren and she shrugged her permission. She carefully cut a few tomatoes and thought about Gabe slipping her dress over her hips, gasping as he cupped her breasts. But despite her attempts to tune Todd out, Lauren couldn't help listening to his story.

It seemed that Todd had been hired by Danforth Associates to take photographs for a brochure advertising its new subdivision, Brattle Woods, in Sudbury. He had put in more than forty hours on the project—at $200 an hour, the highest hourly rate Todd had ever received—and Philip Walcott Danforth III had been very pleased with the results. He'd promised to give Todd more work when the project was completed.

"And then last week," Todd told them, "Phil called and said to come out to his house in Weston, rather than going over to Sudbury. He asked me to bring all my equipment." Todd paused and gave Lauren a look that she knew all too well: "Just give me a chance," it said.

"And then what happened, Daddy?" Drew prodded.

"It turned out that Mr. Danforth was a bad guy," Todd said to Drew. "He wanted me to cheat." He turned to Lauren. "Ol' Phil's plan was for me to photograph some of the details and construction of *his* house—a house I'd guess to be worth well over a million dollars—details and construction that were never going to be part of the Brattle Woods project."

"He was going to use those photos along with your others for the brochure to sell the Sudbury houses?" Lauren asked.

"I don't get it," Drew said.

Neither Lauren nor Todd answered him; they just looked at each other for a long moment. Then Lauren reached over and squeezed Todd's hand. "You're a good guy," she said, surprised at the pride she felt and the tears pricking at the backs of her eyes. She let go of his hand and looked down at her salad, thinking that although Todd might not be the most dependable person in the world, he had to be one of the most ethical. Which is why his unfaithfulness with Melissa had been so upsetting. Lauren raised her eyes. "You did the right thing."

"I still don't get it," Drew said.

Todd picked up a French fry and they dueled for a minute. "Maybe when you get older, you'll understand," Todd said. "The important thing is that Mommy does." He smiled shyly at Lauren.

Drew stood up and announced he had to go to the bathroom. When Todd rose to accompany him, Drew threw his father a disdainful look. "I'm not a baby," he declared. "You stay and talk to Mommy." Then he ran off toward the front of the restaurant.

Todd sat down with a smile. "So our baby isn't a baby anymore."

Lauren stared into her salad. "So he's been telling me."

"What is it?" Todd asked. "Did he get into more trouble at school?"

"Two things—but neither at school," Lauren said slowly.

"Tell me what you're talking about."

Lauren sighed and told him what had happened at the playground and what Drew had done to Bunny.

"Bunny?" Todd's face was creased with concern. "Are you sure? I can't believe he'd hurt that stuffed animal. He loves Bunny—he has since he was born."

" 'Not anymore' is what he told me," Lauren said miserably. "I guess he's learned somewhere along the line that love doesn't last forever."

Todd lowered his eyes. "Should we call Dr. Berg?"

"I did tell Drew he couldn't hurt anything that belonged to someone else—and he didn't. He hurt something of his own. In a bizarre way, he was only following instructions."

"It's still a weird thing for a kid to do—and it sounds to me like things are getting worse. The playground episode could just be little boy stuff, but Bunny . . . Really, Laurie, he dismembered his favorite toy! This isn't something we can easily dismiss." Todd took her hand in his. "I'll call Dr. Berg first thing in the morning."

Lauren nodded.

Todd played with the ends of her fingers. "He's the most precious thing we have. He's—"

"See?" Drew announced, dropping into the seat next to Todd. "I'm old enough to go to the bathroom by myself."

"I see that you are, slugger," Todd said, dropping Lauren's hand and drawing his son close. "I see that you are."

"Can we all go to the movies?" Drew asked.

Todd looked over at Lauren and their gazes held. "If Mommy says it's okay, I suppose we could see what's playing."

Lauren was tempted, but she had planned to spend the afternoon working on *Rebeka Hibbens,* and she knew it was best not to raise Drew's hopes about a reconciliation between her and Todd—although, she had to admit at the moment, the idea did have a strong appeal.

She looked at her watch. "I'd love to, but I've got to meet someone at three," she lied, knowing neither Todd nor Drew would accept working on a book that wasn't due until February as a legitimate excuse.

Drew kicked the table. "Not that guy from your work who came to dinner," he said with a pout.

"Don't do that, Drew," Lauren ordered, grabbing his leg.

Todd's smile disappeared and the pain in his eyes was so acute that Lauren winced. "Are you seeing someone?" he asked.

"Not really," Lauren said, shaking her head. "Gabe Phipps just came over for Chinese food the other night."

"*The* Gabe Phipps?" Todd asked. "Traveling in some pretty impressive company, I see."

"He's helping me with the book. . . ." Lauren's voice trailed off.

"Sure," Todd said, turning his attention back to his sandwich. "I can see where he'd be a great help."

Drew kicked the table again. "I want Daddy to live with us." He glared at Lauren. "It's all your fault he can't—and I hate you." Then he burst into tears.

Todd gathered Drew in his arms and kissed the boy's hair. "It's not Mommy's fault," he said, holding his son close. "It's a decision we both made." But when he looked at Lauren over Drew's head, his eyes glimmered with unshed tears. And she knew that on one level it *was* her fault: She had it in her power to change the situation.

More than anything in the world, Lauren wanted to make Drew and Todd happy, to stand up and say,

"Fine, let's all go home together." But even though her heart ached with their pain—and her own—the memories of Todd's betrayals were too fresh.

She reached over and touched Drew's cheek. "This isn't about you, Mister Boy," she said. "We both love you very much."

But Drew twisted away from her hand and buried his head against Todd's chest. Lauren escaped to the ladies' room.

When Lauren returned, Todd and Drew were waiting for her at the front of the restaurant. Todd kissed Drew and told Lauren he'd speak with her tomorrow. Then, without meeting her eye, he loped off down the street. Lauren and Drew followed at a slower pace. Drew refused to speak to her.

As they walked across Porter Square, Lauren wondered whether she and Todd should stop spending time together with Drew. Not that they did it often, but it almost always ended with Drew in tears—and sometimes Todd and herself too. It was so painful for everyone, and now that Todd seemed to be getting his life in order, it was becoming confusing. As long as Todd was screwing up, no matter what she felt for him and no matter what Drew wanted, Lauren knew that they couldn't be married. But if Todd had really changed, might there be other options? And if there were, what did that mean for her relationship with Gabe?

As they turned the corner onto Upton Street, a toddler careened into Lauren's legs. He fell to the sidewalk, landing on his well-padded bottom, and looked up at her in surprise. Lauren bent down and helped him stand.

The little boy's father, who came running after him, scooped his son up. "Sorry," he said to Lauren, a sheepish smile on his face. He turned toward a breathless woman who came up behind them. "Got him!" he said. "Go bug your mother, you little monkey," he told the boy as he swung him over his head and placed him in his mother's waiting arms. When he planted a kiss on his wife's cheek, Lauren's eyes filled with tears.

As soon as they got home, Drew headed for his room. Lauren watched him go, wondering what she could do to console him. Then she stiffened. The apartment had a strange smell. As if something were burning. She quickly went into the kitchen and checked the stove and the toaster oven. Everything was off and the smell was actually weaker than it had been in the hall.

Sniffing, she checked the living room fireplace. Again nothing, and again the smell seemed weaker. Wondering if she had imagined it, she looked around the room. At first everything looked normal, but then she was overcome by the sense that something wasn't right. With a start, she realized it felt as if someone had been in the apartment. One of the window shades was higher than she usually left it, and the overstuffed chair that neither she nor Drew liked appeared lumpy, as if someone had recently sat there.

She rubbed her arms. No one had been here, she told herself. This was her mind's doing: all this talk of witches and sorcery and black magic. Nonetheless, she checked Drew's room—where he had already managed to cover the floor with Legos—looking under his bed and in his closet. She went into the bathroom and checked behind the shower curtain. Then she walked toward her bedroom.

As she got closer to her room, the odor intensified and she recognized it as incense. She went back down the hall and closed Drew's door, then approached her bedroom again. Slowly, she walked in, noting the unmade bed and yesterday's clothes thrown haphazardly over the chair. The room appeared just as she had left it.

Then she noticed her bureau. Someone *had* been in the apartment. Her things had been moved. With a furtive look at her closed closet door, she advanced toward the bureau. As she got closer, her heart began to pound and she broke into a full body sweat.

On the bureau were the burned remains of two black candles. Between the candles lay a tiny braid of hair. On the edge of the bureau was her hairbrush. It was immaculately clean.

Twenty

LAUREN STARED AT THE GRIM TABLEAU BEFORE HER. Someone had broken into her house. Defiled her space. Left two burned candles and a small, angry-looking braid. She grabbed the candle stubs and threw them in the wastebasket, then did the same with the braid. She was repulsed by the tiny twist of hair, so like a mass of tangled snakes. The knowledge that the hair was her own only added to her disgust.

Did this mean evil sorcerers were after her soul? That she should stop working on *Rebeka Hibbens*? That if she continued with the book, she would soon be dead?

Lauren prowled the apartment again, looking under couches and chairs, in back of bureaus and bookshelves. Furious with this violation, she almost hoped she would find the culprit cowering behind her furniture. She clenched her fists and imagined her fingers encircling a neck, squeezing, squeezing, squeezing. . . .

But as it became clear that no one was in the apartment and that nothing had been taken, Lauren's anger turned to fear. Someone had slid in and out of her home with amazing ease. Someone who had done it once could do it again. She stepped to the phone and dialed.

"Cambridge Police. This call is being recorded."

Lauren hesitated. What exactly should she say? That her apartment had been broken into but nothing taken? That the burglar had removed hair from her brush and made it into a braid? "Is, ah, is Dan Ling there, please?" she finally asked.

The phone clicked in her ear. Finally the dispatcher returned. "Ling's out on patrol. Do you want to speak to someone else?"

Lauren took a deep breath. "There's been a break-in. At my apartment. But nothing was taken, and it's obvious that whoever was here isn't here anymore. I didn't really want to bother you about it, so I figured that because Dan Ling is a friend, maybe he could come by and check it out." Lauren knew she was rambling but couldn't stop herself. "Truth is, I'd feel better if a policeman *did* come—"

"I can send someone over now, or you can wait until Ling gets back. Could be two, maybe three, hours. It's your call."

"Oh, I'll wait for Dan," Lauren said quickly, relieved she wouldn't have to explain the situation to a stranger. "I'll be happy to wait." She gave her name and address to the dispatcher. And then she waited.

She cleaned the kitchen and straightened her bed, barely able to believe that less than twenty-four hours ago, she and Gabe had made love here. Whatever was she going to do about Gabe? Todd had been so sweet at Friendly's; her hands had felt so comfortable in his. But she had a date with Gabe Tuesday night. Did this mean she was going to sleep with him again? Was she actually having an affair? Then her eyes went to the wastebasket and she saw the limp braid. She had bigger problems than Todd and Gabe. She glanced at her watch, hoping Dan would come soon.

Drew let her play space station with him, apparently forgiving her for her earlier behavior. But when, for the second time, she forgot they were orbiting planet Ganymede to save Earth from a wayward comet, Drew suggested, not unkindly, that she go read the paper. Lauren tried but found she was no better able to concentrate on world disasters than she had been on Drew's intergalactic ones.

Finally Dan showed up. Lauren had never seen him in uniform before, and he looked painfully young. "What's up?" he demanded as he strode into the apartment. "Everything all right?"

"Yes and no," she said.

"Let me have it quick," Dan said. "I've only got a few minutes. Helene's in a bad way, and I promised I'd come right home after my shift." He smiled sadly. "I guess our getaway didn't have the effect I'd hoped."

Drew popped out of his room and looked wide-eyed at Dan. "The police?" he breathed, a wide grin filling his face. "Here?"

"This is Dan Ling," Lauren told him. "Remember I was talking to him at the playground?"

"I didn't know he was the police." Drew was staring at Dan's gun. "Is it loaded?" he asked Dan.

Dan put his hand over the holster. "It's only for emergencies."

"Can I touch it?" Drew asked.

Dan shook his head. "Sorry, that's against regulations."

"Dan's just here for a cup of coffee," Lauren told Drew. "Why don't you go back to your space station and I'll call you when it's time for dinner?"

Drew threw one last glance at the gun but did as Lauren asked.

In a low voice, Lauren told Dan what had happened while he scribbled furiously in a small notebook. Then he made her take the candles and braid out of the wastebasket and set them up exactly as she had found them.

"Shit," he said, staring at the bureau. "A real voodoo warning." He quickly but thoroughly searched the apartment. "Anyone have a key?" he asked after finding no signs of forced entry.

"Todd, Aunt Beatrice," Lauren said slowly as they stood in the living room, "and Jackie. There was, still is I guess, a key hanging in her kitchen. . . ."

"With your name on it?" he demanded.

Lauren didn't answer as she tried to visualize the jumble of labeled keys hanging from the wall in Jackie's kitchen. They both knew Jackie well enough to know that a woman who kept an extra key to her own house in the mailbox would most likely have written Lauren's name on her key. Dan called a twenty-four-hour locksmith and told him to come over immediately.

Lauren offered to make a pot of coffee, but Dan shook his head and asked her to recount every detail of her day. When she was finished, he asked, "Who knew you were going to be out this morning?"

Lauren shrugged. "Lots of people. Aunt Beatrice, Todd, Gabe, Drew, Deborah, the other witches . . ."

"Do you happen to know if Deborah has ever been to Jackie's house?"

"At least a few times."

"I'm going to try Conway again," Dan said as they walked to the front door. "Even he's got to see there's a connection between Jackie's death and this break—" He cut himself off as Drew bounded out of his bedroom.

"What's for dinner?" Drew asked Lauren, although he was looking at Dan. "Is it time yet?"

"In a few minutes," Lauren said, trying not to think about Deborah drinking tea in Jackie's kitchen, about Jackie giving Deborah the Deodat Willard print, about Deborah taking advantage of Jackie's openness and generosity. "Go play for a bit and then we'll figure out something fun to eat."

Drew didn't move, his eyes locked on Dan's gun.

"Go," Lauren said, gently turning Drew toward his room.

Drew reluctantly went back to his Legos.

"I've got to get going too," Dan said. "But I wanted to let you know I finally got a copy of the autopsy report." He flipped quickly through his notebook. "It didn't show much. Jackie died from 'respiratory arrest secondary to a fracture of the cervical spine.' In other words"—Dan stuffed his book into an inside pocket of his jacket—"the fall broke her neck, which in turn cut the nerves telling her brain to keep her lungs going."

Lauren closed her eyes against the pictures and pain Dan's words evoked. "I've got something to tell you too," she said softly. "Something weird that happened at the ritual the other night."

"Why am I not surprised?"

Lauren took a deep breath and recounted the story of Nigel Hawkes. When she was finished, Dan didn't comment, but his lips were thin and his eyes cold.

He slammed his hat on his head. "If that locksmith doesn't show up within the hour, call him and tell him it's a police emergency. If he doesn't come right after that, call me and I'll come stay with you until he—"

"You don't have to do that," Lauren interrupted, although she was far from comfortable being alone in the apartment while some crazed maniac ran around the city with her key.

Dan held up his hands to stop her protests. "I'll do what I need to do—and I want you to do the same." At Lauren's quizzical look, he explained. "You need to stay away from RavenWing. If you insist on writing that damn book, and I wish like hell you wouldn't, then write it Phipps's way—without the witches and their chronicle."

Dan opened the door and started down the stairs, then he stopped and turned around. "You may think you need the money from this book to take care of Drew," he said, "but what Drew really needs is a mother who isn't dead."

To Lauren's relief, the locksmith arrived soon after Dan left. She and Drew made Drew's second favorite dinner—after Peking ravioli—hot-dogs slit in the middle, filled with American cheese, and wrapped in puff pastry. They read a whole *Goosebumps* book together before she put him to bed.

Lauren went to bed soon after Drew, but she was unable to sleep. Even with the new locks, the knowledge that someone had been in her apartment made her hypervigilant and edgy. She cruised the rooms in the empty hours of the night, checking and rechecking under every bed and couch, in every closet and cabinet. She looked in on Drew at least a dozen times. The thought crossed her mind that maybe no one had broken in, that the voodoo warning was another of Drew's misdirected bids for attention. But the episode was too bizarre and smacked of the occult. Drew could never have thought of it.

She wandered into the shadowy living room and flipped on the desk lamp, sending a cone of intense white light over the mess of papers on her desk. Lauren leafed through a pile of Jackie's files and pulled out a slim folder labeled: "Coven Members: Biographies." She sat down and opened it.

There was a page on each member of the lost coven. The approximate year of each person's birth was recorded, as were siblings, marriages, and children. After Rebeka's, Foster Lacy's biography was the longest, for he had been a doctor and therefore an especially well educated and revered member of the colony.

Lauren glanced down Foster's page. A Puritan minister, he had studied medicine in England in anticipation of his removal to America. He followed the teachings of the Greek physician Galen, and was known to prescribe vegetable substances and use "the lancet freely."

She slipped the page back into the folder and pulled out Faith Osborne's sheet. Jackie hadn't discovered much information, and the biography was short.

Born: circa 1665. No surviving siblings. Married Ezekiel Hoar (year ?). Ezekiel died: circa 1688. Daughter, Dorcas: 1685. Married Oliver Osborne, important magistrate: 1690. Dorcas hung as witch: 1692. Faith disappeared: 1692.

Lauren stared at the page before her and thought of the pain Faith must have endured. Losing her only child in such a horrid and senseless way. Born in 1685. Dead in 1692. Seven years old. If anything happened to Drew, Lauren didn't think she could survive it. Maybe that's what happened to Faith, she thought. Maybe she died of a broken heart.

Lauren tried to imagine herself as Faith. There would have been no lights in Faith's home to cut through the darkness; she leaned over and turned off the lamp. It would be cold; she took the afghan from the couch and wrapped it around her shoulders. Then she stood, her hand resting on the edge of the desk, and closed her eyes.

"Thou would do well to keep the child away from Rebeka Hibbens!"

Faith looked up from the table board she was readying. She carefully placed the linen napkins she held in her hand on the board cloth and drew her lace shawl more tightly around her. She pulled nervously at the cuffs of her dress. Her husband, Oliver Osborne, stood in the narrow doorway, his arms folded and his face red with fury.

"Rebeka Hibbens 'tis my cousin, sir," Faith said timidly, still slightly in awe of her husband, although they had been married almost two years. "She was most kind after Ezekiel was taken."

"Rebeka Hibbens is a witch doing the devil's work!" Oliver cried. "I've come to warn you off before it is too late to save your child's soul. I have it on good authority that Rebeka has taught Dorcas to cast spells with dead pit vipers stuffed with boar bristles."

Faith busied herself setting the saltcellar in the middle of the narrow table and placing the wood trencher from which she and Oliver would eat in front of their chairs. "Rebeka is the soul of kindness, and Dorcas has great fear of snakes," she finally said.

"Can thou not see the evil hand is upon her? Upon our colony?" Oliver demanded. "The smallpox. The failed wheat. We must unearth Satan's handmaidens before it is too late!"

Faith kept her eyes down, as she did not want Oliver to see the fear within them. Faith knew Dorcas was mischievous and troublesome, with a spirit both wild and wondrous. She also knew her daughter had been spending many hours with Rebeka at Millicent Glover's farm. "I'm sure it is nothing but idle gossip."

"Thou must tell me where the black magic is being done!" Oliver ordered. "'Tis the only way to stop the evil Goody Hibbens and Goody Glover bring upon your daughter and this house!"

"There is no black magic, sir," Faith said, her eyes on the table. "Of this I am certain."

"It matters not that you are my wife, nor that Dorcas is your daughter. If the child is not separated from those who do witchcraft, she too shall be punished!"

"Thou would not protect us?" Faith gasped, unable

to believe her husband would not keep them from harm.

"There is no protection from Satan," Oliver said as he turned and walked from the room.

"Sir!" Faith cried, lifting her hands beseechingly toward her husband. But instead of a lace shawl and white cuffs, she saw a ratty afghan covering the terry cloth sleeves of a bathrobe. And instead of the retreating back of Oliver Osborne, Lauren saw the first rays of morning sun hitting the dark screen of her computer.

Lauren parked her car next to the portico of Gabe's Victorian house. It was one of an impressive queue of mansions that lined Brattle Street as the road ran out of Harvard Square toward Watertown. She had been here before for Gabe's annual department picnics. Looking up at the towering roofline, at what appeared to be hundreds of windows staring down at her, her stomach clenched.

She jerked the car door open, climbed out, and slammed it closed with her foot. Swinging her purse to her shoulder, she marched up the wide stairs of the veranda to Gabe's front door. She raised her finger to the doorbell, then dropped her hand to her side and stood staring at the intricate carving on the huge oak door. Was she doing the right thing? She had been so caught up in her infatuation with Gabe, and admittedly with his position and prestige, that she hadn't carefully considered her actions. Technically, she was still a married woman.

No, Lauren thought, she was *not* a married woman. She and Todd had been separated for more than a year, and just last month she had filed for divorce. They had lawyers and papers and temporary child custody arrangements. Despite Todd's sweetness on Sunday and her own disappointment over her failed marriage, she was single and free and thirty-eight years old. She could go out with whomever she pleased. Lauren jabbed the doorbell.

As soon as Gabe opened the door and ushered her into the house, Lauren knew something was wrong. He kissed her hello and took her coat and offered her a drink, but he seemed distracted, slightly distant. Lines of worry were etched deeply around his eyes.

She followed him through the large foyer, past the sweeping front staircase and the narrow back one and into the kitchen. He handed her a glass of wine, a bright smile on his face. But his smile didn't reach his eyes.

"Is something wrong, Gabe? Should we do this some other time?" she asked, half hoping he would agree.

"Absolutely not," he declared, pointing to a cast iron pot on the stove. "I've cooked up a huge batch of paella, and if you don't help me eat it, I'll be stuck with it for months. And anyway," he walked over and put his arms around her, "this is all I've been thinking about since Saturday night." He gave her a long, slow kiss, and Lauren was glad he hadn't sent her home. Then he pulled away.

Lauren wanted to believe him—and part of her knew that on one level he was being sincere—but it was also clear that Gabe was thinking about something else. She remembered how nice her hands had felt in Todd's and realized that she was thinking about something else too. No, she told herself, Gabe was trying to overcome his worries. She would also.

She leaned over the stove. "Smells wonderful."

"I decided against gourmet," Gabe said as he squeezed water out of three different kinds of lettuce. "Somehow you didn't seem the heavy sauce, artful presentation type."

Lauren lifted the cover off the pot and the most wonderful aroma filled the air. "Good guess," she said. "This—whatever this is—is my kind of food."

"It's the saffron that makes it smell so good." He held up a tiny glass jar filled with fine red, ribbony strands. "Pound for pound, this stuff is more valuable than gold. Wars have been fought over it."

"I've smelled worse reasons for war."

Gabe's laughter filled the room, and for the first time that evening he looked like himself. "I knew there was a reason I was looking forward to your company," he said, raising his wineglass.

Lauren touched her glass to his. Noticing the plants overflowing the window ledge over his sink, she asked, "Do you grow your own herbs?"

He nodded. "More in the summer. These are the hearty ones that survive my benign neglect."

She looked more closely at the neat triple rows of small pots. She recognized basil, mint, and parsley, but the others were a mystery. Leaning over, she took a deep breath. The fresh smell that rose from the herbs was reminiscent of spring and meadows and the place by Hubbard Lake where she had played as a child. "They look pretty well tended to me."

"One of the few positive remnants of my marriage," Gabe said as he chopped mushrooms. "Deborah taught me all about herbs—how to use them, how to grow them—and for that I'll be forever grateful to her."

"But not for much else?" Lauren teased.

Gabe raised an eyebrow. "You know how it is."

Lauren found herself thinking of the many things for which she was grateful to Todd. The appreciation he had imbued in her for the visual beauty that surrounded her every day. The way he had taught her to turn the world on its side and laugh at its absurdity. And, of course, she was grateful for Drew. But she said, "Oh yeah, I know exactly how it is."

They had dinner in the dining room, a formal but surprisingly intimate room, with a circular mural depicting a nineteenth-century fox hunt in deep forest greens and russet earth tones that covered all four walls. The food was as good as any Lauren had had in the finest restaurant, and she marveled at Gabe's many talents.

"So, how'd it go with Deborah on Sunday?" he asked. "Did you get anything worthwhile for *Rebeka Hibbens*?"

"It was pretty much just as you predicted," Lauren said slowly, figuring she'd start with RavenWing and work her way up to Nigel Hawkes and the break-in. "Deborah definitely lives in a world of her own."

Gabe shook his head in bewilderment when she described what Deborah had said about the Immortalis. "It's hard to imagine they could fear life so much that they would be willing to kill themselves to avoid living another one."

Lauren's eyes widened. "Deborah stressed the Immortalis is a reenactment," she said. "I can't believe they'd really kill themselves."

"I hope you're right," Gabe replied, staring off into the fox hunt. "I saw that lancet once. I should have destroyed it when I had the chance. That thing's their holy grail—the symbol of Deborah's misguided evil."

Lauren looked at him in surprise, reminded of how Deborah had referred to Gabe as evil also. Perhaps divorce was the real evil here. "Don't you think that's taking it all a bit too seriously?"

"Those people believe everything Deborah tells them. They think if the lancet is destroyed they will be too." Gabe stabbed his fork into the paella. "Once those poor people realized the lancet was destroyed and that they were still alive, they would be thrown into disarray. That would break down their misguided belief system and end the coven." Gabe's voice had risen and his face was slightly flushed.

Lauren figured it was time to change the subject. "Anyway, after about an hour of listening to Deborah's stories of magic and sages, I had had enough."

"Are you going back?"

Lauren shrugged. "I'm torn," she said. "On the one hand there doesn't seem to be much point, but on the other . . ."

"On the other?" Gabe prompted.

Lauren looked at the laugh lines webbing Gabe's dark eyes, at the interest and compassion on his face. "I've been having strange experiences lately," she said slowly. "Weird dreams at night and even weirder ones during the day—and somehow I keep thinking that maybe Deborah can help me understand them." She briefly told him about the girl in the cornfield and Oliver Osborne and being chained in a seventeenth-century dungeon.

Gabe placed his hand over hers. "I'm sure the daydreams and nightmares are just the result of too much work and too much stress—although be careful you don't get so lost in history that you lose your ability to separate fact from fantasy." He raised an eyebrow. "Like someone we know."

"I'm nothing like Deborah," Lauren said quickly.

"I'm sure you're not."

"Want to hear something else strange?" Lauren asked, encouraged by his response. At his nod, she told him about the break-in and Dan's increased suspicions about Jackie's death. "Dan thinks I should stay away from RavenWing," Lauren said in conclusion. "He says if I have to do the book, I should do it your way—without Deborah's chronicle."

Gabe had fallen silent and pale while she told her story. He cleared his throat. "This break-in sounds serious. Ling is absolutely right—you *must* stay away from Deborah and her crazies." He picked up her hand and rubbed her knuckle against his cheek. "Please let me help you with the book," he said, uncurling her fingers and kissing her palm. "Promise me you won't go back to that store."

Lauren was amazed by the serious expression on

his face, by the concern in his voice, by the pulse of electrical attraction that raced from her palm. "I promise," she said.

Although Gabe seemed pleased with her answer, Lauren could feel his attention slipping away. Not one to pry, she tried to keep the conversation going. They gossiped a bit about Terri and critiqued the plots of a few mysteries they had both read. She mentioned that Drew's turtle had disappeared. Apparently, Herman had climbed out of his dish, but whether he was still in the apartment or had fallen from Drew's open window, they didn't know. She and Drew had looked everywhere, including the bushes and the yard, but Herman was nowhere to be found.

"Is the little guy very upset?" Gabe asked.

"He's taking it pretty hard," Lauren said, touched by Gabe's interest. "But the tough part is that Herman's irreplaceable—unless I take a trip to Spain."

Gabe nodded in sympathy and they struggled on with their conversation, but the cloud around Gabe seemed to darken and, as they drank their coffee, silence fell. She stared into her cup and wondered what consolation she could possibly offer him for a problem he wouldn't share. Lauren decided it would be better for them both if she left. Looking up, she caught him watching her sadly. "Gabe," she began.

"Don't say anything." He took her hands and pressed them between his. "This has nothing to do with you—it's something else entirely. Something I'm not free to discuss." He regarded her with such pain and longing that Lauren's heart went out to him. "I want what happens between us to be as good as it can be."

Lauren nodded. "I understand."

He stood up and pulled her to her feet. "I can't give you all you deserve tonight." They put their arms around each other's waists and walked toward the door. Gabe picked up Lauren's jacket and purse from the living room couch. He helped her on with her jacket, then pressed her close for a long moment. "I've got to go to Washington tomorrow, but I should be back by the end of the week." He kissed her on the forehead. "I'll call you then."

Lauren nodded and, as if in a trance, walked out the door. She heard it click behind her and once again found herself standing alone on the veranda. She didn't know if she was disappointed or relieved.

Lauren called Deborah first thing the next morning and canceled their meeting. "I appreciate all your help, but I've decided to give this book a go on my own," she said. "Reincarnation and the supernatural just aren't my areas of expertise, and I don't see how I can write a book based on them." Although Lauren knew Nat would be furious if he learned she was making this call, she consoled herself with the thought of Dan and Gabe's approval. "I'm pretty sure I can come up with a way of handling *Rebeka Hibbens* that will keep my editor happy," she added, hoping that somehow she and Gabe would be able to make her words come true.

Deborah hesitated before saying, "Oh, that's too bad. I had some good news for you."

"Good news?" Lauren asked, wondering whether she was making the right decision. "What good news?"

"Well," Deborah said slowly, "the coven met yesterday and we discussed the curse of the chronicle. And, ah, after a long deliberation, we decided that it's highly unlikely Jackie's death had anything to do with the curse. . . ." She paused before continuing. "So, this being the case, we thought we'd be willing to share it with you."

"The chronicle?" Lauren breathed, visions of diplomas and royalty checks floating in front of her eyes. "When?"

"There's, ah, one stipulation," Deborah said haltingly, as if she were stalling for time. "I reread the portion of the chronicle that discusses the curse and, ah, my interpretation is that, if the reader participates in a waxing crescent ritual, then he or she will not be susceptible to the curse."

"I already participated in—"

"That was with the Wiccans," Deborah interrupted quickly. "This must be with just the coven."

"Are you saying that if I come to the next waxing crescent ritual you'll let me read the chronicle?" Lauren was incredulous.

"That's right."

Lauren could hardly believe her good fortune. Then she thought about the break-in, and Dan and Gabe's suspicions about Deborah and the coven, and she wasn't sure if her fortune had changed for the better.

"The next waxing crescent is December eighth," Deborah was saying. "Less than three weeks away. And the best part is that it's the night of the Immortalis—when we reenact the glorious 1692 ritual."

"Sounds very interesting." Lauren said slowly. Did she dare risk attending another ritual? Or involving herself with these crazy, perhaps even dangerous, people?

"The Immortalis is a fascinating event. I'm sure you'll enjoy it immensely."

Lauren thought quickly. Dan and Gabe might not want her going to RavenWing or spending time with Deborah, but if all she had to do to make Nat happy was participate in a silly ritual . . .

"I'd-I'd love to," she said, figuring she could always back out at the last minute.

"You won't be sorry," Deborah told her warmly.

"I'm sure I won't."

Twenty-One

AFTER TALKING WITH DEBORAH, LAUREN SAT DOWN TO compile a list of Jackie's occult contacts for Dan. But before she got a single number transcribed, Dan called. They hadn't spoken since he'd come by after the break-in.

"Bad news again," he began. "Lieutenant Conway doesn't think someone breaking into your house and burning candles is—to quote him—'sufficient reason to assume foul play in a completely separate incident,' and he won't open an investigation into Jackie's death. This despite the fact that Deborah Sewall and Cassandra Abbott, along with someone named Bram Melgram, have been on Zaleski's 'cult watch' list for years." Dan paused and sighed. "Conway flashed one of his smiles that says I'm just an overeager rookie, but this time he showed lots more teeth."

"Not a good sign, I suppose," Lauren said.

"Not good at all."

"I'm working on that occult list for you."

"Good," Dan said. "But you know, I've been thinking. What if witches didn't murder Jackie? What if we've been looking at this all wrong? What if the motive was normal human greed?"

"How could greed be the motive?" Lauren asked, wondering if perhaps Lieutenant Conway's assessment of Dan's overeagerness was correct. "Jackie didn't have any money."

"She had the Deodat Willard print."

"Are you saying Simon murdered Jackie to get the print back?" Lauren was incredulous. Then she remembered Simon's fingers digging into her arm and the icy fury of his words. *"Just make sure her name isn't on that book."* Simon Pappas was not a nice man. Still, that didn't make him a murderer. "You think your father-in-law killed his children's mother for a painting?"

"I suppose not," Dan said. "And I've got an even more absurd suspect for you—your friend Gabe Phipps."

"What?"

"Helene was contacted last week about some federal grant Jackie and Gabe did together eight years ago."

"The National Endowment for the Humanities project," Lauren said slowly. As she spoke, she recalled Simon Pappas goading Gabe at the restaurant. She struggled to remember what Simon had said. Something about rumors of trouble and Jackie's records.

"Right," Dan said. "Apparently, the feds discovered a big chunk of money missing, and Jackie's the only one who would have been able to corroborate—or contradict—Phipps's account of where it went. They wanted Helene to go through Jackie's files and see if she could find anything."

Lauren remembered Gabe's glum mood and distraction last night. This must be what he hadn't wanted to talk about. This was why he was going to

Washington. She recalled the worry in his eyes, and her heart lurched in apprehension.

"—couldn't find anything," Dan was saying. "And I guess it means some pretty serious trouble for Phipps. They used words like 'misappropriation of funds' and 'embezzlement.' "

Lauren thought of the last scandal in the department, when an article Benjamin Greerson had written for *The American Historical Review* was found to be plagiarized. Greerson had lost his job, his career—even his wife—and the university had lost Greerson's large research grant, wreaking havoc with the department's budget for years. Lauren realized she was biting her cuticle as she listened to Dan and she yanked her finger from her mouth.

"Gabe doesn't need to embezzle money," she said. "He's got plenty of his own. And there's no way he killed Jackie."

"Just bear with me," Dan said. "Did Gabe ever express any interest in helping you with *Rebeka Hibbens* before Jackie died?"

"Of course not," Lauren snapped. "Before Jackie died I didn't need any help."

"Had he shown any personal interest in you?" Dan persisted. "Why did he choose this particular time—right after Jackie's death—to start up a relationship?"

"What could Gabe possibly stand to gain from dating me—or from helping me with my dissertation?"

"I don't know," Dan conceded. "It doesn't make much sense, but on the other hand, why would a man like Gabe Phipps suddenly offer to help a graduate student he barely knew with her dissertation?"

"Maybe he thinks I'm cute."

Dan chuckled. "Touché."

"I think this whole line of inquiry is off base," Lauren said. "And I think that you do—" She was interrupted by the buzzing of her intercom. "Someone's downstairs. Let me call you back."

"No need," Dan said. "Just give me a ring when you've got that list together and we can take it from there."

As Lauren hung up the phone, there was a knock on the door. It must be Todd. He had keys—to both the front door and the apartment—but she had insisted when he moved out that he not use them unless she wasn't home. As she pulled open the door, she made a mental note to get Todd a key to the new lock.

"Hi," Todd said, striding into the hallway. "I was supposed to be in Boston fifteen minutes ago, but I had to talk to you."

Lauren followed him into the living room, wondering who in Boston was going to be very annoyed. She was glad it wasn't her. "Want some coffee?"

Todd dropped into his favorite chair and put his head in his hands.

"What is it?" Lauren demanded. "Is Drew okay?" Tuesday nights Drew stayed with Todd. She hadn't seen her son since yesterday morning when he had left for school. "What?"

"Drew's fine," Todd said, lifting his head. "Or he's fine physically, anyway."

Lauren sat down on the couch near Todd's chair. "You talked to Dr. Berg?" When Todd had called Dr. Berg on Monday to discuss their concerns, the school secretary had said the psychologist was out of town until Wednesday. "What did she say?"

"One of Drew's paintings from art class is on display in the school lobby, so when I brought him to school this morning he took me inside to see it," Todd explained. "Since I was already there, I stopped by Dr. Berg's office. I told her about Bunny and the little girl in the playground."

"And?"

Todd looked down at his hands then back at her. "She said he's using his anger in very inappropriate ways, and that despite the fact that he hurt his own property, his behavior is cause for great concern." Todd paused and Lauren touched his knee. He let out a shuddering breath. "She said we have to watch him very carefully. That if he does something like this again . . ."

"If he does something like this again?" Lauren prompted, pulling her hand from his knee.

"Then he'll need a complete evaluation by a psychiatrist. She recommended someone at McLean."

Lauren stared at Todd. McLean. McLean was where Deborah had been locked up for psychotic delusions. Where Bram had spent time. It wasn't a place for Drew. Not for her sweet little boy. "I can't believe it would come to that," she said, tears filling her eyes.

"Dr. Berg said she'd check in with him a few more times over the next couple weeks, and that we should be especially loving and supportive."

"We can do that," Lauren said, coming to sit on the arm of Todd's chair. He reached up and hugged her. She kissed the top of his head and held on to him tightly. They sat quietly for a long moment.

Todd jumped to his feet. "I've got to go," he cried, glancing at his watch. As she stood to follow him, he turned and said, "I almost forgot, I've got a favor to ask. I have plans Sunday afternoon, so can you pick up Drew earlier than usual? Say around two o'clock?"

"Sure," Lauren said. "No problem."

"Thanks," he said, his face grim as he opened the door. "See you then."

As Lauren watched Todd walk down the stairs, she thought of how sweet he had been at Friendly's on Sunday, how nice it would be to be a family again, how happy it would make Drew. She remembered a dress she had seen in the window of a consignment shop on Mass Ave. It was short and clingy, yet still casual. Just the kind of dress Todd found irresistibly sexy. She would buy it and wear it on Sunday. They could take it from there.

* * *

Dorcas stood on the edge of a meadow, facing a dense green wood. "Come bunnies, come!" she commanded. She pulled up the hem of her long gray skirt and knelt on the ground. "Now!"

There was a fluttering of underbrush, and suddenly dozens of rabbits leapt from the woods and scampered over to where she squatted.

"Good bunnies, good," Dorcas cooed as the animals jumped on her knees and nuzzled her about the ankles. "Good little bunnies."

"No!" Lauren cried. "You mustn't!" Startled by the sound of her own voice, Lauren became aware of the hum of the car's engine, of the steering wheel under her fingers, of the warmth of the sun on her face. She blinked at the sparse foliage clinging to the tree branches. Autumn, she thought, somewhat dazed, it was late autumn. But where was she? Suddenly terrified, she pulled the car off the road.

Yanking up the parking brake, she took stock. It was Sunday, the tail end of November 1995. She was driving west out of the city, trying to cheer herself with a bit of fall foliage before picking up Drew at Todd's. She looked around at the last wisps of autumn color, the rusted reds and brown-yellows. Yes, she was definitely in western Massachusetts. But how far west? And how had she gotten here?

Icy runners of fear shot through Lauren's chest and formed a knot in her throat. She remembered leaving her apartment at eleven-thirty that morning. She could visualize herself driving through the suburbs of Lexington and Concord, thinking what nice places these towns must be to raise a family. But this was no suburb. This was wooded and hilly and rural—and quite far from Cambridge.

Filled with trepidation, Lauren looked down at the clock on the dashboard. It was one o'clock. She had lost a full hour. Gone. She had descended into what she was beginning to think of as her personal black hole. A black hole in which she had watched Dorcas Osborne tame wild rabbits.

Lauren dropped her head to the steering wheel. Her black holes had been coming more frequently of late, and they were of longer duration. Just yesterday she had forgotten her ATM number. She had stood pushing buttons frantically on the machine, trying to recall a number she had used almost daily for five years. But that small memory lapse didn't compare with her waking fugues. Fugue states that she had initially summoned to better understand the seventeenth century. Fugue states that were now getting out of her control.

The fugues were becoming frighteningly real. She fell into them more deeply and stayed longer. And now they were appearing when she hadn't summoned them. Could there be something physically wrong with her? A brain tumor? Early Alzheimer's? Or were the fugues the not-so-unexpected result of dealing with a divorce, a troubled son, and the death of her best friend? Maybe it was the stress of writing the book, of spending so much of her life immersed in a time and place that were not her own.

Lauren stared, unseeing, through the windshield. Todd and Jackie had warned her about her tendency to use work as an escape from reality. And Gabe had remarked that, if she wasn't careful, she would become like Deborah—so lost in history she could no longer separate fantasy from fact. At the time, Lauren had insisted she wasn't like Deborah, but suddenly she wasn't so certain.

Lauren took a deep breath and turned the car around. She might not know exactly where she was, but she knew it would take her at least until two o'clock—the agreed-upon pickup time—to get to Todd's. As she settled in for the trip, she once again found herself wondering about Todd. And Gabe.

Gabe had come home from Washington on Thursday and called the next morning to see if she was available for dinner Saturday night. "I don't think we should see each other for a while," she had told him. There was silence at the other end of the line, and Lauren's palms began to sweat.

"Is this because of the NEH investigation?" Gabe finally asked.

The department had been buzzing with the news all week. After a number of improprieties had been found, the federal government had begun an audit of all university grants. The National Endowment for the Humanities had been particularly vigilant. While reviewing their records, they had found $100,000 in unsubstantiated charges in Gabe and Jackie's final budget report.

"You don't believe I'd do anything like that, do you?" Gabe asked Lauren.

"No," she told him. "I know you wouldn't. And anyway, it's not like the Benjamin Greerson thing—it's not like it was plagiarism."

"It's just a paperwork screwup," Gabe said quickly. "But my meetings in D.C. were a disaster. It was clear from their attitude that if I don't find the backup receipts to support my position, they're going to hang me out to dry." Gabe's sigh was audible. "They want to send a message, and they figure if they do it with someone as visible as I am, they'll get a bigger audience."

"You haven't been able to find any of the receipts?"

"Nope—and neither has Jackie's family. But they've got to be somewhere. Terri's working on it and so am I. The receipts exist—and they'll prove my innocence—but we may have to go through twenty years of files to find them." He paused, then asked, "So why don't you want to have dinner with me?"

"It has nothing to do with you," Lauren said, which was both true and untrue. It was mostly because of

Todd—and Drew—and her sudden indecision about the state of her marriage. But she had to admit it was also because of the doubts Dan had planted in her mind. *"Why did he choose this particular time—right after Jackie's death—to start up a relationship with you?"* Dan had asked. *"Why would a man like Gabe Phipps suddenly offer to help a graduate student he barely knew with her dissertation?"* Although Lauren knew the questions were ridiculous, Dan's queries had left her uncomfortable.

"It's not you," she repeated, "or anything directly involved with you and me. This is about me. About decisions I need to make in my life."

"Do you still want my help with *Rebeka Hibbens*?"

"Of course I do," Lauren assured him. "But I've got at least a month—probably more like five months—of work to do on my own. I've tons of rewriting and integrating of Jackie's materials, and I'm still collecting new data: from the library, Jackie's notes . . ." She paused before adding, "When I called Deborah to cancel my meeting—as I promised I would—she said she might let me read the chronicle after all."

There was a long pause. "Do you think that's smart?" Gabe finally asked. "Are you going to do it?"

"Let me work on the book on my own for a while," Lauren said, avoiding a direct answer. "And let me work through my personal stuff. Then we'll talk about everything."

"I'm not going to overstep and try to tell you what to do about your personal life." Gabe's voice was hollow with resignation. "Although I wish to hell you wouldn't close me out—"

"I'm not closing you out," Lauren protested. "It's just more than I can handle right now."

"Whatever," Gabe had said. "I just want you to think twice about getting involved with Deborah and her cult. You know she's nuts—and the rest of them probably are too. I still feel very strongly that they, and their chronicle, should be left alone."

Recalling the conversation now, Lauren was touched again by Gabe's concern, but it didn't change her mind about slowing down their relationship. As she drove into Lexington, heading for Todd's, the wind kicked up and the last remaining leaves fluttered in the sunlight. She needed to give Todd a chance. For his sake, for Drew's, and for her own.

Todd had rented an apartment in Somerville not far from the elevated section of Route 93—if you could call his converted garage an apartment, and if you could call the garage converted. Two pretty big "ifs" as far as Lauren was concerned. The garage was squeezed behind two seedy triple deckers, its back pushed up against a rusted chain link fence. The place had no pretensions of being anything other than what it was: an old garage in which indoor-outdoor carpet had been laid and a side door and toilet added. The previous tenant had left a small refrigerator, and Todd had bought a hot plate. Drew thought it was really cool. Lauren and Todd hated it.

Lauren climbed from her car and locked it quickly, checking over her shoulder a couple of times as she walked between the shabby houses toward Todd's garage. But she need not have bothered. On this cold Sunday afternoon, no one was about. The only sound was the roar of the highway.

Drew threw open the door as soon as she knocked. "Look what Daddy got me," he cried, turning and running to an old card table next to the refrigerator. He lifted a videotape and waved it at her.

Lauren followed and grabbed him. "It's nice to see you too, Drew," she said, laughing and nuzzling his neck. "I missed you a lot."

He squirmed out of her arms. "It's about witches, just like your book," he said, handing her the tape box. "*Hocus Pocus*. Can we go home and watch it right now? Please, please, please, please, please? I've been waiting since yesterday." Todd didn't have a VCR.

Lauren glanced over Drew's head to where Todd was sitting on the edge of the bed. Todd stood and she was struck by how handsome he looked. He was wearing a forest-green cotton shirt that brought out the green in his hazel eyes and a new pair of jeans that accentuated the narrowness of his hips and the broadness of his shoulders. His dark hair had been recently cut and, if she hadn't known better, she would have thought he had blown it dry. He gave her a characteristic lanky shrug and grinned. "It was on the buck table at the store," he said.

Lauren blinked, so affected by Todd's physical appearance that she didn't understand what he was saying. She felt breathless and a bit light-headed. "Buck table," she repeated stupidly.

"At Caldor's," Drew explained with exaggerated patience. "We went to get Daddy a clock radio and I saw it on a table. It was only a dollar, so Daddy said I could have it." Drew pulled at her sleeve. "Can we go home now? Please?"

Lauren wasn't listening to Drew. She was still looking at Todd, who was walking slowly toward her. "That's a pretty dress," he said, his eyes never leaving hers. "You don't usually wear that kind of style." He smiled at her. "You look like one of your Puritan women."

Lauren looked down at her long gray dress. She smoothed the crossed linen stays of the bodice, then tugged nervously at the lace cuffs. "I went into the secondhand store to buy a short dress," she said, her voice reflecting the amazement she still felt at her choice, "but somehow when I saw this, it looked so perfect on the hanger, and I-I just wanted it."

"It becomes you, Laurie." Todd kissed her cheek lightly.

"Thank you." Lauren pulled Drew to her as if he

offered protection against the onrush of feelings. She felt the imprint of Todd's lips on her skin long after he'd stepped away. Looking at his craggy, familiar face, she wanted to tell him she had broken up with Gabe, that she wasn't sure she wanted to go through with the divorce.

"I—" she began, but stopped. *"I have plans Sunday afternoon,"* Todd had said. The clothes. The haircut. Lauren suddenly realized why Todd looked so nice. He had a date.

He smiled at her, that big-toothed smile that always sliced through her. "You . . ." he prompted.

She looked down at the videotape in her hand to hide the tears that had sprung to her eyes. "You, ah, you told me you had someplace to go this afternoon," she said quickly, then turned to Drew. "This looks good, honey. It's set in Salem, where the most famous witch trials were held. The same time as my book."

"Can we make popcorn and watch it together on the couch?" Drew begged.

Lauren knelt down and pulled Drew to her. She held him tightly. "Sure," she said. "It'll be fun." She gave him a perky smile, but what she really wanted to do was cry.

When Lauren and Drew arrived home, Drew went straight to the VCR while Lauren made popcorn. By the time she joined him, he was already lost in the movie. Lauren snuggled down next to her son, hoping to lose herself too. But she couldn't rid her mind of the picture of Todd with another woman.

She kissed Drew and whispered that she would be right back. He nodded distractedly. Wandering into the hallway, Lauren heard Natasha, the four-year-old who lived downstairs, singing a "Sesame Street" tune in a tiny, high voice. There was something lonely and plaintive in the little girl's song that wrenched Lauren. She went to the kitchen window and gazed through the bare branches at the empty street below.

Although the leaves on the big oak across the street were past their prime, an amazing number still clung to the tree. Here it was, almost the end of November, and the leaves were still fighting to hang on. Conceding to winter doldrums was no way to deal with her problems. She had an afternoon to spend with her son, and a week stretched before her with no distractions, no mysteries of either the heart or the mind to solve. With no Todd and no Gabe, she would be able to concentrate on her work. With no Deborah—at least until the Immortalis more than two weeks away—she would be able to separate herself from everything associated with the supernatural. She would focus on the historical *Rebeka Hibbens* and give Drew all the love and support Dr. Berg said he needed.

Turning from the window, she headed back to the living room. She picked the little boy up and placed him in her lap, pretending to be as interested as he was in the movie.

When the movie was over, they had a quick dinner and played Boggle Junior until it was time for Drew to go to sleep. Lauren showered and climbed into bed with the latest Anne Tyler novel, just out in paperback. But as much as she loved Tyler, within minutes the book sagged in her hand. Lauren turned off the light and was quickly asleep.

She dreamed she was having lunch with Deborah in Gabe's dining room. Deborah did not look well. She was much older and more worn than when Lauren had last seen her. Deep wrinkles were etched into her skin and the red cloak that hung around her shoulders was ripped and dirty. But Deborah didn't seem to notice how old she had become or how she was dressed. She nibbled on her salad and smiled at Lauren. "A mother is responsible for the fate of her child," she said.

Lauren took a bite of her sandwich and looked at Deborah questioningly.

"If something bad happens to a child—perhaps that child dies—then it is the mother's fault. Especially if the mother did not heed the warnings."

Lauren was filled with terror. What did Deborah know of Drew's troubles? Of the warnings they had received? But before she could speak, Cassandra walked out of the fox-hunt mural on the wall and stood before her. She was as disheveled as Deborah, her dress ripped at the shoulder and her long skirt streaked with dirt.

"You are not only responsible for what has befallen your child," Cassandra screamed at Lauren, "you are responsible for all that has transpired." Then she fixed Lauren with a piercing stare. "You have betrayed us, and for your sins you shall be punished."

Lauren started to stand and inform this awful woman in the soiled dress that Drew was safe in his bed, but when she tried to rise, she found she was frozen in her chair; her arms and legs were like lead and even her lips refused to move. Cassandra had paralyzed her.

"All witches must die," Deborah and Cassandra began to sing in the high treble tones of nasty schoolchildren. "Hung at dawn until dead," they taunted. The singsongy dirge grew louder and louder until it swirled around Lauren and she thought she would smother in it. "All witches must die, hung at dawn until dead."

Gasping for breath, Lauren opened her eyes. She was relieved to find she was safe and alone in her bedroom, although the tinny strains of the horrid chant still rang in her ears and fear gripped her like a vise. Half asleep, she rummaged in her night table drawer for her dream journal and the little flashlight. Shining the light on the page, Lauren scribbled down her dream, hoping she'd be able to sort it out in the morning. Then she dropped her head to the pillow and, surprisingly, fell quickly back to sleep.

It seemed only a moment before it was morning. As Lauren pulled herself into the day, she caught a fleeting wisp of her dream and was once again filled with fear. Anxious to read what she had written, she pushed herself up in the bed and reached for her journal. But when she flipped to the last page, she froze. The handwriting wasn't hers: The letters were narrow and stylized with flourishes and swooping Ss and Fs. And the words were even stranger than the penmanship.

Last night, Rebeka Hibbens and Millicent Glover visited me as I slept. Rebeka was weak and low and her cloak was covered with mud. She spoke of betrayal and punishment. Of how my girl Dorcas might die if I do not heed the warnings. Millicent said it was not only what befell Dorcas for which she holds me responsible, but also for all else that has transpired. I cannot fathom the meaning of their words in the world of the waking; Dorcas lies safely sleeping on her pallet and I know of no warnings.

Although others may laugh at my folly, I hold there be truth in dreams. And I cannot hold back from wondering what to make of this one. I fear it means Dorcas's life is in grave danger, and that Rebeka Hibbens and Millicent Glover wish me dead.

Twenty-Two

CASSANDRA PUSHED A FEW LOOSE HAIRS INTO HER braid and said to Bram, "I think kidnapping her is a bit extreme." She turned to Deborah. "Couldn't we put a watch on her instead, Mahala? Follow her everywhere she goes for the next two weeks? If she hasn't remembered in thirty-odd years, a couple of dreams don't necessarily mean she's going to remember now."

Deborah picked up the lancet from where it lay on the altar behind her. She opened the wooden case and spread the blades into a fan. The members of the coven watched her every move. "Although Lauren only told me two dreams, I feel there have been more," she said. "These dreams are a warning from the sages. We must listen closely and heed their words."

It was the night between waxing crescents, the waning gibbous, two weeks before the Immortalis. An icy rain had forced the coven inside for their ritual, and the six were assembled in the back room of RavenWing.

"I fear it's more than just the dreams." Deborah closed the lancet and laid it reverently on the altar. "Someone is trying to scare Lauren away from us." She told them about the Bellarmine urn and the poppets with their accompanying warning notes.

There was a collective gasp followed by a stunned silence as the full meaning of Deborah's words registered.

Bram's face went white and his eye ring fluttered. "But, but why?" he stuttered.

Deborah shook her head. "The sages do not allow us to know all."

Alva played a few plaintive notes on her flute and then rested it in her lap, but instead of her usual glazed stare, her eyes were riveted on Deborah. Robin moved her chair closer to Alva's and placed her arm around the smaller woman's shoulders, then she turned quickly back to Deborah.

"What should we do?" Tamar asked.

Deborah looked at the small flock huddled before her. They were so frightened, so unnerved. She was their "wise one," their Mahala. They looked to her to reassure them, to teach them, to show them a new way of seeing, of believing, of living.

She smiled benevolently upon her worried brood. "Fear not. There is far too much at stake for a single human to be allowed to stand in our way. We shall reach the sages. And we shall live amongst them forever. I will let nothing stop us," she added, her voice rising.

Deborah stood and walked to the altar. "I will keep Lauren Freeman safe. I will keep Lauren Freeman near. And I will keep Lauren Freeman from remembering." She placed the lancet on the altar behind her. "I'll bind a spell." She turned the altar slightly, facing it north, then realigned the tools that lay on top: obsidian to the east, blood to the west, hangman's noose to the south, the lancet to the north.

Cassandra handed Deborah a cracked mirror. "Do you think it's wise to risk the energy drain so close to the Immortalis?"

Furious at Cassandra's impertinence, Deborah turned her back on the older woman. She placed the mirror in the center of the altar and arranged a black candle on either side. Reaching beneath the velvet cloth, she pulled out the turquoise stone that had belonged to Lauren.

Deborah turned her eyes to Cassandra, who blanched. "If we lose Lauren, there will be no Immortalis," she said, her voice outlining each word in cold steel.

Cassandra bowed and, with trembling hands, placed two small caldrons, one filled with seeds and the other with saltwater, above the mirror. "Of course, Mahala," she whispered. "Forgive me for questioning you."

Deborah nodded curtly. "Let us begin." Everyone stood and she cast the circle. After lighting the candles, she sprinkled saltwater on Lauren's turquoise. She raised the stone. "This turquoise is not a piece of inert rock," she said. "This turquoise beats with life and is covered by flesh. This turquoise *is* Lauren Freeman."

Deborah wrapped her fingers tightly around the stone and closed her eyes, focusing her inner mind on Lauren sitting in the beanbag chair, her knees sticking up in awkward discomfort. When Deborah felt the heat of the stone rising beneath her hands, she visualized a fisherman's net falling over Lauren, enclosing her. "From this waning gibbous until the next waxing crescent, you will stay close and you will stay safe, and then you will willingly and joyously join us for the great Immortalis." She passed the stone to Cassandra, who nodded her appreciation for the simplicity and efficiency of the spell.

"From this waning gibbous to the next waxing crescent, you will stay close and you will stay safe, and then you will willingly and joyously join us for the great Immortalis," Cassandra said. The stone was passed from one to another, and the words were repeated by all except Alva until it returned to Deborah.

Deborah squeezed the stone between her palms and closed her eyes, concentrating on visualizing the event she wanted to take place. She felt Lauren's taut skin give way under the lancet as she, the great Mahala, pressed the blade home. Then she watched Lauren Freeman's lifeless body float out to sea.

Deborah smiled and opened her eyes. She placed the turquoise between the two candles. "I'll bury it later," she said. "Some place close. And some place safe."

Deborah stood silently at the altar as a potent excitement began to fill the room. She allowed it to build for a few minutes, noting the high color on Robin's cheeks, Bram's eyes darting around the table, the sweat gathering above Tamar's lip. "Tonight is a special night," she finally said. "The final waning gibbous of 1995. In only one half of a single lunar month, our great Immortalis will be upon us. And then summerland."

"Summerland," the coven chanted.

Alva raised her flute from her lap and played a long string of notes that echoed the coven's anticipation.

"Tradition decrees that it is time now for our own Summerland to make his great ascent. For him to pave the way, to fly to the sages and announce our imminent arrival." Deborah turned and walked into the store. When she returned she was carrying the bird cage in her left hand.

Summerland sang out his lyrical, gurgling song, his yellow body adding a splash of brightness to the shadowy room. Alva's flute sang along with him. As Deborah opened the door and the canary jumped onto her finger, she returned the bird's smile for the last time. She lifted Summerland above her head. He warbled cheerfully.

Deborah placed the bird on the altar and encircled the back of his head with her left hand. With the sure motion of a trained surgeon, she raised Rebeka's lancet and sliced a tiny crescent into the base of the canary's neck. Summerland's song ended abruptly with a surprised chirp.

"Go to new life, Summerland," Deborah said, thrusting the knife into his heart. The little bird staggered for a moment, then dropped with a tiny thud onto the cracked mirror.

It was mid-afternoon. Instead of working on her book, Lauren was staring at the entry she had made in her dream journal Sunday night. *"Did you ever wake to find a dream recorded in an unfamiliar hand?"* Deborah had once asked. Lauren reread the entry and the book trembled in her hands. Had she had some kind of bizarre dream within a dream? Or could this incident be related to her forgetfulness and fugue states?

She was interrupted by a phone call from Todd. He wanted to know if she could keep Drew for the night. "I know Tuesdays are mine," he said, "and that this is late notice, but how about I swap you for another day next week? You can have two nights off in a row if you want."

"I've no reason to want two nights off," Lauren said coolly. "I'm home working on the book almost every evening. It's nice you've got time for last minute fun."

Todd paused and Lauren knew with the certainty of those long married that he was going to lie. "Ah, yeah. It is a-a last minute thing," Todd stuttered. "A thing I just couldn't get out of. . . ."

Todd had another date, Lauren thought. Her stomach twisted with a pain so potent she had to keep herself from wincing out loud. She grabbed the side of the desk and noticed her knuckles were white. "Well . . ." She was well aware she could stop Todd's date just by saying she had plans for the evening, for despite his faults, Todd was eminently fair in his dealings with her. But the truth was, she would just as soon have Drew for company. "I suppose it's okay."

"Great," Todd said, the jubilation in his voice confirming her worst fears. "Thanks. You're a pal."

Lauren stared at the phone and allowed a few tears of self-pity to fall from her eyes. She swiped her cheeks with an angry gesture. Fine. Todd had a date. She had had dates. She had even had sex. He was free to do whatever he pleased on a Tuesday evening—as was she. But when Lauren thought about what she wanted to do, she realized about the only thing that sounded appealing was a movie. Good. Drew was her date for the night—and Drew was her favorite movie companion.

The two of them shared a passion for film, whether on the big screen or small, and they had no trouble agreeing on a movie showing in Harvard Square. A cold rain was falling, but that was of no consequence to Drew, who was thrilled at this weekday treat. They giggled together on the subway, and when they reached the theater, they settled in with a bucket of popcorn and a large lemonade. As usual, Lauren lost their ongoing argument over the popcorn. She wanted to eat it all right away—she hadn't had much for dinner and preferred not to have popcorn crunched in her ear while the movie was playing—but Drew liked to savor it, kernel by kernel, until the closing credits. She pouted as she handed him the almost full bucket. He shook his head and slipped it under his seat.

But when the feature started, Lauren found she couldn't concentrate on the figures that loomed before her in the darkness. Her mind kept returning to the strange entry she had made in her dream journal. It wasn't just Deborah's prescience or the odd handwriting. What really frightened her was the underlying message that she and Drew were in danger. She thought of the Bellarmine urn and the poppets and Nigel Hawkes. She reached for Drew's hand.

Afterward, running hand in hand with his mother from under the theater marquee to the relatively dry entrance of the Harvard Coop, Drew happily recounted his favorite scenes as if she hadn't just seen them too.

"Come on, let's run," Lauren cried, pulling Drew across Mass Ave. and down the stairs of the brightly lit subway station. Drew laughed at how silly Lauren looked with hair stuck to her face. She assured him he looked no better.

The train pulled to a stop amidst a blast of dirty air. Lauren and Drew climbed into an overcrowded car. She joined the ranks of the strap hangers and instructed Drew to hang on to her, thankful their trip to Porter Square was short.

As they were rocked back and forth by the motion of the train, Drew jabbered on about the movie. "There's one thing I don't get," he said. "At the very end, you know that man Tyrone? Well, was he a good guy or a bad guy? At the beginning he seemed like he was nice, but at the end he wasn't."

Lauren looked down at her son's face, which was filled with the conviction that she had answers to all his questions. Her heart squeezed with love and she wanted to kiss him, but knowing he would be mortified, she restrained herself.

"Very few people are all good or all bad—or all of anything. Tyrone was like that. He was a little bit of both." She paused for a long moment, then continued. "Sometimes it's really hard to know if someone's more good than bad, or vice versa." She thought about Gabe declaring Deborah crazy and dangerous, while Deborah was convinced Gabe was evil and not to be trusted. "It's not always easy to tell what people really are."

Drew nodded solemnly, and once again Lauren was overwhelmed with love. The subway lights flickered off for a moment and, as the car descended into darkness, instead of Drew's face, Lauren saw the half-wolf, half-human face of Cardinal Bellarmine. Once again she smelled the odor of dampness and dead animal that had risen from the urn. The lights came back on and Lauren blinked at their harshness. Suddenly wary, she pressed Drew closer to her.

By the time they arrived home, they were both soaked through to the skin and shivering from the cold. They raced up the stairs and into the vestibule, where Drew shook himself like a wet dog. "Whoever gets upstairs first gets a hot chocolate," Lauren said. Drew dashed to the apartment door.

Lauren followed more slowly. As she passed the mail table she noticed a large box she didn't think had been there when they left for the movies. She checked the address. It was for her. She checked for a return address. There was none.

She stood alone in the large hallway, dripping water on the worn rug and watching the inert box as if it were a rattlesnake ready to strike. She could just throw it in the trash; there was no law mandating a person to open mail with his or her name on it. And yet she knew she wouldn't. She knew she would take it upstairs and see what was inside.

Despite a sense of foreboding, Lauren carried the bulky carton into the kitchen and placed it on the counter. The brown box sat there while she gave Drew his hot chocolate and talked him through his tooth-brushing, clothes-changing, story-reading bedtime routine. The carton sat there, haunting her every move.

Once Drew was asleep, she stood before the box with a large carving knife in her hand. Slowly, she approached the carton. With a quick slashing motion, she sliced the tape. The top flaps flipped open and a stale odor reached toward her.

Lauren stepped back, then gingerly came forward and looked into the box. She gasped. As she had subconsciously suspected, it contained a Bellarmine urn. But when she shook the contents of the urn onto the floor, she found that they weren't what she had expected at all.

For instead of her hair and her fingernails and a heart with her name on it, a tiny blond braid studded with nails and a few dirty fingernail parings slid onto the floor. She touched the braid and a tornado of fear roared through her. She would recognize that hair anywhere. It was Drew's.

There was more. She heard something else rattling around inside the urn. She shook it and had to stifle a scream when a small green object clattered to the floor. It was roughly twice the size of a silver dollar. And even before she recognized the design on its back, she knew. It was Herman's shell. And the shell was empty.

Lauren lunged for the objects on the floor and stuffed them back into the urn. Frantic, she shoved the urn into the carton and raced downstairs. She deposited the box in the garbage closet on the porch, slamming the door firmly behind it. When she got back to her apartment, she called the airport and her parents. Then she began to pack.

Twenty-Three

THE FIRST FLIGHT TO MIAMI LEFT BOSTON AT SEVEN A.M. and, miraculously, two seats were available. Lauren set her alarm for five, but hours before it was due to go off, she was up, drinking coffee and worrying. She worried about the urn, she worried about Drew, and she worried about what she was going to tell her mother.

Someone had broken into her apartment and left her one warning. Now they had sent another. There was no point in calling the police. All she could do to protect her child was run. Always a nervous flier, now Lauren could barely contain her longing for the moment when the plane's wheels would lift off the tarmac and they would be airborne. Airborne and safe.

When she woke Drew at five, he was cranky and complained that his head hurt. She hustled him into the kitchen and force-fed him his favorite cereal.

"I want to go back to sleep," he whined, scratching his back.

"Don't you want to see Grandma Ruth and Poppa

Bernie?" she asked with false cheerfulness. "Go swimming in their pool?"

"I guess," he mumbled and put his head on the table.

Concerned when mention of the pool didn't animate him, Lauren rested her hand on his forehead. He actually did feel a bit warm, so she gave him a couple of Tylenol and sent him off to get dressed. If Drew did have a little bug, he would mend more quickly in the warm sun. Getting him out of Boston was the most important thing. She needed to know he was safe.

"Damn," she said as the bowl she was washing slipped from her hand and shattered on the floor. Lauren crouched on her knees and picked up the bigger pieces. What kind of lunatic killed a helpless turtle?

"Drew!" she called sharply. "Are you ready? It's almost time to go."

But when she went into his room, she found him lying on his bed with an arm thrown over his eyes. His pajamas, as well as the jeans and sweatshirt he was supposed to be putting on, were on the floor. Looking down at his scrawny chest, each rib pressing against his taut skin, Lauren felt her heart turn over. How she loved this skinny little guy. She sat down on the bed and pulled her son to her; he buried his head in her shoulder. "I'll help you," she said, kissing his hair and holding him tightly. "You can sleep on the plane and some more at Grandma's if you want."

Airborne and safe, she thought. In less than two hours they would be airborne and safe.

"Okay," he said listlessly.

"Hands up," she ordered, again with false cheerfulness, telling him how she used to do this for him all the time when he was a baby. As he obediently raised his hands, she noticed a few clusters of red spots on his chest. "Does this itch?" she asked, touching one of the clusters lightly. The spots were mostly small and raised, although some seemed to be filling with fluids.

He shrugged. "So-so."

Lauren pulled the sweatshirt down and pulled her son up. "Time to go," she said, thinking that if Drew hadn't had chicken pox when he was five, she would swear he was coming down with a case now.

When they were both ready, Lauren had Drew wait in the apartment while she went down and put the suitcases in the car. As she passed through the vestibule, she inspected the corners for lurking shadows and threw a glance at the mail table to make sure no new packages had been delivered. Outside in the predawn stillness, she continued her scrutiny, scanning the street in both directions to ensure no one was waiting to harm her child.

After checking between the parked cars, Lauren stowed the luggage in the trunk and ran back to get Drew. She kept her hand on his shoulder from the time they left the apartment until he was buckled into his seat belt. As soon as she got into the car, she locked all the doors.

On the way to the airport, Drew began to perk up, asking whether they would be in Florida long enough for him to do an art project with his grandfather and if he'd be able to go swimming every day. Lauren assured him that he would, weather pending, while she concentrated on getting through the already jammed tunnel and finding a place to put her car in Logan's notoriously undersized parking lots. Everything went smoothly and they were in line at the Delta counter almost an hour before flight time. Which was fortunate, for the line was long.

As they inched closer to the counter, Lauren pushed the bags with her foot so she could watch the crowd while keeping a hold on Drew. After a few minutes, Drew squirmed from her grasp. "Don't!" Lauren cried, her voice too harsh. "Stay close to me," she ordered, grabbing his arm again. When she saw tears welling in his eyes, she was overwhelmed with guilt. "Hey, Mister Boy," she said, ruffling his hair. "Sun and fun comin' our way."

"Uh huh." He pushed his body into hers and allowed her to hug him in a way he hadn't tolerated in public since he was five.

Lauren knelt and took her son's face in her hands. It was cool but slightly flushed, and the red spots were climbing up his neck and onto one cheek. "Just a few more minutes," she said, kissing his forehead.

A woman standing next to them, dressed in a designer maternity suit, smiled at Lauren. She appeared to be about six months pregnant. When her eyes dropped to Drew's face, she blanched and stepped back. "Does he have chicken pox?" she demanded.

"No," Lauren said. "He must've eaten something he's allergic to—he had chicken pox a couple of years ago."

The woman stared at Drew for a long moment. Then her eyes narrowed and she took another step away. "He's not taking the seven o'clock to Miami, is he?"

Lauren pulled herself up to her full height. "Yes," she said. "As a matter of fact, he is."

"Exposure to chicken pox can cause birth defects." The woman lifted her briefcase from where it lay on top of her suitcase, as if shielding herself from Drew's contamination.

"I told you," Lauren said coolly, "he doesn't have chicken pox." She pulled Drew in front of her and turned her back on the woman.

Fortunately, their turn came quickly and they were directed to an agent at the far end of the counter. When their bags were checked, Lauren bought Drew an ice cream cone—which did seem to make him feel better—and, hand in hand, they headed down the long concourse. When they reached their gate and Lauren saw that the plane was parked at the ramp, she was flooded with relief. Grabbing two seats near the door, Lauren smiled. They were almost there.

When first class was allowed to board, Lauren noted that their own seats were at the back of the plane. She stood, swinging her purse and carryon to her shoulder. "Almost our turn," she told Drew, pulling him up from his chair. As she turned, Lauren noticed a cluster of people in navy Delta uniforms conferring at the desk. The pregnant woman with the briefcase stood off to the side; her face was flushed and triumphant.

"Ow!" Drew cried, pulling his hand from Lauren's. "You're squishing my fingers."

"Sorry," she said absently, her eyes never leaving the group of blue jackets. The woman making the announcements nodded and reached for the mike. Don't, Lauren prayed, don't say my name.

"Will Ms. Lauren Freeman and Mr. Andrew Freeman come to the desk, please? Ms. Lauren Freeman and Mr. Andrew Freeman."

"Mommy, that's us," Drew cried. "They called my name!"

Lauren took his hand and walked slowly toward the desk. "Yes," she said through clenched teeth, "they called your name." She glanced down at his face and saw to her dismay that the spots seemed to have both spread and grown over the last hour—and that they did look like chicken pox.

"I'm sorry to bother you, Ms. Freeman," a perky young woman who appeared to be about thirteen said to Lauren, "but there's been a concern expressed about your son's health."

"My son is fine," Lauren said as Drew hid behind her leg. "He's having an allergic reaction to something he ate."

"Would you mind if we took a little look?" the

woman asked sweetly. She reached into her pocket and pulled out a handful of plastic wing pins. She knelt down and held out her hand. "Andrew?" she called before Lauren could stop her. "Would you like some wings?"

"Wings?" the little boy said, poking his head around his mother's leg.

"Here you go, honey." The woman dumped a few pins in his hand while she scrutinized his face. She patted him on the head, then stood and faced Lauren. "I'm sorry, Ms. Freeman," she said, her face suddenly much older looking, "as our first concern has to be the safety of all of our passengers—"

"I told you," Lauren interrupted, desperate to keep the woman from completing her sentence, "it's not chicken pox. He had chicken pox two years ago and I know you can't get it twice."

"I'm sure you're correct," the young woman said sweetly. "But until you give us a doctor's note attesting to that fact, we won't be able to allow Andrew to board the plane."

Drew did indeed have chicken pox, a particularly bad case complicated by infected blisters and a tenacious fever. "It's extremely uncommon but not undocumented to develop chicken pox twice," the pediatrician told Lauren after she examined Drew. "There's a lot we don't know about the disease. But my guess is that your little fellow is in for a rough two or three days."

When Lauren brought Drew back five days later, still feverish with new blisters forming, the doctor shook her head. "According to the literature, second cases do appear to be more troublesome, although I've got to admit this is the most virile I've ever seen."

The pediatrician was well into her sixties, and Lauren was not comforted by the fact that the woman must have seen thousands of cases of chicken pox.

The doctor advised Lauren to cut Drew's nails so he wouldn't scratch the blisters and to give him cool baths in Colloidal oatmeal. "He's still contagious, so keep him at home and secluded," she said. "Chicken pox can be deadly to people with diseases like AIDS—and it can cause birth defects if contracted by a pregnant woman."

Lauren told her she was well aware of the risk posed by chicken pox and packed up her lethargic and contagious son. As she helped Drew strap his seat belt, she once again saw in her mind's eye the urn and poor Herman's empty shell. Had someone cursed Drew with a virile case of the chicken pox? A few days ago she would have thought this question absurd. Now she was far from certain.

With both Todd and Aunt Beatrice out of town—Todd on assignment in L.A. and Aunt Beatrice on an extended visit with her daughter Roz for Thanksgiving—Lauren became a full-time nurse. She swabbed Drew's blisters, ran him baths and encouraged him to eat, sleeping when he slept, not sleeping when he didn't.

By the afternoon of the seventh day, when Drew's temperature had been normal for twenty-four hours and all his blisters were scabbed over, Lauren was too exhausted to feel jubilation at the doctor's pronouncement that he could return to school on Thursday. But Drew was ecstatic, forgetting for the moment that school wasn't his favorite place to be. He was also ravenously hungry and full of energy.

Lauren dragged herself into the kitchen and stared into the empty refrigerator. She opened the freezer and searched through a mound of "mystery packets" so covered with ice that she couldn't tell which bygone leftovers they might contain. Finding a half empty package of hot dogs, she pulled it out, but discovered there was no American cheese or pastry dough to cook them the way Drew liked. Suddenly, an idea came to her, and with it a burst of energy.

After zapping the frozen hot dogs in the microwave, she scurried into the living room and began laying a fire in the large fireplace.

"What are you doing, Mom?" Drew asked from his throne of pillows on the couch.

"You'll see."

Excited by her tone, Drew jumped up and helped her with the kindling and newspapers. Once Lauren got the logs roaring, they found two long fondue forks in the back of the silverware drawer. She impaled a hot dog on each. "Turn off all the lights," she directed Drew, who was more than happy to comply. "We're going to have a dinner just like in the olden days."

Lauren turned down the heat and they huddled together around the fire, darkness filling the corners of the room, warmth and light dancing before them. Drew giggled happily as they cooked their hot dogs over the open flames.

"Can't you just see it?" Lauren asked him. "It's three hundred years ago, and we're early settlers to this wild, new land. We're in our small farmhouse, in the kitchen, and inside our deep, deep fireplace is a kettle and a pot and a set of toasting forks hanging from a lugpole."

"Sure, Mom," Drew said. "I'm a settler." Then he burst into renewed giggles.

But Lauren did see it. She saw the expansive chimney and the lugpole resting on projecting stone ledges within it. She saw a cheery blue and white valance made of calico hanging from the edge of the mantelshelf. And when she turned to smile at Drew, for a single short second she thought he looked just like Dorcas Osborne.

The next morning Lauren began to return the phone calls that had come in over the past week.

There were three from Deborah, two from Dan, and one from Gabe. Gabe said he didn't need a return call; he just wanted to wish Drew a speedy recovery and let her know he'd found the backup substantiation and had been completely exonerated by the NEH. "They even sent a written apology," he said, adding, "I also wanted to tell you that I'm here. No questions asked, whenever you're ready."

She didn't call Gabe, but she did try to reach Dan and Deborah. Dan wasn't home, but Helene, who sounded almost cheerful, promised he would get back to her as soon as he could—probably Monday.

Deborah picked up the phone at RavenWing. As soon as she recognized Lauren's voice, she asked how Drew was.

"How did you know Drew was sick?" Lauren demanded.

"After getting your machine all week, I called your department at the university—I hope you don't mind. I didn't mean to pry, but after the poppets and the Bellarmine Jackie got . . ." Deborah's voice trailed off before she added, "Please forgive me if I've overstepped."

"There's nothing to forgive," Lauren said, not at all sure that was the case. Why had Deborah mentioned the Bellarmine urn? "Drew's fine," she said coolly. "It was just a bizarre case of repeat chicken pox."

"I'm sorry I left so many messages. But aside from being worried, I wanted to let you know about the Immortalis."

"The Immortalis," Lauren repeated slowly. After Drew's strange illness, she had decided she wasn't going to any witch rituals. But now, with Drew recovered and Herman's murder a week in the past, thoughts of Nat and her precarious finances filled her mind. She decided to at least listen to what Deborah had to say.

"It's the eighth. This coming Tuesday," Deborah

said quickly, as if sensing Lauren's reluctance. "Just around the corner. I thought we'd send a cab for you—we're not going to drive any cars up there to avoid a repeat of last time. It's late, though. Will eleven be all right?"

Lauren started to say no, then stopped herself. She'd cancel at the last minute, with some irrefutable excuse about Drew. That way maybe Deborah would still let her read the chronicle. "Sure," she told Deborah. "Fine."

"There's one other thing—although you don't have to tell me if you don't want to. . . ." Deborah hesitated. "Has anything else happened since last we spoke? Another dream or anything else strange?"

"Haven't had a dream in weeks," Lauren lied. "And nothing else odd that I can think of has happened." No way was she going to tell Deborah about her dreams or fugues, and she definitely wasn't talking about Herman's mutilation—if indeed Deborah didn't know about it already. Lauren was trusting no one from now on.

"I just thought you'd like to know that Bram has been searching the Internet for other covens, even solitaries, who use Bellarmine urns, and he's—"

"Why was Bram doing that?" Lauren demanded, wondering once again if Deborah knew more than she was letting on.

"Because I asked him to," Deborah said, and Lauren heard exasperation in her voice. "But the important point is that, as far as Bram could determine, there are no witches anywhere in the world using Bellarmines."

On Thursday morning Lauren walked Drew and Scott to school. She stayed to talk with a couple of other mothers while the boys played on the tire swing. When the bell rang, she went with Drew to his classroom. Drew was annoyed by her overprotectiveness and communicated his dissatisfaction by ignoring her. Ordinarily, Lauren wouldn't have tolerated his rudeness, threatening to withhold television until he returned her "good-bye." But now she didn't care. His safety was far more important than his manners.

When Drew saw her at his classroom door at dismissal time, he glared at her. "Scott and I can walk home by ourselves," he said, stamping his foot. "I'm not sick anymore—and I'm not a baby."

"I know," she said calmly. "I was just in the neighborhood, so I thought I'd take you two for an ice cream cone."

Neither boy commented on that fact that Lauren was almost always "in the neighborhood" at three-fifteen in the afternoon—or that it was rather cold for ice cream. They knew a good deal when they heard one.

As Lauren walked them to school the next day, Drew asked if she was going to do this all the time. "Walking's my new exercise regimen," she told him. "I've decided to walk to your school and then do a loop down to Garden Street every morning." She smiled brightly. "That way I'll keep in shape through the winter."

"Get a NordicTrak," he grumbled, turning from her.

After seeing him to his classroom, Lauren did walk down to Garden Street, clocking a good three miles before she went home to fact check the early chapters of the manuscript. She was deep into verifying details on ergot poisoning when the telephone rang. It was Mr. Procter, Drew's principal.

"You'd better come down here right away, Mrs. Freeman," he said, his usually high voice almost shrill. "I don't want to alarm you, but I'm afraid we've got a problem—it appears some woman has kidnapped Drew."

Twenty-Four

LAUREN RAN THE FIVE BLOCKS TO THATCHER SCHOOL. Coatless, the cold December wind slicing through her thin shirt, she raced across streets and skidded around corners. Her mind was filled with a kaleidoscope of images: Drew, scowling at her from the door of his classroom that morning; Drew riding on Todd's shoulders at Disney World, his eyes huge with wonder as Mickey Mouse shook his hand; Drew, frightened and crying and wanting his mother, being held somewhere damp and dark and scary, by someone who might—

The blast of a horn and the screech of brakes broke into Lauren's panic. She glanced briefly at a teenage boy in a rusted Toyota who raised his fist at her, but she kept running. Running toward the school. Running to hear that it had all been a bizarre mistake, that Drew was actually at the library or the gym or had gotten sick in the bathroom. "We're so sorry to have worried you, Mrs. Freeman," she could hear Mr. Procter saying. "Can you ever forgive us?" She would nod and smile and assure them it was okay. And it would be okay. Because Drew would be safe.

Please make him safe, she chanted to the beat of her feet pounding on the pavement. Please make him safe. But when she rounded the corner across from the school, she came to a screeching halt. Grabbing a telephone pole for support, she stared in numb disbelief. Two police cruisers were pulled up at the front door and another was angled on the small patch of grass between the driveway and the street. All three looked as if they had been hastily parked and just as hastily abandoned. Radios crackled and blue lights strobed. A uniformed policeman leaned out the open door of one of the cruisers, a microphone in hand.

Her vision went black around the edges, and for a moment Lauren thought she was going to be sick. Todd, she thought, pulling herself from the darkness. She had to call Todd.

She sprinted across the street and up the front stairs of the school. The policeman with the microphone gave her a quizzical glance as she flew by, but he didn't try to stop her.

Another cop did. Before she could reach the top stair, a wide-shouldered policewoman stepped from the shadows and stood directly in Lauren's path. "This is a crime scene," she said. "We can't let anyone through."

Lauren stopped, but she found she couldn't speak. She was too winded and terrified. She just stood on the stairs, her hands pressed to the stitch in her side. *Crime scene.* The words burned like acid into her brain and she felt her eyes bug out of her head as she stared at the woman, mutely beseeching her to understand. *Crime scene.*

"You're the mother," the policewoman guessed, placing a hand on Lauren's shoulder. When Lauren nodded, she motioned through the glass. The door was opened from inside by a policeman wearing gloves. "The mother," she mouthed to the man as she led Lauren past him and into the vestibule.

Still unsteady, Lauren pressed her hand against the glazed cinder block walls. This wasn't happening. It couldn't be happening.

"I'll take you to the principal's office." The policewoman's words reached Lauren as if from the wrong end of a long tunnel. "They're waiting for you there."

Lauren managed to put one foot in front of the other and propel herself forward. It was happening. There had been no mistake. Drew wasn't in the library or the gym or the bathroom. He was gone. And no one knew where. Darkness once again threatened to steal her eyesight, and she stumbled. She assumed it was the policewoman who grabbed her elbow and led her on, but she wasn't sure.

She was in a large open office area and it was in pandemonium. Lauren shrank from the painfully bright lights that accentuated the strained faces of the young women and the old women and the middle-aged men who milled between tightly packed desks and file cabinets. She smelled tuna fish and copying machines and noticed the school secretary crying into a handkerchief as a uniformed policeman barked orders into the phone at her elbow. A man in a shirt and tie quickly wended his way through the tumult and stuck an oversize map under the policeman's nose. He pointed to something in the right corner of the map. The policeman nodded.

As Lauren walked through the noisy room, an odd hush seemed to follow in her wake. The change in sound level threw her off balance, made her dizzy. Reaching out to steady herself, she felt two hands grip her shoulders. The grip was solid yet gentle, comforting. She leaned back into the hands and found herself in Mr. Procter's office. As the door closed behind her, Lauren could hear the hubbub rise in the outer office, even louder than before.

She blinked at all the people crowded into the small

room. Ellen Baker rushed forward and pressed Lauren to her. Mr. Procter and two policemen—one was Dan Ling, in uniform, and the other was a stranger wearing a jacket and tie—stood. All three looked pained and uncomfortable. Dan threw her a weak smile. Two other women, whom Lauren vaguely recognized as teachers, looked at her sympathetically. Drew's friend Scott and his mother, Melinda, were huddled in the corner. The little boy burst into tears as soon as he saw Lauren. Disoriented, Lauren shook her head. Were all these people waiting for her? How had Melinda gotten to the school before she had and, more important, what were she and Scott doing here anyway? Then everyone began talking at once.

"Oh God, this is so awful," Melinda said, releasing Scott and starting toward Lauren. "I was helping out in the library—"

Scott let out a wail as soon as his mother let go of him. "I'm s-s-so sorry," he cried.

"I'm sorry too," Ellen whispered in Lauren's ear. She took a tissue from her pocket and dabbed her red-rimmed eyes. "I should have been watching more closely. We were coming from art—on our way back to the classroom—and I was at the front of the line. I know I should have been watching the back of the line too—and if only I had been, then maybe this wouldn't have happened. . . ."

Lauren stared at Drew's teacher and then turned to Mr. Procter, panic welling up from her stomach. She wanted to scream at them: "*What did you let happen to my child? I left him in your care. I trusted you.*" She opened her mouth and then closed it again.

"We called your husband and he's on his way." Mr. Procter came from behind his desk and pressed Lauren's hand, his usually ruddy complexion pasty. "They're going to find Drew for you, Mrs. Freeman. I just know they will." He let go of her hand and motioned to the policemen. "You wouldn't believe all the things these gentlemen have already put in motion. They couldn't have gone far."

"I'm Lieutenant Detective Conway and I understand you know Officer Ling," the policeman in street clothes said. "I want you to know that we're doing everything we can—and will continue to." He regarded her with such compassion that Lauren had to turn away. "We've broadcast a description of your son, as well as the car and the woman, that this young man gave us." He smiled briefly at Scott, who was sobbing in his mother's arms. "And we currently have all available cruisers delegated to cover circumference points."

Circumference points? Woman? What woman? A woman Scott knew? She glanced over at Scott and Melinda. Melinda was seated Indian-style on the floor, her arms wrapped around her son. She was rubbing his back and whispering in his ear.

Lauren winced as a stab of raw pain sliced through her. Where was *her* son? Was he hurt? Did he need her? Was he even alive? She grabbed onto the edge of the desk as the image of Herman's empty shell rose before her.

"I've already got someone checking on any similar incidents in the area and the state police have been contacted," Lieutenant Conway was saying. "We're on the LEAPS computer with a Mass BOLO on your son—"

"BOLO?" Lauren asked, needing to slow him down.

" 'Be on the look out,' " Dan told her.

BOLO, Lauren thought, staring at the policemen. *BOLO on your son . . .* The blackness began at the edge of her vision and thickened toward the center with the nauseating motion of a tidal wave. The room grew excruciatingly hot and there was a loud buzzing in her ears. The floor slanted toward her. . . .

* * *

A horrible, bitter smell assaulted Lauren and she twisted her head away from it. When it came back at her, she swatted at it. *Get away,* she tried to scream. *Leave me alone.* But she was buried under a heavy layer of nausea and darkness and no words could make their way through.

"She's coming to," a woman's voice said.

"Lauren," Todd called. "Laurie, it's me, honey. Are you all right?"

"Let her take her time," the woman cautioned. "It would be best if everyone cleared out and gave her some space."

Lauren heard whispers and the sound of shuffling feet. She opened her eyes. It was bright and hot, and she was stretched out on a hard linoleum floor. The ceiling had a rusty water stain that looked like Bunny. Todd was kneeling over her, holding her hand. "Todd?" she said through parched lips.

"You fainted, Mrs. Freeman," the woman said. When a pair of oversize glasses and a wide band of freckles filled Lauren's vision, she recognized the woman as the nurse at Drew's school. But she was unable to imagine what Ms. Veroff was doing with Todd. "You're at Thatcher School," Ms. Veroff said in a calming voice. "You're going to be fine."

Thatcher School. Drew. She tried to sit up and immediately felt the blackness closing in on her again. Todd grabbed her and she clung to him.

"Stay where you are, Mrs. Freeman," Ms. Veroff cautioned. "Take a sip of water and give yourself a few minutes."

It was true, Lauren thought, closing her eyes again. The worst nightmare lurking in every mother's imagination was actually happening to her. Lauren pushed the water away and buried her head in Todd's chest. The tears she had been holding back since Mr. Procter's call burst through.

"We'll find him, Laurie," Todd said, his voice shaking slightly. He kissed the top of her head and wrapped his long arms tightly around her. "It's got to be some kind of bizarre mistake. There's no reason for anyone to kidnap Drew. As soon as they realize they've got the wrong kid, they're sure to let him go."

Lauren shook her head but found she still couldn't speak. There had been no mistake. Someone had taken Drew because of her. Because of the chronicle and *Rebeka Hibbens* and that damn Immortalis. She'd quit school. She'd wait tables for the rest of her life. She'd do anything, anything, to get Drew back. She shook her head again, more violently this time. She had to get control of herself and tell him what was going on. "I-I . . . There—"

"Shush, baby," Todd said. "The police have everything under control."

Lauren pulled away from Todd and took a large, shuddering breath. "There's, there's more to this than you know," she told Todd, then she turned to the detective. "I've been receiving threats for the last month—"

"Threats?" Todd's face was bloodless, his eyes huge. "What kind of threats?"

Conway glanced at Dan and then said to Lauren, "I've got Zaleski over at RavenWing right now. I'm sorry I didn't take this all more seriously before."

"Take what more seriously?" Todd demanded. "What the hell are you talking about?"

Lauren told him everything, starting with the poppets and Jackie's death and ending with the Bellarmine urn containing Herman's empty shell. Dan and the lieutenant took notes. Todd stared at her, his eyes filled with horror and incredulity.

"Why didn't you tell me about this?" Todd demanded, his face as white and hard as if it were chiseled in stone. "How could you let it go on for so long?"

"Dan and I informed the police twice in the past

few weeks," Lauren snapped. "What else was I supposed to do?"

Conway cleared his throat. "Now, Mrs. Freeman, from your experience with these—"

"When the lieutenant said there wasn't enough evidence to open an investigation," Lauren started to explain to Todd, "I figured it must be some crackpot. . . ." Her voice petered out and tears ran down her cheeks as she realized that it *had* been some crackpot. "Oh," she moaned, "it's all my fault." She covered her face. "If anything happens to Drew . . . If anything . . ."

"Don't," Todd said, pulling Lauren to him again. "Don't."

"I should have known," Lauren protested. "I should have guessed from the—"

"Stop it," Todd interrupted, squeezing her shoulder. "Nothing will be gained by blaming yourself." He turned to Conway. "Tell us what happened," he said. "Everything."

The lieutenant crossed his arms. "Apparently, Mrs. Baker was walking her class down the corridor a little before noon." He looked over at Ellen, who nodded her agreement. "Drew and Scott were at the end of the line. According to Scott, as they passed through the front vestibule, a woman approached them, explaining that she was a kindergarten mom who needed help bringing some things in from her car."

This time he looked at Scott, who also nodded. "Then both boys followed the woman outside to a white station wagon parked in the driveway. Suddenly, the woman grabbed Drew, threw him in the backseat, and sped away. Scott ran into the school to get Mrs. Baker. And that's about all we know," Lieutenant Conway concluded. "Unfortunately, the kid's descriptions of the woman and the car are less precise than we'd normally hope to get."

Lauren pressed a hand to her mouth. A moan, deep

and low and full of pain, escaped from her lips and she leaned against Todd. "I-I want to go home," she whispered. Maybe it's a mistake, she thought. Maybe they had already dropped Drew off and he was waiting for her at the apartment.

But Lieutenant Conway misunderstood her reasoning and nodded. "I've already talked to the D.A.'s office about setting up a wiretap at your house—if that's okay with you?" When Lauren didn't say anything, he continued. "Officer Ling will take you both over there now. We'll keep a policeman and a VWA—"

"A VWA?" Todd asked.

"Victim witness advocate. A support person provided by the state to answer your questions and help you get through this."

Lauren and Todd both rose slowly to their feet. "Fine," Todd said, putting his arm around Lauren's shoulders. "Anything—" His voice cracked and he took a deep breath. "Anything we can do."

Dan stood too and gestured toward the door. "I'm going to need some more information if you're up to it, Lauren." His dark eyes were full of sympathy. "Some of it'll be a repeat of what I already know," he shot a glance at the lieutenant, "but for the record, I'm going to need details on your work, the witches, the break-in—and on Drew. A full description of him, pictures, dental records . . ."

Dental records. Lauren stumbled and Todd caught her arm. *Dental records.*

Lauren lay stretched out on her bed, fully clothed, daring the medication to take affect. Two policemen, Ms. Maher—the victim witness advocate—and a telephone man were in the living room with Todd, waiting for some crazy person to call demanding a ransom in exchange for her son. Tears slid down her cheeks, wetting the pillow. She felt empty and hollow yet full of pain, as if someone had ripped out her insides and left her a vacant, aching shell.

She had told Dan everything she could think of that might be relevant—even though he already knew most of it. Then she told it all over again to Detective Zaleski. She described Drew and tried to remember exactly what he had been wearing that morning. Todd gave them a recent photograph and telephoned Drew's dentist. Conway called both the state police and the FBI. When a state trooper and an agent from the FBI's regional office showed up, she told the story twice more.

They also wanted to know about the status of Todd and Lauren's marriage. How long had they been separated? Was a divorce imminent? How was Drew dealing with the situation? Was there any chance of a reconciliation? Lauren and Todd were sitting on the couch, holding hands. At that question they looked at each other for a long moment. Lauren finally dropped her eyes and whispered, "It's always a possibility." Then she burst into tears.

When she couldn't stop crying, Todd called her doctor and got a prescription for sleeping pills. Lauren had protested that she needed to be awake and aware in case there was a call, but Todd assured her he would rouse her if there was any need. Completely exhausted and bereft, she had finally agreed, sure that no matter how many pills she consumed, she would be unable to sleep.

To her surprise, Lauren felt swirls of seductive, velvet sleep wrap around her. The swirls called to her, urging her to come rest with them. She fought. She fought as long and as hard as she could and then, with a sigh of submission, she let the swirls take her.

But they took her to a place she didn't want to go.

She was standing amidst an angry crowd on the edge of a rocky outcropping. The wind cut through her thin cloak and the chill of the earth seeped through the holes in her boots. The sky was steel gray and overcast, the same color as the ocean that lapped at the bottom of the hill.

Along the steep promontory lumbered a cart. It was crammed full. Several women and one child clung to each other as the overloaded conveyance jerked up the rutted trail. Confused, she stared down the hill. Her stomach wrenched with fear and her hands began to tremble when she saw that Drew was the child in the cart. She didn't know how and she didn't know why, but she knew with the certainty of the dreaming that Drew was going to die—and that it was her fault.

As the cart crested the hill and came to a stop under the thick, spreading limbs of an ancient oak tree, the crowd roared.

"Mommy!" Drew called to her over the bellows of the crowd. "Mommy!"

Lauren tried to run to him, to snatch him from the cart and the hangman's noose. But hands grabbed at her. They held her feet and her shoulders and her hair. She was immobile. She was forced to stand facing the horrible oak.

As the noose was slipped around Drew's neck, Lauren felt the rough hemp on her own skin. "No!" she cried, straining to escape her captors. "Drew!"

"Mommy!" Drew called again, reaching his arms toward her, his eyes huge against his pale face. "Mom—" His last word was cut off as the noose broke his windpipe. He dropped his head, shuddered, and was still. Until the wind picked up his small body and he swung gently from the branches of the towering tree.

Twenty-Five

LAUREN BOLTED STRAIGHT UP IN BED, SCREAMING Drew's name.

Todd rushed in from the other room. He immediately stretched his long body against the length of her own and wrapped his arms around her. "It's going to be okay, Laurie," he murmured, kissing her hair. "You've got to believe he's going to be okay."

"No!" Lauren cried, punching Todd's chest and shoulders. "He's not okay! I know it—I just know it. We've got to do something. We've got to help him. My baby, my baby . . ." she moaned. The vision of Drew's body hanging from the tree was so disturbing, Lauren covered her eyes to block it out. But she could not make the image go away. It was a sign. A horrible, terrible sign. She began to shake uncontrollably and tears poured through her fingers. She struggled to stand up, but Todd held her fast.

"There's nothing we can do," Todd said, his voice hoarse with emotion. "We've got to let the experts—"

"He needs me!" Lauren cried. "I'm his mother."

She wrenched from Todd's arms, flinging her body with such force that she hit the wall next to the bed with her shoulder. She yelped in pain and collapsed to the floor. Todd knelt down next to her and took her in his arms again. This time she didn't pull away; she stayed where she was and sobbed like a child who had lost her mother. Or a mother who had lost her child.

Lauren felt another presence at the bedroom doorway but didn't look up. She heard mutterings about "doctor" and "something stronger," but she couldn't take in anything except her pain. Please don't let Drew die like Dorcas, she prayed. Please don't let my mistakes harm him the way Faith's mistakes harmed her child. I'll find out what Faith did and make sure I don't do it, she bargained, knowing it was senseless. I'll stop working on *Rebeka Hibbens*. I'll never read anything about the seventeenth century again. I'll move from the state. I'll do anything. Anything . . .

Somewhere around the edges of her black anguish Lauren felt Todd's arms around her, heard his voice whispering in her ear. She was vaguely aware of someone else kneeling next to her and of a sharp prick on her arm. Then she fell into a darkness so deep and so thick that she knew she would never emerge. And she was glad.

When she did open her eyes, it was daylight and she had the strange sensation that many days had passed since she had last been awake. Disoriented and groggy, Lauren glanced down and saw she was wearing jeans and a sweatshirt. What was she doing in bed? Why was she—

As the memories flooded back, she cried out in pain. The bedroom door opened in response to her cry. She turned toward the sound, expecting Todd, anxious for news. But instead of Todd, Drew hurtled himself at her. He wrapped his bony arms around her neck and buried himself within the curve of her body.

"Mommy," Drew sobbed. "Mommy."

Todd stood in the open doorway, tears streaming down his cheeks, a huge grin on his face.

Lauren had been in a drugged sleep for almost forty-eight hours, and while she slept, Drew had been found by a law student on her way to the Suffolk University library. He was huddled behind several garbage cans in an alley on the back side of Beacon Hill.

"I'm lost," he called to the student as she passed by, a backpack slung over her shoulder. "You look like my mom. Can you help me get home?"

The young woman took him down to the police station, where he was immediately recognized. By early afternoon, he was back at the apartment, waking his mother. His clothes were dirty and there was a long scrape on his cheek, but other than that he appeared to be unharmed.

According to Drew, the woman who abducted him had been very nice, although he thought it strange that "her hair changed to red" after they got to a building "near lots of other buildings." She promised if he was a good boy and did everything she asked, he would get to go home soon. So he did what she asked—mostly staying quiet and keeping his eyes closed—and then, on the second night, when she thought he was sleeping, he pushed his cot up to the window of his basement room, broke the locked window with a hammer, and slid his little body out into the alley. He had seen someone do it in a movie.

Although Drew grudgingly admitted to being "a little" scared, he maintained that it hadn't been all that bad. He told them the woman, her hair alternately long and blond or short and red, had brought him Peking ravioli for dinner both nights and put him in a rec room with a VCR and "a zillion" videos. But he sobbed for a long time in Lauren's arms—as did she—and was unwilling to leave either Todd or Lauren's side.

"It's over," Lauren told Deborah awhile later on the phone. "All of it: *Rebeka Hibbens*, my dissertation, the Immortalis." Holding the portable phone to her ear, Lauren walked into the hallway and peeked into the living room where Drew and Todd were pressed together on the couch watching television. "Drew's back and he's safe and that's the way he's going to stay."

There was a long pause before Deborah said, "I understand."

Lieutenant Conway—they were now calling him Steve—and two state troopers had just left. Although it had been dark for hours, it was the first time since Drew's return that afternoon that the three of them were alone. But before she could revel in the return of her family, Lauren had wanted to spread the word that she was cutting herself off from the witches. Tears welled in her eyes as she looked at the unruly tufts of Drew's hair rising helter-skelter over the back of the couch.

"I'm really glad everything worked out so well," Deborah was saying warmly. "And if any of it had anything to do with us, words can't possibly convey how sorry I—we all—are."

Lauren went back into the kitchen, both to keep from disturbing Drew and Todd and to keep them from overhearing her conversation. She understood the message in the kidnapping, and she was going to do everything in her power to make sure there was no reason for anyone to send her a message again.

"To tell you the truth," Lauren said, "I think it *was* about my involvement with the coven—and that's why there's going to be no more involvement." Dropping into a chair, she was suddenly overwhelmed with exhaustion. "The police are opening an investigation into Jackie's death."

"They were here for hours yesterday and came back again this morning," Deborah told her. "They talked to Bram too."

"I guess you know they're far from convinced of your innocence."

"They made that quite clear," Deborah said dryly, then changed the subject. "So tell me what happened. Drew's okay?"

"Amazingly so. The clever little monkey escaped through a window." Lauren barked a laugh without humor and wondered if Deborah was already familiar with what had transpired.

"There wasn't a note?" Deborah asked. "No message?"

"Oh, there was a message all right—and it came through loud and clear." Lauren shifted in her chair to look out the window, but all she saw was her own disheveled reflection in the dark glass. "The police are more than a little mystified. On one hand, they think it might have been a professional job. 'Very slick and clean,' the detective said. But the lack of a ransom demand and the fact that the woman was dumb enough to allow Drew to escape, don't fit with a professional MO. So they're going to keep the case open with a high priority. Both Drew and I are under twenty-four-hour surveillance. I assume they're watching you too."

Deborah's sigh was audible over the phone line. "I wish there was something I could do to make up for this mess I seem to have gotten you into."

"Well," Lauren said slowly, "as a matter of fact, I could use a couple of favors. . . ."

"Name them."

Lauren looked into the black glass and tried to comb her messy hair with her fingers. When she saw she was just making it worse, she turned her chair. "I'd really appreciate it if you could get out the word that I'm not going to be writing *Rebeka Hibbens,* or reading the chronicle, or going to any of your rituals."

"Have you told your publisher or professors yet?" Deborah asked.

"Tomorrow," Lauren said. She figured Gabe and Paul Conklin, who had taken over as her committee chairperson after Jackie's death, would be more than supportive, but she was not at all anxious to break the news to Nat—or to dwell on the financial repercussions of her decision.

"I'll call everyone in the coven as soon as we hang up," Deborah promised. "And I'll ask each one to mention it to anyone who might be remotely interested. What's the second favor?"

"It's actually more of a question," Lauren said, then she briefly described the dream she had had about Drew. When she finished there was a pause on the other end of the line.

"And your question is?" Deborah finally asked in a voice that sounded faintly alarmed.

"What I want to know is—well, do you know if Faith Osborne was responsible for Dorcas's death?"

"I thought you were abandoning your research. . . ."

"This isn't about the book," Lauren said. "I know it sounds crazy, but I've got this idea that if I can find out how Faith endangered her daughter, then I'll be better able to protect Drew."

Deborah was silent for a long time, and when she spoke her voice was thoughtful. "You're right, it *was* Faith who caused Dorcas to be hanged."

Lauren's chest constricted and she forced herself to take a series of deep breaths. How had she known this? Faith had never been mentioned in any of the books she had read, and yet her subconscious had somehow guessed what had happened. "How?" she demanded.

"I'm not free to say just yet," Deborah said slowly. "Give me a day or two to think it through."

"But you have to tell me now," Lauren said. "We have to break off all contact after this. I can't—and won't—chance anyone thinking I'm still involved with you or *Rebeka Hibbens*."

"Understood," Deborah said. "I won't do anything to jeopardize your safety." Then the phone went dead in Lauren's hand.

Lauren walked slowly into the living room, sorry she had brought up the dream and trying to decide what to tell Todd about her conversation with Deborah. There had been far too many secrets between them of late, and if they were going to reconcile—as she was starting to believe they might—it was a bad way to start. But he would be furious at the idea of her having even the most fleeting contact with anyone in the coven.

"All taken care of?" he asked, a wide smile filling his face.

Lauren smiled back and dropped a kiss on Drew's head. "Yup," she said, sitting next to her son and putting her arm around him.

They watched television together in companionable, and grateful, silence. When Drew's head fell to her shoulder, Lauren looked up at Todd. Their eyes met and a stab of pure physical desire torched her body. Todd gently untangled their sleeping child from her arms and carried him to his bedroom. Lauren followed.

As she watched Todd pull the covers over Drew, she thought about what troopers both her boys were. Todd had been steadfast and optimistic from the first moments at the school. He'd never broken down and had soothed her when she did. He'd stayed awake during the entire ordeal, never once blaming her for what had happened. On the contrary, he had repeatedly assured her that none of it was her fault.

Drew had been just as tough. After his emotional return, he had sat through interminable interviews and helped with the tedious job of working up a composite sketch of the kidnapper with a patience and calmness she wouldn't have believed possible. Even Steve Conway had remarked on Drew's composure and maturity.

Suddenly, Todd's knees seemed to give out. He dropped to the side of Drew's bed and buried his head next to his son's. His shoulders began to shake in silent, racking sobs.

Lauren went quickly to his side and wrapped her arms around him. "Come on, babe," she whispered. "It's okay. Come with me." Todd stumbled to his feet and she helped him from Drew's room to hers. To their room, she thought. It had always been their room.

Todd sat on the edge of the bed and cried while Lauren held him. She began to cry too, and they cried until, after a few minutes, they both began to laugh. Eyes red-rimmed and cheeks streaked with tears, they laughed until Lauren's side hurt and Todd started to hiccup.

"I-I guess this is hysterical relief," Lauren finally managed to say. Todd started to speak and then hiccuped again, sending them into renewed gales of laughter. When Lauren regained her composure, she placed her hands on Todd's cheeks and kissed him. It was a kiss full of love and gratitude and passion. If there was one thing the last couple of days had taught her, it was that family was all that mattered, that being with the people you loved was the most important thing in the world.

When they pulled apart, Lauren looked into Todd's eyes. All was right with the world. They were a family again. "I've been thinking about little baby girls," she said, a shy smile playing on her lips.

Todd pressed her to him and then stood abruptly. He walked to the window, keeping his back to her, and said nothing.

"What?" Lauren asked, her passion chilled to fear. "Don't you want to try again?"

He turned slowly and faced her. His eyes were dark and troubled, the web of lines surrounding them suddenly deep and visible. "I-I do," he said, his voice gravelly with emotion and confusion. "Or I'm pretty sure I do. But something's come up." He threw his hands in the air. "Something I never expected to happen. And, and I'm torn."

"There's somebody else," Lauren guessed.

"Yes," Todd said miserably. "Yes, there is."

"Is it serious?"

"I don't know," he said. "It's only been a few weeks, but you know how it is at the beginning, when everything is clicking, when you think you've found the perfect person and—" He stopped abruptly, apparently realizing how much his words must be hurting Lauren. He stepped toward her, but she backed toward the door. "I'm sorry, Laurie. You, you just can't control these things. I wish it hadn't happened—but it did."

Deborah was furious. In all of her lifetimes she had never been filled with such a boiling rage. She saw her own aura swirling around her: It was red and orange and white hot. Someone—or something—was trying to keep Lauren from the Immortalis, trying to keep Deborah from reaching her destiny.

It was just before midnight and Deborah was sitting in the darkness in the back room of RavenWing, waiting for the coven to gather. Everyone was there except Alva, but nobody spoke. Deborah's rages were legendary, and there could be no doubt in anyone's mind that Deborah was more angry than ever before.

After Lauren's phone call earlier in the evening, Deborah had almost believed the sages did not want her, that Lauren's call was their way of telling her the Immortalis should not take place. But Deborah knew better. She had had visions and dreams and messages from the raven. The coven was to ascend to the sages at the last waxing crescent of the year 1995, of this she was certain. This was not the work of the sages. This was the interference of a human. Deborah slammed her fist down on the altar. This she would not allow.

As Alva slipped into the room, Deborah pulled the chronicle from beneath the altar. "It is two days until the great Immortalis and, as planned, we shall read the final—the first—book of Mahala. Then you shall all disperse and I shall contact the sages for their final instructions."

"But, Mahala," Cassandra interrupted, "the energy drain so close to the Immortalis. The—"

"Silence!" Deborah roared, her anger inflamed by her fear that Cassandra was right. "I shall not be questioned! I shall do what needs to be done."

"I'm, I'm so sorry, Mahala," Cassandra stuttered. "I was just so surprised—"

Deborah silenced the woman with a fierce look. She opened the chronicle and began to read.

Rebeka Hibbens had been privy to the tales. She had heard tell of what had transpired in Salem Village, and knew it would soon come to pass in Cambridge. Once the ferreting out of witches began, these superstitious humans, believing they had come to a land ruled by the devil, would hang many of their own in the name of their God. Rebeka could not allow this to happen, for it was she, and those whom she loved best, who would be among the first to be executed.

Rebeka mixed her herbs and cast her spells and spoke with the sages who ruled the afterlife. But, as she was well aware, the sages never intervened directly in human events, and, as always, they would not intercede now. They did, however, guide her in the devising of a magical ritual to save her coven from the hangman's noose. On the night of the next waxing crescent moon, with the aid of heliotrope, malaxis, and christianwort, the seven would ascend to summerland, home of the sages, leaving the realm of the human for all of eternity. Rebeka named her ritual the Immortalis, and when the others heard of it, they began to call her Mahala, the wise one.

Things did not go well in the town. Young girls began experiencing unexplained fits, which were seen as evidence that the devil was near. "The evil hand is upon us!" the townspeople cried. "It surely be witchcraft."

And indeed, when the girls were asked to name their tormentors, they claimed they saw shapes flying in the night that bit and pinched them. They named the old woman who lived alone down by the river and the Negro slave who, it was said, practiced the black arts. And when the girls named Martha Cory, a respectable matron, and her slow-witted husband, Giles, Rebeka knew she and her coven would surely be arrested before the next waxing crescent moon.

So Rebeka went to visit her cousin, Faith Osborne, who was married to Oliver Osborne, one of the most influential magistrates in the Massachusetts Bay Colony. Rebeka had a deep and abiding love for her much younger cousin, but with the birth of Faith's daughter, Dorcas, the most powerful soul Rebeka had ever encountered, their bond had grown.

Faith was a sweet and rather timid woman, but her new husband was as ambitious and self-obsessed as he was powerful. If Oliver Osborne could be convinced it was in his best interest to allow the witchcraft accusations to die down, Oliver Osborne would do what was best for Oliver Osborne. It was well-known that Osborne was mad for Faith, his hale and well-looking third wife, and Rebeka hoped a few soft words spoken by Faith into his ear in the darkness and privacy of their marital bed would go far.

"There's talk that this smallpox is a sign that the Lord has turned away from the unworthy," Rebeka told Faith as they sat in the front hall of Oliver Osborne's house. "The inquests and warrants grow closer to us."

"Do you really think it be so?' Faith asked, her blue eyes widening in fear. "Is Dorcas in danger? Are you?"

"It is a great possibility," Rebeka said. "Which is why I come to warn you never to speak of Glover barn and to beg you to intercede with your husband on our behalf—and on behalf of all that is right."

Faith's face was pale and the teacup in her hand trembled. "I shall do all I can, dear cousin. Rest assured, I shall do what I can."

Rebeka thanked Faith and pressed her to her breast as she took her leave. But despite Faith's words, Rebeka was filled with dread.

And it came to pass just as Rebeka had feared. For the next evening, Dorcas slipped into Rebeka's farmhouse. "My mama, my mama . . ." the girl said as she sobbed in Rebeka's arms.

"What is it, child?' Rebeka asked, apprehension clutching her heart. "Is your mama hurt?"

Dorcas shook her head vigorously. "I-I heard through the floorboards," she stuttered. "Mama told him. She told him about you and Goody Glover and Mercy and Dr. Lacy."

"She told your stepfather?" Rebeka asked softly, so as not to let the child know of her terror.

"And he plans to arrest Goody Glover and you and everyone else as soon as he is able!" Dorcas began to cry even harder.

After she had calmed the child, Rebeka called the other five members of her coven together. The sages had helped her devise a powerful magic elixir to ensure the coven's safety until the Immortalis, and she wanted the seven to partake of the potion immediately. She knew Dorcas had spoken the truth. They had little time.

The coven crept to Millicent Glover's barn under cover of darkness. Rebeka quickly cast the circle. As they stood, linked by held hands, heads bowed to receive the liquid in Rebeka's crucible, Rebeka called to the sages to protect them. But before the sages could respond, the doors of the barn were thrown open and a deep voice roared in outrage.

Oliver Osborne stood there, full of righteous fury, a band of goodmen on horseback behind him. "Give glory to God!" he cried, ripping the crucible from Rebeka's hand and pouring its contents into the dirt. "Arrest these witches before they do any more of the devil's work!"

It mattered not a whit to Oliver Osborne that his stepdaughter was one of witches.

There was a deep silence as Deborah closed the chronicle.

"It was so horrible," Bram whispered.

"They threw me in the dirt and stepped on my hand." Tamar wiped a tear from her cheek. "Horrid, horrible men."

"If only Faith hadn't told him," Robin said. "If she had kept her mouth shut everything would have been different."

Deborah looked at Robin and nodded. "I make this promise to all of you now: What happened in 1692 shall not happen again. In two days, we will celebrate the final Immortalis. In forty-eight hours, the soul of Faith Osborne will finally be destroyed and we will all be free!"

One by one, each touched the crescent-shaped scar at the base of his or her neck and left the store.

After locking the door behind them, Deborah returned to the back room and pulled a grass mat from between two bags of bulgur wheat. Laying the mat before the altar, she slipped to the floor in preparation for a message.

She arranged her body in a receiving position—legs straight and open, hands resting palm up on her knees—closed her eyes and concentrated on contacting the sages. *Speak to me,* she demanded. *Tell me. Empower me so that I may overcome those who attempt to stand in my way.* She focused all her anger and fury until she felt it fuse together. It became smaller and yet more powerful than it had been before, like a dying star collapsing in on itself to form a black hole. She cried out in triumph as thunder rolled overhead and forks of lightning lit up the room. The veil between the worlds parted, and she slipped through.

Deborah flashed through darkness and through light and into darkness again. Borne by a fierce, fiery wind, she was whipped above a rocky shoreline and then hurtled inland. Beneath her, she saw herself scrambling up a steep mountain, the chronicle clutched to her breast. The sages were waiting at the peak. They had a message for her. But when Deborah reached the crest, she found Lauren instead of the sages. Infuriated by the sight of the human, she opened the chronicle, ripped out a handful of pages, and shoved them at Lauren. As soon as Lauren took the pages, she vanished and the wind became soft and warm and quiet. Deborah heard Summerland's sweet song swirling around her.

Deborah glided in the twilight, along a meandering river that snaked through an evergreen forest studded with startling white pines. All was right with her world. When the trees fell behind her, she slid into the light of a wide, open beach and saw herself again. It was the night of the last waxing crescent moon. Cassandra, Bram, Tamar, Robin, and Alva were all with her. The six of them were gathered in a circle around a towering bonfire. Waves crashed on the sand.

Suddenly, Deborah's view was obstructed by the black raven. He was bigger and blacker and shinier than ever before, and when he saw her, he opened his mouth. But before he could tell her anything, his body exploded and he broke into half a dozen ravens, all of whom plummeted into the ocean and disappeared without a splash.

With the raven gone, Deborah's view was clear once again, and she saw Lauren step from a break in the trees and approach the circle. Lauren was winded and disheveled, and her expression reflected both fear and excitement. As Lauren surrendered herself to the circle, Deborah felt the heft of Rebeka's lancet in her hand. She flashed the blades in the moonlight and smiled. The message was clear: Lauren would come and destiny would be fulfilled.

Twenty-Six

LAUREN WANDERED AROUND THE APARTMENT, RUNning her finger along dusty bookshelves and staring out at the bare trees. She looked at the piles of books and folders and notes scattered on her desk. She knew she should be ecstatic, that yesterday at this time she would have given her life to have Drew back safely. She glanced at his school picture sitting crookedly on a bookshelf and felt a bit better, but she couldn't help wondering if she had done the right thing in sending him back to school so soon.

Ms. Maher and Dr. Berg had both insisted. "He needs to get back into his normal routine as soon as possible," Ms. Maher had advised. "That's what's going to make him—and you—begin to feel safe again." And even though Lauren had walked him to school and checked to make sure the policeman was on duty outside his classroom, she wasn't so sure. She didn't feel safe. She felt jumpy and nervous and exhausted. She wasn't sure if she'd ever feel safe again.

She reminded herself that in a remarkably short time she had done everything in her power to assure

Drew's safety, including keeping almost all the promises she had made in the depth of her despair. In less than twenty-four hours, she had called Nat to cancel her book contract, informed Paul Conklin that her dissertation was dead, and told Deborah to spread the word that she would have no more contact with witches.

Dropping onto the couch, Lauren stared up at the ceiling. Although she knew she had done the right things, she couldn't help feeling overwhelmed by the consequences. What now? she wondered. No dissertation, no husband, no money—worse than no money; she was now deeply in debt to Boylston. And although she knew it was the least of her worries, the idea of turning her back on the seventeenth century left her desolate and forlorn.

Both Paul and Nat had been understanding. Nat assured her he supported whatever decision she wanted to make, although he was clearly disappointed. And Paul offered to brainstorm new dissertation topics with her. "I don't think I'm quite at that point yet," Lauren had told him, wondering if she would ever be, if maybe it was best to drop out of the PhD program and come up with an entirely new career plan. "But I'll hold you to your offer when I'm ready," she had added just in case.

Staring at the paint peeling off the cornice above the bay window, Lauren considered taking Drew and moving to Florida to be with her parents. Todd wouldn't like it and might even try to fight her in court, but custody law heavily favored the mother and she figured she could pull it off. It would serve Todd right anyway. Another woman, she thought, punching a throw pillow. Probably Melissa, the "meaningless mistake" that had ended her marriage the first time around.

When the phone rang, Lauren threw the pillow to the floor and went to her desk. It was Terri, the department secretary, calling to say Gabe wanted Lauren to come over to talk with him as soon as possible.

"You mean now?" Lauren asked, filled with hope at the idea that she might have somewhere to go, something on which to focus.

"Mondays are one of his 'writing days,' so the calendar's clear until he goes into high gear for the conference. He's got a few luminaries to escort around late this afternoon and I think he's planning on taking the six o'clock shuttle to New York."

"For 'The Today Show'?" Lauren asked. Everyone knew Gabe was to be the keynote speaker at the annual conference of the American Historical Association, which was being held in Cambridge this year and started tomorrow—and that he was being interviewed in the morning by Bryant Gumbel.

"Yes," Terri gushed. "Isn't it just the most exciting thing? Isn't Gabe just fabulous?"

Gabe was pretty fabulous, Lauren thought, her face flushing as she remembered that night in her bedroom. But if Terri was calling, Gabe's interest wasn't personal this time. "What's up?" she asked, trying to keep her voice light. "Why does he want to talk to me?"

"Let's just say it would probably be in your best interests to hear what the great leader has to offer," Terri said mysteriously.

So Lauren went straight to school. Gabe ushered her into his office with a chivalrous bow. After she was seated across from him, he offered her a part-time job as principal investigator on a grant to the Lexington Historical Society to study the contribution of Colonial women to the winning of the Revolutionary War. A job that would pay her enough to live and allow her to begin reimbursing Boylston for her advance. It would also give her a dissertation topic that was in the eighteenth, not the seventeenth, century.

"So what do you think?" he asked when he finished

presenting the offer. "Is this perfect, or what?"

Lauren stared at him across the littered expanse of his desk. She ran her fingers through her hair, overwhelmed by his offer. "I, ah, I don't know what to say."

"You're perfect for it and it's perfect for you—even down to the fact that there's very little public speaking involved." Gabe stood and walked around his desk, dropping into the chair next to her. "I've been searching for months for the right person for this position. I thought of you for it, of course, but with *Rebeka Hibbens* and all, I knew you wouldn't be interested. But now that's all changed." He reached over and touched her knee. "At least say you'll meet the board of directors."

"I'd love to," Lauren stuttered, overwhelmed by Gabe's generosity and very aware of his close proximity. "But I don't understand—how do you even know about this job, let alone happen to be in the position to offer it to anyone?"

Gabe leaned back in his chair and let out a full-bodied laugh. Lauren was glad to see he was his old self again now that the NEH lawsuit had been dropped. "Oh, you know me, I get around," he said. "When I was first married, we lived in Lexington and I got involved with the society—and I guess I just never got uninvolved. My friend Pat has kept me on the board of directors, and she twisted my arm into helping them write this grant. She's also the one who put me in charge of the PI search committee."

"A committee?"

"It's a committee of one," Gabe said. "All you have to do is pass muster with the board of directors, which, with my endorsement and your background and charm"—he flashed her a grin—"will be no problem at all." He reached over to his desk and twirled his calendar around. "There's a meeting a week from today. If you give me a résumé, I'll fax it to all the members—we'll take it up next Monday and set up an interview then."

"You're going to hand this job to me on a platter?" Lauren asked, afraid it was too good to be true. "What's the catch?"

"Don't you see?" Gabe asked. "You're doing *me* the favor. We've had a bitch of a time trying to find the right person to take the reins."

A jolt of electricity zapped through Lauren as Gabe smiled into her eyes. She remembered the feel of his naked body against hers, the way he had cupped her breasts, the fact that Todd now had a girlfriend.

"It's new territory for the society, and I've been worried that if we couldn't find anyone," Gabe was saying, "I'd have to direct the damn thing myself."

Lauren's mind whirled with the possibilities. It was as if her fairy godmother had flown down from the sky and waved a magic wand. But before she could say anything, Gabe leaned over and kissed her. It started as a light kiss, but Lauren found herself responding with a passion she wouldn't have thought possible a few hours earlier. Then they were standing and Lauren felt him hardening against her as she melted into him. "Whoa," she said, finally pulling away.

"Got those personal issues taken care of?" Gabe asked.

Lauren hesitated for a second, then nodded. "It's all been worked out—I think."

"Then do you want to go out and celebrate?"

She glanced at her watch and laughed. "It's eleven o'clock in the morning."

"We'll have an early lunch in the square," Gabe suggested, grabbing his black cashmere coat.

They had an elegant lunch at Rialto, the restaurant at the Charles Hotel. When they walked up to the maître d', he bowed deeply to Gabe and showed "Dr. Phipps and his guest" to "the best table in the house."

Gabe smiled broadly as he waved Lauren to precede him.

Lauren wished Todd could see her being fawned over by pretentious waiters as she ate endive and walnut salad with a world-renowned man. But as lunch progressed, Todd grew further and further from her mind. They talked about Drew and the NEH lawsuit and the Lexington job. They giggled over a story Gabe had heard in Washington about a senator who got caught where he shouldn't have been. When lunch was over, they went to Gabe's house.

"So was this Lexington job just a ruse to get me here in the middle of the afternoon?" Lauren teased as they stood in the vestibule smiling foolishly at each other.

"Not even funny, Lauren." Gabe's expression was suddenly serious. "The society's professional, not personal. You could walk out of here right now—never talk to me again—and I'd still recommend you to the board." He stepped away and gestured toward the door.

Lauren closed the distance between them and wrapped her arms around him. "And if I don't?" she asked.

"That's even better," Gabe said.

Their coats ended up on the floor, along with Gabe's jacket and Lauren's sweater. As he kissed her and pressed her to him, she felt a warmth flowing through her limbs. This was a good thing, she thought. Gabe was a good man. A great man. She was lucky to have found him. She began to unbutton his shirt, kissing his neck and chest as she worked her way downward. "Where's your bedroom?" she asked, her knees beginning to buckle. "I don't think I'm going to be able to stand up much longer."

Gabe took her hand and led her up the wide staircase to a large, airy room at the front of the house. Bay windows at the treetops let in light but allowed privacy. They undressed each other slowly, savoring the anticipation in a way they had been unable to do that first night in Lauren's apartment. The afternoon sunlight danced suggestively over their bodies, increasing Lauren's passion.

"Let me look at you," Gabe said when they were naked. He reached out and trailed a finger along her hipbone. "You're beautiful," he said, his voice husky with desire. "So beautiful." Lauren pulled him to her.

Afterward, lying in Gabe's arms and staring at the treetops, Lauren felt strangely let down. Although the sex had been great, she had a hollow feeling inside, an empty place Gabe had been unable to touch. She realized she missed Todd and the silliness that always accompanied their lovemaking. She missed the teasing about her prehensile toe, the giggling while having sex on the kitchen floor, the playacting that she was a nurse. Gabe was a wonderful lover, skilled and serious, but she longed for Todd's laughter.

Stop it, she told herself as she turned toward Gabe. Todd had someone else.

After leaving Gabe, Lauren wandered through Harvard Square, wondering what she was getting herself into. She felt lonely for Todd, but there was a warm, pleasant throbbing between her legs. She recalled Gabe's serious dark eyes, deep with passion, watching her as he brought her to orgasm. She thought of how thoughtful and dependable Gabe was, how handsome and charming—not to mention rich and famous. Any other woman would be thrilled that such a man wanted her. As Lauren headed down the stairs to the subway, she decided that she was too.

Emerging from the glass triangle of the Porter Square T station, she glanced up at the red metal sculpture turning in the wind above her; three abstract shapes floating past each other at different rates and angles, each carried by the breeze on its own path. She stood in the middle of the brick plaza contemplating the inexplicable gyrations of life. Then she noticed the time. She had less than twenty minutes before she had to pick up Drew at school. Lengthening her stride as she headed toward home, she realized with a pang of guilt that she had hardly thought of her son since arriving at Gabe's house.

Lauren climbed the porch stairs, lost in thought, and was disturbed by the sense of another presence. Someone was in the shadows, sitting in the creaky rocker some long-ago tenant had left behind. With a start, she realized it was Deborah.

Deborah was holding a large manila envelope in her lap. A bulky package wrapped in brown paper rested against her leg. She had the appearance of a woman who had been waiting patiently for some time and, as she silently watched Lauren's approach, Lauren had the uncomfortable feeling that Deborah knew exactly where—and with whom—she had been.

"What are you doing here?" Lauren demanded, looking up and down the street.

"I'll only be a moment," Deborah said, rising from the chair but staying in the shadows. "I have some things for you." She proffered the envelope but held onto the package.

"I told you to stay away," Lauren said, not moving forward. "I'm afraid for Drew."

"Take this," Deborah said, her calm voice brooking no argument. "It may help you help him."

Figuring that the best way to get rid of Deborah was to do as she asked, Lauren took the envelope.

"The answers you need are in 'The Book of Mahala'—the portion of the chronicle that tells the story of the first Immortalis—and that, as I've explained, I can't give you until you've completed a waxing moon ritual with us."

Throwing another look over her shoulder, Lauren stepped into the shadows. "Then what's this?"

"Our chronicle is different from your Bible in that it has two distinct parts—call them the sacred and the profane. The profane is a series of historical analyses of the places and epochs in which the coven has lived. It's much closer to history than religion. It's not about witchcraft or magic or anything personal."

"So who wrote this?" Lauren couldn't help asking, remembering Gabe's story of finding Deborah typing the chronicle on an IBM Selectric. "Who did the historical analysis?"

Deborah smiled and shifted the package from one hand to the other. "As I told you before, we did. Harriet Reardon Smith wrote the portion I just gave you in the late nineteenth century."

Lauren placed the envelope under her arm. "Thank you," she said with a curt nod, indicating it was time for Deborah to leave.

"A portion of Faith Osborne's story," Deborah continued as if Lauren hadn't spoken, "along with pieces of lots of other people's stories, is used to analyze the economic and social conditions in the Massachusetts Bay Colony in 1692. Oddly enough, Jackie was interested in this particular piece."

"How do you know that?" Lauren demanded, curious despite her nervousness.

"She phoned me the morning she died and said she needed to talk to me about the part of the chronicle that reinterpreted the importance of religion in Colonial America—the Faith Osborne part. But I was handling the store by myself and couldn't talk with her. We arranged to meet the next day to discuss it."

"You need to go now," Lauren said, motioning toward the stairs. She had forgotten Jackie had said she was going to call Deborah that morning, but it sounded as if Jackie had wanted to speak to Deborah about something very different from what she had wanted to speak to Lauren about. Whatever it had been didn't matter now. What mattered was keeping

Drew safe. "Thanks for your help. I appreciate it—really I do. But I need you to leave."

Deborah moved out of the shadows. "What's in there is only a small part of what happened to Faith and Dorcas. The rest—the part I think will help you figure out how best to protect Drew—is in 'The Book of Mahala.'" She thrust the bulky package into Lauren's free hand. "This is Jackie's Deodat Willard print. My way of making amends for the trouble we've caused you."

"The best way to make amends is for you to leave me—"

"The Immortalis will be held at midnight tomorrow," Deborah added. "If you change your mind, we'll be at White Horse Beach."

Then she swooped down the stairs and disappeared around the corner.

Twenty-Seven

SCOTT CAME HOME WITH DREW AFTER SCHOOL. AFTER giving the boys a snack, Lauren meandered into the living room and sat down at her desk. Noticing Jackie's Deodat Willard print leaning against the wall, she was reminded that she had to call Simon Pappas. But she also had sixty exams to grade and return to Paul Conklin by tomorrow. As grading was now her only source of income, grading came first.

Pushing aside stacks of books and scribbled notes for *Rebeka Hibbens*, as well as piles of unpaid bills and unopened mail, Lauren searched for the exams she had picked up from Paul last week. She found them under the envelope Deborah had just given her. Fingering the edge of the envelope, Lauren thought of her promise to stay out of the seventeenth century. She glanced at the Deodat Willard and remembered she had also vowed to find out what Faith Osborne had done to cause Dorcas's death.

An explosion of giggles jolted her as Drew and Scott bounded through the doorway. "Can Scott stay for dinner?" Drew asked. "Dinner's part of the game we're playing and it won't work if Scott has to go home," he explained.

Lauren was overwhelmed by an almost irresistible urge to reach out and touch her son, to reassure herself that he was indeed alive and safe. But for Drew's sake, she restrained herself. "If it's all right with Scott's mom, it's all right with me," she said. "But we're just having frozen pizza."

"Couldn't we have hot dogs over the fire again?" Drew begged. "That's what would fit our game the best."

Lauren shook her head, uncomfortable with the memory. "That was a special treat."

"Okay," Drew said, knowing when to quit. "Thanks," he added over his shoulder as the boys raced back to his room, slamming the door behind them.

Lauren pushed Deborah's envelope under the blue books and grabbed a handful of exams. It was safer for Drew if she stayed away from Deborah Sewall and the seventeenth century. She opened the first blue book and skimmed a few paragraphs to get a feel for the general level at which the students were working. She opened a second and did the same. But by the time she was skimming the third, she found her thoughts drifting back to the afternoon she had just spent with Gabe.

What exactly did she feel for Gabe? It wasn't love. She had been in love once—perhaps she still was—and she wasn't experiencing any of the dizzying ups and downs of that state: the feverish excitement, the terror that her feelings might not be reciprocated, the intense longing to be with Todd every minute. Nor was she having any problem thinking about other things. Like Ed Zaleski's report that he had been unable to find any covens or sorcerers who worked with Bellarmine urns. Or Steve Conway's discovery of an abandoned apartment with a broken basement window near where Drew was found on Beacon Hill. Or Todd's tormented expression as he had left her apartment yesterday.

So what was it? Lust, Lauren decided. She was in lust with the great Dr. Phipps, the country's best known living historian. For although they had had a great afternoon, filled with candid conversation, good sex, and the savoring of their easy companionship, she wasn't the least obsessed.

They had talked about everything from Todd and Deborah, to the existence of God, to Gabe's longing for a child. "Deborah felt it was unfair to bring kids into a world that was so screwed up," Gabe had told her. "And ironically, by the end, when all those weird people with their crazy ideas and nutty books were all over the house, I was just as glad. Can you imagine the effect that kind of insanity would have had on a child?"

Although she had enjoyed Gabe's company immensely, Lauren found herself more than happy to have time away from him. Between now and noon tomorrow, when he would open the week-long American Historical Association conference with his plenary session address, he was "doing the media bit," as he had put it: flying to New York City to be on "The Today Show;" taping a simultaneous public radio broadcast that was to be aired by over fifty stations nationwide; being interviewed for a feature article by The *Boston Globe*. Then, after opening the conference, he would have to play host for the rest of the day to the world's most renowned historians.

He had apologized profusely for not being able to include her at dinner and had promised to meet her at her apartment as soon as he could get away. "I'll be out of there no later than nine," he had told her as she left his house this afternoon. "Thirty-two hours away from you seems like thirty-two years." Lauren glanced at the clock. Only thirty more to go.

With great resolve, Lauren pulled a copy of the test from the first blue book, once again reminding herself that until she got the Lexington job, grading was a financial imperative. After scanning the complicated essay questions, she groaned. It might take her all thirty hours to complete the damn exams.

It was one o'clock in the morning and Lauren had been lying in bed for hours, unable to sleep. Deborah's envelope had been calling to her and she felt her willpower crumbling. She slipped out of bed and with a furtive glance over her shoulder, slunk into the living room.

Her heart was pounding and her palms were damp. Like a thief in the night, she closed the blinds before turning on the light. Then she went right to the envelope. With the relief of a dieter reaching for that forbidden bag of cookies, she opened it. And with the gluttony of that same dieter, she sat down and began to read.

She flipped quickly though the more academic portions of the pages until she found what she had been longing to read: the Faith Osborne story.

Following the execution of her seven-year-old daughter, Dorcas, for witchcraft in 1692, a warrant was issued against Faith Osborne, wife of Oliver Osborne, a powerful magistrate of great renown in the Massachusetts Bay Colony. An extremely beautiful woman, Faith married Oliver after the death of her husband, Ezekiel Hoar, a landless man who hired himself out. It was well-known that Faith had been content as a poor woman, tending to Ezekiel and her pots and her daughter, but after two years of raising her daughter by herself, she had sought to escape her poverty and loneliness by entering into a loveless marriage with Oliver Osborne, a man twenty years her senior.

It was this marriage that led to her downfall, for Oliver was an ambitious and prideful man. After Dorcas was ex-

ecuted, Faith refused to live in Oliver's house, claiming that she too was a witch. She wandered around the town, crying out her guilt to any who would listen. Despite the fact that a declaration of guilt usually freed a woman accused of witchcraft, Oliver had Faith arrested to prove to the colony that no one, not even his own wife, was above God's law.

The accusations against Faith Osborne were numerous. Her neighbor, Sarah Walcott, claimed that she, Sarah, went into a fit after Faith "did steadfastly fix her eyes upon me." She also alleged that the day after Faith Osborne warned that the chimney on Goody Walcott's house "shall be falling down," it did. Another neighbor, Elizabeth Cloyce, claimed that Goody Osborne's "shape did come into my room at night" and that "her specter was biting and pinching and pricking my body." But by far the most damning evidence was given by Oliver himself, who, after watching Elizabeth Cloyce enter his house, had seen a blue boar run back through the gate only moments later. This proved beyond a doubt that Faith was a witch. Had he not seen with his own eyes that she did turn Goody Cloyce into a boar?

Faith Osborne was imprisoned in Cambridge Prison, tried, and found guilty. When she changed her story and refused to acknowledge her sins, she was subjected to peine forte et dure*—an English procedure in which heavy weights were progressively piled on a prisoner's body—until a confession was procured. She was then reprieved and released. When Oliver Osborne refused to pay her prison fees, claiming that "no witch is any wife of mine," she was imprisoned once again.*

The luckless woman, Lauren thought as she rubbed the goose bumps on her arms. Faith was struggling to support and raise a child on her own and, because she had allowed herself to become dependent upon a man whose ego and ambition were greater than his feelings for her, she had been destroyed.

Lauren remembered her dreams: of Millicent and

Rebeka in Gabe's dining room, of Drew being hanged. None of her dreams matched anything in the chronicle, yet Faith's story felt so familiar and Lauren felt such a strong empathy for the woman. And there were the fugues: making soap with a high-spirited daughter, arguing with her husband about the witch trials, watching wild rabbits being drawn from the forest as if they were tame circus animals.

Questions she didn't want to answer assaulted her. Could Deborah and Cassandra be right? Did the soul reincarnate and perhaps even remember pieces of its previous lives? But then she caught herself: What was she thinking? Was she saying she believed she was the reincarnation of a seventeenth-century soul? That she, Lauren Freeman, had once been Faith Osborne? Forcing her thoughts away from the unthinkable, Lauren reminded herself that one didn't need a PhD to recognize the similarities between Faith's struggles and her own.

She flipped through the remaining pages and found she had to disagree with Gabe on one point: This work was anything but a "nutty book." The chronicle read like sophisticated history written by a learned and serious scholar. It was also clear that Gabe *had* been right about another point. This was clearly the work of a contemporary historian.

For the author, undoubtedly Deborah Sewall, had used a technique that was unheard of until recently—she'd used actual data to compile an equation comparing the economic conditions of various groups in the Massachusetts Bay Colony. In another example of twentieth-century scholarship, Deborah had then taken episodes from the lives of ordinary people—one of them Faith Osborne's arrest for witchcraft—to posit the argument that economics, not religion, was the primary force behind the witchcraft hysteria. Deborah went on to use this as a basis for a reinterpretation of all the institutions in Colonial society. Despite having been written in the twentieth century, this was an extraordinary piece of work, exploring ideas that hadn't entered mainstream historical thought until Gabe's own book, *A New Social History of Colonial America,* was published in 1990.

Although Lauren knew she should go back to sleep, she couldn't resist reading a few more paragraphs.

It has been posited that the witchcraft hysteria, so widespread in seventeenth-century America, was the natural outgrowth of the repressive Calvinist doctrines to which almost all colonists adhered. Other explanations range from mass hysteria to a fungus in the bread that caused wild hallucinations. Based upon careful analysis of dozens of individuals who were accused of witchcraft, it appears that economic considerations are by far the most powerful in explaining the phenomenon. For every . . .

Before she could get caught up in the narrative, Lauren stuffed the pages back in the envelope. She reminded herself that, although there was clearly much to interest a student of seventeenth-century America here, she was no longer that student. She knew she should go back to bed, that she would be exhausted in the morning, but she remained at her desk. Lauren closed her eyes and imagined what it must have been like to be married to Oliver Osborne.

She was in a small room with a low ceiling, the walls covered by wide panels of rough pine. She was scared. Terrified. Unable to see her way through to the thing she must do. She wrung her small hands, hands that had been red and rough from work just a few seasons past, hands that were now pink and white and pampered. Pampered by the wealth of Oliver Osborne.

Faith's mind bobbled from one impossible choice to another. To tell Oliver that Rebeka, Millicent, and the others did meet in Glover barn was to bring the witch-hunters upon them. The goodmen of Cambridge would arrest them and try them and surely find them guilty of the most absurd of crimes. Crimes for which they would be hung.

But if she did not tell, Dorcas would face the hangman's noose.

Faith pulled at the lace cuffs of her dress. Rebeka was her dear cousin. Rebeka had cared for her as a child, had taught her the fox and glove stitch for knitting suspenders, had brought food and comfort to her home after Ezekiel died. Millicent Glover had always been kind, and the others were without guile.

But Dorcas was her child. Her only child. And barely of seven years.

How could she betray Rebeka, who had begged her never to speak of Glover barn? How could she align herself with the witch-hunters she did so detest?

She thought of Dorcas sleeping soundly on her pallet overhead, of her daughter's tinkling laughter, of the wonder with which the child gazed at the world.

Faith stared into the knots of the pine, as if within their design she could find the answers she sought. Oliver had promised that Dorcas would be spared if Faith told where Rebeka and Millicent did their black magic.

Faith stood and pressed her damp palms to her shirt. Dear Lord, she prayed, forgive me for what I do. Then she stepped out of the room to tell her husband of the goings-on at Glover barn.

Tuesday dawned gray and forbidding, the first snow of winter huddling within the slate-colored clouds. After Lauren had finally returned to bed, Drew had woken twice, his body quivering with fear, his mind full of monsters. After the second awakening, Lauren brought him in with her. She lay beside him, stiff and wide-eyed, as he thrashed and muttered and cried out in his sleep.

That morning he didn't want to go to school, begging her to let him stay home. But Lauren remembered the psychologist's words and made him go. When they arrived, there was no policeman on duty. She called Steve Conway, but he wasn't available, and the woman she spoke with was surly, grudgingly offering to send someone over in half an hour. Lauren had waited in the hallway until the policeman showed up.

Her hands deep in her pockets and her jacket zipped to the neck, Lauren had headed home, reminding herself that Drew was safe and that events had taken a remarkable turn for the better. But she didn't feel reassured. She felt tired and ill-tempered and had the uncomfortable certainty that something bad was about to happen.

When she got home, she called Todd to remind him to pick up Drew from school. "I know what day it is," he snapped. "I only forgot that one time when he was in kindergarten—I think you should let it go." She tried to explain her nervousness, but he would have none of it. "I'm perfectly capable of caring for my son for the night," he told her.

Lauren put the receiver down and glanced at the clock. She had promised Paul that the exams would be on his desk half an hour ago. Annoyed with both Todd and herself, she gathered the blue books and raced over to the university.

Paul's door was locked, so she headed for the department office to leave the exams in his basket. The large open room was the usual bustle of activity. Lauren murmured the appropriate hellos while dropping the exams in Paul's box. She checked her own mailbox, then headed to the ABD office.

ABD stood for "all but dissertation" and was used to designate those graduate students who had finished their course work and passed their comprehensive exams, having only a doctoral thesis to complete before being awarded a PhD. The ABD office was much larger than the one used by the other graduate students, and each ABD had his or her own desk and phone in a private carrel.

After checking the other carrels and finding them empty, Lauren put her backpack and mail on her desk. She dropped into her chair and began flipping through the envelopes—the usual assortment of free textbooks she didn't want, solicitations for more textbooks she didn't want, and job announcements for which she wasn't qualified. Full of jittery, undirected energy, Lauren played with her junk mail and watched the clock: more than two hours to kill before Gabe's speech.

She could go home, clean the apartment, maybe make a batch of chili for Drew, but there really wasn't enough time. On the other hand, now that her course work was completed and she was momentarily dissertationless, there wasn't anything she needed to do on campus. She could begin her research on Lexington women, but it seemed presumptuous to begin work on a job she didn't actually have—and it might jinx her chances for getting it.

It was so peculiar; after years of always having too much to do, too much pressure, too little time, she was suddenly free. But instead of feeling relief, all she felt was edgy emptiness. She zipped up her backpack and left the office. As she walked out of the building, part of her brain felt uncomfortably vacant and useless.

Then she thought of Faith Osborne, of the horrible decision she had imagined Faith making in an attempt to save her child—an attempt that Lauren knew had failed. She remembered Drew crying out in the night and wondered where Faith had gone wrong. Walking along the sidewalk, she saw the wide steps of the library spread open before her. The building tugged at her like a magnet drawing her to it. Despite her promise to stay away from the seventeenth century, she knew it was important, imperative even, for her to learn all she could about Faith and Dorcas.

A computer search netted a sum total of zero citations for her query on Faith Osborne, but she found numerous references to Dorcas Osborne and forty-seven books in the library system that contained "anecdotal accounts" of the Colonial witch trials. She headed down three floors into the depths of the stacks, where the oldest and mustiest of the books were shelved.

Only four of the sources on Dorcas were in the library, and it didn't take Lauren long to determine that, with the exception of one, their references to the child were limited. Half the other books were out on loan and a quick skim of the table of contents of most of the others indicated they were going to be useless for her purpose. Six of the titles, including Gabe's *A New Social History,* looked promising. Glancing at her watch and noting that over an hour remained before Gabe's speech, she carried the books to a study carrel and sat down.

The carrels in this part of the library always made Lauren think of livestock corrals: pens of desks lined up in rectangular configurations in the bowels of the building. Lauren flipped on the study light over a desk, casting a small triangle of brightness into the gloomy, overheated room. Pulling at the collar of her sweatshirt to get more air, she glanced down the spines of the books.

She couldn't resist a peek at the jacket of Gabe's; he beamed out at her, his charisma on full wattage, and she felt a warm, melting sensation. Although the book had been published more than eight years ago, Gabe looked remarkably the same now as he had then: handsome, intelligent, his sense of humor webbing his sexy bedroom eyes. He was a bit grayer at the temples now, she thought, scrutinizing the picture. A few more lines, perhaps. But overall, he was the same "world-renowned scholar of American history," the same man who had kissed the inside of her elbow yesterday afternoon and told her he hadn't fallen this fast or this hard since he was sixteen. "It makes me want to do something adolescent and crazy," he had said. "Like run off to Las Vegas." She had laughed at his joke then, but she couldn't help wondering now how much of a joke it had been.

She closed the book over Gabe's picture. She had read his book years ago—one couldn't study American history at the college level without being assigned Phipps—although now that she thought about it, she had done a lot more skimming than reading. Still, she knew it to be a general text that presented a new theoretical overview of Colonial society. Lauren put Gabe's book down and reached for one of the more promising in the pile.

She was unsurprised to find a fairly long segment on Dorcas and wondered why she and Jackie hadn't included this information. Then she remembered that, of course, Dorcas hadn't been a member of the coven.

As she read on, her interest mounted. According to this account, Dorcas had been arrested with the other coven members in Millicent Glover's barn. In September of 1692, Millicent, Rebeka, Foster Lacy, Bridgit Corey, Abigail Cullender, and Mercy Broadstreet as well as Dorcas—"the seven firebrands of hell"—had all been found by Oliver Osborne "doing the devil's work" at Glover Farm. What was Dorcas doing with them? Lauren wondered. Where was Faith?

The others were all taken to Cambridge Prison, but in deference to Dorcas's "young years" she was examined and tried immediately. Upon finding "devil's marks" on the little girl's body—"numerous unnatural markings of the flesh upon her cheeks," which sounded to Lauren like freckles—and eliciting a confession from the confused child, Dorcas was sentenced to death the next day.

Dorcas was hung the following dawn, from the branches of an ancient oak tree on Gallows Hill. Lauren shivered as she remembered her dream about Drew, once again unnerved by her strange prescience. She was certain that before reading this account, she hadn't known the details of the girl's execution.

The book went on to briefly discuss the fate of the other six, summarizing the story Lauren knew so well: the trial, the imprisonment, the unexplained disappearances. But there was no mention of Faith. As far as this author was concerned, Faith Osborne had never lived, had never been a part of the coven, had never vanished without a trace. Although Lauren knew it was not unusual for a relatively minor player to be missed in historical accounts, she found the omission of Faith ominous.

Lauren closed the book and stared at the scarred face of the carrel wall. *Parkinson was wrong: Time only contracts* was scrawled in red-brown ink. *You suck* was written neatly under it. She swung her chair around to catch a bit of light from the high, narrow windows behind her. Although still morning, the sky appeared to be darkening, its color now the same no-color of the cement foundation framing the small panes. She shivered again.

Stop it, she scolded herself, turning back to the books. There was no point in coming unglued because she had had a dream about an unknown event whose details she could have easily surmised. Nor was any purpose to be served by wondering why some sloppy historian had failed to include Faith in his discussion of the coven.

She picked up Gabe's book and examined the index to see if he had included anything on Faith or Dorcas. As she had expected, he had not. Turning to the table of contents, she saw that his opening chapter summarized his reinterpretation of Colonial life, and she flipped to it to see if his sounded anything like Deborah's analysis.

She began to read Gabe's discussion of how he had turned the philosopher Georg W. F. Hegel on his head to derive a "neomaterialist interpretation, deflecting attention from the institutions traditionally considered to be the seats of social control." He then described how he had combined Marxist philosophical tenets with the more conservative structural-functional approach of the great sociologists Talcott Parsons and Robert Merton, and added in a quantitative analysis to derive his "triangulation of perspectives." Lauren smiled. All a bit multisyllabic and academic for the witches. Then she skipped down a few paragraphs and read:

It has been posited that the witchcraft hysteria, so widespread in seventeenth-century America, was the natural outgrowth of the repressive Calvinist doctrines to which almost all colonists adhered. Other explanations range from mass hysteria to a fungus in the bread that caused wild hallucinations. Based upon careful analysis of dozens of individuals who were accused of witchcraft, it appears that economic considerations are by far the most powerful in explaining the phenomenon. For every . . .

She reread the paragraph and then raced through the next few, sweat gathering above her lip and prickling beneath her arms. She pulled the pages of Deborah's chronicle from her backpack and spread them out on the table.

Lauren now knew why the chronicle had sounded so familiar—and it had nothing to do with witchcraft or reincarnation. Gabe and Deborah's words were exactly the same.

Twenty-Eight

LAUREN SAT FROZEN, THE LIGHT OF HER CARREL THE only bright spot in the dimness. So Gabe had spoken the truth. The chronicle was a wild lie, a hoax, a farce. Deborah had made the whole thing up—after she'd copied Gabe's work. Lauren looked down at the book and the photocopied pages, stark and three-dimensional in their small cone of light. No wonder the chronicle was brilliant; it had been written by a brilliant man.

The vertical partitions of the small carrel seemed to bend in toward her. The murky light outside the high windows grew murkier and the low ceilings even lower. Lauren stood. Grabbing Gabe's book and Deborah's pages, she headed through the maze of stacks. She needed air. She had to get out of this dark and musty place.

As she walked along the deserted rows of forgotten tomes, she was reminded of her long-ago dream of Oliver Osborne, leaves clinging to his bushy hair and mud caking the hem of his cloak, chasing her through the dark library stacks. He had held a shiny knife in his hand. Lauren shivered at the memory.

She blinked as she caught sight of light over the open stairwell at the end of another narrow corridor of books. A wide shadow appeared at the opening. A dark figure in a long cloak was coming toward her, his cloak brushing the stacks as it passed. The figure was backlit, so she couldn't see the face, but she could see that he was striding quickly and purposefully toward her. Lauren grabbed onto a shelf for support. Just as she was about to turn and run, she recognized who was approaching and began to laugh. It was no menacing figure; it wasn't Oliver Osborne or some other evil apparition. It was Gabe, his black cashmere coat billowing open as he walked.

She grinned and waved. "Gabe," she cried. "What are you doing here?"

He was upon her in a second. He grabbed her up in his arms and kissed her passionately. "I had a few minutes before my keynote and I needed to get away from the adoring throngs," he said with a self-effacing smile. "I came down here because it's usually deserted, but you, my love, are an unexpected—and extremely welcome—surprise."

"As are you," Lauren said, a bit breathless from both the kiss and the scare she had given herself. She smiled up at him, for a moment forgetting what she had just discovered.

"What have you got there?" he asked, pointing to *A New Social History*. "Looks vaguely familiar."

"Some boring historian," Lauren said, raising the book. As she did, Deborah's pages slipped from her hand and fell to the floor. Together they knelt to pick them up. When Gabe's hand brushed against hers, Lauren felt the burn of the contact all the way up her arm. She thought of them as they would be later that night, naked and entwined in her bed. Yes, she thought, she was definitely in lust.

"You're not going to believe what I found," Lauren

said as she gathered up a fistful of pages. "It's the most—" She glanced over at Gabe and the words caught in her throat.

Gabe's face was set in harsh, hard lines. "Where did you get these?" he growled in a raspy whisper.

Lauren stared at him, at the anger gathering on his face, at his fingers crumpling the pages in his hands.

"I thought you'd cut off all contact with Deborah."

"I, ah, I . . ." Lauren began, but stopped in confusion. "How did you know I got these from Deborah?"

Gabe didn't say anything as he struggled to control himself. His angry expression was replaced by stony calmness, but a tinge of anxiety remained in his eyes. "I told you," he finally said, dropping his gaze and smoothing out the pages he had crumpled, "I've read their ridiculous chronicle."

"You knew she plagiarized your book?"

Gabe pulled the rest of the pages from Lauren's hand. He shrugged. "What do I care what a bunch of crazies write?" But his gaze shifted uneasily around the stacks.

Lauren looked up at her lover, his handsome face in shadow, his broad shoulders throwing a wide swath of darkness over her, and rocked back on her heels. What if she had the scenario all wrong? What if it wasn't Deborah who had plagiarized Gabe's work? What if it was Gabe who had stolen from Deborah?

"You never wanted me to read the chronicle," Lauren said, her voice barely a whisper. "You did everything to keep me from it." As she heard her own words, another much more terrible thought blazed through her mind. Although plagiarism was one of the worst violations that could be committed within the academic community, it was a theft of mere words and ideas, a crime against the profession. It wasn't kidnapping—or murder.

"I told you," Gabe said, coming toward her. "I

don't think the chronicle has any place in historical analysis. I didn't want your first major work to be contaminated by inappropriate data."

Lauren heard Deborah's words in her ears. *"We never read history . . . male-biased, patriarchal conjecture . . . by old white men who weren't there . . ."*

Suddenly, Lauren saw it all. Deborah had never read Gabe's book; it had been published after their divorce, after she had discontinued her academic studies. If Deborah had copied the chronicle from Gabe, she would never have given it to Lauren or Jackie. They were Gabe's student and colleague, and Deborah would have known they'd have read *A New Social History*. Only someone who had never read *A New Social History* would have done such a thing. Someone who had let her husband read her own writings, never guessing he would steal them.

As Lauren watched Gabe stuff Deborah's pages into his coat pocket, she knew she was right.

He reached out to take her in his arms. "I just didn't want you to be laughed at."

Lauren swatted his arms away as her last conversation with Jackie replayed in her mind. *"I've found something big. . . . Not what you think,"* Jackie had said. *"I was reading this section on religion in Colonial life. . . . It posits a much more reduced role for theology than I've ever seen before . . . It's pre-Phipps. . . . "*

Jackie must have discovered Gabe's plagiarism. And Jackie had died within hours of that discovery. . . .

Had Gabe murdered Jackie to silence her? Lauren's mind raced so fast she could barely keep up. Had Gabe been trying to keep her from also discovering the plagiarism? By wooing her? By scaring her away from Deborah with poppets and Bellarmine urns? She looked up at Gabe in horror. Was he responsible for Drew's kidnapping?

"Lauren," Gabe began, his charismatic smile in place, "you can't possibly think—"

She backed slowly away. Had she made love with the man who had kidnapped her son? The man who had killed her best friend? Lauren was hit by a revulsion so powerful that for a moment she thought she would be sick. She couldn't look at him. She couldn't be near him. She turned and ran.

She ran back into the stacks, away from Gabe, but stupidly also away from the exit. She threw a look over her shoulder and saw he was following her.

"Lauren," Gabe cried. "Wait! Stop!"

But Lauren wasn't about to stop. She took a sharp turn and then another. Her nightmare was coming true, but instead of Oliver Osborne behind her, it was Gabe. The great Gabe Phipps. The man with whom she had been eating and sleeping and laughing. She heard his footfalls thundering through the empty stacks. He was gaining on her. Horror roared through her as she skidded into the rotunda. Slipping on the flagstone, she righted herself and raced up the stairs.

"Lauren!" he called, only a few steps behind her. His voice was loud enough to attract the attention of a group of students heading down into the stacks. They craned their necks in fascination at the sight of the eminent Gabe Phipps running through the library.

"It's not what you think!"

Lauren didn't want to hear it. Her heart pounding and her breath coming in gasps, she took the stairs two at a time. Elbowing her way through the clusters of people on the main floor, she flew out the door. She heard him behind her on the sidewalk, but it sounded as if the distance between them had lengthened. She turned and saw that Gabe had stopped, that he was sitting on a stone bench in front of the library, his head in his hands.

Lauren kept going. She burst through the doors of the student union and, without conscious thought, got in line for lunch. The room was chaotic and noisy and smelled of turkey gravy. Just the place she needed; she would lose herself in the anonymity of the crowded cafeteria and try to figure out what to do.

She set her tray down in the center of a long table, a group of Asian students on one side and a couple of youngish professors on the other. Lauren sat quickly and stirred her yogurt; she slopped the thick mixture over the sides of the container and all over her tray. When she tried to wipe it up, the napkin slipped from her shaking fingers and fell to the floor. She looked around self-consciously, but no one was the least bit interested in her. From the conversations at the table, she quickly ascertained that the Asians were in the botany department and the professors in English. She sighed, feeling relatively safe caught between the academic conversations, safe enough to confront what frightened her most.

Maybe it was as Gabe had said. Maybe she was jumping to some pretty outrageous conclusions. Just because Gabe had stolen some words—and, she had to admit, some theories and insights—from the chronicle, that didn't mean he was guilty of kidnapping and murder. Lauren looked around the crowded room full of academicians and overachieving students, a room full of towering intelligence and towering egos. A man of Gabe's stature might do anything to maintain his reputation—murder, kidnapping, pretending a love he didn't feel.

She had always known Gabe was a great performer. She saw him charming America on TV, charming Nat on the phone, charming her in his bedroom. Could the whole thing have been an act? *"I just want to start this relationship being honest,"* he had told her. *"Everything out in the open."* Could he have killed her best friend and terrorized her son and then held her in his arms and told her how much he cared for her? Lauren felt dirty, violated, used.

She remembered Dan's suspicions about Gabe. Dan had pointed out that Gabe's interest in Lauren had coincided closely with Jackie's death. And Gabe had always been adamant in discouraging her involvement with Deborah and the chronicle. Gabe knew about poppets and Bellarmine urns. He could have gotten the key to her apartment off the wall in Jackie's kitchen, broken in, burned the candles, taken Herman. . . .

Lauren stood and dropped her uneaten lunch into the trash. She knew what she had to do.

Lauren slowly made her way to Sibley Auditorium. As she entered, she heard Gabe's voice pumping through the sound system. She couldn't believe how normal he sounded. He was even cracking jokes. The standing-room-only crowd roared with approval. The TV minicams whirled. She used the telephone in the lobby.

Steve Conway answered on the first ring. He was mostly silent through her recital of the story, interrupting only to clarify a few points. When she finished he asked, "Did you ever hear of a company called SFE Realty?"

"No," she said impatiently. "But I'm really concerned that—"

"How about Brattle Enterprises or P&P Associates?" he interrupted.

"What do these companies have to do with anything?" she demanded, annoyed by his lack of interest in what she was telling him.

"I'm still trying to untangle the web of ownership," Steve said, "but it looks like P&P is the holding company that controls the property at 57 Anderson Street—that's where we think Drew was held."

"But what about everything I've been telling you?"

"The fax is coming through now. I'll meet you at the auditorium in five."

"I could be all wrong," Lauren started to say. "I'm not at all—"

"We'll talk about it when I see you."

Lauren paced the anteroom. She picked up a conference program and flipped through the pages, trying to keep from feeling the full brunt of all she had learned and surmised, trying not to focus on what might happen next. Her gaze drifted to the title of Gabe's keynote address: "The Place for Morality in Historical Analysis." She snorted in derision.

Steve arrived, accompanied by a uniformed officer. A cruiser pulled up on the sidewalk, and Steve told her there was another circling the perimeter of the building. "Before we go in, I want to let you in on the plan," he said. "If our suspicions are correct, Phipps is a very dangerous man and we must approach him as such. But if he's innocent, he's a very famous man who has done nothing wrong. So we're going to take it carefully, quietly."

Lauren nodded. Her throat felt as dry as sandpaper. She wasn't at all sure she could speak. *"Phipps is a very dangerous man. . . ."*

"The only fact we have at the moment is that Phipps is the owner of the building Drew was held in. That's it—and it's not much. Everything else is conjecture. If we don't handle this situation very carefully, we could end up with nothing." He waved to the policeman behind him. "After the big man finishes his speech, Greenho here and I will go up and talk to him real nice."

"But—" Lauren began.

"No second guessing." The lieutenant shook his head. "I've seen guys like this before—if you catch them off guard, there's a chance they'll crumble right at your feet. So you stay in the back," he told Lauren. "Out of sight. And one of my men will be around to get you when it's all over."

Lauren was numb as she watched the two policemen disappear through a side doorway, her thoughts swirling in a wild kaleidoscope of images: Gabe smiling at her over lunch at Rialto; Gabe touching her wineglass and toasting *Rebeka Hibbens*; Gabe staring at her naked body in wonder, telling her how beautiful she was. Then she saw Drew, running to her with tears streaming down his face after his kidnapping. She felt his skinny arms clutching at her, her own holding him as if she would never let go. Lauren's heart felt like a fist of cold stone in her chest. She turned and entered the auditorium.

She did as Steve had instructed, standing along the back wall with the undergraduates who had been unable to afford the price of the conference, but who were unofficially allowed in to hear the words of the great Dr. Phipps as long as they didn't take up a seat. Although she could barely make out his face from this distance, Gabe's towering, familiar voice gave him a nearness that unnerved her.

"It is our job as historians," Gabe was saying, "to keep the moral values of our time from inadvertently coloring our analysis of another epoch. And yet, in order to truly appreciate that other epoch, we must understand the code of mores that underlies the fabric of their world, that gives meaning to their culture. . . ."

Lauren inched forward, driven, despite Steve's admonition, to get a closer look at Gabe. To see from the expression on his face if he too recognized the irony of his discussion on morality in light of what he knew she had discovered. But as she drew closer to the stage, she saw a Gabe Phipps who was as calm as ever. He stood at the podium, confident and in control, acting like any man who thought himself the greatest living historian would act before an assemblage of his adoring peers: wise, witty, and regal.

A flame of white hot anger gusted to life within Lauren. How could he? How dare he? Her hands trembled with rage. She grasped them together to still their shaking.

"And so, I leave you with this thought," Gabe was concluding. "To know the code of ethics of an epoch—to know what to them was irrefutably right and reprehensibly wrong—is to know that epoch." He paused to let the brilliance of his statement filter through the crowd. Then he gave a wise nod and added simply, "Thank you."

The applause was thunderous. It swelled and filled the huge auditorium until Lauren felt no more sound was possible. Gabe dropped his eyes, as if embarrassed at the emotion he had evoked both within himself and his audience. Then he raised his head and looked out over the adoring throng, acknowledging their homage with a slight self-deprecating smile.

When Gabe held his hands out for silence, mimicking a gesture Lauren had seen the Pope use to still a crowd gathered below his Vatican window, her fury was overtaken by disgust. Suddenly, she didn't care about Steve Conway's plan to go carefully and quietly. Her fear of public speaking vanished as her desire to humiliate Gabe before his peers grew. More than anything, she wanted to take his huge overblown ego and dash it to bits before the people whose opinions he most respected.

Lauren stepped into the open aisle and called into the silence Gabe had commanded, "Aren't there some things that are *always* considered 'reprehensibly wrong,' Dr. Phipps? No matter what the historical epoch?" Out of the corner of her eye, she saw Steve Conway move to the edge of the stage curtain. He shot her a furious look. But Lauren couldn't stop herself from adding, "Aren't there some universals—some moral absolutes? Say, for example, rules against plagiarism? kidnapping? murder?"

Channel 7's minicam turned its lens from her to Gabe.

Gabe smiled benevolently, but she was close enough to see the cold glint in his eye. "While one might make the argument that all societies find murder repugnant," he said evenly, "one must also look to the various forms of murder that exist. Is an executioner hired by the state guilty of a moral wrong? Or a soldier killing the enemy of his country?"

Enraged by his smooth segue, Lauren stared at Gabe, her eyes full of hatred. He was smiling out into the audience, but she knew him well enough to detect the fear hovering beneath his composure.

"You're arguing semantics," she called up to the stage, "and I'm asking a question of moral commonality. I'm asking how all societies—all human beings—feel about someone who selfishly takes another life just to protect his own reputation."

"That, ah, that's a very interesting question, young lady," Gabe said, his self-confidence wavering. "Of course there are some moral absolutes. And, ah, the one you suggest is as good an example as any."

"And do you subscribe to that absolute, Dr. Phipps?" she demanded. "Do you hold yourself to the same moral standards as everyone else in America? Or have you put yourself above the code? Have you done things that people in this room would find reprehensible?"

Gabe shrugged his shoulders and shook his head sadly at the audience. "Of late, this young woman has shown up at every one of my public functions. I'm not sure what her problem is, but it appears from her vague and persistent accusations that there might be some mental instability involved." He smiled at Lauren with great compassion. "I think it's best if you go now, dear."

Lauren was struck speechless by Gabe's blatant lies and was only dimly aware of shuffling behind her. Suddenly, hands grabbed at her. They held her arms and her shoulders. Adrenaline burst through her and, with a mighty shove, she wrenched free of her captors.

"That's your method, isn't it?" she shouted at Gabe. "Whenever anyone threatens you, you declare them insane." More hands came at her, and once again she batted them away. "Are you planning to commit me to a locked ward, just like your wife? Do you think that will protect you from what you've done?"

The knuckles of Gabe's fingers were white as he gripped the podium. "Are you accusing me of something?" His voice roared through the sound system. "Something of which you have proof? This bizarre scenario you've concocted in your own mind has a lot more to do with your craziness than does any so-called guilt on my part."

Lauren was acutely aware of the silence of the hall, of the musty odor of damp wool and too many bodies pressed close together, of the whirl of the minicam. She flicked the last of the hands from her shoulders and looked straight into the camera. "They aren't just *my* accusations." She pointed at Steve Conway and Sergeant Greenho, who had taken a few steps onto the stage as she was speaking. "There are two gentlemen here who have some questions for you."

As the audience sucked in its collective breath, the policemen walked up to the podium. Steve Conway took Gabe's arm and led him to the back of the stage.

Lauren leaned up against the wall and closed her eyes.

Twenty-Nine

LAUREN RETRIEVED HER BACKPACK AND COAT FROM where she had left them in the library and went to the police station. The building was undergoing renovation, so she had to follow hand-lettered signs and wend her way through a maze of broken concrete and yellow tape to a rear door. She entered directly into a large room that was a tumult of activity. Phones rang from almost every desk. A group of policeman sat in a corner drinking coffee and laughing uproariously. An enraged citizen berated a resigned-looking policewoman for her inability to find the thieves who had broken into his apartment. A man in a sport jacket and tie kicked a soda machine and, when no can rolled out, kicked it again and walked away.

Lauren approached the female dispatcher seated at a makeshift front desk. After explaining who she was, Lauren was waved to a wooden bench and told to wait. "Sorry about the zoo," the woman said as a buzz saw screamed from the next room. Lauren just nodded, too preoccupied to be concerned with the disorderliness of the police station.

A few minutes later, Steve Conway emerged from an inner office. He also apologized for the untidiness, and for keeping her waiting, but he told her it would be at least another hour before he would be able to speak with her. "We're in the middle of taking Phipps' statement," Steve said. "It could be quite awhile."

"Did he confess?"

Steve moved closer and lowered his voice. "He's just at the beginning of his story, but let's just say that, although your ability to follow directions isn't top-notch, your intuition sure is."

Lauren smiled sheepishly until the full impact of his statement hit her and she once again heard Gabe talking to Nat. *"You know me,"* Gabe had told his editor, *"I always get what I want in the end."* She felt an odd clutch of fear in her stomach and was glad she was sitting down. "My intuition on everything?"

"Later," Steve said, shaking his head. "Is there anyone else you can think of who I should talk to? Anyone with additional information who could help me get a better grip on this mess?"

She explained a bit more about Deborah and Gabe's relationship and reminded him how much Dan Ling knew.

"I've got Ling working on it right now. Looks like I owe that boy one hell of an apology—you too, I guess."

Lauren waved her hand. "Who could've known?"

"Why don't you take a walk?" he suggested. "Get some air. A bite to eat. Come back in about an hour."

Lauren found a pay phone in a drugstore on the next block and called Todd. She reached him at his darkroom. "It looks like they've caught the kidnapper," she said. "And maybe Jackie's murderer too." Feeding the phone change as she went along, she told him the whole story. When she finished, there was silence on the other end of the line.

"Please deposit twenty-five cents for an additional three minutes," ordered a whiny recorded voice.

Todd waited for the ding of the coin before he spoke. "How are you doing?"

"A little shaky at the moment, but I'll be fine."

"It's just so incredible. Gabe Phipps. You never really know people, do you?"

Lauren barked a laugh without humor. "Ain't that the truth."

"Oh, Lauren, I didn't mean—"

"It's all right," she interrupted. "I deserved it."

"You want me to come down there?" he offered. "I can call Aunt Beatrice and see if she can take Drew for a couple of hours."

"No, I'm okay. Really. You spend some time with Drew—he had another tough time last night."

"Well, he apparently had a better morning."

"What do you mean?"

"I just got a call from Dr. Berg. Remember she told us Drew's behavior in the next few weeks would be crucial in determining whether his inability to control his anger was serious?"

"Who could forget the threat of McLean?"

"Well, apparently Drew became very frustrated this morning in school—something about a girl in his group not letting him do the part of the project he thought he was supposed to do. Anyway, instead of lashing out at the girl, Drew stormed out of the classroom and went down to Dr. Berg's office. He marched up to her desk and demanded, 'Okay, now what am I supposed to do?' "

"And this is a good thing?" Lauren asked slowly.

"According to Dr. Berg, it's great progress. She thinks it's a pretty strong indication that the intervention is working. That our boy is headed in the right direction."

"Well," Lauren said, her mood beginning to lift for

the first time all day. "That's really great. Terrific even."

"Do you think I should tell Drew about Gabe?" Todd asked. "Maybe it would make him feel safer if he knew the kidnapper was caught."

Lauren's spirits sagged again, and she stared around her at the old-fashioned drugstore; it actually had a scuffed hardwood floor, but the pharmacy counter was staffed by a tall woman with reddish purple hair and black fingernails. "Let's wait until I've talked with Steve Conway. Things aren't always what they seem."

"Ain't that the truth," Todd repeated her words with a laugh. "You know," he added, "this really is terrific news."

"I guess." Lauren flipped the coin return slot on the phone. "It just hasn't sunk in yet."

"It's all over," Todd said. "The creepy packages, the looking over your shoulder, the worrying about Drew—and about you. You can even go back to *Rebeka Hibbens*. Finish your book and get your degree like you planned."

"I can, can't I?" Lauren asked as the enormity of what had occurred began to dawn on her. She might have lost a potential job, a lover, and a good deal of her innocence, but she had gotten her safety and security back—as well as her dissertation. With a start she realized that the Immortalis was tonight—and that there was now nothing to keep her from going. "I hadn't even thought . . ."

"Something else is over too."

Lauren caught her lower lip between her teeth. "Oh?" she asked, her heart pounding.

"I broke it off with Kara."

"Todd, I can't even begin to think about—"

"Can you think about little baby girls?"

When the recording started demanding money again, Lauren said, "Let me run. I'll talk to you after

I've had some sleep and some time to think. Give Drew a kiss for me and tell him I'll pick him up at school tomorrow."

"And the baby girl?" Todd asked, a teasing tone to his voice.

Lauren laughed. "I'll give her some thought too." The phone clicked dead in her ear before Todd could answer.

Lauren bought a sandwich and a soda from a mom-and-pop deli across the street. It was too cold for the walk Steve had suggested, so she returned to the police station. Reclaiming her seat on the hard bench, she tried to eat but ended up throwing the sandwich in the trash. She drank the soda, wondering what was happening to Gabe.

Before she got far into her speculations, a hand gripped her shoulder. She looked up into Deborah's white-brown eyes.

"They told me a little bit about what happened over the phone," Deborah said. "That man's even worse than I'd thought."

Lauren motioned for Deborah to join her on the bench, and they sat in uncomfortable silence until Lauren finally said, "I guess you were right and I had it all backward. The evil wasn't supernatural at all—it was all too natural: self-interest and greed."

"The human ego is a powerful thing to behold," Deborah said. "And not to be underestimated."

"If you hadn't given me those pages from the chronicle . . ." Lauren let her sentence trail off and shrugged her shoulders, still unable to meet Deborah's eyes. "We might never have known. He might have gotten away with it all."

"These things tend to work out in one fashion or another," Deborah assured her. "The sages have a way of keeping the balance."

Lauren finally looked directly at Deborah. "I'm sorry I didn't believe you."

"Sometimes the most difficult part of belief is letting go of what we hold to be true," Deborah said.

Lauren nodded. "I wish I could make amends to you all. To you. To Cassandra and Bram—"

She was interrupted by Steve Conway. "Sorry to keep you waiting so long, Lauren." He looked at Deborah. "Officer Ling will be with you in a few minutes."

As Lauren stood, Deborah held onto her hand. "There are no amends to make," she said. "But if you want to extend them anyway, you're welcome to join us tonight at White Horse Beach."

Lauren smiled warmly at Deborah. "I might just do that." Then she turned and followed Steve down a hallway and up a flight of stairs.

Steve had the largest desk in a narrow room with *Detective Bureau* stenciled on the door. He sat down and motioned her to the chair next to his. He leaned toward her and touched her knee. "You okay?" he asked.

Lauren was surprised when her eyes filled with tears. As the tears spilled over onto her cheeks, she began to laugh. "I'm usually a pretty tough person," she said, her voice quivering. "But you seem to catch me at my weak moments."

"From what I witnessed today," he said with a smile, "weak is not the word I'd use to describe you. It's not easy to stand up to a man like Gabe Phipps."

"Thanks." Lauren wiped her cheeks with the back of her hand. "So tell me what's happened," she demanded. "You said my intuition was right. Do you mean about *everything*?"

Steve leaned back and crossed his arms over his chest. "Gabe has requested a chance to tell you about it himself. You don't have to do this if you don't want to—and I'd actually recommend against it—but he says it's important you hear it from him. That it's the only way you'll get the whole story."

Lauren hesitated, not at all sure how she felt about this turn of events. One part of her wanted to confront Gabe, while another part wanted to stay as far away as possible. "Has he been arrested?" she asked.

"His statement is still incomplete." Steve's tone left little doubt that Gabe's arrest was imminent.

Lauren stared at Steve. Gabe had done it. He really had. He had killed Jackie because she had discovered his plagiarism, then he had seduced her so she wouldn't discover the same thing. He had made love to her, then lied to her; then, knowing full well what it would do to her, he had kidnapped Drew. She felt a fury building within her unlike any anger she had ever known. It started at the core of her being and pushed outward until she felt it in the tips of her fingers. How dare he? How *dare* he?

"I want to hear it," Lauren said. "I want to hear it from the scumbag myself."

Steve stood. "Follow me." He led her to a room that looked as if it might have been the waiting room of a small hospital—except that it was unlocked for them by a uniformed policeman. The policeman locked the bolt behind them after they entered, then returned to his position next to the door.

Gabe sat slouched in a yellow vinyl chair. His suit was wrinkled and his tie askew, but aside from that he looked remarkably intact. A woman holding a flip phone and balancing a pad on her knee sat to his left; she was clearly his lawyer. Most likely the hotshot from Hubbard and Hobbs he had bragged about.

Gabe bolted upright when he saw Lauren. She stepped back and bumped into Steve, who grabbed hold of her arm and held it.

"Lauren," Gabe cried. "I want to explain."

Lauren stared at the handsome man before her. The man who had been on "The Today Show" this morning. The man with whom she had made love yesterday afternoon. The man who had terrified her child, who had murdered her best friend. Lauren clutched her fists into tight balls at her side.

Steve Conway touched her shoulder and nodded to the door, then to the policeman guarding it. Lauren nodded in return, and Steve slipped out of the room.

"Once you've heard how it all happened," Gabe was saying, "I know you'll understand that it wasn't my fault. I know you'll find it in your heart to forgive—"

"This is a very bad idea," snapped the woman sitting next to Gabe. "As your attorney, it's my duty to instruct you not—"

"Lauren deserves to hear the truth, Allysa," Gabe interrupted. "And I'm going to tell it to her. I'm sick of all the lies."

"Then do it some other time and place," Allysa ordered. "This is suicide. The policeman is right here—"

"I don't care where the policeman is," Gabe interrupted her again. "I'm going to explain it to Lauren now, after which I'm going to finish explaining it to the police."

"Then you'll have to do it without me." Allysa dropped the phone into her briefcase and capped her pen. "It's impossible for me to represent you if you refuse to take my advice."

"Fine," Gabe said calmly. "You may go."

Allysa stood. "You're a foolish man, Dr. Phipps."

"That is quite evident, Ms. St. Gelais," Gabe said, a self-deprecating smile creasing his face. "Quite evident."

As the lawyer left, Lauren sat down in a beat-up chair across from Gabe, thinking that despite it all, even in his darkest hour, Gabe could still be charming. *"Don't be fooled by his power and charisma,"* Deborah had told her. *"The man is evil."*

But Lauren had been fooled.

"Lauren," Gabe said softly, charmingly, utterly sincere. "I need you to know that this isn't what it seems. I'm a victim too—a victim of a series of accidents. Horrible, terrible, ghastly accidents, true, but accidents just the same. Will you listen? Will you hear me out?"

Gripping the arms of the muddy brown chair, soiled fuzz poking between her fingers, she said, "Talk."

Gabe nodded. "As you've surmised," he began, "I did borrow some of Deborah's materials for *A New Social History*."

"Borrowed some of Deborah's materials?" Lauren was incredulous. "I saw what you 'borrowed'—and it sure looked like plagiarism to me."

"But it wasn't intentional, nor was it just for myself," Gabe explained. "You saw her work. You're an historian, you can understand. It was brilliant, extraordinary—bordered on genius. I tried to rewrite it using my own words, I really did. But I just couldn't put it as simply and as elegantly as Deborah."

"Are you trying to justify what you did based on the fact that Deborah's a genius? That she writes elegantly?"

"No, no." Gabe shook his head. "I'm not trying to justify anything—I'm just explaining my thought process. You see, I figured that, since no one was ever going to read her chronicle, I was actually doing the historical community a favor by sharing her ideas with them."

"That's bullshit!" Lauren exploded. "Complete and utter bullshit. I don't care about your convoluted excuses for what you did to Deborah, I want to know about what you did to Jackie—and to Drew." Her eyes filled with tears and she angrily blinked them away.

"It was all an accident," Gabe said. "I never meant for her to die. I just wanted her to keep quiet."

Lauren sucked in her breath. Gabe *had* killed Jackie. Then he had stood staring sadly out Simon's window, pretending a grief he didn't feel. The bile of hatred soured Lauren's stomach. The man was disgusting, despicable. As Deborah had said: He was even worse than she had thought.

"After Jackie called to tell me she had read the chronicle," Gabe continued as if unaware of Lauren's reaction, "I went to her house to try to reason with her. But she resisted my appeals to our friendship, to the university, to the prestige of the department. She insisted she was going to the dean first thing the next morning."

Gabe's eyes glowed with self-righteousness. "I became so angry at her stubbornness, I reached out and grabbed her by the shoulders. I shook her. I probably shouldn't have, but I was so upset that she refused to see it from my perspective. And I needed to make her understand.

"She caught me by surprise and kneed me in the groin. I had to let go, and when I did, she fell and hit her head on the leg of the dining room table. I didn't kill her. She fell. She fell. You've got to believe that."

"Is that when I arrived on the scene?" Lauren asked, her voice dripping with sarcasm. "When you ran out the back door and left Jackie to die?"

"I didn't know what else to do," Gabe said. "I was confused. Disoriented. So I just grabbed the chronicle and got the hell out of there."

"Was it fun playing the angry sorcerer? Sending Jackie and me poppets and Bellarmine urns?" Lauren clenched her fists to keep from hitting him. "Breaking into my house. Lighting candles. You stole Herman. You killed him. And then, and then . . ." She couldn't even say the words.

"I never meant to hurt you—or Drew. I just wanted to scare you away from the coven so you wouldn't read the chronicle. I was forced into more and more drastic actions because you refused to take my threats seriously."

"So you're telling me it was my fault?" Lauren spat. The great Dr. Ego, Deborah had called him. *"Never underestimate the power of a man with limitless ambition,"* Deborah had said. But, once again, Lauren had failed to heed Deborah's warning.

"No, no, of course not." Gabe ran his hands through his hair. "You know, I'm starting to believe there really *is* a curse on that damn chronicle. Because all this is so bizarre. So capricious. So unlike me. Why else would I have returned the chronicle to Deborah? Why would I have done something so stupid unless there was a powerful force making me do it?" he demanded, his eyes begging Lauren to agree with him. "There has to be some powerful, awful, evil force."

Lauren just shook her head.

"A couple of nights after Jackie's death, I dreamed a raven ordered me to bring the chronicle back to Deborah. So, like some idiot in a sleepwalking limbo, I got up in the middle of the night, got dressed, and did what the bird said. Now why would I do what some dumb bird told me to do?" Gabe dropped his head to his hands. "I haven't slept in weeks," he said. "It's been so awful for me. Hiding so much. Hurting you. Deceiving you."

"It hasn't exactly been a picnic for me," Lauren snapped. "Or for Drew."

"I was desperate." Gabe lifted his head, and for the first time that day, Lauren saw a flicker of remorse in his eyes. "When you told me Deborah had offered to let you read the chronicle, I was beside myself. I knew once you read it, the whole thing would blow wide open. So I came up with the kidnapping idea—but I was never going to hurt Drew, I swear I wasn't."

"Well, you did hurt him, you hurt him plenty," Lauren said. "And you hurt me too." How could she have been so stupid? she wondered. So blind?

"But I never meant to hurt you," Gabe cried. "That's the part you've got to understand. I hired a really nice woman and then I made sure she was especially kind to Drew. I explicitly told her not to scare him, to be gentle, to rent him a bunch of videotapes, and to get him his favorite for dinner: Peking ravioli." He looked beseechingly at Lauren. "You said that was his favorite. Didn't he tell you that's what he had to eat?"

Lauren nodded. This was unbelievable. Incomprehensible. Gabe Phipps—the powerful, the wealthy, the brilliant—was using Peking ravioli to justify the kidnapping of her son. He'd lost all sense of proportion, of right and wrong. At every fork, he had taken the road most easily traveled. And now, true to form, he was choosing the easy way out: denying what he had done, abdicating responsibility for his actions. He was hollow at the core. Again, just as Deborah had said.

"It had to be the curse that's caused it all—that's causing my downfall now. There's just no other explanation." Gabe's eyes filled with tears and his voice began to shake. "I never wanted to hurt anyone. Never. That's why I planned to release Drew, unharmed, the very day he ran away. The fact that he escaped doesn't negate my good intentions." He covered his face with trembling hands and began to sob. "It doesn't negate my good intentions," he repeated.

Lauren watched Gabe in silence, her anger suddenly replaced by overwhelming sorrow. So many losses, she thought. And for what? For what?

Lauren didn't leave the police station until after ten o'clock. As she stepped into the cold December night, she looked up at the sky. It had cleared since morning, the snow that had been threatening blown far out to sea. Although most of the stars were hidden by the city lights, she could see the waxing crescent moon rising in the east. She thought how nice it would be to join Deborah and the coven for the Immortalis, but she knew she was far too exhausted and wrung out to make the trip.

Everything had taken so long. After talking with Gabe, she had been questioned over and over again by so many different people—Steve Conway, an FBI agent, The *Boston Globe*, The *Cambridge Tab*, Channel 7, even a student from the university daily—that by the end, she was sure her story was completely incomprehensible. No one seemed to mind; they all had been extremely kind. The dispatcher even ordered in Chinese food for dinner.

Lauren headed to the T station. The crowds had thinned by this hour, and she had the sidewalks almost to herself. It seemed incredible that this was still Tuesday, the same day she had walked Drew to school, dropped exams off at Paul Conklin's office, and gone to the library to kill a few hours by researching Faith Osborne. As she turned the corner past a brightly lit but deserted laundromat, she pictured the comfort of her bed and the safety of her apartment. A safety that was now assured.

The train came as soon as Lauren reached the platform and she was home in no time. Despite her exhaustion, she prowled the apartment, unable to relax. She washed the dirty dishes in the kitchen sink and put away the laundry that had been sitting in the basket for days. She circled the living room and wandered down the hallway to Drew's bedroom. Then she walked the loop again. Finally, she forced herself to stretch out on the living room couch. But she couldn't get comfortable. Her leg kept shaking and her mind kept whirling.

Her eyes darted to the Deodat Willard print leaning against the wall and, once again, she promised herself she would call Simon Pappas. Climbing slowly from the couch, she knelt before the strange little print. She didn't want to give it back. It was a part of Jackie, and somehow it was also a part of herself.

The young girl in the picture was dressed as a prim matron. She wore a long skirt covered by an apron with a narrow binding of lace. On her head was a tightly fitted cap. But despite the unflattering hat and the restrictive clothes, the spirit of the child burst from the print. Lauren reached out and touched the girl's cheek.

The child turned and looked straight into Lauren's eyes. She released a high tinkling laugh. "Mama!" the girl cried, clasping her hands together. "I've been searching for you everywhere."

Lauren was startled but strangely unafraid. "I would've thought you'd be angry with your mother," she said.

"Why should I be angry when I know you thought me asleep on my pallet that night?" Dorcas asked. "'Tis clear you told your husband about Rebeka and the others to save me from the gallows."

"But I didn't save you," Lauren whispered, once again seeing the tiny, lifeless body hanging from the towering oak tree. She closed her eyes against the image. "You had run to Rebeka's. You were in Glover barn. . . ."

Dorcas was silent. "Things do not always turn out as we plan," she finally said. "A mother who puts her child before all others is not a person to be scorned. She is a woman to be admired."

Lauren opened her eyes.

"You are far stronger than you think, Mama," Dorcas said, her voice growing fainter. "And so much more is possible than you allow yourself to believe."

"But—" Lauren began and then stopped. The small print was still and silent. Dorcas was turned away from her toward the corn, as she had always been.

Thirty

THIS TIME, LAUREN HAD NO TROUBLE FINDING HER WAY to White Horse Beach. When her headlights lit up the pair of gnarled birch trees standing sentinel on either side of the dirt road, she turned onto a lane that was as tight and rutted as she remembered. Naked tree branches scraped against the sides of her car. As she pulled into the parking lot, it was just before midnight. Turning off the motor, she stared into the shadowy silence for a long moment, then grabbed a flashlight from the glove compartment and climbed from the car.

Zipping her jacket high against the night air, Lauren could hear the distant lapping of waves, but little else. She walked slowly toward the dense forest. But even with the flashlight, she had difficulty finding the break in the trees that led to the narrow beach path. She nosed her way into the woods a few times, thinking she had found the trail, only to become caught in a mass of impenetrable underbrush. Finally, she found it. As she stepped carefully around saplings and rocks, she could smell the salt and hear the surf.

She felt the knot of dread the ocean always tied within her, but she kept walking. The path seemed much longer and more circuitous than she remembered. Finally, she pushed through the last of the trees and stepped onto the wide, open beach.

They were all there: Deborah, Cassandra, Bram, Tamar, Robin, and Alva, barefoot and apparently naked under their long white robes. They were gathered in a circle around a bonfire, with a brass pot hanging over it. A white bush with strange braided roots was at their feet. With a start, Lauren recalled Deborah had left a similar bush on Jackie's casket.

"Lauren." Deborah glided across the sand, her white cloak trailing behind her. Through the split in her robe, Deborah's naked body glistened in the moonlight. She appeared unaffected by the cold. "I knew you'd come."

The others followed more slowly, expressions of dazed amazement on their faces. Cassandra was the only one beside Deborah who actually approached, touching Lauren's arm as if she couldn't quite believe she was real. The rest kept their distance, forming a wide, ragged circle around her. They were subdued, almost as if they had been drugged, staring at her in bewilderment.

Lauren looked into Deborah's pale eyes. "I've come to find out what is possible," she said. "And to find out who I am."

Deborah took Lauren's arm. "I have your robe. It is time to begin." Together the seven walked single file across the sand.

They approached the fire. Whipped by the wind, the flames shot wildly in every direction, eating at the bottom of the pot. A wooden dipper lay nearby in the sand. Lauren looked out at the ocean and a shiver of dread ran through her body. But when Deborah placed a white robe around her shoulders, Lauren's apprehension slowly abated. Cassandra took one of her hands and Bram took her other.

They formed a circle around Deborah, who lowered the dipper into the pot, then lifted it before her. "Heliotrope, sage, malaxis, christianwort, heart of lubin, aconite," Deborah chanted, her voice vibrating with power. "To live, one must die."

"To die for future life is the privilege of the few," Cassandra answered.

As Deborah returned the dipper to the pot, Cassandra began the story of the Immortalis. "We come to this ocean that carves the edge of the earth to perform the great Immortalis," she said. "It is a deep magic, crafted to insure our seven souls shall be reborn together again, and again, and again."

"One plus zero plus one," the coven chanted.

"One plus zero plus one," Cassandra repeated. "And in each new incarnation our coven shall grow in knowledge and in power and in the magical crafts."

When Cassandra finished speaking, Deborah tugged the ribbon that gathered the neck band of her cloak. As the white cloak fell open, she pulled Rebeka's lancet from between her breasts. She opened the lancet, fanning the four blades above her head. "I wield the lancet of heaven. The touch of this divine blade shall ensure breath be with us for all eternity." Deborah touched each of the four blades to her nose, to her lips, and to the soft spot at the base of her neck, then passed the lancet around the circle. Each member did as she had done. It came to Lauren last.

So this was Rebeka's lancet, Lauren thought as she held it in her hand. The mysterious and powerful lancet of which Deborah had spoken on the day she had first given them the chronicle. Lauren turned the lancet so she could view it from all sides. It was a truly beautiful object, the carvings—the serpents, pinecones, frogs, and a winged caduceus—forming a remarkably pleasing although decidedly odd design. She looked up at the circle and saw everyone's eyes upon her.

Slowly, she raised the lancet, pressing the first blade to her nose. But as soon as the knife touched her skin, Lauren caught her breath. The heavens had shifted and she knew she was in a different place in time. The stars were much brighter, and in a slightly different formation. The near stars stood out in front of the Milky Way, which lay against a sky that was the deepest velvet black she had ever seen.

Lauren gazed around the circle in amazement. The bonfire was much smaller and the brass caldron much larger than they had been a moment before. Tamar and Robin were gone. Instead, Abigail Cullender, her eye swollen shut, and Bridgit Corey, her arm hanging uselessly by her side, stood across from her. As did Mercy Broadstreet, Foster Lacy, and Millicent Glover. Rebeka was standing next to the bonfire, shriveled and old in her muddy red cloak.

Rebeka's voice echoed down the long corridor of time: *"The sages have rendered judgment upon you, Faith Osborne. You must sacrifice your life."*

She felt the unyielding grip of Rebeka's hand over her own and saw the lancet rise in front of her throat. The surf pounded in her ears and the salty taste of fear filled her mouth. Horror flashed through her body and she was back in the present, her every nerve ablaze with fiery terror. With the clarity and certainty of yesterday's memory, she knew exactly what had happened to her in 1692.

As the circle of familiar faces rose before her once again, Lauren felt the heft of the lancet in her hand and Gabe's words filled her ears. *"There were descriptions of weird rituals involving suicide and murder.... There was going to be another mass suicide like the one at Jonestown—with Deborah as the next Jim Jones."* These people had killed her once before, and they were going to kill her again. Her eyes skidded from the dark woods to the restless sea. There was nowhere to run.

Lauren closed her eyes to hide the terror she knew they contained. She forced her trembling fingers to be still and touched the blade to her lips. Slowly, as they all had done before her, she touched each of the four blades to her nose, to her lips, and to the soft spot at the base of her neck. Then she jerked the lancet from her face and sprinted toward the break in the trees, her robe falling from her shoulders as she ran.

"She knows!"

"Get the lancet!"

Clutching the lancet, Lauren moved as fast as she could across the beach. But the sand sucked at her sneakers, slowing her down. She tripped on an exposed rock and fell. Scrambling on all fours, she gathered the coordination necessary to stand and ran.

"Wait! Lauren!" Deborah called. "This isn't like the first Immortalis. It's as I told you—this ritual's symbolic. A reenactment. No one will be hurt."

Lauren kept running. She could hear them behind her. But when she turned and looked over her shoulder, she saw that, although their bare feet were helping them cross the sand, they were bogged down by their long robes. Cassandra tripped and Alva stopped to help her up, but Bram and Deborah and Tamar and Robin kept coming. Still, Lauren ran. The woods, she thought. In the woods her sneakers would give her the advantage she needed. She could get to her car. Get away.

She heard labored breathing behind her, and a painful stitch twisted in her side. Her wind was almost gone. She wasn't going to make it. They were going to kill her. Lauren looked behind her. Bram had thrown off his robe. His naked body shone white between the dark trees and his eyes gleamed with madness. He was gaining on her. Deborah was right behind him.

Then she heard a cry and a thump and knew someone was down. Adrenaline pumped through her and she crashed through the underbrush, sliding on rocks, grabbing onto saplings to stay upright. A break in the trees opened before her; it led back to the beach instead of to her car, but it was the only way she could go and still maintain her lead. Lauren raced ahead.

But as she stepped onto the sand, a hand grabbed her from behind, yanking her backward and halting her momentum.

"You shall do as we do," Deborah said in her ear. With a powerful twist of her wrist, Deborah forced Lauren around. With her other hand, she wrenched the lancet from Lauren's grasp.

"I-I won't," Lauren gasped, trying to jerk away from Deborah. But Deborah's fingers were bands of iron on her arm, and Lauren was held fast.

The witch's eyes were completely white in the moonlight. "You shall enter the water with us and then you shall do as we do."

"No!" Lauren cried, struggling vainly to free herself. She was not going into the ocean. She was not going to kill herself.

One by one, the others gathered in a tight circle around her.

Deborah's laughter rang out over the beach. "You shall do as we do or your precious Drew will be dead."

With a painful tug, Deborah drew Lauren toward her. Their faces were inches apart and Lauren could smell the metallic odor of Deborah's breath.

"If you impede this Immortalis," Deborah said, her voice vibrating with rage, "if you stop me from reaching my destiny, I swear upon the sages I will kill your son." She pulled Lauren even closer. "In a terrible and painful way."

As Deborah's hateful words filled Lauren's ears, she

thought of the phantoms that haunted Drew's dreams, of how he had cried and clutched her in the night, of all the pain she had already brought him. His image rose up before her and her terror swelled, engorged by rage. Deborah would not hurt Drew. Lauren would not allow it. There had to be a way out. She scanned the beach and the sea and turned back toward the woods.

The coven drew closer. Lauren heard their labored breathing. Smelled the sweat of their excitement. Tasted her own panic.

"Look at me," Deborah ordered.

Lauren turned and was caught within the eerie whiteness of Deborah's unblinking stare. "I-I . . ." she stuttered.

"You shall do as we do," Deborah ordered. "You shall say what we say: 'To live, one must die.' " Her gaze burrowed deeper and deeper into Lauren's eyes, deep into the core of Lauren's being. "For if you don't," she whispered gently, "it will be Drew who will die."

Lauren's eyes were fixed on Deborah. It was clear the woman was mad, and it was also clear she would make good on her threat. And Lauren knew, just as Faith had known, that she had no choice but to do as Deborah asked. "To live, one must die," she repeated in a stilted and disembodied voice. "To live, one must die."

Deborah nodded to the others and then turned to the dark water, its waves ripped wild by the force of the new moon. As five sets of hands grasped onto Lauren, Deborah let go. She walked across the sand and into the ocean, stopping when the water flowed just above her waist; her cloak swirled as it rode the restless waves. She turned and beckoned for the others to follow.

As if in a trance, Lauren approached the shoreline. A knot of fear twisted in her stomach and overwhelming sadness blurred her vision, yet she was strangely unaffected by her own emotions. She watched, as if she were seated in the clouds, as Cassandra and Bram drew her over the slippery rocks and into the sea. She was amazed to see herself enter the ocean as if she had never feared the water, as if the waves whipping about her were no more than ripples in a bathtub.

Slowly, the six figures made their way to where Deborah stood. They clung to one another, fighting the powerful waves at their waists and the pull of the undertow at their feet. As she held and was held by Cassandra and Bram, Lauren came back into herself. Suddenly aware of the flesh-numbing cold, she was suffused with a sense of inevitability. This was her destiny, just as it had been Faith's. She was putting her child before all others. She was giving up her own life to save Drew's. She submitted to her fate.

Deborah raised the lancet, and its many knives flashed in the moonlight. "To summerland!" she screamed above the roar of the pounding surf. Then she placed the lancet in Lauren's hand, her fingers pressing it deep into Lauren's palm.

Lauren felt the deep ridges of the lancet's engravings. She imagined the serpents and the pinecones and the winged caduceus slicing their shapes into her skin. As she wrapped her fingers around the knife's hilt, she could feel the lancet's power pulsing outward from her hand until it permeated her entire body. Her entire being.

"Go to new life, Lauren Freeman," Deborah said, her eyes searing into Lauren's. But Lauren also heard Deborah's voice from another time and place. *"If the lancet is ever lost or destroyed, the coven will be too."*

The lancet, Lauren thought through her haze. The lancet had the power. The lancet was the way. Dorcas had told her she was stronger than she thought. So had Steve Conway. *"These people believe everything*

Deborah tells them," Gabe had once said. *"They think if the lancet is destroyed, they will be too."*

Deborah gently lifted Lauren's hand and placed one of the knives against her neck. "To new life."

Lauren closed her eyes. Before her stood her own death. A cold and shadowy void. A death that would deprive Drew of his mother. A death that would give Deborah her victory. And in that moment, Lauren rebelled against the void. Rejected it with all her being. She was suffused with an energy, a powerful resolve. She would not die. No matter what the risk, she would fight to live.

Her fingers were beneath Deborah's, the lancet in her grasp. She could feel Deborah's cockiness loosening her grip. It was the chance she needed.

With every ounce of strength within her, Lauren ripped her hand free of Deborah's and threw the lancet as far across the water as she could. She was amazed at her own power. The lancet flew as if it had wings, arcing upward, twisting over itself again and again, its blades blindingly white in the moonlight, until suddenly it dropped straight into the black waves.

"No!" Deborah screamed as if she had been stabbed. She dove into the water and started swimming toward the spot where the lancet had fallen. With wails of outrage, the other members of the coven followed.

As soon as Lauren was free of the coven's hold, she lunged toward shore. But the ocean fought her every effort. A powerful undertow grabbed at her feet, dragging her out to sea, while waves slammed into her back, pushing her forward—and down. She fell and went under. She came up coughing and flailed against the crosscurrents. She couldn't allow her fears to stop her now. She had to reach shore. She had to live.

The ocean floor was rocky and hard to traverse. She

fell again, pushed herself up, struggled on. Finally, after what felt like aeons, Lauren stumbled out of the water and collapsed onto the sand. She looked out to sea and thought she saw heads bobbing on the waves, but she couldn't be sure. She had to get up. Reach her car. Get away.

Shivering uncontrollably and covered with sand, Lauren struggled toward the woods. Still coughing, she sobbed as she stumbled along the seemingly endless path. Pushing her battered body forward, she covered the final distance, wrenched open the car door, and threw herself down onto the seat. Her head dropped to the steering wheel. As she sucked in deep gulps of air, she thought she heard sirens in the distance. Certain she was hallucinating, she lifted her head and saw blue lights strobing through the trees. A line of police cars was screaming down the dirt road.

A Cambridge police cruiser came first, followed by three with *Moorscott* written in large black letters on their sides. The four cars sped into the parking lot and stopped with a massive screech of brakes and a powerful updraft of dust. Dan Ling, in uniform, jumped from the lead car and ran to her.

"Are you all right?" he demanded as she climbed from her car.

"The witches," she gasped. "Six of them tried to kill me." She pointed toward the path. "On the beach. In the water."

Dan waved the policemen in the direction she indicated. They took off at a run. Then Dan led her to his car. He pulled a blanket from the trunk and wrapped her up in it.

"Come sit," Dan said, opening the door and indicating the backseat.

Two cruisers from Lynn pulled in. Dan told her to sit again and walked over to one of the cars. He came back with a patrolman. "Officer Walbrom will stay with you—I'll be right back."

Still leaning against the car and shivering inside her blanket, Lauren said, "I don't understand. What are you doing here? How did you know where to find me?"

"Gabe Phipps," Dan said. "I stopped by to see him when I was coming off my shift. He said that after you left, he began thinking about what he had read in the chronicle, and figured out the witches were planning to kill you tonight. He was frantic—nearly hysterical. He convinced us to go to your house and make sure you were safe. When you weren't home—and Lieutenant Conway remembered you telling the Sewall woman you might join her tonight—we came here."

"But—"

Dan placed his hands on her shoulders and turned her toward the open door.

"I'm coming with you," Lauren argued, struggling to stay on her feet. But under the gentle pressure of Dan's hands, her knees buckled and she collapsed gratefully onto the seat.

"I'll be right back." Pulling his gun from its holster, Dan ran toward the path. Officer Walbrom climbed into the front.

Before Lauren could begin to get her bearings, a policeman emerged from the woods. He jogged to his car and yanked a transmitter from its housing. Lauren could tell from his body language that something big was taking place. She looked at Officer Walbrom, but he shook his head. Within minutes, Dan came down the path and climbed into the backseat next to her. He took her hands in both of his.

"What?" she demanded, fear hammerlocking her heart. "What?"

"There's nobody on the beach. Just a weird bush and a pot and the remnants of a fire."

Lauren wrapped her blanket more tightly around her.

"My guess is they're all still in the water," Dan said. "The Coast Guard's been called and they're coming with boats and helicopters. The Moorscott and Lynn police are going to continue to search the beach area—and I'll need information from you to get out an APB on everyone who was here."

Dan paused and stared out the window. She followed his gaze and they watched the police lights strobing the knobby white birches blue, then black, then blue again. Dan cleared his throat and turned back to Lauren. "They say the ocean's bad tonight. Strong undertows. Crosscurrents . . ."

Lauren closed her eyes, but still the lights strobed across her vision. As did the image of six small bodies being carried into the vast blackness by the swiftly moving waves.

By daybreak, the Coast Guard had recovered five bodies and were certain they would find the sixth in the shoals of an unnamed island to the southeast of Moorscott. After spending the morning being interviewed by detectives, Lauren returned to White Horse Beach. But the police wouldn't let her go beyond the yellow tape strung between the trees at the edge of the sand.

She stood at the tape, staring across the beach at the dead embers of Deborah's bonfire, searching for something that would explain what had happened here. But the crashing waves told her nothing. Neither did the blackened wood. Nor the birds flying and diving overhead.

Epilogue

Cambridge, Massachusetts
December 1996

THE LABOR WAS LONG AND HARD, AND WHEN SHE FInally felt the baby slip from her body, Lauren greeted her daughter's birth with as much relief as joy. Todd, on the other hand, was a portrait in ecstasy.

"Look what you've done, Laurie," he whispered as he gazed down at the new life in his arms. "She's the most beautiful thing I've ever seen."

Lauren watched her husband with a deep welling of emotion. "That's exactly what you said when Drew was born."

"But this time I mean it," he said, a wide sheepish grin on his face. "She truly *is* beautiful. I've never seen a baby with such incredible eyes. The color is just amazing."

"All babies have blue eyes," Lauren told him, glancing over at the nurse for verification.

The nurse nodded and smiled tolerantly. "And all new fathers are a bit daffy."

"Not this one," Todd crowed as he sat down on the edge of Lauren's bed and swung his daughter up for her inspection.

Lauren caught her breath. The baby's eyes were an eerie white-brown, and at the base of her neck was a tiny birthmark in the shape of a crescent moon.